# 2s

# AND

# 3s

## JACK GANNON

## CYNDI WILLIAMS-BARNIER

ISBN-13: 978-1-7349515-8-5


YBR PUBLISHING, LLC

Jack Gannon – Co-Owner, Production Manager
Cyndi Williams-Barnier – Co-Owner, Marketing Manager, Production Editor
Bill Barnier – Co-Owner, Senior Editor
Loreen Ridge-Husum – Art Director, Independent Contract Illustrator
Michelle Owens – Marketing Agent

## To Our Fathers

*Commander John H. Gannon, Medical Service Corps, United States Navy*

*Dallas Williams, Chief Jailer Beaufort SC County Sheriff's Department,*

*Thank you for the inspirations of leadership and attention to detail, may our stories honor your memories…*

"2s & 3s" by Jack Gannon and Cyndi Williams-Barnier is a psychological thriller. September 11, 2001, changed many lives forever. A new Task Force has been created to take care of terrorist cases that law enforcement can't handle, and four military specialists staff it. In Richmond, Virginia, a bus explodes, and there are only two survivors – a small child called David and the bomber. A priest adopts David, a man who appears to the world as a kindly man, but he is different behind closed doors, and David suffers badly. A serial killer is hunting in Virginia. Every two years, he commits three murders and leaves a biblical quote at the scene of every murder, earning himself the name, The Biblical Bomber. The Task Force takes over the hunt for him when a Senator's wife becomes a victim, with the brief of taking him down whatever it takes, but even they struggle to find and stop him. Turning to a private company for help, the special agents step up their efforts to find him before he kills again. Can they succeed before the next bomb goes off?

"2s & 3s" by Jack Gannon and Cyndi Williams-Barnier is one of those "wow" books. Full of suspense, this is one psychological thriller that will leave you reeling. The action is non-stop all the way through, with twists and turns to send you off in one direction before roughly grabbing you and sending you in another. The pacing is excellent. It leaves you no time to wonder what's coming next as the action slams you between the killer and the agents in a game of cat-and-mouse like no other. The characters are excellent, well-developed to the point where you feel like you know each one intimately, including the antagonist, a man you may even start to feel some sympathy for at certain points in the story – but not too much. The main plot and the subplots are weaved inextricably together, culminating in the explosive ending. If you are looking for an edge-of-your-seat page-turning thriller, this is it.

~Anne Marie Reynolds

Readers' Favorite, LLC

**CHAPTER 1**
**APRIL 1993, RICHMOND, VIRGINIA**
**BIRTH BY FIRE**

THA-THA-THA-THUMP burst from the machine gun. Ejected empty brass clinked on the floor and rolled in all directions. A homemade bomb had been magnetically fixed to the bottom of the bus, at the front entrance.

"Everybody, stay in your damn seats and you might stay alive!" The middle-aged attacker stood at the front of the bus, firing his AK47 into the roof again, making jagged holes. His eyes were wild with fury, teeth bared into an animal-like display. Shards of metal, paint and plastic rained down on everyone's heads. Seventeen terrified passengers screamed with the gunfire, coughed, covering their ears. Some crouched on the dirty floor in a futile attempt to hide or look smaller. Panicked eyes were steadfast, glued to the gunman. The terrified bus driver was frozen in place, hands on the steering wheel, eyes searching the street ahead for any sign of help.

The smell of cordite filled the air, and an unexpected quiet returned. Beams of summer sunlight stabbed through the bullet holes, and the gunman seemed to appear from the settling dust as if the devil himself was present.

At the back of the bus a little boy cried as his mother pulled him close. "Shhh, David, be quiet, mommy and daddy are here." His daddy reached over and took David's hand in his. The panic on the bus was palpable. David felt a sense of dread roll through his little body, not understanding the noise, the gun, or the screaming man.

The five-year-old, with wispy blond hair and sharp blue eyes looked on as the bad man screamed into a walkie-talkie. "ONE million NOW, or this baby goes up in one freakin' fireball!"

After the call came in, the one-block area around the bus was cordoned off without delay. Less than thirty minutes later SWAT units surrounded the city's square block, hiding behind buildings, in doorways, and on rooftops. They evacuated stores through back doors, and through PA speakers in their squad cars they urged pedestrians off the streets. Bomb technicians suited up in the back of a bomb squad vehicle as it sped to the scene.

"Stay calm," squawked the voice from the walkie-talkie. The policeman spoke slowly and deliberately. "No reason for anyone to get hurt. We want everyone to go home safe tonight, okay?"

"One trick, I see one uniform, and this baby explodes. Got it?" He slammed the walkie-talkie on the bus dashboard with a loud thud. The panicked driver jumped in his seat in surprise.

The slender gunman was drenched in sweat. Dark hair plastered his forehead, and glasses slid down his nose. He was forced to nudge them back up with a forearm. Perspiration stains spread from his armpits to his chest, turning the light green shirt to a darker shade of green.

Everyone watched helplessly as the mad man extended his arms into the air above his head, gun in one hand, detonator in the other.

He began, "Father, forgive me," praying aloud, shouting scripture, asking God to grant him money and freedom and an easy end to the insanity to which he'd been driven. The passengers made no attempt to move or speak. They didn't want to alarm the man, forcing him into another shooting spree, perhaps aiming at one of them.

David hadn't yet fully developed a sense of time. He couldn't tell if they'd been there for minutes or hours. 'How long is one million anyway?' He thought. Time seemed to drag. With its engine off, there was no air conditioning on the new city transit bus. Although it was already eighty-one degrees outside, the inside of the bus was heating rapidly. Sweat was rolling off the passengers, and the stale air was stifling. A mixture of perfume and body odor wafted about. Skin and clothing stuck to the uncomfortable fiberglass seating. Someone quietly lifted a dirty window, letting in some fresh air without notice.

David stared at the man with the gun. He was mesmerized by the beads of sweat that trickled off his face and down his neck. Leaning awkwardly against the railing at the front of the bus, the man's head hung low, breathing heavily, muttering to himself, "One, I can do with one million. Maybe that's not enough. Two, I can do with two, yeah, I'll tell 'em two million."

The man sensed he was being watched. His wicked eyes rolled upward; strands of wet hair hung off his forehead. He stared directly into the little boy's eyes. Another bout of fear seized David, and he could hear his own heartbeat inside his ears. The bad man studied the boy and half a grin crept across his face as he felt absolute control over the child. David was subconsciously memorizing the bad man.

There was a flash of light outside the bus window, then something that sounded like fireworks. Police attempted to launch a flash-bang grenade, but it failed to penetrate the open window on the bus. The man yelled into his radio, "I'll see you in hell!" David wet his pants, terrified. A stain on the front of his khakis appeared and spread fast. Embarrassed that he'd peed on himself, he felt like everyone was staring at him.

David's parents jumped up. They threw their bodies over him, trying to protect him, falling to the floor almost in slow motion. Out of the corner of his eye, he saw a flash of light, then another brighter flash of light, and the loudest boom David ever heard. He felt a violent rumbling from the bottom of the bus. The explosion lifted their bodies upward, then back down, hard on his back.

The bomb blast blew out large sections of the bus, sending parts soaring upwards and outwards. Police and fire personnel watched in horror as fire balls, steel and body parts rained down. Storefront windows shattered. The bus looked surreal, miss-shaped in a bizarre, twisted way. Axles protruded and a lone tire bounced and rolled aimlessly down the street. Pinned down by flames and debris, they were sure the bomber fled from the bus micro-seconds before the explosion, as if carried away by the first billows of smoke. "It'll be a miracle if anyone survived that," one of the policemen muttered. "Wonder why he didn't stick around to negotiate his ransom."

Minutes passed. David felt heat and heard the fire crackling around him, the weight of his parents kept him from moving. "Mommy, Daddy, get off me, it hurts." He smelled something familiar. 'Gasoline! Daddy told me about gasoline. The lawn mower. It could be dangerous.' David thought about it, more frightened than ever, he sobbed out loud. Cold water came in from everywhere, gurgling and swirling under his arms and legs. He heard men's voices, loud sirens, and muted sounds barked from walkie-talkies. "We got a live one!" someone yelled as they heard the boy's cries. Firemen, still extinguishing the flames, pushed the two limp bodies aside to lift the small boy.

Three firemen cleared the debris and lifted him from the carnage, taking care as they moved about. Two of the firemen held onto him, another checked his tiny body for injuries. He touched one of their yellow jackets and stared at their helmets that dripped with water. "You okay, little fella?" asked one of them. Sluggish and dazed, David looked at the three firemen, their faces covered in soot and dirt. "One, two, three," David counted out loud, a shaky finger pointed at each fireman in unison.

Looking down he saw his parents, motionless, and bloody. Shards of glass and steel were embedded in their bodies. His brow furrowed into worry lines. "Mommy, Daddy, wake up? One, two," he pointed downwards and counted again, his voice cracked as he spoke. The firemen looked at each other. One spoke, "He's probably in shock, but thank God this one's alive. Tell the paramedics."

Body parts were strewn about in what was left of the demolished bus. A woman's burned severed head sat precariously upright on a nearby seat. Tears welled in David's eyes, not understanding what he saw. He asked the firemen, "Where's the bad man? How come Mommy and Daddy won't wake up?" The three looked at each other again and wondered what to say to the boy. "The bad man got away, kiddo, but you're gonna be okay, we'll get you to a hospital." They didn't know how to answer the question about his parents. They were more concerned now with injuries, or perhaps a concussion. Someone else would have to explain the tragic details later.

Two paramedics met the firemen as they brought the boy out of the smoking wreckage, handing him over and placing him on a gurney. They examined him in detail, listened to his lungs, checked his pupils, felt his extremities for broken bones. He became listless as moments passed, disjointed from his surroundings. "I'll call in to the emergency room, tell them to prepare a unit for him, and try to find some relatives."

His head hurt, body ached, everything spun around. David stared into the distance and numbly contemplated that his parents were dead. Feeling alone, he knew the bad man was out there somewhere, and David was afraid he would come back. His little world crumbled in on him as he remembered the face and eyes of the bad man. "ONE, ONE million, TWO, TWO million." David repeated the bomber's words aloud to no one in particular.

## CHAPTER 2
## APRIL 1993, RICHMOND, VIRGINIA
## JOURNEY TO AN ANSWER

Mark and Jan had been inseparable since childhood. They played together as they grew up, went to the same schools, birthday parties, local events and dated all through high school. They were best friends, in love with each other, and Mark longed for the day he could propose to Jan. Mark and Jan's parents knew the two would eventually marry. Both sets of parents talked, thought out their plan of action whenever the event might become official.

All four adults were also best friends, attended high school together, college, marriage, and expected babies at the same time. It was no real surprise that Mark and Jan were destined to be together.

Mark Jason came from a wealthy family in Richmond, Virginia. In 1971 his father, Zachary, founded Jason Enterprises in Richmond. There was no board of directors or stockholders, only a staff of vice-presidents who ran the various divisions that made up the company. Zachary established a second location ten years later in Washington D.C. after it began winning exclusive contracts with the Federal government. Over the years it became an international business that could have been a Fortune 500 company, or listed in Forbes Global 2000, if it weren't for the fact that it was a private 'technologies' corporation. Mark's mother, Peggy, was content to stay home and take care of the many social commitments to which the Jason's had obligation, oversee the various charities Jason Enterprises supported in the city, as well as run the household staff.

Tall and fit, eighteen-year-old Mark often followed his dad into work on the weekends. Other boys of seventeen or eighteen played baseball or basketball or lazed around the house and played the popular new PlayStation. But his high IQ and inquisitive nature often allowed him to expand his knowledge of science and engineering, and to treasure the times he helped his father with secret projects.

He never forgot the time his father gave him a 'grunt job.' A federal agency hired JE to retrofit six dozen sniper rifles to specifications that couldn't be bought on the open market. Mark's father gave him access to the secure 14th floor and let him disassemble the rifles, engineer the components, and reassemble everything, just to see what Mark could do. Once the rifles were redesigned, Mark tested each one in the indoor firing range at JE, which Mark greatly enjoyed. Such work allowed him nearly unlimited target practice, and by the time high school graduation neared he already scored at expert proficiency. He loved the feel of the rifle in his hands, aiming the guns in total darkness, exhilarated when he hit the target each time. His work on the latest project reduced the rifle's noise by fifty percent, and its recoil to nearly zero. He'd tinkered with the piston system, reset the trigger, attached night vision and lasers, and added a few other prototype items. The small project intrigued him, and he wanted to learn more. Interested in micro-technology, he studied, researched on his own, and hoped one day to move into the technologies field in the military. He became so engrossed with the work on the 14th floor, he never realized his father watched him covertly from one of the multitudes of security observation rooms and scored his work after each project's completion.

Mark knew he would eventually take over JE but wanted first to follow in his father's footsteps and join the Navy. He'd been in JROTC all through high school, worked out every day, even jogged every morning before school. By the time he was done with high school, he was more than fit for Navy basic training. When he'd met with his recruiter, there was no doubt that Mark excelled in science, mathematics, technology, or any number of fields that the Navy offered. He worried about Jan, the marriage, and a military career right away. Or worse, that he'd join the military and be stationed far away. There would be long stretches of time when he couldn't see her while he was in basic training or on deployment. He was torn, but he absolutely wanted to marry her more than anything. He'd known it for years.

Jan, a petite girl of eighteen with long red hair, was very much in love with Mark. She was intelligent, attractive, and had good grades all through school, although not quite so high as Mark's near-straight 'A's. She often felt she wasn't worthy of Mark's love and attention because she rarely equaled his scores despite her countless hours of study. She didn't want to win him with simply great looks (all those freckles notwithstanding, she always complained). She also wanted to be his intellectual equal.

Her parents, Thomas, and Evelyn Churchill didn't have the same social status or income as the Jason family, and it had become an irksome issue for her since they began dating. Her own family took in a higher-than-average income, but it couldn't compare to Jason Enterprises. She'd been his date at all the Jason-sponsored social events, company parties and celebrations. Her parents held a couple of parties a year, such as their wedding anniversary, or Jan's birthday. She began to wonder if she was going to become little more than 'just a wife' whenever Mark popped the question and she said "yes."

What she didn't fully realize was Mark didn't much care about any of the requisite 'social standing'. He never compared what his family had or did. He wanted her first and knew it in his heart without question. Because he grew up in wealth, his classmates and peers often saw him as lucky or fortunate. Because he excelled so much, his classmates often felt his successes were bought instead of earned. And unfortunately, Jan thought that on occasion. She thought Mark knew truly little about money or its value because he often appeared oblivious to money issues or his status at school or in the community. He seemed more concerned with his future goals than present reality. He ended up with the underserved reputation of being aloof or 'better' than his schoolmates.

Jan knew Mark wanted to join the Navy, and her dilemma first and foremost was to let him go. The military meant time away from her for training and deployment, months, perhaps years without him. As graduation crept closer, Jan struggled with offers to attend colleges, or not go at all. She had a part time accounting job at a local law firm, rather than her father's accounting firm, as her desire was to eventually study law. If she was to be with Mark, then she wanted to specialize in corporate law.

Mark lay on his bed, hands behind his head, staring at the ceiling, contemplating his future with Jan. His bedroom was bland for a teenager, his friends found the environment to be 'nerdy.' He didn't have the usual posters on the walls, clothes thrown about, or week-old pizza crust hidden under the bed. Mark had a workstation, more than the usual desk with a computer. The setup was quite large, with two computers, two monitors, and two printers. His thought was to always have a full backup suite in case one crashed. The walls were shelved with books on science, space, engineering, architecture, theory, psychology. It was rare he would read a book of fiction just for sheer enjoyment. Another corner held a laboratory of sorts, one his dad helped him build over the years. It had a worktable with a microscope, pipettes, syringes, calibration equipment, incubator, spectrophotometer, centrifuge, and a host of other specialized equipment. No expense was spared if Mark needed a new "toy". After all, his dad wanted Mark to be prepared for Jason Enterprises. The more Mark studied and experimented, the better prepared he would be to take over one day.

Mark had planned for weeks to ask Jan to marry him. He thought about proposing at their favorite movie theater, their usual Friday night date spot. He knew that wouldn't work; she'd want something more intimate, romantic. As Mark lay on his bed, a thought came to him, sending him to an upright position. "I've got it," he said out loud.

As he dialed the phone, he could barely contain his excitement. In a thick Italian accent, she answered. "De Luca Ristorante, how may I help you?"

"Mrs. De Luca, hi, it's Mark Jason."

"Mario, it's-a-you!"

Giulia De Luca always addressed Mark as Mario. Years ago, she told him it meant 'sailor of the sea'. She knew his love of the Navy and his plans for going into the military, so she lovingly dubbed him "Mario."

"I have a favor to ask of you, Mrs. De Luca, I hope it's okay."

"Anything for my sweet young Mario! I wish my boys had-a turned out like-a-you." Mrs. De Luca over-exaggerated her Italian accent, but the customers loved it.

Mrs. De Luca could go on forever about her two boys, and often did whenever there was a set of ears which had never heard about her sons. Mark interrupted. "I was wondering, Mrs. De Luca, you know how Jan and I come in every Friday night after the movies, for dinner?"

"Yes, yes, of course."

"Well, um, I was hoping I could reserve a table for two, way in the back where it's kinda quiet, and private. I'm, well, gonna propose to Jan Friday night." Mark shuffled his feet as he held onto the phone. "I thought your place would be sort of, you know, romantic, when I gave her the engagement ring." Mark blushed as he 'confessed' his love over the phone.

"Oh, Mario, you and-a-Jan, getting married! You make-a-me cry! Si! Of course, I make-a-special place for you in-a back. You don't worry, Mama Giulia takes care of everything for you. Eight o'clock okay for you? You know, my-a sons, they will never give-a me grandbabies."

Mark rolled his eyes and dreaded to hear another long story about her sons. He interrupted for a second time. "Yes ma'am, eight will be fine and thank you so much." Hanging up the phone, he knew he had to tell his dad, then pay a visit to Jan's father. He wasn't sure which visit terrified him more.

◆

It wasn't exactly Jason Enterprises official business. Mark felt this had to be done. He decided to tell his dad of his marriage proposal plan in the big office at the top of the Jason Enterprises building in downtown Richmond. He'd been on the executive level and 'the office' scores of times. Today, he felt like he was about to meet Zachary Jason for the first time.

He waited patiently in Zachary's secretary's office as a day-long parade of businessmen came in and out as scheduled. Zachary knew his son was waiting and was making this a lesson on the importance of scheduling.

Finally, all the meetings for the morning were done. Zachary welcomed his son into the office. "So, to what pleasure do I owe this unscheduled visit?" Zachary said with some jest mixed in with the education.

"Well," Mark began, "I, um, I just wanted to tell you that, um, I'm going to—"

"Propose to Jan?" Zachary interrupted.

Mark sat in his chair in total dumbfounded shock. "How did you know?"

Zachary smiled. "You want to run this company one day son? Then get to know everybody around you better than they know themselves. Strive to seem almost psychic or invincible to everyone else. They'll respect you and not be afraid to come to you with concerns, because they'll believe you'll be able to help them. You can't buy that kind of loyalty and trust, you earn it."

Mark had to agree. He'd never seen even one disgruntled employee any time he came to the office.

"So, how did I know?" Zachary continued. "I've watched you your whole life, son. I've seen you happy, sad, angry, hurt, furious, and obsessive. But whenever Jan is on your mind, well, I'm not going to tell you how I know, you'll find that out with children of your own. But right now, that 'Jan look' is all over your face, the biggest I've ever seen."

Mark could only smile at the 'first answer his dad never really gave him'.

Zachary laughed. "I've taught you to keep your feelings controlled so they can be useful. But love can't be controlled, let alone hidden.

"You never cease to amaze me, Dad."

"A trait to guarantee loyalty, friendship, and trust, among other traits. So, Mister-About-to-Propose, let's go get a beer for me and an iced tea for you and you tell me about your plan. We'll tell your mother about it after Jan says 'yes.'"

◆

Visiting with Jan's dad at his office was nerve-wracking for Mark, but it was the right thing to do. It had been a nightmare for Mark the day he had to go through the 'interview' process with Jan's parents so he could ask her out for their first real date, despite that both families had known each other all their lives. Zachary told Mark that this was propriety, and he will do the same thing with his own son or daughter one day. Right now, though, Mark had to corral all the butterflies which caused havoc from the inside.

As he walked up to the two-story CPA building, Mark thought about some of the comments Thomas Churchill could possibly make, "You wanna do what? Take away my little girl? Deflower her? Get the hell out of my office!" He'd pound his fists on his desk and get red in the face. Mark shook the vision out of his head, knowing it wouldn't be that bad, maybe. Perspiration stains showed around the armpits of Mark's shirt when he got out of the elevator. He thanked God for whoever created the sports coat.

To Mark's relief, the visit went well. Thomas nearly jumped out of his chair to shake Mark's hand, and commented it was about damn time the two got hitched. The stout man lit up a celebratory cigar.

"I better open a window though or I'll be gettin' hell from my secretary. She hates the smell. Not supposed to smoke up here anyway." Opening the window, he asked, "Well, when you gonna ask her? Thought of a date? Wanna a big wedding, invite the whole town, or a small, intimate one with just the family?" Mark hadn't thought much about any of it. He stared at the floor and searched for answers in the blue-green carpet.

"I-I don't know, sir; guess I hadn't really thought it all through. All I've really thought about is marrying your daughter, nothing else really matters. Oh, I did plan on asking her this Friday, though."

As he rounded the desk Thomas said, "Well, don't worry 'bout it. Girls love to plan that stuff anyway. Don't matter whatcha want, she'll get her way no matter what. And knowing Peggy and Evelyn, us fellas don't stand a chance in hell of gettin' a suggestion in any way!" He gave a hearty laugh; his belly shook as he clenched his cigar in his teeth. He patted Mark on the back. "Welcome to the family, son!"

◆

The next day Mark went to Jenson's Jeweler's downtown to pick out an engagement ring. "Size, what size is her finger?" Mark repeated back to the sales lady. "Um, I don't know, I never really thought about it." Dumbfounded, he came to realize that despite all his studies in so many subjects, he didn't know much at all about rings. As she talked, he debated if Jan liked gold or silver, if she wanted a solitaire, heart, marquis, round, oval, princess, his and hers matching bands. He received a long lesson on cut, color, clarity, and carat size of a diamond. After an hour, his head spun, not to mention the exorbitant prices that pinched at his wallet, as he wanted to stay within his allowance savings. "She's real petite, with tiny hands. Can you help me make decide? I want so much for this to be a surprise."

The sales lady smiled; she'd gone through this routine dozens of times with customers. "Well, based on the description you've given of her personality, clothing style, that she's not very frivolous, and the fact that she's petite, may I recommend a one carat, square, solitaire diamond, with matching his and hers bands with three small square diamonds in each? Probably size 6 or 7. The rings can always be resized if they don't fit."

"Are you sure?"

"Well, no one can be absolutely sure, unless you let her pick it out herself."

"No, it really needs to be a surprise. Okay, but make it two carat, and white-gold, I can afford it, though Dad may kill me," he smiled.

◆

Mark and Jan went on their usual Friday night movie date. They often went to the new premieres, and always went to the late afternoon shows to have more time together in the evening afterwards. After the movie Mark asked, "You ready for some dinner?"

Giggling a bit, "Yep, Mama De Luca's food was calling to me all through the movie." Mark sighed in relief at the perfect coincidence. Since the restaurant was luckily her choice anyway, none of what Mark had planned would be suspicious. Mark didn't usually take her to see romantic movies, but tonight he took her to see 'Indecent Proposal'. Mark said he was a Robert Redford fan, but Jan thought he just wanted to see Demi Moore nude on the big screen. While there was a minute or two of her partially nude, he was refilling their snacks at the concession counter right then, so Jan believed Mark was telling her the truth, and never said a word about what had run around in her head nor what he missed on the big screen. On the other hand, she had to admit Demi was gorgeous, and Robert Redford, well, he was Robert Redford!

Mark dressed a little nicer than usual. He wore his normal Izod shirt, but also put on a sports jacket. Jan commented on how nice he looked. Mark shrugged it off and smiled, saying he just wanted to impress his beautiful date.

Mark took her arm and they walked through the lobby and to his car as usual. He quietly admired her beauty as he helped her into the passenger seat. He couldn't help but notice the extra high slit in her skirt that teased him with a longer view of her porcelain-toned leg, and nearly caught his fingers in the passenger door as he shut it. Mark rounded the back of the red Mazda RX-7, a present from his parents when Mark turned eighteen. The new '93 model was the best in design, purred like a kitten, and went from zero to sixty in only five seconds. Jan wasn't so fond of the five second portion, as it threw her head backwards and always knotted her stomach. She thought they would wreck one day or get a ticket. She admired the car however, and thought Mark sure looked good driving it.

"Mark, you missed the turn to the restaurant." Jan pointed out the window, and watched the street go by.

"I know."

"Where are we going?"

"You'll see in one second."

Mark slowed the car and pulled off the side of the road in front of Fountain Lake, at Byrd Park in downtown Richmond. The sun was setting. Hues of orange and yellow from the sky mirrored onto the lake. A tall fountain sat in the center of the lake. Water shot high into the air and created ripples that ringed out toward the shore. Giant oaks stretched long green reflections into the water, melded with the other tints, and created nature's portrait at its best.

Jan sat forward in her seat and unbuckled her seatbelt, "Oh, Mark, it's beautiful! Look at the colors!"

Mark turned off the ignition and unbuckled as well. "I know. You like?"

"Yes, is this why you brought me here, to see this?" Jan leaned over and gave Mark a kiss on the cheek.

"Come on, let's get out for one minute, then we'll head off to dinner," he said.

They got out and took a seat on a bench. Mark reached to place Jan's hand in his. Waving his other hand dramatically toward the lake he said, "I, Claude Monet, painted it just for you, Mademoiselle," mimicking a heavy French accent.

She didn't even attempt to laugh at his comedic gesture, instead looked up into his eyes, "I love you, Mark." Her comment was simple, but the sincerest words he'd ever heard. He took her in his arms and kissed her long, and with passion. Children rode by on bicycles and snickered as the two kissed, which prompted the lovers to move apart. They giggled too and, hand in hand they walked back to the car and off to the restaurant.

The couple entered De Luca's at exactly eight o'clock, greeted by the maîtres d' and escorted to their table. Mark was getting more nervous by the minute. Thoughts of doubt raced through his mind: *what if she says 'no'?* He'd be embarrassed, but worse, devastated. Their table was in a far corner, at the back of the restaurant, situated in a platform area, accessed by three small steps. His hand fiddled in his pocket, and checked for the millionth time, to make sure the ring was still there.

In his nervousness, Mark's shoe caught on one of the steps leading to their table. He lurched forward, balanced with the other foot as it came down sharply on the next wooden step. "Mark, are you okay?" She looked back and smiled at his clumsiness. He was hunched over slightly as he caught his fall.

Standing straight he ran his fingers through his hair, "Yeah, missed a step, that's all," he said as he feigned a half-hearted smile.

"Look-a-who's here!" Mrs. De Luca rounded the corner and up the stairs, a short, stocky woman in her late fifties. Her dark eyes beamed with happiness, a smile with perfect white teeth seemed to stretch from ear to ear. "Give Mama a hug!" both arms extended wide. She embraced Mark and Jan at the same time and stood on tippy toes to give them both a kiss on the cheek. She smelled of garlic and onions, not an unpleasant fragrance for an Italian restaurant. Her once-jet black hair had tints of gray and was pulled back in a bun. A lock fell forward and gave her a disheveled look of her work all day in the kitchen. "My-a two favorite babies, here again. Aw, but not-a babies anymore, ah, Mario? You graduated and all grown up-a-now, si?"

Jan eyed Mama De Luca, thoughtful of her attentiveness this evening, wondering why they weren't being seated at their usual table by the front window.

"You sit-a-here tonight, okay? I have-a new lasagna recipe, I test it on-a my favorite babies! I trust-a you to tell me is-a good! This-a be on the house, since you are being beautiful guinea pigs, eh! I get it for you in-a-no time." She waddled off to the kitchen as the maîtres d' opened a sconce and lit a candle. It provided ambient light in the darkened, curtained corner. He proceeded to pull back a chair for Jan, "Signorina, please have a seat." Hesitantly, Jan sat as he scooted her chair toward the table and formally placed a cloth napkin in her lap. Mark sat as well and gave a shy grin at no one in particular. He'd not expected such elaborate service. A napkin was on its way to Mark's lap as well. Mark looked up at the man, took hold of the napkin, "Got it, thanks," and finished setting it down himself.

"And now, what may I serve for your drinks this evening?"

"Just water," Jan and Mark spoke in unison, and chuckled when they realized they'd both spoken at the same time.

"Water it will be. Your server will be right with you." The maîtres d' gave a short bow and departed.

Jan leaned forward, "Mark, what in the world is going on? They're being extra nice and all. Look, our normal table is open, why'd she bring us all the way back here?" The waitress was at the table in no time, serving glasses of water and placing a steaming basket of garlic toast on the table. "And, wow, Mama was laying on the Italian accent heavy tonight!" Jan giggled.

Picking up a piece of toast, "I don't know, Jan, maybe she's got a group party or something later? But it's kinda nice, huh?" Mark nervously reached for his water, knocked it over, and sent cold water forward and onto Jan's lap. Instinctively, she jumped up, bumped the table, the candle toppled over along with her glass of water.

*"This is NOT going well at all,"* Mark thought as the waitress helped clean the mess and tidy the table back to normal. He sat forlorn, chin in hand, and stared at Jan.

"It's ok, Mark, it's just water," she said, smiling, trying to cheer him up.

Lasagna was served, Mark being extra cautious that no other disasters happened throughout dinner. After the first bite they both agreed that Mama had achieved another culinary success, and Mark gave her a 'thumbs up' when she stopped by to ask how they liked it. She waddled away, giving herself a big hug. They carried on their normal chit-chat, and to his relief, all went fine. *"This is it, the big moment,"* he thought. *"Don't screw this up!"* Taking Jan's hand in his, "Jan, there's been something on my mind, something I want to talk with you about."

The candlelight on the table flickered between them. It sent varied patterns of shadows and light against Jan's bare arms, accented the freckles on her shoulders and biceps and bridge of her nose. Her red hair practically glowed when the candlelight hit it. "What is it, Mark? Everything okay?"

Mark inched his chair back, its wooden legs screeched on the floor, and attracted the attention of other nearby patrons. He stood and reached into his pocket. *"Oh my God, could it be?"* Jan thought. Her eyes widened and her face flushed at the thought of what might happen next.

Mama De Luca shushed everyone else in the restaurant as she pointed toward the corner table. Mama, the patrons, waitresses, and maîtres d' craned their necks in silence, and waited for the answer they prayed would be cause for cheer.

He knelt before her, oblivious to the sudden silence in the restaurant. He focused on nothing but this moment. Mark looked into her eyes, and was suddenly calm, confident, and happy. He brought forth the ring case and opened it, "Jan, my love, will you make me the happiest man in the world and marry me?"

The restaurant became vacuum-silent as everyone held their breaths. Jan stared solidly at Mark, not in shock, not taken aback in the least, and hopelessly in love. She reached out for his hand

and the ring and smiled. "Mark, my dear sweet man, YES! I'd be honored to be your wife!"

A roar went up throughout the restaurant, clapping and shouts exploded at hearing Jan's answer. Both Mark and Jan involuntarily jumped at the clamor and blushed with embarrassment. They never realized they were being watched. Mama gave the newly engaged couple a big bear hug as wait staff brought out bottles of champagne for all the restaurant guests, on the house.

## CHAPTER 3
## APRIL 1993
## A PRAYER ANSWERED

He bolted down the steps and out the open double-door, turned left and ran around the front of the bus. He hit the detonator button just as policemen were starting to charge him, but the sudden explosion sent everyone back to cover, allowing him to escape on foot. In the distraction of the rain of flaming bus and body parts he dropped the AK47, detonator button and gloves in a trash can when he was out of sight. Replaying the whole scene in his head, he ran. Thoughts bombarded his brain: their rundown home, the need to renovate, upkeep on the clunker of a car, the debts that his church had incurred. It all seemed too much, and the man had given in to his desperation. No money from his poorly thought-out plan, and now he had to deal with the fear of being caught. The thought that he had just killed a dozen people never even entered his mind, so furious was he that this simple plan was ruined. He never meant to kill anyone, but they forced his hand and he had to reply with the righteous fury at his disposal. He ran until he felt no one followed, found a quiet alley, and fell to his knees and sobbed, not in sadness, but in complete anger. He wanted to lash out, hit someone, anyone, but he was alone in his turmoil of emotions.

## 2s and 3s

The explosion was heard a mile away, according to the paper. Over coffee the next morning, his wife continued to pick the last pieces of glass, metal, and other shards from his back. He didn't escape unscathed, but also never felt the hot objects penetrate his clothing and skin. He only winced once from the pain as he scanned the morning's headlines in haste.

*Mysterious man escapes after bus bombing in city*
*Demanded millions of dollars*
*Only survivor five-year-old boy*
*Child turned over to local children's home*

The article went on, taking up most of the front page. Graphic pictures of the scene were pasted in full color throughout the article. His wife swallowed heavily as she glanced at the paper. Her eyes filled with tears, but she dared not say anything. She knew what would happen if she did. She knew too well the monster he'd turned into over the years.

"Woman, we barely have the house and our church, just those TWO."

"Yes, dear." Bent forward, she continued with the tweezers to remove small pieces of glass from his back.

A thought struck the deranged man and his eyes widened, then narrowed as a plan began to form in his head. "We will have our THIRD child!" He slammed a fist on the table and glanced backwards at his wife.

She jumped involuntarily at the outburst. "Yes, dear! But we've been over this. The doctor says I can't have any more children, you know that."

Father DeVeaux crumpled the paper and threw it on the floor and glared at her, "Don't contradict me, woman! We're gonna have a THIRD child, I have the perfect one in mind. We'll have our THREE children, and maybe even afford to raise them all simply fine." He jerked his chair backwards, knocked his wife off balance momentarily, she dropped the tweezers to the floor. "Yes, everything should be perfect with THREE children now, we just have to be patient and be our perfect TWO selves."

JULY 1993

David sat on the bottom bunk in the children's home, wide-eyed, as a man in a black suit and white collar knelt in front of him. He shared a room with three other boys his same age for the past three months and had been given the bunk no one else wanted. The walls were painted a cerulean blue, dotted with baseball pendants and posters of Teenage Mutant Ninja Turtles and Michael Jordan. The posters of Michael Jordan were David's favorite, both basketball and baseball. He often thought about how he used to shoot hoops in the driveway with his dad before the bus incident. Every time he thought about his parents, David cried.

Prospective adoptive parents were interviewed for weeks. There was no mention of David's accompanying inheritance, however. The DeVeaux family and their Episcopalian Church were well respected in the community and seemed to be a perfect fit for David, therefore little 'background' was done on Father DeVeaux and his family.

David had gone through a long bout of depression since the bombing. Therapists worked with him, tried to help him deal with feelings of abandonment and grief. They had yet to understand his fixation of counting the numbers two and three at random moments. It was usually when he saw two or three of anything grouped together. They would continue to help him, even after he was adopted.

A woman and two small children, a boy, and a girl, stood solemnly behind the man with the white collar. They were nicely dressed, but quiet, like statues without facial expressions. David's mind wandered, he thought they might be just as afraid as he was.

Three months had passed since the bus explosion, and no family members came forward to claim David. Both his parents had been only-children, so there were no aunts or uncles to take him in. One grandfather died in Vietnam, the other in a traffic accident before David was born. One grandmother was in a nursing home, and the other was living in England but couldn't be reached. He was placed in a local children's home and quickly put on the adoption list. His parents had been wealthy from well-worked Wall Street investments. They'd drawn up a will when David was born, denoting a large trust fund to him, should they die simultaneously. The attorney had fretted over the situation at the time, knowing someone could possibly adopt David and abuse the sizable amount of money. They finally decided that a portion of it was meant to aid in raising David in a new home, should a tragedy occur. The rest went to a trust fund to be given to him at age eighteen.

The DeVeauxs were approved for the adoption and given the details about David's financial backing. Father DeVeaux felt weak in the knees and fought hard against the urge to either scream for joy or pass out. Financial burdens had miraculously been lifted and a third child was finally among his flock. His prayers seemed to be answered.

Extending his hand in greeting, "Hi, I'm Father DeVeaux, how are you, David?" David shyly lowered his head, narrowed his eyes, but kept them set steadfast on the Father's face. He didn't return the offered handshake, and kept his hands firmly squeezed between his knees, without a response. The Father's nostrils flared, and heat built up behind his collar and in his ears. Tolerating disobedience was difficult for the minister. While he preached that patience was a virtue, he failed to heed his own sermons more times than not. He feigned patience and smiled as he lowered his hand.

"That's okay, David, I know you don't know us, and you're probably scared of everything right now. We know what's happened in your life recently. Let me introduce you to your new family. This is Mrs. DeVeaux, and your new brother and sister, Henri and Elise." David had never heard names like 'on-ree' and 'ai-lees' before, he wasn't sure they were real names. He motioned to his wife, then the two children: a skinny four-year-old boy with neatly combed brown hair, and a freckle faced three-year-old girl with blonde hair tied into two ponytails. Both children stared at David with blank expressions. "Say 'hello', family." In unison, all three mumbled something incoherent. David closed one eye and cocked his head sideways. "THREE," he said aloud, pointing to the mother and children, then pointed at the reverend and his wife and said, "TWO." Everyone looked at each other with curiosity, horrified that the boy mimicked the Father's 'ways'.

Father DeVeaux knew, however, recognizing exactly what he thought was going through David's mind. He smiled and looked expectantly into David's eyes. Taking hold of David's arms, he shook him in excitement. "I have THREE of you now, THREE of you, isn't it wonderful?"

Despite the black suit, white collar, and the family that stood behind him, David thought he recognized Father DeVeaux as the man who blew up the bus. He was sure of it. The police had talked with David after the bombing, and gently persuaded David to give a description of the man. "The bad man on the bus," he thought as he stared at the Father. "The man who killed mommy and daddy." David became solemn, breathed heavily, and his eyes darted to the floor. The sparse, blue bedroom began to spin around.

DeVeaux lifted David's head by his jaw with an index finger. Staring into his eyes once again, he spoke slow and soft. "David, you do exactly as I tell you, and we'll get along simply fine. Got it?" David swallowed hard, and tears welled in his eyes. Despite his young age, he somehow knew his little world was falling apart even more than it already had.

**CHAPTER 4**
**JULY 1993**
**"I DO"**

As planned, Mark would report to Great Lakes Naval Base in late August. The wedding was held in early July, after the Independence Day holiday weekend. Mark's daily routine was to get an early start, a strenuous workout each morning in the family gym, then run several miles through the neighborhood. He would always take a different route to not be predictable. He realized that if JE could be a possible 'target' then so could he and his family. Extra precaution and discretion were always top priority.

Mark felt invigorated. The exercise gave him a natural high. Today though, he cut his time in half. He hated to lose out on 'workout' time, but today was special.

Showered and shaved he felt mentally and physically fit, more than prepared for the noon wedding ceremony, or so he thought. The wedding was held at the family's church. Both families attended the same church for years. Every pew was filled, and well exceeded the two hundred occupancy limit. Extra chairs were placed throughout the church. Work associates, family, friends, school buddies, were there for the big day.

The old church was large. Colorful stained-glass windows ran the length of the church, from ceiling to floor. Next to each window were gold plated plaques, each with a different bible scripture. A framed, backlit stained-glass portrait of Jesus was displayed prominently behind the pulpit. The Savior knelt on the ground beside a large rock, hands placed together in a prayer as He stared up into the heavens. The large portrayal seemed to jump out almost three-dimensional, mesmerizing to look at with all its bright colors. The old oak pews had been renovated years before, now set with light green cushions for comfort.

The Maid of Honor, Bride's Maids and Jan hovered in a small room on the second floor of the church. They attended to each other's hair and makeup, to look perfect. Jan fidgeted at every detail. She sat on a stool; tears pooled in her eyes as friends toyed with the bridal bouquet. "Who would the next bride be?" she wondered in silence.

"OK, Jan, come on," said Ann, the Maid of Honor. "Straighten up now, your makeup's gonna run." She dabbed a tissue to Jan's face and tried to soak up a few tears.

Jan stared into the mirror and recalled the days of little girls who sat in the driveway, blew bubbles from a wand, and drew chalk marks for hop-skip-jump. "I'm gonna miss all of you," the words came out blubbered more than spoken.

A Bridesmaid spoke up, "We're always here for you Jan, you know that. Nothing's changed just because you've got that rock on your finger!" They all crowded around for a delicate group hug but, assured hair and makeup stayed in place despite their sincere affection.

The photographer drifted from the bride's room to the groom's room. He staged and captured secret moments in time, as each prepared for their debut.

Mark sat alone in his small anteroom, his mind wandering a bit. Throughout high school Mark trekked off to the JE offices on school holidays and weekends. He interacted and worked with employees throughout the building, interested in the research and development areas. The burgeoning computer and engineering offices were added in the high-security areas, and he wanted to be in on all of it. As the wedding day approached, employees chided him, "Shouldn't you be somewhere else today?" He ignored the friendly banter.

Before anyone was truly prepared, sounds from the organ downstairs bellowed throughout the church, and prompted the wedding party to assume their positions. All shuffled downstairs and took their places as rehearsed, nervous.

Jan was anxious as she walked down the aisle with her father, attuned to every detail, especially her mother in the front right pew. Jan's mother smiled, dabbed at a tear, happy and sad at the same time.

Mark had picked out a white tuxedo instead of the traditional black, with Jan's approval, and looked very handsome standing at the front of the church. Jan matched beautifully in her white Vera Wang bridal gown, a one-shoulder basket-weave with a dropped waist, and draped bodice with organza petals and a traditional lace veil. Mark was overwhelmed by her beauty. A lump caught in this throat, and he felt tears well up in his eyes. With his right hand he pinched the top of his left hand as hard as he could. The pain cleared his head in an instant and the thought of tears vanished.

A young girl and boy preceded Jan, throwing rose petals haphazardly. They were the twin children of close friends. The boy tripped and dropped his basket, which caused Jan and her father to stop as everyone watched on in silence. The boy bent to scoop up the petals, and snickers were heard from nearby onlookers. He dutifully got back into step and continued to throw petals as if nothing had happened. Jan proceeded, "Thankfully," she thought to herself.

The Bridesmaids and Groomsmen were dressed in baby blue gowns and tuxedos, a color Jan had picked. Mark didn't like the choice, but had given in, just as Mr. Churchill advised him. Seeing the five men on the left and five women on the right, he was in awe of the formality and beauty. "She's right as usual," he thought to himself.

Throughout the ceremony, Mark and Jan spoke their rehearsed vows carefully, nervous as hundreds watched and listened. Within minutes the marriage ceremony was over. The couple happily walked down the aisle, to the front steps of the church, and paused for pictures along the way under a shower of rice.

The couple headed for the limousine at the front of the church, only to be delayed again by their parents and the photographer. "Not so quick, you two. Gotta get a few more photos on the church grounds before the reception." A few moments turned into twenty minutes as the photographer posed the happy couple in front of large oaks, weeping willows, and rose bushes.

The session was finally over, not realizing it was a stall tactic made by their parents. Mark and Jan ducked into the limousine and noticed all the guests had disappeared. "Mark, we're late for our own reception!"

"Better than being late for our own wedding," he said in reply. "Bet they won't start the reception without us."

**CHAPTER 5**
**JULY 1993**
**"HE CALLED ME MRS."**

The reception was lavish but was also tasteful and met with all the parents' satisfaction. It was a half day affair held at a large private estate on the outskirts of Richmond. Both moms selected the location for its extravagant surroundings, far enough out in the country to warrant privacy and heavy, though discreet, security, and removed everyone from the city noises of car horns and the sight of high rises. Most of the guests opted to attend.

The limousine took the newlyweds to a far corner of the employee parking lot. They were surprised that they were not being dropped off at the estate house. Instead, they were greeted by two men in black tuxedos with tall, black top hats. Staring at the hats, Jan grinned and whispered, "Mark, they look like Abraham Lincoln."

"Mr. and Mrs. Jason, please step this way," one of the men waved a white gloved hand toward an open-air white carriage, pulled by two white horses.

"Wow," Mark mouthed in a juvenile gaze, dumbfounded by the opulence of everything in white.

"Wow, he called me 'Mrs. Jason'!" Jan's face beamed with happiness.

Jan pulled him forward and up into the carriage. Her billowing gown fit in with the Cinderella-like scene. Mark sat half on her gown just to fit side-by-side. Jan didn't mind. The men climbed onto the driver's seat and gently urged the horses forward.

The fairy tale ride approached the mansion entrance, and the couple appeared wide-eyed as they passed the mass of guests lined along the cobblestone entrance. People spilled over into the grass and waved at the happy couple. The photographer pushed his way forward and snapped photos that would soon be bound in a wedding album and placed on their coffee table for years to come.

Making their way from the carriage to the pavilion, the couple was greeted with enthusiasm and happy smiles, and shook hands with prominent guests and embraced everyone with tearful hugs. After one couple passed through the receiving line, Jan turned to Mark with her mouth wide open. "Oh, my God, Mark, that was the President!"

Mark looked at her, nodding, "Mm, hmm," as calm as he could. At last, it dawned on her that this was not the first time Mark had met the President of the United States and First Lady. She punched him in the arm. "Smartass," she whispered.

A male peacock strutted his way through the mingled crowd. His eye-dotted, full tail plumage spread large and wide; the blue-green feathers were breathtaking. Letting out an irksome, high-pitched screech, the guests gawked at the bird, and watched as the bland gray female ran a few yards behind. Pointing at the bird, "Hey, Jan, there's you, running after me." Mark spoke before thinking, getting a second punch to his arm. Snickers and laughs came from the crowd as they all headed into the outdoor, air-conditioned pavilion.

At the request of both mothers, the reception began with heavy hors d'oeuvres and champagne in the pavilions, and guests were free to view the mansion or wander about the lush, sprawling grounds. Secret Service agents were stretched throughout the estate and stayed as out of sight as possible.

After a few quick snacks, the couple was persuaded by the photographer to retreat to the grounds for more wedding memories. Photos were taken in the gardens next to exotic flowers, century old boxwoods, magnolias, and oaks. They would later discover the most beautiful photo of all would be the one in a grassy field in front of a pond. Mark held Jan close, bent her slightly backwards, and placed a gentle kiss on her lips. The photo would later be enlarged, framed, and placed prominently in the living room, a silent remembrance of their love for each other.

After many photos and much more champagne and wine for the guests, a light luncheon was served for everyone.

Later in the evening, men stood outside in groups talking over cocktails and cigars. Fireflies twinkled in the fields like winged pixies. Lanterns hung low from old oak trees, producing an orange hypnotic glow throughout the grounds. Other guests danced to music in the ceiling-to-floor glassed rooms, while some played billiards in other rooms. In silence, Jan and Mark made their way to the observation deck on the roof. It overlooked the massive stretch of land and the Rappahannock River Valley. Holding each other, "I can't wait to get you back to the hotel tonight, then off to Hawaii tomorrow," Mark whispered into her ear, nibbling on it since he was in the area anyway.

Whispering back, "I can't wait to get us both out of these outfits and into a shower," Jan nuzzled closer to Mark and pulled him to her. They kissed long and hard.

Mumbled words escaped from Mark's lips, "Jan, when can we leave, soon I hope?"

## CHAPTER 6
## JULY 1993
## FLY ME TO THE HONEYMOON

The next day, Mark's dad put the newlyweds on the company jet for a honeymoon trip to Waikiki, Hawaii. The Gulfstream IV had just been through its annual inspection in Savannah, Georgia. A security detail of three men was sent along for a 'working vacation', to assure the couple was safe throughout the trip. The staff was instructed to let the young couple go their own way as much as possible, but stick by them, unnoticed, always.

One of the security staff spoke up as he boarded the plane, "Sure am grateful Mr. Jason picked me for this assignment. It's damn time I got a little vacation." The other two guards mumbled a reply, all thankful for time away, even though work was involved.

"Man-o-man, would ya look at this." The last security guard to board had never been on the luxury jet and was taken aback by its extravagance. "Look at the room in this thing, damn, a Rolls-Royce for the air. What, seats about twelve, lots-a leg room, got a bar and a TV? Yep, gonna love this trip." He fell silent as the Jason's boarded and moved forward.

"Have a seat everyone." The senior pilot emerged from the cockpit; the trip coordinator stood just behind him. "Buckle up till we get to altitude then make yourselves at home. Gotta straight flight plan to LA, 'bout five hours, grab some fuel, then off to Hawaii, 'bout another five hours. Then some sun, fun and re-laxation. Well, at least for the Jason's that is." The staff and newlyweds clapped in accord, excited about the trip.

The pilot returned to the flight deck. "My name is Brenda, and I'm your social coordinator for the trip," the lady announced in a high-pitched southern drawl. "Y'all just let me know what you'd like, and I'll see that it happens."

Mark looked at Jan, then back to Brenda. "Well, are we old enough for some champagne on this jet?"

Brenda smiled, nodded her head "yes," and stepped to the galley while the young couple and guards took their seats.

Once in the air, drinks and snacks were served and typical chit-chat abounded. The first hours of the flight were spent in small talk about the wedding and various details.

◆

At 30,000 feet, the pilots prepared to land in Los Angeles. One pilot talked with Air Traffic Control and was advised of their descent and approach instructions to the runway.

A sudden loud noise emanated from the front, and the plane pitched and went into an unexpected sideways dive, falling about 2,000 feet within a few seconds. Drink glasses sailed across the cabin, and everyone was thrown from their seats. One of the guards yelled, "What the hell's going on?" He slid down the aisle and grabbed hold of a chair frame.

Mark landed closest to the flight cabin door. He steadied himself and grabbed hold of the door and jerked it open. He saw the pilots fighting with the yolks. "What's happening?" he demanded.

"Something exploded in front of the plane!" The pilot yelled.

"What! Someone tried to shoot us down?"

"I don't know, sir! Give us a minute!" The pilot answered with impatience. He proceeded to contact LAX for an emergency landing and advise them of what he perceived to be the problem.

"Mark!" Jan screamed, in semi-panic mode. Mark turned and climbed 'down' to reach where she and the security guards were, most already back in their seats and buckled up. Jan pulled Brenda into the seat next to her. The woman was semi-conscious with a nasty gash on her forehead. Jan tightened the restraints to keep her in place and held a tissue to her forehead to help with the bleeding. "It's ok, Brenda, just hold on." The jet continued to shake and grumble.

"What happened?" yelled Jan over all the noise.

"I don't know yet," Mark yelled back. "I'll ask them when they get the plane under control."

"Oh my God, are we gonna crash?" She looked at Mark, at his stoic face. "How can you be so calm?"

"I'll panic later when the crisis is over," he replied, trying to offer up a soothing voice. He looked back at the open door to the flight deck.

He heard the copilot yell, "I got a green light on the number two engine."

The pilot answered, "Then hit it, by God! Advance to 100% power."

Everyone felt a rumbling surge in the superstructure as the engine restarted and the jet began to level out. The passengers had no idea it had been shut down, and worse, everyone was panicked at the uncertain situation.

Tense moments passed as if they were hours. Mark stood behind Jan's seat and wrapped his arms around her without regard to being strapped in. The jet seemed back to normal, and the quakes came to a stop. "Calm down, honey, everything's gonna be ok."

The pilot yelled back, "We're back to normal again, Mr. Jason. Lost an engine temporarily, lack of air flow from the explosion most likely. Airport has us on an inbound approach, down to about 5,000 feet, approaching around 220 knots. We're about six to eight minutes out. Everyone buckle up. We're ok it seems. Oh, and don't be alarmed when you see the emergency vehicles, it's just precaution."

Air Traffic Control put all other planes in a holding pattern around LAX as the JE jet was led in. Fire and EMS units assembled along the taxiway as a precaution, and Airport Security was enroute to meet the jet when it landed. The occupants stared out the windows in disbelief as emergency units took their positions along the taxiway, lights flashing. Wheels gently touched the tarmac as the jet landed, and everyone tilted slightly forward as the brakes were applied. A sigh of relief could be heard throughout the plane, though no one said a word. Mark made a quick cell phone call to his father to let him know what happened and everyone was ok.

## CHAPTER 7
## JULY 1993, LOS ANGELES
## THERE'S GOOD NEWS AND BAD NEWS

Private FBO parking ramp staff with muff ear protectors, bright yellow vests and orange signal wands guided the jet to a cordoned off area, where the jet could be inspected and repaired if necessary.

Paramedics boarded the plane and began to assess Brenda's injuries and prepared a stretcher for her. Airport Security boarded the plane as well and escorted all passengers off and into security vehicles. Everyone was taken back to the FBO and into a conference room for what would turn into an exceedingly long debriefing.

A terminal security agent spoke. "Mr. and Mrs. Jason, I beg to report that Air Traffic Control advises they think you were targeted by a ground-to-air missile. It appears to have exploded ahead of you in flight and the concussion most likely knocked out your number two engine."

Jan's hand flew up to her mouth, covering it so no sounds could escape.

"Any idea who did it, or why?" Mark asked calmly.

A man stepped into the office as Mark asked the question. "Fred Zimmerman, Chief of Airport Security. Mr. Jason, I received a call from your father regarding the incident. I informed him what I'm about to tell you. A fax was sent to our airport as well as to most local media affiliates in the area. The media's already run with it I'm afraid. I have a copy here and will read it to everyone."

Chief Zimmerman took a seat and proceeded to read, "'We have shot down the Jason Enterprises plane, killing all on board. We have proven that the rich capitalists are not as invulnerable as they think they are.'

Mr. and Mrs. Jason, you look quite excellent for dead newlyweds," the Chief chided.

"Did they identify themselves?" Mark asked.

"No, sir. The FBI is already at work on it. The FAA and NTSB are on their way here as well."

"How's the jet?" one of the pilots asked.

"Crews are taking a look at her, sir. Afraid you're grounded for now though. Will take two or three days to get a full inspection, repairs if any, and an ok to go," Zimmerman replied.

Jan whispered to Mark, "Oh, my God, Mark, this is too much to take in. I can't believe what's happening! What about Brenda? We've got to check on her, Mark, we can't leave her alone. What do we do about our reservations?"

"It's ok, Jan, we'll go check on Brenda. We'll get everyone to a hotel here and I'll fix the reservations in Hawaii, don't worry."

◆

After a couple of hours of discussion, two FBI agents were escorted into the conference room to meet with the Jason's and the crew. Zimmerman rose to greet the men, shaking their hands, as everyone else stood to stretch their weary bodies. Whispered chit-chat could be heard but not quite deciphered. "Everyone, these are Agents Cooper and Fernandez from the FBI." Zimmerman briefly introduced the group, trying his best to remember everyone's names.

"Please have a seat everyone," Agent Fernandez took control of the meeting, motioning everyone to sit once again while he stood. "We've been working this for several hours now and we're here to give you a quick briefing of our findings, then you'll all be free to go. I'll come right to the point. There was definitely an incendiary device launched and was meant to contact the Jason aircraft. Luckily, it missed and exploded in front of the plane." Pointing to the pilots, "You were correct in your speculations that the blast caused a lack of air flow and one of your engines was temporarily shut down due to compressor stall. The technicians are looking at the jet now and so far, have only found some minor damage to that engine. It should be repaired, inspected, and certified for flight within a day or two. You all are INCREDIBLY lucky, the size of that missile would have, well, destroyed the plane and everyone in it. Sorry to be so blunt. That's the good news, however."

"Can it get worse?" Jan asked in frustration. Jan contemplated that this was NOT how she imagined her honeymoon.

"We've had our radar on a paramilitary group if you will. They call themselves the AAE, American Army for Equality." Fernandez took a seat to finish out the frightful details. He interlocked his fingers on the table and continued. "The AAE seems to be a diverse coalition of people whose ideology is marked by a rebellion against what they consider capitalists."

"Capitalists? What the hell?" Mark started to get up, only to have Jan put a hand on his shoulder and gently encourage him to settle.

"Mr. Jason, I'm just trying to explain what these people are about, so you'll understand. And no, you're not gonna like it. They take violent resistance against people who they perceive are destroying the American way of life, people that might profit from corporate advantages, tax breaks, and things of that nature. They want to protest and fight against what they think is an excessive or rich way of life. Mr. Jason, no disrespect, they just think people like you and your family have unfair individual liberties."

Mark closed his eyes and shook his head. He was barely able to take in all the information the FBI was feeding him. Jan stared at Mark, afraid to speak. "So, now what?" Mark asked.

"Well, we think some of these people are actual military personnel, using stolen logistical inventory out in Nevada. Others are just radicals tagging along as muscle, looking for the same fight. They've done this before, and we have a good bit of intel on 'em. We just didn't see this one coming, unfortunately, sir. Not to worry, we got an eye on 'em now. We know their every move."

**CHAPTER 8**
**JULY 1993**
**THE CALL**

In Virginia, Zachary Jason slammed the phone receiver down and looked up at his security chief. "Get the security staff into the conference room, NOW!"

Zackary briefed his security staff about the near-miss in California. Angrier than they'd ever seen him, he barked orders left and right. He commanded the staff to put the building and its employees on high alert. "And put a twenty-four-hour detail on my house. You go where my wife goes, got it?" Everyone nodded in the affirmative. "She'll give me hell for that, I'm sure."

Zackary spent enough time in the military to know how to access information, the kind that was unavailable to the public. Pointing an index finger at one of his employees, "John, you're now my liaison with the FBI, I'll tell 'em you'll be calling. Keep me briefed on every damn detail, 24/7. No one's sleepin' 'til we get this in the bag. Damn S-O-B's. You men sit here and work out your security plans. I got something to do."

Zackary left the room and slammed the door behind him, harder than he intended.

◆

Zac took the large clunky cell phone from his office drawer. He extended the antennae and punched in the numbers. He heard static, clicking then finally a ring. He touched the gold key on his desk as he waited. The person on the other end picked up but said nothing. "Charlie, Zac. Need a favor."

## CHAPTER 9
## JULY 1993, SOMEWHERE IN NEVADA
## CELEBRATING A JOB WELL DONE

The Mojave Desert can be one of the most beautiful places in the world. But tonight, it held an aura of mystery and desolation. A variety of barrel cactus occupied the area near the old, dilapidated Quonset hut, as did groves of Joshua trees, Yucca plants, and various shrubs. The moonless night was darker than usual as cloud cover obscured any stars that might ordinarily shine through. June bugs made crinkling noises as they moved about. Cicadas with their multi-veined wings dove back and forth and made loud buzzing noises.

The tranquil quiet was disturbed by the rumbling of an engine. The stolen Jeep Wrangler rolled along the sandy desert road. During the day, mounds of rippled sand dunes could be seen for miles, surrounded by low rolling hills made from ancient volcanic cinder cones. A 2 ½ ton military flat bed, also stolen, followed close behind, an empty rocket launcher was bolted to the back. Both vehicles rolled up next to the hut near a large grove of Joshua trees. The stolen FIM-92 Stinger missile had blown up the JE jet, or so the men thought. The surface to air missile had been converted from its hand-held homing format, adapted, and bolted to the truck, taken to its proximity, and launched. The launcher had a small ejector motor with a solid fuel sustainer that ran on argon gas, which produced a low thermal conductivity. It was easy to shoot, easy to carry, easy to conceal. A layman would hardly be able to tell that anything had been fired from the truck.

The militant group had stolen numerous Stingers and stored them in the upstairs portion of the Quonset hut, along with other weaponry. The Stingers were easy to come by. Thousands were in military warehouses throughout the United States and abroad. Tonight's mission seemed to be easy, both vehicles left immediately after the launch so as not to be detected. The launch team never looked back.

Six men got out of the vehicles; the inside lights illuminated the darkness. They were relieved that no one had followed them. They shook hands for a job well done, some gave high-fives. One of the men produced a flashlight and opened a cooler in the back of the jeep. The 'whish' sound of a can being opened led to quick silence as other flashlights clicked on in response.

"Hey, man, you didn't tell us you brought beer."

Shouts of "woo-hoo" and "alright" broke the silence as more whishing sounds followed in succession. The sticky night air had only gotten down to a 'cool' 89 degrees. The men were sweaty and thirsty, and downing the first beer took less than a minute. As they drank, large moths flitted about, seeking light from the flashlights. A few hungry long eared bats appeared and dove at the unsuspecting moths. One man with a thick Mexican accent jumped about at the 'bat attack'. Sounding much like Cheech Marin, his voice raised an octave, "What the hell, man, get these things away from me! They're making me spill my beer!" As he bobbled around, he backed into a barrel cactus, and screamed in pain as the needles penetrated his backside. Several kangaroo rats scooted out from underneath the cactus during the commotion, upsetting the man even more.

The men leaned against the trucks and laughed, shook their heads, and enjoyed the show as they drank. Once the performance was over, they grabbed more beer from the cooler, as well as their weapons, and piled into the Quonset hut.

The hut contained two rollup doors, one on the east side in front, and one on the west side in the back. The leader disbursed the men to each door, and upstairs for security, and they joined the six other men who had already been in the hut on guard duty. Each carried stolen military rifles and ammo. The hut was stifling and musty, holding in the heat from the one-hundred-degree day. They decided to open the doors halfway. A light breeze passed in one door and took the heat out the other. The metal shell building 'ticked' every few seconds as it cooled.

The hut was anchored to a concrete slab, and a desk and several chairs sat in the middle on the first floor. A battery powered TV sat on the desk, rabbit-ear antennas extended outwards. Someone had placed tinfoil on them to get better reception. Next to the TV sat a portable bag phone. Lanterns and various other battery powered camp lights were switched on, just enough for the crew to see where they were going as they fanned out inside the building. The leader sat in the center, turned on the TV and searched for a channel as others gathered around. "Why didn't we install cable in here?" one of the men questioned.

"And where the hell would the cable come from?" The leader asked. "You see any electricity in this shack, dumb-ass?"

The others snickered as their boss hit the side of the TV. He'd hoped for a better signal. "We need to see a news report about the jet," the leader explained. "Boss is gonna be really happy with this one. Textbook all the way. Message signed, sealed, and delivered, boys! And we'll get paid well, very well."

"Shoulda been paid first," one of the men grunted as he fiddled with an antenna, and finally got a semi-clear station showing a newscaster.

"There, leave it there!" The leader snapped.

"Yeah, that's one hot babe reading the news. Wonder how she'd read me?" one man spouted off.

"Aah, shut yer ass."

They listened to the newscast.

**CHAPTER 10**
**JULY 1993**
**CAUGHT WITH THEIR PANTS DOWN**

Six dark figures moved like smoke from within Joshua tree clusters, slow and deliberate.

The strike team wore standard bullet-proof gear and was dressed in an advanced style of black BDUs. The uniform was an experimental prototype, using a material that was potentially bullet-proof, acid-proof, fire-proof, and impenetrable. They blended perfectly in the black void of the night. Each one wore a state-of-the-art tactical headset with parabolic audio enhancers.

Radios were clipped to their belts, and a first-of-its-kind wireless, hyper-sensitive throat microphone was affixed to their necks. Waterproof night vision goggles with heat enhancing thermography were affixed to the headset and offered a clear panoramic view of their entire surroundings. People, animals, or other objects could be seen in the dark, and through the walls of the building. They gave off grayish, almost ghost-like silhouettes. Things that emanated a higher temperature were easier to see through the goggles.

There were no manufacturer trademarks or patent numbers on any of the gear. There was no way to connect that the equipment was developed by Jason Enterprises, should it be left behind for any reason.

"Damn, these goggles are heavy," whispered one of the women as she walked forward. "Wish the lab would find a way to make 'em lighter."

"I told ya, gotta exercise those neck muscles more, like pushups, up, down, up, down. You can practice on me later," one of the male team members whispered back. Light chuckles could be heard through the headsets from the other male team members.

"Shut up, Joe."

"Everyone shut up," the team leader demanded. "Get a good fix on everything around you. Know where everything and everyone is located."

Outside, heat signatures were noted from the two vehicles, engines still hot from their trek through the desert. One of the men noticed a strange hot spot on the ground just a few feet in front of him, squinted at it, and tried to make out what it was. An odd, circular pyramid shape that progressively got smaller at the top. It sat upon a rock, still hot from the earlier hundred-degree heat. He thought it looked like a tall pile of dog crap. Then he heard it, the unmistakable warning rattle from the snake, then a lunge toward him. "Shit!" he said louder than expected. He felt the thump against his leg as he jumped backwards. The uniform kept the snake's teeth from penetrating the material.

"What is it?" the team leader whispered an irritated bark.

"Rattler, sir," the man puffed air in and out, obviously shaken. "All's OK, no problem." He watched the image of the rattlesnake slither off into the brush as his heartbeat slowed back to a normal rhythm. Though their special BDUs were meant to stay cool in the summer and warm in the winter, he felt sweat dripping from his forehead, armpits, and back.

The team members took in their surroundings through the goggles and were able to see through the metal of the arched building with ease. Heat signatures were evident. The team crouched outside to watch and listen. Six men sat or stood around a table. Some were smoking, the tips of the cigarettes showed a darker gray because of their hot spots. Most had rifles hanging across their chests, some were drinking from cans, and one was even picking his nose. All six men stared at a box on the table. The team finally discerned it was a TV once they homed in their audio sensors and were able to hear the ongoing discussion about a jet crash, waiting for the news announcement to air on the TV.

"Close the doors, it's cooled off enough in here now." Noticing movement near both doors, the strike leader gave a hand signal for all to hold their positions. Four more men appeared, seemingly from nowhere. All held rifles as well, and cranked the half-open doors fully shut.

"They must have been keeping guard on the doors, maybe hiding behind boxes or furniture," the leader whispered to his team. "Let's pull in a little closer. Andy, check out the trucks."

Andy, the team's biological engineer, headed toward the trucks. He took an environment detector device from his vest pocket and scanned both vehicles. After a few minutes, Andy reported his findings. "This is it, boss. Rocket launcher bolted to the back of the big truck, traces of argon gas and signs that it's been fired in the last few hours, minute amounts of carbon scoring. Also picking up an unknown from the jeep. No wait, just beer, sir."

They approached the metal structure without a sound and split up to each side of the hut and the doors at either end.

One man stationed himself at the door on the east, another on the west. The remaining four positioned themselves equidistant on either side. The four on the sides donned special black gloves with fabric-lined magnetic surfaces on the palms and fingers, another prototype. In unison the four began to climb up the sides of the two-story structure. Their ascents made no sound.

They placed electronic detonators along the metal surface.

Two climbers stopped mid-way to the top and hung in place. The other two made it to the top of the curved structure and quietly moved toward two air vents.

The leader of the strike force was at the front door. "Status," he commanded in a hushed voice.

"Two on the second floor, one at each window," said one of the team's women.

Another said, "Ten on the bottom, they're movin' around. Two at each door. Four at each lower window. One sitting midway, one standing beside him, ah, and I read an extra heat sig as an old-fashioned TV, the output seems like it's on battery instead of AC. In fact, I don't read any electricity coming in here at all."

"There's a few low-powered lights, battery operated," said a third voice. "I make out the inside to be mostly dark."

"One comin' at ya, boss," said another voice.

The leader and his partner shied back into the overgrowth near the eastern front entrance. The door rolled up about three feet and they watched as a man hunched down, stepped out the door and stopped a few feet outside. He pulled down his zipper and began to urinate.

The urine stream gave off waves of heat in their goggles. The commander gave his partner, who was closer to the man, a three-finger signal, followed by a fist and "OK" sign.

The partner waited for the man to finish his business and put his pants back together. The strike team member lunged forward, grabbed the man, covered his mouth, and plunged a knife into his back. The man slowly sagged to the ground, dead.

The second guard inside became impatient, hunched over, and stepped outside to look for his friend. The boss reached out from the shadows, grabbed the man's head with both hands and twisted, snapping his neck, sending him to the ground, dead.

Two other uniformed men slipped inside the open door. "If you meet 'em, take 'em," he ordered into his throat mike.

Across the building the other team members silently entered via the upstairs windows and slithered in under the other door. The only sounds heard were the "phht"s of silencers. While the inside men died, their attackers moved forward to catch their bodies as they fell, so as not to alarm the two watching the TV. Within minutes the only people alive were the strike team and the two men at the television set in the middle of the first floor.

The missile team leader was still seated at the desk as he waited for the bag phone to ring. He also waited for the newscaster to get to the story about the jet. The news segment ended, as did the weather segment, sports, all interrupted by incessant commercial breaks that curdled his stomach. Finally, the local newscast ended with a story about schools that would prepare for the new school year, and no mention of the Jason jet exploding in the air. "What the hell!" he yelled as he stood.

"There shoulda been something!" said the second man. "Maybe it crashed too far from the airport? They didn't see it, or haven't found it?"

"A missing plane would still make the news," said the first. The bag phone rang, and the leader answered immediately. "Maybe they just didn't have the story ready for the evening edition, sir," the leader started.

"YOU IDIOT!" The voice on the phone was so loud the second man could hear him. "THE PLANE LANDED!"

The strike team commander said into his throat mike, "Trace the call."

The man at the desk said into the receiver, "That's impossible, sir! We had the plane targeted! We saw the rocket explode. The plane—"

"You saw the rocket explode IN FRONT OF THE DAMN PLANE!" screamed the phone voice. "It landed safely at L.A. this afternoon!"

Still holding the phone to his ear, he looked over at his comrade and pointed at him, "Which means," the leader took a long pause before he continued, "they're looking for us. I TOLD you not to send out the message until after the crash site was found!"

"You told me? You said it was a great idea!"

"We gotta get outta here before we're found." He called out to his crew across the building, "We're leaving, now! Everyone get out of here!"

No sounds came from within the Quonset. "Tom! Rick! Gary!" There were no replies.

The television suddenly exploded. The men turned around and saw two men in black military uniforms with weapons aimed. One shot the television to get their attention.

The voice on the phone yelled, "What's going on?"

**CHAPTER 11**
**JULY 1993**
**TIME TO SAY GOODBYE**

The leader of the fledgling Army for American Equality loosened his tie while his face turned a peculiar color of red. He sat at his desk in his suburban Richmond home, and yelled into the phone again, "What's goin' on over there?" His office was in shambles. Newspapers and magazines were thrown about. Articles about corporate wealth, stock market averages, all cut out and haphazardly taped to the walls.

He heard the phone on the other end drop with a sharp thump, then distant voices and a mixture of strange and confusing noises for another minute. The muffled sounds of gunfire, yells, overturned furniture, and a final dull thud.

The chubby man wiped sweat from his forehead. Fear took over and his mind raced. He knew the operation had been compromised and his men were probably dead.

Still holding onto his end of the phone, he heard a few seconds of silence. He heard the slow, methodical steps of someone walking closer to the phone on the other end. It was picked up and a man spoke, unhurried and deliberate. "We have you." The man opened his mouth, but nothing came out. His eyes scanned his office and peered at the window into the darkness. He saw nothing. "There's one more thing," the voice on the phone said as the receiver was set down and sounds of feet scurried, debris crunched underfoot, and people ran. The boss's eyes widened as the silence turned into a percussion of explosions before the connection fell silent.

He knew immediately that he had to escape. He gathered a couple of briefcases and started to assemble various papers and files to take with him; everything that would connect him to the AAE, if any of it was discovered. He lost track of time as he scooped up page after page.

Finally, he had everything packed and headed for his office door. However, the door opened slowly blocking his exit. A man in black paramilitary clothing stepped in and pointed an M-9 with a silencer at the man. He wore a black cloth cap, on top of which sat a strange looking headset with a parabolic shell over the left ear. Flat black glasses hid his eyes. The only visible skin was his mouth and jaw.

The AAE leader stumbled backward into the wall and stared down at the desk beside him. *If I had just grabbed my damn gun,* he thought.

"Your 'army' is dead," said the black-clad man as he walked forward. "The Jasons send their regards from their honeymoon, courtesy of Zachary. Uh, uh," the soldier said gruffly, pointing to the man's sneaking hand. "You just move aside little boy, you shouldn't play with stuff like that, you could accidentally shoot yourself."

The soldier guided the man to the side of the room by gunpoint until he was on the backside of the desk. He took a miniature metal detector from a pocket in his ammo vest and waved it over the desk. It beeped in response to something metal in the top drawer behind the pencil shelf. He kept the man cornered and extracted another hand-held device from a vest pocket and activated its systems. "No bugs, no trip wiring, no alarm. Good boy," he said as he returned it to its pocket. He opened the drawer and removed a .38 special pistol. "Now, here's what we're gonna do…"

◆

"Yeah, the wife heard the gunshot, came in and found him like this," the Sheriff's Office Sergeant explained to one of the detectives. The forensics team was scouring the office for clues, taking photos, carefully placing pieces of evidence in bags, and marking each accordingly.

"Nasty way to go," one of the team members commented. "Brains all over the back of the chair and the wall. The crazy ones, they always put it in their mouth. Makin' a statement, I guess."

The sergeant continued, "Looks like he was part of this Army for American Equality people. The ones that tried to shoot down that plane in California. Papers and shit everywhere talking about equal rights, down with the rich man. Took his .38 and ate it. Found it on the floor, found him like that." He pointed to the dead man.

He sat somewhat prone in his chair, his head rested backwards slightly atop the chair, eyes open wide. His mouth hung open, blood stained his chin and white oxford shirt. Bits of hair, skull, and brain tissue spattered in all directions. Red blood dotted the tan walls like an abstract painting.

"Doesn't look like a murder, they already found gun residue on both his hands. Probably turned the gun around and pulled the trigger with his thumbs. No signs of forced entry. Guess he got sick and tired of it all."

The sergeant nodded in agreement.

◆

About the same time in deep rural southern Nevada, a metal building was found melted to the ground from a massive explosion and fire. Investigators found two sets of vehicle tracks but no vehicles.

The Army for American Equality was never heard from again.

**CHAPTER 12**
**JULY 1993, HONOLULU, HAWAII**
**MAHINA MELI**

Two days later, the Jason party landed at Honolulu International Airport in the company jet (its safety verified by technicians and engineers in Los Angeles). The pilots taxied to the Executive Terminal where they would leave the plane for the week. The passengers piled off, stretched, and yawned as they gathered luggage and headed for a limousine that waited for them in front of the private building. The plane staff would finish their post-flight details then grab a taxi to the hotel.

Seven miles later, the limousine arrived at a Waikiki resort spa that Mark's dad reserved for everyone. Not one dime was spared on the luxury resort. The oceanfront rooms sported grand accommodations, the largest televisions available, and spacious kitchens with fully stocked bars. Two hot tubs were provided in each suite: a small intimate one in the bedroom, and a much larger one in the living area should one need to invite guests over for a soak and martinis.

Unfortunate for the security staff, they wouldn't be doing much soaking or pouring of martinis. They went right to work setting up miniature camera surveillance and sound systems hidden in the hallway. Seven oceanfront rooms had been booked, all in a row. There was a room for Mark and Jan, and the rest of the rooms for the flight crew and security staff.

Mark and Jan made themselves right at home and took advantage of the bedroom hot tub as soon as possible. They stood on their balcony that night and surveyed the skyline. It was dotted with high rises and resort hotels up and down the beach as far as the eye could see.

Jan, scarcely dressed in a pink negligee, pulled the covers back on the bed. "Mark, you don't think security put cameras in our room, do you?" Jan looked around, and half expected to see tiny black boxes affixed to the ceiling or doorway.

"Don't be silly, they don't do that. They only put in the listening devices." Mark grinned as he fluffed the bed pillows. Jan momentarily stood still and blinked in disbelief. Finally getting the joke, she tackled Mark onto the bed where they passionately remained for the next ten hours.

◆

The newlyweds emerged from their room around mid-morning, aware their security would follow them at a discrete distance. The security staff had been awake and dressed for several hours. Two of the men took the lead and paced to the elevators. "'Bout time those two came out, I'm starvin'," mumbled one to the other. One security guard got on an elevator with Mark and Jan and the other two took the stairs. They would all meet up in the downstairs restaurant yet remain a close but detached distance from the couple.

Throughout the week the newlyweds enjoyed time on the warm island beaches and waded in the blue-green clear waters. Brisk winds made for tall waves that broke with great force on the north shore. Surfers flourished and took advantage of the ocean at its best. The couple shopped on Kalakaua Avenue, named after Hawaii's King Kalakaua. Jan was eager to take in shops like Louis Vuitton, Prada, and Cartier. They dined in restaurants and cafes on Kuhio Avenue and went to some of the popular nightclubs on the same street. Mark was not at all surprised they had a front row table at a Don Ho concert, where Don serenaded the newlyweds after his opening number. Mark prodded Jan to get up and sing with the Hawaiian crooner. She gave in and joined him in a rendition of his popular "Tiny Bubbles".

The security staff hustled, trying to keep up with the couple and blend in wherever they went. For them, the nightclubs were the worst. They felt inadequate and outdated amongst the younger crowds and ordered Ginger Ale and Cokes instead of liquor. The trio felt like stalkers as they spread out at different angles to the couple.

During the day, the couple watched surf competitions and outrigger canoe races. At night they took in outdoor performances and hula dances. The week was fast paced and non-stop. Security was grateful when the couple finally went to their room at night, giving everyone another few hours to recuperate. No one complained about late breakfasts after the first day.

The couple returned home a week later, well-tanned, relaxed, and full of stories. The two lived with Mark's parents for several weeks, temporarily, waiting to see where the Navy would send them. Jan finally let him go so he could spend his afternoons with his dad getting a rudimentary, yet formal, introduction to JE during his remaining days before reporting for training.

**CHAPTER 13**
**AUGUST 1993, RICHMOND, VIRGINIA**
**FIRST LESSON**

Zachary and his security chief sat across from each other at Zachary's desk. He was reviewing the text from various news reports of the suicide across town and the warehouse explosion in Nevada. He read them several times while his chief sat in silence.

Eventually he set the papers in both hands, jogged them so they were neat and aligned, and put them in the open manila file folder on his desk. He closed the folder and sat forward, elbows on the desktop, fingers interlaced. "It appears a message was delivered, but the sender is unidentified."

"Yes, sir," the chief said.

"I assume the inventory on the 14th floor is verified?"

The chief handed him a stapled report. "Per standard procedure, all property in testing and development has been visually verified. The inventory report is ready to present to Washington."

"Very good. Fax it now. On your way out tell Mark he can come in."

◆

Mark greeted the security chief as the burly man left his dad's office. Zachary closed the office door and motioned for Mark to take a seat in the cozy part of the office. Mark unbuttoned his jacket and took a seat on the couch. Zachary sat in a plush chair angled at ninety degrees to the couch.

"I've been watching the news," said Mark with a serious look on his face. "No word of who tried to shoot us down."

"You won't." Zachary sat slouched forward in his chair, fingers intertwined.

Shaking his head, Mark looked at his father. "I don't understand. What do you mean 'I won't'?"

Zachary stood, walked to his desk, and reached for the gold key. He tapped the ring end of the large gold key in one palm. "Family, Mark. It's all about family. EVERYTHING is about family. Nothing is more important. You ever thought about who your family is, son? Your family is your mom and me, and now Jan's family, a good number of family members, between our family and in-laws. But the day you walk through that door," he said as he pointed at the office door and held the gold key in front of Mark's face, "as the occupant of THIS office, your family will be everyone who works on every floor below you in this building, and every JE office in other cities, by the time you take charge. And their families will be your family. Their friends will be part of your family."

Zachary walked to the sliding glass doors leading to his private balcony and looked out on the city. "Son, when you take possession of this office your life is gonna change. You're gonna have to wear two faces: the face the financial world sees, the warm compassionate face, the head of Jason Enterprises; then, the cold, calculating face of a man that will do anything to protect his family. Sometimes, you'll have to protect your entire family in ways that are not exactly…oh, shall we say, by the letter of the law. Don't get me wrong, son, I'm a full advocate of law and justice. It's just sometimes justice requires a different solution. You may find yourself having to protect your JE family one day, without benefit of law enforcement, in public, or away from the limelight."

Zachary turned back around and stared at his son on the couch. "But you protect them boy and teach the lesson. You destroy whoever attacks you, even those working for you. You destroy them mercilessly and completely. In the end, you must know that your actions have been vindicated, and your entire family, Jan, your mom and me, Jan's family, your employees, their families, and friends, are safe for another day. And you'll face this challenge every day, making sure every single one of them is safe day after day. You must be warm and inviting to succeed. You must also be cold and relentless to protect. There can be no second guessing. There can be no questioning." Zachary placed both hands on his desk and stared carefully into his son's eyes across the room. "Feeling remorse makes you human. But there can be no guilt. Feeling guilty makes you dead!"

As he listened to his father's speech, Mark put things together in his head without another question. Whoever was responsible for trying to shoot them out of the sky was gone, forever. He knew his dad had everything to do with it, and nothing to do with it, both at the same time. The shock of such a thing, never mind that his father was responsible for it, overpowered his senses. The man he admired more than anyone else in the world, the man he needed to respect him and eventually hand over control of the company to him, was suddenly a complete mystery man to him. He looked up at his father, struggling to control the growing anger in his voice, "All those people, dead. You caused it. You ordered their deaths! And you treat it like some everyday damn business deal. My God, Dad! How can you stand there so calm? Isn't there somewhere inside you that feels any sympathy? Do you feel guilty at all?"

Zachary walked toward his son. For a moment there was an expression of remorse and sorrow in his visage, instantly replaced with cold impassion. Zachary lifted Mark by his muscular shoulders firmly so that they were standing face-to-face, eye-to-eye. "Listen to me, boy, and listen good, 'cause I'm only gonna say this once. Those people were worthless wastes of skin. They tried to kill my son. MY SON! They tried once, and they failed. I made damn sure they don't get a second chance, because the second time they might succeed. So, do I feel guilty about protecting MY ONLY SON?

"Not one damn bit."

**CHAPTER 14**
**AUGUST 1993**
**"SAY HELLO"**

Mark's plan was to take college courses online at some point while enlisted. He wanted to stay in the Navy for many years, then, with a business degree in hand, he would take over JE.

He finally got orders to Naval Station Great Lakes in Illinois, just north of Chicago, for basic training. He learned that most sailors called the place "Great Mistakes" as a pun on the eight-week boot camp. There he'd receive orientation and training, then would be sent to an apprenticeship, or "A-School", somewhere in the U.S. for further training in an occupational specialty. Mark hoped his specialty would lie somewhere in advanced technologies.

A week before he was to depart for Great Lakes, Mark lay in bed with Jan. His muscular arms held her as she rested her head on his chest. Her long red hair cascaded downwards, divided over her neck. Cool, white satin sheets enveloped them and added comfort and seductive allure to their privacy. The sheets had been Jan's idea, a present she'd delighted in when she made up the bed earlier.

"You have an important mission, sailor," giving him a poke in the chest with one finger.

"Yeah, what's that?"

"We need you to come home safe and sound, you know."

Mark smiled back. "Sweetie, I'll be home before you and all the folks realize I've been gone."

She crept up onto her hands and knees, the sheet slid down her back. Mark marveled again at her supple body. "No, silly," Jan said softly as she slowly moving one hand to her bare belly. "WE."

The gears in his head came to a screeching halt when he understood her inference. Open-mouthed and eyes wide, he sat straight up in bed without any support. He focused on her body while thoughts scrambled through his brain. He placed his hands on her slender arms and traveled downwards until he placed his hands on her small belly. Their fingers intertwined near her navel. "Jan," he whispered.

"Daddy, say hello to your new baby."

He released her hand and wrapped his arms around her and squeezed gently. "I love you so very much!"

She in return wrapped her arms around his neck and pulled his head to her chest. Any fear she had about breaking this news was long gone. "I love you back! Oh my God, I love you, Mark!"

**CHAPTER 15**
**SEPTEMBER 2001, OUTSIDE WASHINGTON, D.C.**
**IT WAS GOING SO WELL**

After Mark finished basic training, he mapped out a personal goal for his naval career. He didn't want to stick with just one "A" school, but he could only pick one. He sought to include extensive training in Naval Engineering, Intelligence, Leadership, and Personnel Development Command. Even more, he wanted to be trained in Surface Combat Systems, IT, and Cryptology. After that, he wanted to go on to all training for Navy SEALS. In doing so, he'd travel to Florida, California, and his home state of Virginia. Included were his on-line college classes, a tough act to follow. Mark knew he was an overachiever, always had been. He simply liked it that way. He thrived on the stress of the challenge.

Over the course of eight years, Mark amassed several commendations and awards. His accomplishments in covert operations and engagements led to early meritorious promotions. He attained the rank of Lieutenant in a few short years. When not on assignment or deployment, he flew home to spend time with his family. He could usually find a military hop on a C141 or a C130. Otherwise, he bought a ticket for a commercial airline to get home. As a special favor, he once grabbed a lift on the "Snoopy", a European C130 atmospheric research aircraft with a red and white weather probe mounted to its nose. It just happened to be going his way and the "higher-ups" felt generous. Mark laughed when he first saw her, and thought she looked much like a mosquito and not at all like the cartoon canine.

At work and at home, Mark followed a strict personal regimen of physical fitness. He'd developed an even greater musculature even professional athletes would envy. The SEALs required stringent and at times severe preparation.

◆

Eight-year-old Angela, their only child, had fallen asleep early. A tall, thin, gawky girl with brown eyes and shiny jet-black hair, she was the love of their life. Much like her daddy at the same age, she was obsessed with books and showed a particular interest in science, history, and mathematics. She, too, was considered a "nerd" in school, like her father. She didn't care. Angela had a mind of her own and proudly stated she was a "non-conformist", a word she'd heard from her dad all too often, although she didn't exactly understand what it meant.

Twenty-seven-year-olds Jan and Mark usually went to bed early, just like Angela. Jan assumed a position of comfort in their bed, nestled up to Mark after another long, busy day, marveling at his growing physique. Mark continued his college studies wherever they were stationed and picked different subjects to read nightly. Business, logic, military tactics, psychology, micro-engineering, computer technology, anything he could get his hands on he read with focused intensity. He didn't have a photographic memory, but had developed a great skill for studying, and retained much of what he read through simple discipline. His grades were near-perfect, but it was an average with which he wasn't satisfied. He aspired to be totally perfect in all things, a goal he realized was impossible to attain as time went by. He therefore focused on being the absolute best he could be in everything he studied or did.

Tonight, though, with a book in hand, he stared off into the distance. The recent terrorist attacks in New York City,

Washington, D.C., Pennsylvania, and Virginia had set Mark's blood fever into full gear, as it did with most military personnel. He thought about how he had requested an immediate reassignment to wherever the terrorists were found. The news of the attacks shouldn't have taken him by surprise. After all, he'd gotten bits and pieces of intelligence on numerous activities playing out world-wide in his missions. The recent attacks were exactly what he trained for, but they were too close to home. Richmond wasn't that far from Washington, D.C. An assault like this one still surprised him.

He was stunned and angered as all his requests were denied each time he climbed up the bureaucratic chain of command, his constant questioning boarded on insubordination. Not only were his requests for reassignment denied, but he'd also been disengaged from all SEAL activity and relocated to an administrative post in Washington, D.C. Beyond being confused about his mysterious reassignment, he was not told what his new job would be or where to report. He was essentially on "active-duty vacation". He knew he could help strike against the unseen enemy. He was also an officer and knew when to keep his mouth shut and follow orders, even if he didn't understand or agree with the decisions made by his superiors. They told him he was on a "need to know basis" and didn't "need to know" right now. His disappointment was palpable, and Jan had tiptoed around him for days. Tonight, he stroked her long red hair, saddened at the tragedy, and worried about their family's future.

## CHAPTER 16
## GRANT AND MICHELSON, THE PENTAGON
## A DIFFERENT CHRISTMAS PRESENT

Admiral Harrison Grant was situated in his Pentagon office at two a.m. Christmas morning. He sat hunched over his desk and perused files and various documents. Even at this late hour, he could hear personnel and contractors busily walking up and down the long corridors. All doors now remained closed for security purposes. Reconstruction still took place after the September 11th terrorist attack where a jetliner plowed into the building and killed 189 people. Most of the work was nearly complete. Flags, plaques, glass cases, etc., were being replaced. The offices on his side of the building had received only minor damage.

The sound of Lieutenant Commander Adele Parkinson's black Oxford military dress shoes made a light quick step to his door. She was the admiral's personal aid and gently knocked on his door but entered the office without waiting for a response. The office was dark except for a small desk lamp. "Sir, here's the rest of the portfolio you requested."

Looking up at the officer, "Very good, Lieutenant Commander, have a seat for a minute and let's go over it." He took the folio and began reading. Parkinson sat and faced the Admiral at attention in the chair. She hoped he'd be pleased with the background she'd worked on for so long and searched his face for any expression. She felt a hair move across the nape of her neck, and discretely reached around to the back of her head. She made sure the blonde hair was pinned up nice and tight, not touching her collar. "Your hair's fine for O-two-hundred, Adele, quit fiddlin' with it, and sit at ease," the Admiral said without looking up.

She grinned. Always wanting to make an impression on the admiral, a man old enough to be her father, or perhaps grandfather, she couldn't tell his age for sure. Looking around the room for the millionth time in five years, she couldn't help but notice how sparse and cold the office remained. The walls were stark white with no pictures, accommodations, or plaques. The only source of life to the room was the lone picture of the admiral's family on his desk: his wife and two children. The photo was taken ten years ago, prior to their fatal car crash, and it was a story he never discussed with anyone.

"Sir, permission to speak freely?"

"Shoot."

"Your new office, it's dull, bland, it says nothing, sir."

He cocked an eyebrow at her boldness, but never looked up from the paperwork. "Yeah, that 'bout sums it up. Kinda like me, dull and bland." He looked up and smiled at his aid. "Don't wanna go and get big-headed on anyone now, do I? Like it plain and simple." He shook his head, "No ma'am, no braggin' rights here."

Grant, a forty-year veteran, was in excellent shape for a man of sixty. The only thing that revealed his age was a full head of silver hair in a crew cut. He looked at the young woman and saw the eagerness in her eyes despite her best efforts to suppress it. It painfully reminded him of his deceased daughter.

"Everyone you selected has been reassigned stateside and at a base within a couple hours' travel of the Capitol, sir," she reported. "Their new COs have been reporting they're all wondering what their new billets are and are not happy with 'active-duty vacation' status."

Smiling, Grant said, "Hope they get the word I don't give a flying shit about their unhappiness. They'll all get over it. Thank you, Lieutenant Commander. Well done, indeed. From these we find the four."

JANUARY 2002

"So, the world's going to hell in a handbasket, eh, sir," Colonel Tom Michelson calmly stated as he entered Admiral Grant's office.

Tom held a striking appearance in his Marine Corps uniform, though he only stood about 5'5". He felt squared away in his khaki shirt, green trousers, and shiny black Oxfords. They were spit-shined specifically, a task he dutifully undertook every morning. The perfectly aligned silver eagles on his collar stood out proudly, denoting authority and demanding respect. A variety of ribbons and medals adorned his flawless shirt, tucked in straight and neat. His Distinguished Service Medal and Purple Heart Ribbon announced his time in battle and reported to all that not only had he been wounded in action but survived.

With piss-cutter tucked under his arm he took a seat in front of Admiral Grant's desk. Tom was a man of forty, already a career Marine with twenty-one years' service. He continued, "Yeah, I'm just surprised we're not already at full war with the entire Mid-East by now."

The admiral nodded. "The whole country is beyond pissed if you believe what the polls say. A poll, hell, a poll of 1,200 or 1,300 doesn't represent millions of actual people. Look at the flags poppin' up on houses across the country. Americans want more than justice, they want retribution. The President wants everyone to live their lives normally. I may be an ole southern fellow, Tom, but those of us trained in military ops wanna kill the sons-a-bitches. Oh, but enough 'bout that, I could go on all day. I called you in for another reason."

Sitting back, he crossed his legs at ease. "What's up now, Admiral? We already have Homeland Security. Tell me they don't want something else now?" Tom asked in reply.

Admiral Grant sat back in his old executive leather chair, rested his hands on his belly and looked over his glasses at Tom. He pursed his lips for a moment before he answered. "Tom," He paused to gather his thoughts. "I've known you a long time, son. And even though you aren't in the same branch of the service as me, I asked to be the one to conduct this talk with you."

"Uh-o, here it comes," Tom mumbled as he sat forward, lowered his head and grinned. Reminded again of their long-time friendship meant one thing, more work. Hard work, he suspected. There was also an air of mystery, based on the way Grant spoke.

"You're a combat vet. Survived a lot of high-risk missions. Tehran, Desert Storm, shot in the ass, too." The admiral stopped to snicker at the momentary recall. "Your record's impeccable; intuition, inventiveness under pressure, taking and keeping command." He leaned forward and placed his hands on his desk. "This one's got your name written all over it."

Head down and still grinning, Tom shook his head back and forth. "Leave it up to you sir, to put me right in the middle of things, again. And it wasn't just my ass, sir. It was the back of both legs, and my shoulder." Sitting up straight, he continued, "Seriously Admiral, I'm here for you. Tell me what you need and it's as good as done."

"That's what I like to hear, my boy. You have that go-get-em attitude we need. So glad we got you on here a few years back. Well, the Joint Chiefs of Staff have been brain-storming again."

"Oh, no, that's always scary," Tom interrupted.

"All sorts of crap goin' on out there since nine-eleven. I don't mean the terrorists; I'm talkin' about crazies comin' outta the woodwork. Hell, crap's been going on since before then, too. I'm talking about crime, son, big crime, the federal stuff. The stuff the locals can't get to, the states can't figure out, matters the feds need to get their hands into. They've proposed to put together a task force of such."

"But, sir, the FBI, CIA, all the others. We already have that."

"No, son," the Admiral shook his head. "This is different. Under approval from the White House, we're gonna form a new operation. We'll take several people from each of the armed services, Navy, Army, Marine, and Air Force. Create a new covert field team, small. Each member will specialize in an area of intelligence, exploration, infiltration, and pursue-and-capture. Different, specific, extremely covert. Think of your team as CIA and FBI Ninjas on steroids if you will."

Tom laughed and shook his head again.

"They'll be trained to work as a team, or as partners, or individually. You'll run this new division. Receive info from all intelligence sources. You'll answer to me, I'll answer to the Secretary of Defense, then up to the President. The Joint Chiefs will be kept apprised so they can oversee it, watch how it's going, make policy changes, as necessary. You'll be given discretionary control over the missions you assign to your team from the briefings you receive. As well, your agents should be able to adapt to all conditions, at any time, be observant at all times. They may end up starting a mission on their own based solely on what they notice. But if captured or detected they will be disavowed."

"But, sir, what kind of missions, I'm confused?"

The admiral handed Tom a thick, bound publication. "In here are all the specifications of what we have in mind for this division. Read it, son, you'll get the big picture, you'll understand the missions."

Tom looked at the cover:

TASK FORCE DIVISION
CLASSIFIED INFORMATION

"Sensitive information in there, son. Only for you and your team to read and follow. You all got the highest security clearance needed, I made sure of that."

"Do you already have candidates in mind?" Before he finished the question the Admiral passed him a manila folder. Tom read aloud, "Lieutenant Marshall Gray, Commander Calvin Geffers, Captain Patricia Nichols, Captain James Peterson, Lieutenant Commander Mark Jason, and Lieutenant Andrea Eddington."

Michelson stopped reading the list of names and looked up. "I don't know any of these officers, sir."

"Get to know 'em. But under no circumstance do you approach them, just yet. Learn everything you can on each one, determine what each has as a best, let's say, specialty, and decide if he or she is the right one to start, or be put in line as a, um, replacement, down the line."

"You expect we're gonna lose these agents in missions, sir?"

Tapping his index finger on the desk, "You're not getting super-heroes in that list, Tom. And likely most missions you assign will be suicide missions at worst. You find the best and design a training protocol. We'll help you assemble a set of trainers, technicians, and others to make your division operational. Yes, as with any action, you have to be prepared for agents to be killed. You'll have to replace 'em while you and your personnel grieve. You've done it before, 'cept it was out on a battlefield. This time it's just downtown U.S. of A....and maybe even outside." Grant leaned forward and starred in the Colonial's eyes. "Can you do the job, son?"

Tom closed the folder and placed it atop the book in his lap. "Mission accepted, sir."

"Good," said Grant. "First thing, I need you to retire your commission."

◆

Weeks passed as Tom went about his retirement process from the Marine Corps. At the same time, he studiously absorbed every single word in the manual that Admiral Grant had given him. He worked in an obscure state of disbelief that his life could change so sudden and drastic. Asked to retire his commission with numerous years of possible promotions and pay grades ahead still bothered him. In his heart, he knew he'd done the right thing. He trusted Admiral Grant, not only as his superior but as a close friend. He thought, if Grant bought off on the idea from the White House, then so should he.

With the aid of Admiral Grant, a committee was quietly established to help hire a staff of technicians, computer experts, medical personnel, and more. A location had already been decided, an obscure warehouse in the outskirts of Washington, D.C., and renovations were underway. From the outside, it simply appeared like a new business was being established. Plans for a future multi-story building were being drawn up, but not yet ready to build anytime soon. Inside, all the latest security and technological systems were being installed. Support personnel were being trained, tested, and approved for their new security levels, and Michelson studied the list of agent recommendations.

Seated in his suburban Washington, D.C. home, he read the operational book given to him by Grant. The outline specified the field team would be made up of four service personnel to start. Since the Posse Comitatus Act forbade military personnel from engaging in civilian law enforcement, each, like he, would be required to retire to be part of the team. Tom's inclination was to select the team members with the fewest civilian connections, fewest family members, fewest friends, and wanted them not to be well-known. If he was going to lose people in these missions, *the less connections the better*, he thought.

The outline recommended that new agents be known under code-names instead of their true names, for protection of themselves, friends, and family. It simply read: "Agents Spy, Adventurer, Hunter, and Mimic".

Tom settled in and lounged on his sofa. "Grant said they weren't super-heroes, then he goes and gives them super-hero-type names," he chuckled. "Well, Admiral, I like 'Spy' and 'Hunter,' simple and straightforward. 'Adventurer' is a helluva mouthful, so how about, 'Searcher'? Nah, don't like that." He rested his head on the back of the sofa and closed his eyes.

Frank, his Siamese cat, tiptoed across the top of the sofa. The cat head-butted Tom and begged for a good belly scratch and some attention. Without opening his eyes, Tom reached up and grabbed Frank. He threw the cat onto the couch on its back and scrubbed at its belly; the cat mimicking a half-hearted fight with love bites and pawed at his master's arm. "Old Blue Eyes, you thought you could sneak up on me, didn't you?" He'd named the cat after Frank Sinatra because of its brilliant blue eyes and laid-back demeanor. Besides, he thought Frank was a cool masculine name for a cat.

"OK, Frank, 'Adventurer' is supposed to be a world-traveler, like Indiana Jones, I guess. What did he do? He looked for stuff, sought answers, right?" Frank sat and stared at Tom. The cat meowed; three subsequent expletives escaped from the cat's mouth. "Mow, wow, wow." Tom narrowed his eyes as he stared at the cat and took in its unusual language. "Sought? No, find? No, seek! That's it, Frank, SEEK. OK, the new name is 'Seeker'," he decided as he crossed through the original name and wrote in the new one. Frank purred in approval and stretched out his long body on the couch.

"Now for 'Mimic.' What a lame name. Needs to be better." He set his paperwork down on the coffee table so he could think. Frank stood, letting out an ear-piercing yowl. "Whoa, boy, must be time for dinner, huh?" At the word "dinner" the cat jumped from the sofa and headed for the kitchen. Tom knew no work would get done until Frank was fed and satisfied. He got up, grabbed his empty coffee cup, and headed for the kitchen.

He fumbled around in a cabinet for a can of cat food and mused on the name 'Mimic'. "I know there's a better name for an agent. Fish or chicken, Frank?" He looked down at the cat, expecting an answer. "Row," was the answer. "Fish, just as I thought." He dug for the coffee can and cat food, slid a can of soup aside, and his eye caught the words "Protein 2g" on the back of the can. "Wait, protein, from school, Greek Mythology." He closed his eyes, dug through the fog of memories since college, and finally found what he searched for in his mind. "'Proteus'! That's it, Frank! It means flexible, versatile, and adaptable. It's perfect." Much to Frank's disapproval, Tom ran back to the living room to write down the name, Frank fast on his heels, protesting vehemently. Grabbing the outline, he crossed out "Mimic" and wrote over it "Proteus."

"Row."

"Yes, Frank, dinner. We'll begin assembling this Task Force right after dinner."

◆

Several weeks passed during which Tom researched the list of candidates for the new Task Force field unit. He realized it would take time to fully outline the performance assignments of each agent, with common training programs to work as a cohesive team, as well as work individually on missions.

It was easy to fill the positions of Hunter, Seeker, and Proteus. He decided that the Spy would be the team leader, based on the administrative, executive, and intellectual requirements of the position. He had two highly qualified candidates: Marshall Gray and Mark Jason. Jason's personnel jacket detailed him with so high honors it made him sound like "soldier-of-the-century". Based on his infallible missions and performance as a Navy SEAL, he seemed too good to be true. Tom was concerned that Jason was a family man from a prestigious family in Richmond and Washington, as well as his family being a major supplier of military armaments, R&D, and specialized material. *Bit of a concern, looks like possible double-dipping if I choose you, Jason.*

Gray was a few years older, and while his jacket scores were impressive, they didn't hold a candle to Jason's. Gray was single, no known significant others, and most of his family had already passed on. "A prime candidate for the team," he mused. Michelson spent the next few days researching deep into both "Spy" candidates' lives and histories, almost knowing both men better than they knew themselves. The decision to choose one of them gnawed at his gut, indecisive to the end. Ultimately, he resolved to go with Gray as his "Spy", only because he didn't have all the family ties that Jason did. Tom felt slightly uneasy about the decision but based on protocol Gray was the best fit.

Sitting at his desk in his home office, he closed the personnel folders of both men. Tom noted in his report that Jason would be placed in line as a backup for the Spy position. Should that station ever open in the future, Jason would still be fit enough to qualify. *SEALs never seem to fade away*, he thought.

With his first team leader and back-up named, he moved to the next position. Agent Hunter would have to be well-versed in weapons as well as improvisation and be unsurpassed at tracking. Marine Lieutenant Mei-Lae Kolama seemed to fit the bill perfectly, but Tom wished she were a few years older. He marked her as potential back-up after a few more years in the field, and recommended she be returned to track down Al-Qaida operatives in the Philippines with her previous Marine squad.

"REE-OOWRRR!" Frank growled.

"Yeah, I agree." Tom went back to his folio. "Calvin Geffers. He speaks eight languages, degrees in sociology, nah, he's not a Hunter, he's a Seeker."

Tom continued his personnel review throughout the night, with Frank Sinatra performing a purring serenade beside him on the couch.

## CHAPTER 17
## MARCH 2002, RICHMOND, VIRGINIA
## LIVING BY TWOS AND THREES

"As it's written in Luke," Father said, slamming the well-worn open Bible on the table, "'The servant who knows the Master's will and does not get ready or does not do what the Master wants will be beaten with many blows. But the one who does not know and does things deserving punishment will be beaten with few blows. From everyone who has been given much, much will be demanded; and from the one who has been entrusted with much, much more will be asked'. That's your lesson, all THREE of you. Now eat and be quiet, or there shall be blows!"

They all sat at the dinner table, quiet, and staring at each other. Their father and mother sat at one end of the rustic, old table, an antique that had been passed down for generations. Their father sat on the end and their mother on the side next to him. The three children were made to sit on the opposite end of the table. Henri sat at the end, with Elise and David on the sides. Two adults on one end, three children on the other end; they were always grouped in twos and threes, just how their father liked it.

The small A-frame house was modest and simple, with light gray walls, no wallpaper or fancy trim. The original layout was that of a one-story home with a bedroom, kitchen, bathroom and a combined living room and dining room. When the children came along, Father DeVeaux took out the pull-down attic stairs and built actual stairs up to the attic. He refitted it so there were two bedrooms with an adjoining bathroom in the center, right above the downstairs bathroom. The ceilings in the upstairs rooms were slanted, leaving little room for furniture, much less for moving around.

With David coming to the family, the boys ended up sharing a bedroom. It was even more crowded than before with truly little privacy. Everyone studied on their beds in the evenings. The other half of the upstairs was walled up, used mostly for storage space. Tiny doors in both bedrooms lead to the creepy uninsulated space. When the children were small, they made up stories about monsters living in there, and any creak during the night would send them into dreadful chills.

Their father allowed no televisions or radios in the house. The outside world would corrupt his family with fictions and blasphemies if he ever allowed those devices in the house, he always declared. Their father allowed very few personal items, simple furniture, no carpeting, no decorations, nothing ideological. He felt if Jesus didn't need it, neither did the DeVeaux family. Their mother was, however, allowed to have a washing machine, which resided in the bathroom. The laundry requirements of the family were quite large. No dryer though, he demanded that the clothes be dried outside on the line, in God's clean fresh air.

Their father made sure every bedroom had a large crucifix hanging on the wall over each bed. Jesus looked down on the family, a crown of thorns atop his head. They were placed there to remind the family that they sinned every day and punishment and death were a way of life.

Dinner was eaten in silence in the small, sparse house. David had quickly learned the rule of silence, but occasionally forgot when he didn't concentrate, like this evening. Their father ruled with a quick iron fist while touting and extolling his version of the Bible's teachings. David wanted to hit him back but was afraid to find out what "an eye for an eye" really meant. David looked up as the eyes of Jesus stared down at him from a painting on the wall in the dining room. A judgmental portrait, synonymous with his father, he supposed.

Tonight, was a simple dinner: fried chicken, corn on the cob, lima beans, rolls, and water. He abruptly thought of the nice, sweet tea his real mom used to make for dinner but forgot what it tasted like. His stepfather only allowed water for the children, while they drank wine.

Dinner usually ended quietly. The children set their utensils down in tandem, each asked to be excused to go to their rooms to study before changing and getting into bed. When father nodded an approval, the three took their dinnerware to the kitchen counter, cleaned off the scraps into the trash can, placed their ware in the sink for mother to wash, and walked quietly up the stairs. During school nights, there was no outside time permitted.

## 2s and 3s

Over the years David had noticed Elise' unusual affinity for round objects. It didn't matter what they were, baseballs, bowling balls, or ball bearings in father's garage. On this Saturday morning, she sat on the porch steps blowing soap bubbles, soft colorful orbs floating delicately upwards in the breeze. He and Henri were playing marbles on the sidewalk outside of their tiny house. Marbles were the only thing his new father let him bring from the orphanage. When David saw how much Elise loved the bubbles, he looked through his marble collection and found a particular one.

He got her attention by waving his hand near her eyes. "Here, Elise, you take this one." David handed her a perfectly clear marble, with no flaws inside and no scuffs on the outside. A broad smile emerged from her sad face. She took it in her hands, rolled it about, gazing into it intently as if in another world. She didn't thank David. It was not surprising, as she rarely ever said anything at all.

David stepped back, allowing Elise time to relish her new gift, but tripped as he turned and fell half on the walkway and half on the grass. Henri ran up to him as David got to a sitting position and pointed out a trickle of blood on his wrist. Henri said, "That looks like a nasty cut. You better get that cleaned up before you trail blood in the house."

David looked at his hand and considered Henri's warning. "I hate that you're right, Henri." David looked at his other hand, then at the sidewalk. He crossed his feet, right toe behind left heel, and stepped forward so he would fall again, this time landing on his uninjured hand. Without a sound of pain or discomfort, David pushed himself to a seated position. He looked at his hands, and then showed his palms to Henri. "Look, two hands, both cut and bleeding. Look closely. Total of three scratches. Won't Father be pleased now?"

## CHAPTER 18
## SEPTEMBER 2003
## CHANGE OF COMMAND

After ten years in the Navy, leaving was a hard decision for Mark. He was halfway through a military career with thoughts of retirement long down the road. His dad Zachary had fallen ill, however, and someone needed to take over Jason Enterprises. This was, after all, what he'd trained and studied for his whole life, to replace his dad as President of the corporation. He didn't think it would come this early, though.

Mark parked his Mercedes convertible in the reserved family section of the garage attached to the Jason building. He walked down to the street level and onto the decorated plaza outside the front entrance. The building was magnificent, with the front covered in dark, mirrored glass all the way to the twentieth floor. Employees could look out, but those passing by couldn't see in. The glass reflected blue skies, and the green manicured garden and seating area next to a fountain out front. In the spring a variety of azaleas offered an array of color that reflected from the building. However, during cold stormy winters the building took on an eerie gloom, almost dark and menacing.

Mark took a heartfelt moment and stared upwards to the top right corner of the building. "This is gonna be my new workplace, my home," he thought. He felt mixed emotions, awkward and sad without his Navy uniform. At the same time, he was thrilled to be in a business suit, presented with hundreds of challenges to meet in his new future. He knew he was in no way seasoned or as wise as his dad, and he felt his young age of twenty-eight might intimidate some of the employees. They might think he was too young to be the President of such an important company. It was something he would have to deal with as time went by.

He had been in the Jason building thousands of times as a kid, to work and visit. After joining the Navy, he and his family would stop by on occasion to visit with his dad and other employees, pleased with the improvements and new technologies. He was always enthusiastic and bold whenever he entered the front doors. Today though, the butterflies in his stomach protested. This was the first time he would enter those doors as "the boss".

"OK, Mark, you can do it," he encouraged himself out loud.

He looked at the Rolex on his left wrist, the time showed 6:59 a.m. He shook his shoulders, buttoned the front of his blue suit coat, and with a throat-clearing "harrumph", started for the entrance. A uniformed security guard opened the door as he approached the building. "Good mornin', Mr. Jason," the man said with a smile and a heavy Irish accent.

Mark maintained a cool composure and expectant attitude as he peripherally glanced at the guard's name tag. "Good morning, Greg. Thank you very much."

"A good day to ya', Mr. Jason."

Mark glanced back over his shoulder at the security guard and provided a silent grin in response. He walked through the sizable black and white marble-floored lobby, the sound of his Austin Wingtips clicked with each step and echoed throughout the room as he maneuvered toward the reception desk.

An art deco copper waterfall stood off to the right. The feature stood twelve feet high, and water cascaded down the front into an airy pool filled with water plants. Mark had engineered the waterfall years before. His dad liked it so much that he hired artists to construct it.

Mark stared at the massive desk area as if it were the first time ever seeing it. It expanded nearly a hundred feet around in an oval shape. He knew the desk served as more than just a reception area. It also provided limited security, printers, copiers, faxes, computers, cameras, a PA system, alarms, and phones. It was virtually a one-stop shop and the first set of "eyes on" when anyone walked into the building. It also spoke volumes when prospective clients entered the area. It gave a sense of adequate opulence but also announced it was a company that had its security act together. Several uniformed staff members occupied the area, answered phones, checked systems, and were aware of Mark's presence.

Behind the reception desk was an enormous bullet-proof glass wall, which gave view to another expansive area that housed nearly thirty trainees and new hires on the first floor. A security office and security entrance were stationed behind and to the right of the reception desk and next to the work area. Employees swiped a coded key card at the reception desk then proceeded to a security door to enter the work area. A fingerprint and eye scan station were attached to the glass wall.

Mark stopped at the desk and looked down into pools of teary, droopy blue eyes. "Hi, Dad."

Slow and deliberate, Mark's dad rose from the wheelchair. Shaky and withered, his right hand maneuvered its way to his forehead, and formed a stationary salute from the former Navy officer. A small grin crept up one side of Mark's face as he stood at full attention. His heels clicked in place and returned the salute to the most honorable man in his life. Lowering hands simultaneously, they reached to shake hands. "Dad."

"Son."

Mark grabbed hold of the emaciated man, hugged him fiercely and couldn't help but feel the distinct skeletal frame of the once sturdy man. "How ya doing, Dad?" he asked as tears filled his own eyes. Nearby employees busied themselves and pretended not to notice the willful exchange of life and death that switched places before their eyes. Cancer had set in years before, and now was taking its final toll on the man once full of life, now only in his late fifties. Zachary had kept the cancer a secret, refused treatment, until the disease was so invasive, he couldn't hide it any longer.

He sat back in his wheelchair and stopped momentarily to catch his breath. Tears gone, his eyes twinkled like a teenager, happy to see his son. Rubber tires squeaked on the floor as he turned the electric wheelchair around with the push of a button and headed toward the elevator. Mark stared at his father from the side, now a shell of a man with a face lined with wrinkles and a head full of thick gray hair. "Well, come on, boy! I'm so damned proud of you. This is your big day, you know, you ready?" he said as he smiled wide.

Mark looked down and replied quietly, "As ready as I'll ever be, I guess."

Out of the corner of Mark's eye he spotted movement up on the second-floor walkway. He narrowed his eyes as he spotted his mother, Jan, and Angela. "Sneaky ladies," he thought, "left after I did and arrived before I did. What's up with them anyway?"

Zachary wheeled into the elevator and punched the button for the second floor. Before the door closed, a lone security guard slipped in beside Mark without a word. "Come on, son, let's get your first day started off right. Lots to do, you know. Busy day ahead of us."

"But, Dad, the office, it's on the twentieth floor."

The older man looked up at Mark and grinned. "Gotta start from the bottom up, right?"

"Right, Dad, whatever you say."

The elevator hummed and ascended to the second floor. "Just follow me throughout the day and the next few weeks. You'll be the best of the best, not that you aren't already. You've been a damned strong-willed kid, all these years. Went and joined the Navy, turned into one of those SEALs." He punched Mark in the arm, "Just kidding with you, kid. I'm proud as hell of you, you know that. Followed in the old man's footsteps…though I was never one of those fancy guys." Mark offered a patient grin as the security guard silently smiled in the background.

The elevator dinged softly as it reached the second floor. All three men disembarked and headed toward the meeting hall. It was an impressive room, designed to be multi-purpose. It served over the years as a board room with multiple seats. It was also used for training seminars. Banquets were held during Thanksgiving and Christmas, and many other occasions. As he walked into the room, Mark was taken aback. It was filled with company officers, executives, supervisors, and as many support staff as it could hold. His sudden realization of the "welcoming party" hit him like a brick, unexpected.

Despite his frailty, Zachary displayed no trouble in commanding the room's attention. "Ladies and gentlemen!" he announced and slapped the arm on his wheelchair. "Thank you for joining us here today." A round of applause exploded throughout the room. The feeble man raised an arm and motioned for everyone to sit and be quiet. "I can't believe it's been thirty years already."

"Thirty-two," bellowed his wife from the back of the room. Laughter and mumbles from the crowd developed. "I stand corrected, um, I sit corrected, that is." The reply drew more laughter from the employees.

As the chuckles came to a stop he continued, "I'm sure you're all tired of looking at this old Jason face, so today you get to see two Jason faces. The face of the old boss," he pointed at himself, "and the new boss," he pointed at Mark. "Son, you've spent so much of your youth in this building, with these people, and your adult years out there keeping us safe. Now it's time for you to keep THESE people safe and working." He reached into his jacket breast pocket and retrieved a large gold key. "Now, this key doesn't fit one damn lock in this building, but this has been my good-luck charm for thirty years."

"THIRTY-TWO!"

The man scowled an eye at his wife, which caused more chuckles all around. "As I was saying, this has been my good-luck charm for thirty-two years. And with this on my desk this company has grown every year. I'm passing it on to you now, son, so you put this back on YOUR desk, you'll see the spot. You've got a great crew here. They're the best at what they do, and they work for you now. Congratulations, Mark! Ladies and gentlemen, I introduce to you Mark Jason, your new President of Jason Enterprises!"

Mark shook his father's hand as the staff erupted into loud long applause. Mark's mom, Jan, and Angela, teary eyed, made their way toward Mark with hugs and kisses all around.

Though it was only the start of the morning shift, a huge sheet cake imprinted with the JE logo was rolled out and several bowls of punch and platters of finger sandwiches were scattered about the room. The catering staff moved seamlessly through the swarm of employees. By 10 a.m. the festivities ended, and employees returned to their offices and the Jason family headed for the elevator. The catering staff cleaned the room and tables were disassembled. The top floor was dubbed "The 20th" by the employees, some even called it "Executive Row." The President, Vice-Presidents and senior staff occupied the entire top section. People headed back to their offices, most all stopped to congratulate the Jason men as well as the Jason ladies.

The executive office suite was at the far end of the corridor. As he stopped his wheelchair at his secretary's door, the elder Jason looked up at the younger, "It's your office now, son...you first."

Mark noticed that every vice-president and secretary stood in the hallway and watched the Jason family. With a glance at Jan, Angela and his mom, Mark took a deep breath and for the first time set foot in *his* office.

**CHAPTER 19
APRIL 1, 2007
EVOLUTION**

"If you leave this house, by God there'll be hell to pay!" the children's father bellowed every time he and his wife left the house. The children had become used to it over the years: the shouts, his flared temper, the abuse, and it left them scarred and warped. Psychologically, the children were far from normal, especially David and Henri. Over time, the boys began to act odd.

Church was a different story, however. It was a small Episcopal church on the outskirts of town, built nearly a hundred years ago. On any given Sunday, there'd only be fifty or sixty in attendance, more on Easter and Christmas holidays. Father DeVeaux was boisterous, loud, and high-spirited with his sermons, he screamed quotes from the Bible, slammed his fist on the pulpit, even ran up and down the aisles in his black cassock, its band cincture flapped as he walked, the white collar stained with sweat. His eyes were hard fast on the sinners in his congregation. He'd done the same thing for nearly thirty years, and his devout followers adored him and were moved to shouts of "amen" and "hallelujah" as he preached.

Until he adopted David the money put into the offering plate wasn't enough to keep the church solvent, let alone enough to keep the family going, but since his adoption and his inheritance it all changed.

After one Sunday service, Father DeVeaux knelt on the prayer bench at the altar. With head bowed in hands, he let his mind wander. His introspection and postulation made him appear as if he were praying, but he didn't pray. In his selfishness, he reflected to days long ago. The days of hijacking a bus, demanding money, and adopting a small boy to make his children a group of THREE. He knew David couldn't access the full trust until his eighteenth birthday, and this gripped at him endlessly. He knew the clause stated the funds would be released upon the death of any foster parents, but the Father knew that wouldn't happen anytime soon. The inheritance funds were beginning to run low, after all the years of repair and refurbishing of the church building and his house. The Father contemplated how to get David's trust fund money when David turned eighteen soon and make it his own.

## 2s and 3s

At home, the children followed his day-to-day orders as best they could. They learned to become silent and numb when the shouts and punishment started, it was the only way they could survive. On occasion, they'd break one of their father's twisted "Bible rules", and that was when the belt came off and the beatings would begin.

Recently the boys were taking longer than usual to take out trash and clean up dinner dishes in the kitchen. There was laughing and whispering coming from the area. Their father sat in the living room and speculated. "Rebellion, disobedience, they're in there whispering, plotting against me again, coming up with antics out of spite," he thought. His paranoia kicked into high gear. His green eyes glared as he stared toward the kitchen. Henri was seventeen and David had just turned eighteen within the last few days. David didn't realize it at the time, but he was now eligible for his trust fund money. His adoptive father had never shared that fact with him. His warped mind distrusted his children and accused them of infractions if anything was out of place, even in the slightest amount. He had no problem with any rough punishment. He needed to have his THREE children, but at the same time, hated his THREE children.

"The Bible says obey thy mother and thy father!" he screamed from the living room. "Get in here now!" The boys emerged from the kitchen, stoic, they knew what would come next. "Drop the pants, boys, both of you." Elise sat in a chair, reading a book. "You talking about me behind my back? Slacking off? I heard you in there!"

Henri piped up, "Father, no! We weren't doing anything but cleaning up, we promise."

It didn't matter. Their father was too closed-minded to listen to reason. The two closed their eyes and defiantly took the punishment, embarrassed their sister had to watch. She'd learned to cover her eyes now that the boys were older. She knew it wasn't right. The boys liked it even less that she was forced to see the bloody strap marks left behind. They dared not make a sound. When they were smaller, they used to cry. It was like fuel for the fire, the more they cried the harder he would swing the belt. It didn't matter where the belt hit, so long as it contacted flesh. Their father kept the upper hand and maintained control over them, and almost longed for reasons to beat the boys, his need for dominance overpowered all reason. He was unaware of his sickness, but the children knew, and his wife knew. They knew to be silent.

"Now, what do you say?"

"Thank you, Father," David spoke first, followed by Henri.

He forced the boys to thank him after any reprimand. He believed reproaches should be accepted, taken as a lesson, and received with gratitude.

The two took off for their upstairs room. David slammed their door, both ready to be out of their father's sight. When they got upstairs, Henri noticed something. "Your back's bleeding through your shirt, David, lemme take a look." Henri attempted to raise the back of David's shirt to see if he could help. He ignored the pain of his own lashings and the spreading warm sticky wet feeling on his own back and bottom. David spun on his heel, eyes glaring. Fury consumed him to the core, and he was out of control. His face turned a deep shade of red. When he spoke, spittle flew from his mouth and onto Henri's face. Henri squeezed his eyes closed and turned his head.

"Get away from me, dammit! That son-of-a-bitch is gonna get his, just wait and see."

Henri wiped the spit from his cheek, angry at first then troubled at David's fury. David fell onto his bed and pulled the pillow over his head. An exasperated heat burned inside his brain as he lay there for hours and plotted. The sting of the earlier lashing smoldered on his back as it became the fuel for his near future revenge.

## 2s and 3s

Elise escaped her father's wrath for the most part. Her mother shielded the girl because of her disability. It began with a severe bout of strep throat about six years earlier, and her parents neglected to seek medical attention for the condition. At the time, her father popped off about how she liked to pretend she was sick, and only wanted sympathy. The untreated illness left her mostly deaf, able to hear only loud sounds and voices. On her own she had learned to match mouth movements to what she could still hear by looking straight at someone and comprehending most of what they said. She was unable to hear her own voice however, and her speech pattern degenerated to where she seldom spoke in public.

"I can't stand to look at you anymore, girl," her father yelled on one occasion. He shook a finger in her face as he scowled. "This is MY punishment from God. He punished me by giving me a girl, a stupid girl like you!" His eyes glared and the prominent anger lines on his forehead wrinkled, forever etched in place. Elise stared at him and those angry lines. Tears fell from her eyes. Her father walked away. He couldn't bring himself to hit her or berate her any further.

Her maladies led to severe shyness and kids picked on her at school. She rarely made eye contact with people and stayed close to home, made few friends other than her two brothers. Her mother insisted on home-school for Elise as her impairment worsened, though her father protested vehemently.

She was thankful to be out of school, away from the bullies. Her shyness and depression had worsened, so being at home was a relief. She was developing odd behaviors of her own, however, from her father's cruelty. She remained aloof for hours on end, hiding out in her bedroom. She began collecting things that she found outside or around the house, oddities like rocks, pearls from her mother's broken necklace, coins, broken glass, most anything that had a perfect round shape. Her good-luck charm, and the most valued of all, was the marble David had given her years ago, one of the few kindnesses she could remember. She would hold the perfectly round glass ball and stare deep into it, as if another world existed within. Most times, she just held it in one of her hands throughout the day.

David and Henri contemplated leaving, but neither had the resources. They didn't want to leave each other behind, especially Elise with her problems. They feared for her sanity in the house of hell, knowing they would need to take care of her. "It will take the TWO of us," he pointed at Henri and himself, "to take care of the THREE of us," David said. *It will always be the THREE of us, even after the TWO are gone*, he thought. The TWO were their father and mother. The boys agreed there would be strength in numbers. David hated that he sounded like his father after all these years, but he couldn't help himself, and it infuriated him.

The boys sat together in rocking chairs on the front porch. White colonial columns stood dominantly on either side of the front steps. Paint hung in patches, peeling away after years of neglect. "We need a plan, Henri. We gotta get out of here." The old rockers creaked on the wooden porch, and Henri stared down into a crack at the dirt underneath the house.

"David, we can't. We have no money. No way to take care of Elise. You keep talking about this. We'll stick together, yeah, all three of us, but the time's not right."

A cool breeze blew, and branches swayed. A ray of sunlight dotted in and out, hitting David on the face. He felt the warmth, and the sensation sent waves of comforting goosebumps down his limbs. His memory recalled the last time he experienced such light and heat on his body, the day his life changed forever. He took it as a sign, a SECOND sign, that his life was to change again. This time, David would be the one doing the changing over his father's life. Squinting one eye, he looked over at Henri, "No, it's time."

## CHAPTER 20
## APRIL 5, 2007
## BEGINNING OF THE END

David excelled in school, especially in science, and received excellent grades on every test. He checked out books from the library to study, more than his curriculum required, fascinated with biology, chemistry, even architecture. He often volunteered to work with his engineering teacher after school on the pretense of learning more, but only wanted to deliberately challenge him. David's temper with his professor often became volatile. He believed in his mind that he knew more than the older man, had studied, and surpassed the man in knowledge and skill. Their discussions often led to heated debates and David usually stormed out, only to apologize to him the next day. It was a roller coaster ride for the old man, but he knew David was extremely intelligent, so he tried to tolerate the outbursts.

His father sat in his chair in the living room one afternoon and looked up at David when he came home from school. "All 'A's', good for you, boy," his father mocked when David presented him with the next quarterly report card. "Hard work never killed anyone. You keep at it, one day you'll actually make something of yourself. Right now, you're just nothin'. Eatin' up my food, taking up space. Yeah, you'll get by though."

"Yes, sir, thank you, sir," David feigned a polite reply then headed for his room. "Some 'thank you' that was. Good work, David; keep it up, David; hard work, David; never killed anyone, David. Killed, never killed." David hated his father, and now sat on his bed and contemplated. Weeks before, he'd told his father of his desire to become an automotive engineer, perhaps to specialize in design. Combustion techniques intrigued him more than anything, chemicals, reaction mechanisms, temperature, ratios, fuels, even micro combustion. He didn't share that last part, though.

David took a twisted pleasure in sitting with the old man one evening, staring deep into hateful green eyes, telling a story with a two-sided meaning as his father drank.

His father waved a hand into the air, "Enough about all that engineering crap, boy, I don't understand a damned thing you're talking about." His father was mellow from his drink, and spoke softer than usual, though remained in his normal ill mood.

"I'm a genius, father," David chuckled as he stared at the man, shook his head, and smiled. "You made me this way; don't you get it? I just want to thank you for making me who I am today." David looked forward to playing mind games, any chance he got.

Sitting up in his chair he pointed a finger at David's face, "Get the hell outta here and go on to bed. And I DID make you what you are today, don't you ever forget it. The TWO of you boys, all THREE of you, as a matter of fact." His father belched; the drink started to take its effect.

"Yes, sir, goin' right now, up to my bed, Father. You have a nice night now."

David's father glared at the boy as he walked away. He'd seen the change in David over the last few years and knew he couldn't intimidate him like he used to. He thought maybe he was just getting too old. Then he contemplated that perhaps David had turned out to be just like him. He smiled. "Maybe that boy's gonna be worth something after all. Only took a dozen damn years."

### 2s and 3s

His father finished his fourth drink of the evening. David kept an eye on him, but somehow lost count of the number of drinks. It didn't matter, because when he came downstairs to check again, his father was asleep in his recliner, the light from the dying flames in the fireplace flickered in the darkness. He snored, and drool dribbled down his chin, David knew he was out for several hours.

*Here we go,* David thought to himself. *Better now than never.*

Over time, David had constructed a collapsible metal ladder in shop class. He'd brought it home and hid it between his mattress and box springs. Tonight, he planned to retrieve it one last time, and use it to climb out his second-floor bedroom window. Henri was sound asleep. He was able to sleep through any noise and never knew of David's comings and goings during the night.

David tiptoed across the grass, down his father's well-worn path to the car. David didn't want to leave any footprints or drop any tools, as his father's inane yard inspection would show proof that something was amiss. David worked on the car only a few minutes each night, afraid his father would awaken, or a neighbor out for a late-night dog-walk might spot him. He couldn't be seen, under any circumstances. He'd get the beating of his life, and the plan would be ruined if he were caught. It almost didn't matter, though, as tonight would be the last night. David took great pleasure in the evil thoughts that rolled around in his head.

It took time to run wire to the gas tank. The wire ran deep inside the car's structure, through joints and insulation. The trick was to create a wire capacitor near the battery and hide it near the engine block without notice. His father checked the oil and fluids regularly and would notice anything amiss. David checked the gas gauge. It was at a quarter of a tank, perfect. Thanks to his father's obsessiveness, he always refilled at exactly one quarter tank. It had to be done tonight or wait another two to three weeks.

He clicked on a small flashlight and placed it between his teeth. David took a spark plug and attached it to the end of the wire and fed it inside the gas intake door, behind the license plate.

He shook his head thinking how his father had kept the '88 gray Fleetwood around this long and managed to keep it running. He attached it to the inside with epoxy, closed the door and replaced the plate. Without a sound, he opened the passenger door and clicked off the interior light. David looked around. No one was about and no lights were on in the house.

*Safe for now,* he thought. *Let's get this done.* He opened the glove box, attached the trip wire to the door clutch, taped the ends to prevent slippage and put the door back in place, being extra cautious when securing the clutch so as not to set off his trap while he was in the car. He took a piece of paper from his shirt pocket and wedged it into the glove box; just the edge showed. He hoped it would be enough of something seen that would catch someone's eye and prompt them to open the compartment.

David's mind raced. *The TWO of them, just the TWO of them!* He was content. *At last.* He silently cursed at himself for thinking like his father again, he just couldn't help it. "Those damned TWOs."

With everything set, he returned to the metal ladder and back up to his room. He pulled the ladder up and accidentally dropped it to the floor with a thud. Panic set in. He slammed the window in haste, shoved the ladder under the mattress and dove into bed under the covers.

The sudden noises woke the sleeping tyrant, and David heard him trying to sprint up the stairs in his drunken stupor. He knew the man would rip someone's ass apart for even getting up for a drink of water in the night. He squeezed his eyes shut and turned his back to the door, forced himself to breathe slowly as if in a deep sleep. The door was flung open by the inebriated old preacher. "What the f—" He realized all was quiet and dark. The half-dressed man proceeded over to Elise's room and pushed her door open with a thud. He found her asleep as well. "Stupid kid couldn't hear me if she wanted to," he said out loud.

David smiled to himself as he heard Father DeVeaux stumble down the stairs, cursing as he went. *The last time, father, that's the last time,* he thought.

## 2s and 3s

Showered and shaved, David dutifully dressed and came downstairs for breakfast. On his way to the kitchen table, he saw his father's lighter out of the corner of his eye. It sat on a small table, next to his father's Bible, beside his living room chair. David looked around, scooped up the lighter and took a seat at his usual place at the table. He was thankful he could look out the window and down the road, especially this morning. He crossed his legs momentarily and slid the lighter down his sock and into his shoe.

Henri descended a minute later, Elise a step behind him, and all three teens were at their seats when their father appeared from his downstairs bedroom. He gave a frown of approval as he reached for his car keys, cigar case, and lighter. He growled, "Where the hell's my lighter? Boys, turn out your pockets, NOW." Both boys obediently stood, reached into their front and back pockets, and pulled them inside out. David's shirt had a breast pocket, and his father slapped at the pocket with the back of his hand. David, a couple inches taller than his father, stared down at the tormentor. Built up anger screamed to get out, but he remained silent. "All right, boys, looks like you're clean this time. I'll look for it later. Either of you see it, put it on my table, next to my Good Book, UNDERSTAND ME?"

"Yes, sir," David and Henri nodded and spoke in unison. They leered at the man as they took their places at the table again.

"We're headed into town for a meeting. You stay in this house or there will be hell to pay. GOT IT?"

*The same shit he always says,* thought Henri. "Yes, sir," they replied in unison a second time.

Their mother hurriedly placed breakfast plates in front of each as their father expelled a half sincere prayer of thanks, and everyone began to eat. He rushed through his food, "Hurry up, woman, you eat so damn slow." She'd downed a few bites of scrambled eggs and half a piece of toast. She rushed to grab her purse and join her husband. "We gotta stop and get gas for the car before the church committee meeting, so come on."

Waving her hand to get Elise' attention, the mother got the girl to look up to lip-read whatever she was trying to say. "Honey, why don't you come with us? You know how much you enjoy going to the church when it's empty."

David panicked and almost choked on a piece of bacon. "NO!" Their father turned his head from the opened door and gazed hell-borne daggers at him. David said, "I-I apologize for my outburst, it was totally uncalled for, and I swear to do penance while you're gone. What I meant to say is, that while you're gone, we were gonna surprise you by cleaning the house." He coughed the lodged piece of bacon out and continued. "Elise just didn't know yet, but we're putting her in charge. She's gonna tell us what to do, and we're gonna clean bathrooms and everything."

Elise grinned as she read the words that came from David's mouth, happy that she'd get to boss the boys around.

"Alright. Elise," said her mother, "just don't let these boys start to push you around. We'll be back in a few hours."

Elise waved at her mother, and immediately began barking orders to the boys. Her speech was muffled, and words came out with minor nasal overtones. The boys were used to it and understood her with no problem. Their father, in half-disbelief, stood in the doorway for a few seconds. Hand on hip, he watched. "Half-wit, ignorant girl, can't understand a damn thing she's saying," he said to himself. The boys followed her instructions, picked up dirty dishes, and started washing pots. "Let's get the hell outta here," he snapped at his wife. He huffed in derision, accepted that David's apology and excuses were valid but contemplated a leather-based conversation with him later in the evening for his outburst.

David watched through the window as the car started and drove off. "Goodbye…'Father'…"


## 2s and 3s

Father DeVeaux reached into his pocket for his cigar case, withdrew a cigar, and stuck it in his mouth. He reached in his pocket again for the lighter. "Dammit, I forgot it was missing."

"There might be one in the glove box," his wife said. "Wait, there's a paper sticking out."

"Well, pull it out, lemme see it," he said as he put the key in the ignition.

She slid the paper out and gave it to her husband. He unfolded it and read aloud, "'He will wipe every tear from their eyes. There will be no more death or mourning or crying or pain, for the old order of things has passed away." Father recognized the passage from Revelations and gave an upside-down smile of approval, although the font was unusual and he didn't recognize it, crumpled up the paper and threw it out the open window. "Now how in the hell did that get there anyway? You got my lighter yet, woman?"

"I was just waiting for you to finish, dear." She reached forward and pulled the clasp to the glove box.

**CHAPTER 21**
**APRIL 6, 2007**
**END OF THE END**

The explosion caused the plates to rattle in the kitchen cabinets, but none broke. Henri and Elise felt the jolt and looked up. A small grin appeared on David's face as he left the window and went to the China cabinet and straightened the plates and glasses that shifted from the vibration. Everything had to be in its place. *Father always required things to be neat and straight. Heaven forbid it would be any different starting now,* he thought. Satisfied that all was as it should be, he went to his father's chair and table, took a cigar out of the small humidor, and stepped out the front door.

He watched the burning shell in the driveway that contained what was left of his mother and the bible-thumping dictator. He lifted the cigar to his teeth, and took the lighter from his shoe, lit it and inhaled his first mouthful of smoke. He removed the cigar and stared at it for a few seconds, and realized that he liked it, very much. David returned the cigar to his mouth, shoved his hands in his pants pockets and leaned against one of the porch beams.

Henri joined him outside and stared at the flames and smoke that came from their parents' car. He crossed his arms and asked with feigned innocence, "What happened?" David took the lighter from his pocket with one hand and flipped open the top. With his thumb he rotated the wheel, ignited the wick, and stared at the flame for a few seconds. He did this three times. "THREE, Henri, THREE. They were TWO, but we are THREE." David was calm, pensive. Henri took a seat in a rocker, stared at his brother, and wondered. "Hell's been paid, dear brother," David replied at last. "It's just the THREE of us now."

## 2s and 3s

The police, ambulance, and fire trucks arrived without delay. The neighbors called 911 when they heard the explosion and saw the car on fire in the DeVeaux driveway.

Unable to hear the explosion, Elise went to look for the boys when she recognized no work had been completed in the kitchen. She was in charge, after all, and couldn't let things fall behind. She found them on the front porch, goofing off, was her first thought. She stood and stared at the burning car. Without expression, she dropped a soggy sponge from her hand, and it fell onto the wooden porch with a quiet flop. A muffled "Mother, Father," was all that came out of her mouth as she recognized the car and realized what had happened. "NO!" she screamed and began to run down the steps toward the car. Henri ran after and grabbed her, held her tight, and shielded her from the inferno.

"Henri! Look shocked, surprised, like we planned, got it?" David whispered loudly, though Elise couldn't hear him anyway.

"Got it, David," Henri replied through gritted teeth, agitated. To hold Elise like this gripped at his heart and mixed emotions filled his gut.

## 2s and 3s

David and Henri contrived their grief when the police arrived. Elise' grief was very real, however. She sat on the living room couch and sobbed while the female detective attempted to interview her. Elise blubbered, inaudible, "Who would do this to mother and father?" She wailed over and over.

Looking up and shaking her head at the Sergeant, "I don't know sir, she's deaf, and I can barely make out what she's saying."

Two other male detectives attempted to interview Henri and David, without much success. The boys wept as well but controlled their emotions better than their sister. She sat across the room, inconsolable, and they watched. Henri was traumatized for his mother's sake more than anything. He did indeed partly love her. David, being the eldest, put on an air of trying to be strong, attempting not to cry. He also knew he'd just inherited two wonderful things, his siblings and his new-found trust fund which held millions. He'd found the paperwork in his father's desk a few weeks prior, overwhelmed with anger that he'd kept it from him.

The officers were done with their questions, apologetic they had to ask so many. "Sir, may I see in the car?" David asked. "I really need to see them, one last time."

"Son, I don't think you wanna see what's out there. It ain't pretty, it could be more than you can handle."

David stood, "No, sir, I gotta see for myself. I can handle it, really." David shoved his hands down into his jacket pockets and stared at the detective, eyes dry now and sincere. In his mind, he did need to see their dead bodies. He needed the proof that vengeance was carried out, stored by an image that could be locked away in his mind forever, an impression he would relish and look back on for the rest of his life.

The detective crossed his arms, shook his head, and stared at his feet for a second or two. "OK, kid, I really don't wanna take you out there, but I will. But you're NOT gonna take that little girl out with you." He pointed at Elise. "It would be too much for her."

David looked back at Elise, who still sat in the living room, almost totally cried out. "No, sir, no, just me."

"Alright, if you're sure you can handle it. I sure as hell don't know why you'd wanna, though. Come on." The two walked down the driveway. Yellow crime scene tape was strung throughout the nearby area of the neighborhood, wrapped around trees and light posts, it cordoned off the car and all the debris from the explosion that flew so incredibly far. The street was packed with firefighters and policemen, neighbors stood in their yards and awkwardly gawked at the annihilation.

As he approached the car, David's palms began to sweat. His heartbeat increased and his pupils dilated slightly, he was excited and anxious. A wall of stench hit him. He thought it smelled like a cross between gasoline and burned bacon, but worse. He slowed his pace and closed his eyes to take in the 'aroma', he wanted to savor it, remember it.

"You OK, kid? I told you this would be too much for you."

"No, I'm fine, let's keep going."

The detective lifted the crime scene tape, and both ducked under. "Whoa, wait a minute," a Police Sergeant held his hand up as the two approached.

"It's OK, Charlie. The kid insists on seeing his parents. I couldn't talk him out of it, so just let us through."

David heard other detectives as they talked off to the side and turned to look at them as he walked. He felt like his feet were treading through mud. Everything moved in slow motion, even the blinking of his eyes, and the voices echoed a low, monotone in his head. "No, can't find a cause yet. May have better luck when everything cools down. Maybe an explosion from the gas tank area. This is gonna take a while, we got shit all over the place." One officer pointed to scorch marks on the driveway.

David arrived at the driver's side window and stopped. He turned to face the ghastly charred remains of his parents. He withdrew one hand, made a sign of the cross in insincere reverence, then shoved his hand back in his pocket. He stared at the skeletal remains of his father. The man's mouth was open wide, frozen in a perpetual scream. White teeth emerged through the blackness of the well-cooked skin. His hands still gripped the steering wheel, boney fingers locked in place. David bent down and looked over at his mother, who looked much the same, but more in a fetal position. He noticed the glove box door was open and a small grin crept across his face. He couldn't revel in it now, he was being watched, and the smile disappeared as he stood erect and closed his eyes.

"Son, come on now, you've seen more than you should," said the detective. He took David by the arm and began leading him away.

David looked back and took it all in, the debris, the bodies, and the smell. He listened to the sounds of walkie-talkies that seemed to all chatter at once.

One of the detectives approached the Chief Detective. "Sir, we found this near the car, over in the grass from the driver's side."

"Well, let's see it." The detective handed over a crumpled piece of paper in his latex-gloved hand. The Chief Detective, also wearing gloves, took it and unfolded it. "What is this, a poem?"

David made a pretense of glancing down and reading, "'He will wipe every tear from their eyes. There will be no more death or mourning or crying or pain, for the old order of things has passed away'." He looked up after reading it aloud to see both detectives looking at him. "Sorry, detectives. That's from Revelations. Father was absolute in our learning the Bible forwards and backwards. It mighta been his, a sermon he might have been workin' on. He was always preparing for his next sermons."

"Well," said the Chief, "get this to forensics. See what they can come up with. Could be nothing." The detective took the paper back and headed to the evidence gathering team. The Chief turned to David and said, "Look, David, here's my card. If you think of anything that might help us, just give me a call. Don't matter what time of day or night, you just remember I'm here to help you, ok?"

David took the business card. "Thank you," he said as the Chief Detective turned and walked back to the smoldering car. David also walked to the car, but in a more meandering stroll, until he came to a stop and stood for a few minutes.

Standing just outside the yellow tape, David registered that someone was speaking to him. It was one of the ambulances EMT's. "Damn, that's a shame. He was such a great guy, you know, real inspiration to so many people. Both of 'em." The man looked over at David. "I'm sorry, this is gonna be so rough on you kids. You gonna be ok?"

David lowered his head and with his tennis shoe he kicked at the dirt. David thought to himself. "He was a 'great man, a real inspiration'? This guy was obviously corrupted by my father as well. He should join him in HELL!" David was pissed that the man dared speak nicely of 'The Father'. David's brain shifted gears. A brand-new feeling of euphoria and fury combined washed over him like an ocean wave, then experienced a sudden new and liberating feeling within. It felt like hours to David, though it was only seconds. The EMT saw David's expression go from red-faced and ready to explode, to calm and serene seconds later. The EMT stood still and blinked. He wished he could take back his words. He realized the kid was shaken and he shouldn't have said anything.

"Yeah, we'll be fine." David sounded as broken-hearted as possible. He followed the EMT back to the ambulance in casual conversation and made note of the ambulance's unit number and the man's name tag.

**CHAPTER 22**
**APRIL 6, 2007**
**END OF THE BEGINNING**

Later in the afternoon, soon after the investigation wrapped up, David walked to the garage. He assembled more wiring and spark plugs. Henri and Elise stayed in the house, consoled by neighbors and friends. Elise wondered where David was, but considered he might be out, grieving in his own way.

The hospital was only about a mile away, David walked by it a dozen times over the years. He told everyone gathered in the house he thought he'd stop by to pay a visit in a while, to thank the men on that ambulance for all their help. First, he needed a piece of paper, his Bible, and a computer.

### 2s and 3s

The next morning, the newspaper headlines outlined two bizarre and unexplained bombings in the city. The first detailed the explosion of a vehicle, and the death of Father DeVeaux and his wife, leaving behind three teenage children. The second article disclosed tidbits of information about the bombing of an ambulance and the death of its three occupants at a local hospital.

The three EMTs had just gotten an emergency call and boarded the ambulance when the blast occurred.

The Richmond Police Chief was perplexed by the bombings and deaths and wondered if he might have a serial killer on his hands. Because of the possibility of explosives being used the Federal authorities were advised of the situation and were called in to assist local and state agencies.

Two agents arrived the next day from the Federal Task Force Division out of Washington, D.C. to do a workup. Police detectives worked with the Task Force agents and presented the crumpled two papers with the Biblical quotes. Trace evidence was meager, no accelerant was evident, and no signs of bomb making parts were found. Tom Michelson read the contents of the second crumpled piece of paper to the assembled investigators, *"'For our light and momentary troubles are achieving for us an eternal glory that far outweighs them all.'* It's like they just simply blew up for no reason. We've never seen anything like it. We have the vehicles over in the forensics garage. Still going over them with a fine-toothed comb."

The funeral for the DeVeaux parents took place a few days later. Relatives of the parents took care of the arrangements, allowing the three children to continue grieving. The Episcopal Church replaced Father DeVeaux right away. Another minister lived in a nearby town and was able to accept the position. The new pastor led the funeral service.

At the cemetery, the couple was buried in a single grave but in separate caskets, one atop the other. David mused in silent satisfaction when his father's casket was placed on the bottom. *Closer to the hell he always talked about,* David thought.

Church members, friends and townspeople crowded into the cemetery. Most of their classmates attended. David was surprised that even the twin Taylor sisters, who always teased David because he fancied them, were especially polite to him. "Why the hell did they drag their stupid boyfriends along?"

David and Henri forced themselves to tear up a bit during the funeral, but Elise sat in dazed silence. She was too shocked to even cry.

After the service there were many handshakes, hugs, and condolences. David did his best to act as he should under the circumstances, but the demons in his head screamed at him to remain cold and heartless. David gathered up his siblings to head home. He was now the "head of the family".

The cemetery was lush with green grass, and numerous old oaks shadowed the gravestones. David glanced to the side as he walked and saw a yellow school bus parked behind some of the oak trees. He hadn't noticed it until now that it was a bus from his school. He looked up at the bus number above the driver's window. It was the same bus the three of them took to school every day and had been used to shuttle fellow students to the service. A large banner was attached to the side of the bus: "WE LOVE YOU MR. AND MRS. DEVEAUX!"

He stared at the banner as they walked, and fury boiled up inside his gut again. "No one is allowed to LOVE them! Idiots, how could they do that?" The veins in his temples pounded and David felt something snap inside his head; he literally heard it. Fury surged through his body, and he momentarily stopped to cover his eyes with his hands.

"David, what's wrong?" Henri asked as they all stopped. Elise placed her hands on David's hands and brought them down to his sides. David's eyes were red, and tears of anger rolled down his cheeks. Henri looked over at the school bus then back at David and knew. He knew it would be a THREE, and that was simply fine with him.

## 2s and 3s

A few days later, there were more newspaper headlines. The first one read: "SCHOOL BUS DESTROYED BY BIBLICAL BOMBER." A crumpled paper was found at the scene with the passage, "*A good name is better than fine perfume, and the day of death better than the day of birth*" written on it. The bus was filled with students embarking for their trip home at the end of the school day. Again, evidence was lacking, and the notes were the only connection. Authorities were advised by the Task Force to warn local businesses and residents to be wary of any suspicious activity. The Task Force was able to produce a vague profile of the bomber, trying to link the DeVeaux couple, the on-scene ambulance, and the school bus that was at the funeral.

◆

Jason Enterprises President Mark Jason sat at his desk on the 20th floor of his building in downtown Richmond. The newspaper headline looked ridiculous to him, like something expected in a tabloid magazine. "'Biblical Bomber'," said Mark. "Gotta be the stupidest name I ever heard." He sat back in his desk chair. "'Biblical Bomber', indeed."

◆

The Task Force called local law enforcement into a special meeting. They were prepared to give an internal statement about a possible profile.

Tom Michelson of the Task Force Division spoke to the rest of the gathered law enforcement, "Our profile concludes the person is probably a white male in his early twenties. No doubt a sociopath with many forms of psychoses. This may be someone with a long history of physical and mental abuse as a child, and perhaps socially snubbed because of an obvious personality flaw or physical deformity. Sociopaths can also be the very opposite. They can be friendly and outgoing and oftentimes outspoken and big-headed. We just don't know about this one yet. The person probably has an extremely high IQ, smart enough to undertake the methodology of making undetectable explosive devices. Since the bombings were so closely intertwined, the person is most likely vengeance driven, trying to even a score of some sort. No remorse or regrets." Grumbles were heard around the squad room as Tom continued, "Now, this killer is leaving cryptic notes for fun, sort of a 'catch me if you can' statement, which tells us he's bold, daring and not at all afraid. This, my friends, makes him more dangerous than first thought. The fact that all the notes were Biblical quotes could be just to throw us off or is telling us something very obvious. Otherwise, the person probably indeed has a strong religious background and truly is making some sort of statement, an extremely sick one. Maybe religion was crammed down his throat for years. Three bombings in one week, I'd say we have a serial killer on our hands. We'll be investigating people from Father DeVeaux's church, the family, and other leads."

◆

Foul play was obviously suspected in all three bombings, but it was never proven conclusively. Police and Federal agents began calling them an actual "perfect crime". After several weeks, the insurance company for the DeVeaux family finally gave the children the payout via the family lawyer. Being the eldest child, David received the payment. He requested the insurance payment be made in cash.

"David," said the attorney, "there's also going to be the payments from your trust fund from your natural parents' to which you are now entitled. We're talking a lot of money, a couple million dollars. Would you like to invest any of it? Stocks, bonds, business shares?"

"Cash," said David.

The attorney's eyes widened in surprise. "David, if I bring you that much cash it will raise alarms with the Fed and you'll be investigated for who knows how long, bring more attention on you now—"

"OKAY, FINE!" David growled. "Then divide it all into three different accounts, one for each of us, in two different banks. Set up regular payments to me to care for us, and to keep us off the radar. We want to be left alone…"

**CHAPTER 23**
**APRIL 8, 2007**
**DOUBLE-HEADER, TRIPLE PLAY**

Mother's aunt and uncle took Henri and Elise back to their house the next day, while the authorities still cleaned up the destruction scene outside the house. They felt the sight of the massacre was too much for the children to process. The children needed time to heal, and they would keep them at their home for a while. Though David was adopted, it didn't matter to the aunt and uncle, they loved him just as much as the other children. He was always a charmer with them, on the outside. Inside, he really didn't care less about them. His aunt begged, "David, please come stay with us. You need to get away from here for a while, you don't need to watch what's going on outside."

He politely declined however, and insisted he had a duty to stay and oversee the cleanup. He declared himself responsible now for his younger siblings and wanted to make sure the house and grounds would be ready for their return. They understood and hesitantly agreed with him.

David was relieved to be rid of them when they all packed up and left. He was only slightly concerned about Henri and Elise. After all, he'd grown up with them. He sat on the front porch, smoking one of his father's precious cigars, watching the stupid detectives with their gloves and fingerprint kits. "I'm glad you're gone forever. You thought I didn't know all these years that you killed my real parents. Yeah, I knew, you son-of-a-bitch. All those beatings. Burn in hell, the TWO of you." David sat and contemplated. He felt no remorse or sorrow.

David slowly rocked back and forth in the wooden rocker on the porch and inhaled from the cigar. He learned he liked to let the smoke fill his mouth and nose rather than inhale it deep into his lungs. Lost in thought, he inspected the tip as it burned, and smoke rose to the top of the porch. He'd watched his father for years, how he'd clip the end of the cigar, hold the lighter at the cut end, and dragged in to fully ignite the tightly wrapped tobacco leaves. The expense of the cigars, their aroma, and the fire from the old silver flint lighter, all brought him pleasure. It was his to own and enjoy now, not his wretched father's. He sat and savored and delighted in the cigar, especially the last two days. All the planning and scheming had paid off. *The end justifies the means. Father and his damned followers, all in hell together, where they should be,* he thought.

Another thought occurred to him as he sat and rocked. He knew something else was missing from his newfound, self-professed pleasure. It finally dawned on him that his father had special stashes of alcohol around the house. Since he was a small child, he recalled secretly spying on his father from the kitchen or from atop the staircase. Curious, he watched as his father retrieved bottles that were hidden in closets, under the kitchen sink, in his desk, in the garage, and even one in a hollowed-out Bible on the bookshelf. After his father and mother's death, David did a complete search-and-seizure, and came up with ten bottles of scotch, whiskey, and bourbon. He settled on a bottle of already-opened Jim Beam, took it into the kitchen, took down a water glass from the cabinet and filled it with ice, just as his father used to do. He began to fill the glass with bourbon but stopped halfway. "What if I don't like it?" he pondered aloud. "Why wouldn't I? I already like his cigars, why not his booze?" He sniffed at the fluid in the glass and was surprised by the oak-like aroma. He slowly tilted the glass and the alcohol flowed to his lips.

The sudden burn was both surprising and enjoyable. The liquid had only just touched his lip and already he knew he liked it. He parted his upper lip from the glass and the bourbon flowed in gently. His mouth suddenly exploded in wet fire, but he refused to spit it out. David's eyes watered as he forced himself to accept the burning heat in his cheeks, gums, and tongue. After what seemed to be an eternity the wet fire began to cool, and tears flowed from his eyes. David forced the liquid down his throat and experienced a second wave of burning sensations from his neck to the middle of his torso. He fought the urge to cough, refused to spew it back out. *If father can do this, I can do it*, he thought.

After several long moments, the flames within his body subsided and were replaced by a warm sensation from teeth to stomach. His vision cleared and he found himself bent over on his forearms on the kitchen counter, still holding the glass and the bottle.

David looked at the bottle in his hand, and slowly rotated it so he could read the whole label. He groaned, "Oh, you are some GOOD SHIT!"

Several minutes later David was well on his way to a good inebriation. He sat in one of the two rocking chairs on the porch. He was quite tipsy as he poured his third tumbler of bourbon on ice and his second cigar. Suddenly a dim light clicked on in his mind, "T'ree drinks, smoke two cigars. HA! A-nuh'er 'two and t'ree'. Hope you damn proud of yourself, you hypocritical bastard," he cursed his father. "Lef' me with yer damn twos-n-t'rees, and yer forbidden ALCOHOL!"

David was contemplating killing the whole bottle when a red Firebird pulled into his driveway and parked. Two teenage blonde girls got out. "Ah, th' Taylor twins," David slurred to himself. "Can it get any worse?" He continued to rock in the rocking chair.

Penny and Jenny Taylor, identical twin sisters, had been in nearly every class with David throughout high school. They liked to bully him because they always saw him looking at them and used their feminine wiles to tease him mercilessly. Penny's boyfriend was the quarterback on the school's football team, and

Jenny's was the star pitcher for the baseball team. They always flaunted those facts to everyone around. Whenever they got an opportunity, they'd flash their bra-covered breasts at David (or any other nerdy-type guy) or lift their dresses to show their thong underwear. They loved to belittle him. "Nerd like you could never get anything this good, ever wonder what it would be like? We'd do your daddy before we'd ever let you touch us."

He didn't care why they came to see him. He figured they probably wanted to tease him like always. He didn't look at them, he really wasn't interested. "Hi, David," said the one that drove the car. They were so identical he could never tell them apart. "We came to tell you how sorry we are for what happened." They walked up the steps to the porch.

"Did you?" he grumbled back sarcastically, not even trying to hide his near drunkenness. He felt that if anyone deserved to join his dear father in hell it was these TWO. "These TWO, these TWO… hmmmm…" He took a long puff on his cigar, let out the blue smoke slowly, and sipped another mouthful of bourbon. "Lemme guess, you gonna set up a practical joke on your fav-rit nerd punchin' bag again." He took another swallow. "Get the hell outta my yard. I'm not in a mood fer yer shit today."

The one on the right said, "Jenny and I aren't here to tease you, David. We're sorry, really sorry for your loss." She gently placed a well-manicured hand on his upper leg and smiled politely.

David sat forward in this chair and felt the fury-flame ignite in his soul. "My 'loss'?" he said, staring coldly at them. "An' wha' exactly did I 'LOSS'?" He took another sip.

The first girl, Jenny, lowered her head and replied, "We're sorry for a lot now, David. You've lost your parents in a tragedy. We understand, we really do."

Penny continued, "We lost our parents when we were eight, adopted a few months later, then moved here."

"I didn't know," David said, truly not interested. "You TWO do every guy in school 'cep' me. You TWO always gave me hell."

He stopped for another sip. "Why the hell are you TWO here now?"

"We were awful to you, David, but you never said an unkind word to either of us," said Jenny. "Yeah, we hung with the big stars, but when we saw the funeral and the fund raisers everyone had for you and your brother and sister, we realized you were really liked by a lot of people, and we just wanted to apologize and say we were very wrong, David."

"We were really wrong for hurting you," Penny chimed in. "We just felt like we needed to come by and say that we're sorry."

"And do what we could to help you," Jenny said. "It really is the least we could do after how we treated you in school all this time."

The bourbon was working well on David. The fury he felt minutes before was already snuffed out. His head felt like it was going to fall off, however, and there was no feeling in his neck. He concentrated as hard as he could to focus his eyes, but they felt like they were looking in opposite directions. "I don-need help, 'especially from you TWO sluts," he mumbled. He surrendered to the alcohol. The cigar fell from his hand to the porch and rolled off. He closed his eyes, and all went black.

## 2s and 3s

Several hours later, David opened his eyes wide. The numb feeling from the alcohol was less prominent and his vision was fuzzy. He felt a cool breeze from the ceiling fan, and a cushioned surface on his back.

He looked around in the darkness, finally recognizing his parents' room after his eyes adjusted to the darkness. He looked to his left at the alarm clock. The time read 3:01 a.m.

The bed didn't feel right, as though it weren't level. He sat up slowly and reached for the light dimmer switch behind the bed and gently increased the lighting in the bedroom. A hammer knocked at the back of his head, which indicated a rather good hangover.

He turned the light knob to about twilight brightness and was able to make out the silhouettes of two nude bodies lying in the bed next to him. They were the Taylor twins, one precariously lying atop of the other's chest. Both sisters were asleep and breathing deep. There was an empty bourbon bottle at their ankles. Even though his own head was spinning, he bent over to smell their breath. They'd apparently finished the bottle after he passed out on the porch. "So how did I end up in bed with them?" he mused.

The top one stirred and rolled off her sister, completely revealing herself as well. "Well, they're totally identical, no doubt about that!" David smiled. "But it still doesn't answer the question."

"Davey?" the top sister said sleepily. "Whatcha doin' up?"

"I woke up," he answered honestly and rubbed at the back of his aching neck.

"I woke up, too," she smiled at him. In a soft voice, so as not to wake her sister, she said, "Wow, we had no idea you were so hot! You did us good, what, two times? You been holdin' out on us."

"Just how exactly did we end up here?" he asked, slightly ticked.

"We couldn't just let you sleep out there on that porch, so we brought you in. Then we drank the rest of your booze, and you started waking up, and, well, we got a little carried away." She gently got to her knees on the bed and reached for David's hand. "You feel like going again? Jenny got her second, but not me."

David felt the adrenaline flow in his body, the alcohol effect dimming. *Now this is a TWO-and-THREE worth having over and over,* he thought as he knelt onto the bed and put his arms around her waist.

**CHAPTER 24**
**JULY 4, 2007**
**TEA FOR TWO**

"Come on in, girls."

Penny and Jenny Taylor came in through the kitchen door. Henri was sitting at the table eating a lunch of peanut butter and jelly sandwiches, potato chips, and soda in the largest glass in the house. Ever since their father and mother died and David took over, he enjoyed the summer days and ate whatever he wanted, whenever he wanted.

He eyed the twin sisters as they sat at the table across from him. He studied them, but still didn't know how to tell them apart, so he always waited for a clue before saying a name. He noticed that both were developing uncharacteristic dark shadows under their eyes, and it certainly wasn't their makeup. The sister on the left said, "Davey around?"

"Nope," Henri mumbled with a mouth full of chips. "Took off outa here before sunrise, ain't seen him since."

The sister on the right said, "He told Penny and me to be here now. Wonder where he is?" Henri noted, *Jenny is wearing the diamond earrings, Penny wearing the opal earrings. Got it. Now I can tell 'em apart today.* "David won't like you wearing different kinds of earrings you know," Henri said in a matter-of-fact manner. The two girls looked at each other, and suddenly realized his implications. They took the earrings off and put them in their purses. "He didn't tell me where he was going or that you were coming," he said with a mouthful of sandwich this time.

## 2s and 3s

In the weeks since their first visit to offer genuine condolence to David, the twins became near-daily guests to the house. Early in this new relationship David asked Henri if any of his friends still had the "good stuff". He intended to give it to the twins to keep them around. "Yeah, I know some guys," Henri had replied. A few days later Henri gave his brother a bag of white powder. "Coke?" David asked.

"Better results for what you want."

"Good job, little brother," David smiled.

David secretly dissolved the drug into sweet, iced tea, the twins' beverage of choice whenever they visited. The sisters quickly developed a habit of returning every day to have drinks with David and seemed to enjoy themselves more and more. Visiting David became their new habit.

## 2s and 3s

Elise entered the kitchen, a furniture rag in one hand and a can of spray polish in the other. She ignored the sisters and said to Henri, "Don' fo-ge', pu' yoh diffez ina sink," she said as clearly as she could.

The twins looked at each other. The first time they met Elise, they were in the living room with David. Elise walked through and spoke to David in her normal jumbled tone. The twins had laughed at her disability. David exploded into a furious rage for teasing his sister. "Don't you EVER make fun of my sister, even if you are a TWO! Father did that to her, that's her scar from him!" he had roared. They didn't understand but apologized to Elise immediately. Elise had long ago learned to ignore people laughing at her. After Elise left, they apologized to David, and apologized throughout the night. Satisfied with their groveling, he took them out shopping the next day. He bought them expensive matching gold watches, and then brought them back home for cocktails from one of his father's special bottles of booze…the one David had slipped the drugs into. David knew the evening would go well.

## 2s and 3s

Several days later, the twins and Henri sat at the table in the dining room, chatting. They saw an unusual car pull into the driveway outside the kitchen door. Staring through the glass in the door, they all got up to see who it was. Elise followed behind when she saw their movements. All four stepped outside and stared at the fire-engine red Hummer in the driveway. David exited the driver's side and walked around. Everyone stared in disbelief at the huge new vehicle in the driveway. David had never hinted about a vehicle. It wasn't as though they didn't have the money, it was just the surprise. "Well, I'm glad everyone's here! Whatcha think?" he asked, dramatically waving a hand at the Hummer. "It's very me, isn't it?" No one said anything, still in shock at the red, shiny monster-of-a vehicle. "I said, it's very ME, isn't it'?" David said sternly.

The twins leapt forward and gave him a dual hug, giggling in delight, their hands rubbing up and down over his leather bomber jacket. Henri said, "Looks good, brother. Got one for me?"

"Just might, you never know, do ya?"

"But isn't there a record now of you buying a car?"

"Not a problem, brother. I technically didn't buy a thing today." David smiled at his own genius, and Henri shrugged his shoulders.

In his right hand he held a black plastic shopping bag. He opened it and took out two identical black leather bomber jackets and handed them to the twins. "Put 'em on," he said, more order than request. He reached in the bag and took out another jacket, brown suede, and handed it to Henri, "For you, brother. Hope you like it!" The last jacket was a pink leather blazer. He dropped the bag on the ground, turned the jacket around so the inside faced away, walked to his sister's back, and guided her arms into the jacket without saying a word. He turned Elise to face him, and gently freed her shoulder-length hair from under the collar. With his hands on her shoulders, he smiled and bent down until he was eye to eye with her. Inquiring eyebrows went up, searching for a response. She smiled back at him, tilted her head to the left, and nodded. She loved her new jacket.

## 2s and 3s

Penny and Jenny didn't like the way David treated them sometimes but loved the lavish gifts he provided and semi-understood that they were being sucked into his world. It was turning into a love/hate relationship for all three. He never actually asked what they liked or wanted. Not that he really cared. It was only a ploy to keep them around so he could have his TWO now as revenge for them bullying him earlier.

They also realized they needed David, his attention, but more. They didn't feel right without him. They didn't understand why they felt this way. They needed to share time with him in some bizarre way, and the sudden unexplained need for the "special family tea" that was always on hand. They craved it more and more and couldn't understand the sudden attraction. David would never say it, but he needed them as his TWO. He wanted their company, more as a status symbol that he could control. He demanded they always dress identical in every aspect, even down to the color of their underwear and the shade of polish on their toenails. He felt it to be a small request if they ended their day with him, and they felt relaxed and euphoric.

David also came to the realization that he liked sex with the twins, very much. It was a newfound habit for him, and he wasn't about to give it up. The rougher it was, the more he liked it. It gave him a whole new means to take power and control of his TWO. David convinced the twins to give up their boyfriends so he could spend all his time with them and spoil them. They had no problem in doing so. He was true to his word, and lavishly spent money on them one minute, then was cruel, controlling, and manipulative the next. They were becoming too dependent to even know the difference.

He took the twins to a high-end furniture store to help him pick out new furnishing for the entire house, especially his bedroom, his father's former bedroom. He wanted to purposely adorn it extravagantly, his personal vengeance on his father's soul. The twins had picked out everything, with his final approval. The two picked out masculine furnishings to include cherry-wood furniture, darker dresser lamps with matching shades, and much more. He sat in a nearby chair in the store, staring at their choices. Head cocked to the side he nodded, "Nice, very nice. Father would hate it. We'll take it!" he shouted to the salesman, who jumped at the sudden outburst.

Cable, satellite, computers, internet, wireless capabilities were all set up in every room of the house. Henri and Elise genuinely appreciated the new modern conveniences David was providing. Henri especially enjoyed finally having a room that was all his own.

## 2s and 3s

The next day, David bellowed for all to meet him in the kitchen. Everyone complied. "Brother, we're goin' out and get you whatever car you want, right now." David beamed at his own generosity. "Henri, lock up the house," David ordered. He began waving the girls out of the kitchen door and told them all to get in the Hummer. Jenny said, "Davey, we'd love to, but our folks are having a special dinner party and—"

David glared at Jenny as his face reddened. He gripped her chin and pulled her close to his face. "Did I ASK you if you wanted to go?" he said through gritted teeth. Everyone stood and stared at David, dumbfounded at another drastic mood swing. He let go and contrived a smile. He ran a hand through his hair, regaining his composure. Then slowly ran a single finger over Jenny's throat, between her breasts, and ended at her belly button. "This won't take long, my girls, after all, you choose things so perfectly. You can do that for my dear brother, can't you?"

The twins shook their heads. "We're good, lover," said Penny. "Just let me call home and let Mom know we'll be late."

David leaned forward and gave Jenny a deep kiss, Elise turned away not wanting to see the display. "That's my lovely TWO." Then, pointing toward the back seat, he ordered, "You TWO in the back with Elise, now. Henri rides shotgun." All got in the car as instructed. "Yep, got my THREE girls in the back, TWO guys in the front, just as God meant it to be. Much better than our father's TWOs and THREEs, wouldn't you say, brother?" Henri nodded in silence as David backed out of the driveway and grinned.

## CHAPTER 25
## AUGUST 23, 2007, 5:45 P.M., FOUNTAIN LAKE
## SEEING EYE TO EYE

David was very calm and comfortable.

He was seated at the center of three tables in front of the pavilion that faced Fountain Lake. Despite the high 80s temperature he wore his favorite bomber jacket and didn't feel at all hot. Wearing dark aviator sunglasses, he was able to hide his eyes while he kept watch on his surroundings. He didn't trust anyone too close to him, especially if he didn't know them. Behind him were more tables in groups of two, each in a circular concrete area. "Everything set up in TWOs and THREEs, nice," he thought to himself. It was a beautiful area with a dock for boats and water cycles on either side of him.

Seated at the table with him were the Taylor twins, one on either side, his arms wrapped tightly around their shoulders. They wore matching miniskirts, and the leather bomber jackets he'd given them. One of them kicked off her shoes and curled her feet up under her legs. "Isn't this perfect?" he said, more to himself than the sisters. "I've got my TWO girls, seated at the front of THREE tables between TWO docks, looking at a fountain dividing the lake in half."

"Yeah, Davey, nice," Jenny said sluggishly. She couldn't figure out why she felt so numb. She cast a lazy glance at Penny, and her sister looked like she felt.

"You sound comfy, my little TWO." He reached his hand over her shoulder and down into her bra. He cupped her breast and squeezed tight. He looked to his right and did the same to Penny. "Yep, love my TWO."

"Mm-hmm," Penny mumbled and squirmed, not knowing if the squeeze registered hurt or pleasure.

David heard footsteps approaching from behind and deftly withdrew his hands. He casually rested them on the girls' shoulders. Three people stepped past and sat at a bench close to the left dock. At first glance, he noticed it was a man and two women. Taking a closer look at the man's profile, David discerned he was older, maybe in his forties. He was extremely muscular and had thick brown hair and a matching short, boxed beard. He was impressed with the man's physique, and realized his arms were bigger around than both of David's legs. "Looks like 'The Hulk', ready to bust outta that shirt," David mused.

His attention moved over to the two women. "Um, sexy ladies. Lucky man. Got his TWO like I got my TWO," David whispered to himself. He stared at their long hair that hung over the back of the bench, one red-head and the other with nearly black hair. One wore a short dress and had legs like porcelain. The other wore a T-shirt and shorts. They faced away and he couldn't tell their ages.

"Wha, you say sumpin', Davey?" Penny slurred.

He slapped her in the back of her head. "Shut up unless I ask you something," he scolded, a little louder than intended. The big guy turned and glared at David. His stare was harsh and questioning. David had sunglasses on and turned his head slightly away from the man as if all were normal. David's head stared forward, but his eyes looked to the side, and watched the man who was watching him.

In an attempt not to panic, David gently rubbed his hands up and down the sisters' arms, in a contrived gesture of comfort.

Intentionally, and almost a dare, David turned to look at the man. David grinned and stroked his lady's arms. He knew the man heard something but couldn't know how much. He didn't need any trouble today.

"C'mon, you TWOs, time to go," David said in a soft voice. The jostling movements made the girls sit upright, wondering what was happening. He forced them up by their elbows and made them walk back to the Hummer, intentionally not looking back at the muscular man and his two women. The sisters could barely walk, especially Jenny. They stumbled as they stepped. David wrapped his arm around Jenny, almost having to carry her to the car.

"Ow! My toes," Jenny moaned. She'd left her shoes behind, and her toes and feet scraped along the pavement as she stumbled and was dragged along. David looked behind and saw her shoes under the table.

"Damn bitch!" he growled. He opened the back door of the Hummer and shoved Penny onto the back seat. He sat Jenny down on the floorboard and pushed her inside and saw the bloody bottoms of her feet. "Don't you even think about bleeding on my carpeting, you dumb-ass bitch! You both be quiet 'til we get home." He slammed the door closed and walked to the driver's door. To his surprise, the dark-haired woman from the threesome waited for him at his door. He noticed the same stare in her eyes. It matched the man's stare. *She's probably his daughter,* he thought. David leaned forward slightly, asking, "Can I help you?" sterner than intended.

The young woman smiled and raised her right hand. "One of your girlfriends left her shoes behind, and I noticed they were quite nice and probably very expensive," she said in a gentle voice. She held the pair of Valentino pumps, with pointed toes and spiked heels with gold mini-pyramids adorning the straps and trim. "Pretty pricy pair to leave behind."

He looked down at her feet and saw she wore sneakers and no socks. "And just what would YOU know about designer shoes?" David huffed at her.

The surprised expression on her face amused him. "More than you know, sir. No reason to be rude, I was just trying to help."

"I don't need your help," David grumped as he got in the driver's seat. He took the shoes and tossed them over his shoulder into the backseat. Without another word he closed the door, started the engine, backed out, and drove off.

Jan Jason joined her daughter Angela in the parking area. "Everything okay, Angel?"

"Oh, I'm fine, Mom. Can I be honest?" she asked.

Jan looked at her and smiled. "Of course, honey! What is it?"

Angela nodded at the Hummer as it turned onto Blanton Avenue and continued driving away. "He was an asshole!"

## 2s and 3s

It was night when David drove the Hummer into his driveway. Out of frustration he stepped on the brake so hard the car skidded the last few feet behind the twin's Firebird. He got out, slammed his door, and noticed the house was dark except for lights upstairs. A waxing moon provided illumination all around. Walking around to the other side of the car, he opened the back door. The twins were in the same place he'd put them earlier and could barely get them awake.

He dragged Penny out by her feet. At one point her foot kicked him in the face, in reflex. He roared in anger, pulled her shoes off, and threw them to the side. He tossed her out onto the ground, and she slumped there like a rag doll. Jenny, only barely awake, realized that David pulled her out by her bloody feet. The movement exposed her pink lace G-string panties. He dropped her on the ground also, beside her sister. The heroin, from the earlier tea, had them totally incapacitated and he couldn't understand why. Kneeling beside Penny, he thought he saw black panties, different from Jenny's pink panties. "Something's off, dammit, my TWO have to match perfectly, always!" He grumbled loudly as he reached for her dress hem. In a rage, he yanked her dress hem up. "You bitch!" His voice echoed inside the driveway. "My

TWO must always match perfectly!" He screamed aloud. "How dare you not be a TWO, damn you!"

David dragged Jenny into the house and to his bedroom. He went back for Penny and deposited her as well. Henri heard the commotion from his upstairs bedroom. He pulled on a pair of shorts and descended the stairs, in time to see David's bedroom door slam shut. He thought nothing of it, thinking David was on one of his sexual rampages. He noticed the kitchen door was open, which was strange, and went to shut it when he noticed the Hummer's backseat door was open. *That's odd, why would he leave all these doors open?* he thought. Henri walked outside, looked around, and closed the car's door. He came back into the house, closed, and locked the kitchen door. He heard thumping and bumping from David's bedroom. He shook his head, knowing David was on some sort of weird kick again with his girls.

### 2s and 3s

Jenny woke up slowly, having no idea where she was. She felt sick to her stomach and her head hurt. She realized she was lying face-up and her arms were above her head. She tried to move her arms but couldn't. She tried to move her legs and suddenly realized she was tied down. She lifted her head to see where she was.

She was naked. She could see that her legs were tied at the ankle to a bed footboard, and when she looked up, she saw her arms were similarly bound. She was tied spread-eagle on David's bed. A glance to her right revealed Penny lying beside her, just as naked and bound. "Wha-what's going on? David?"

He stepped into her view. In his hands he held a long, thick leather belt. "You didn't follow my instructions, my lovely TWO. Father taught me well how to discipline disobedience."

Jenny began to cry and pulled hard at her bonds. "What? What did I do?" she screamed.

David plucked their panties from the foot of the bed. "You..did..not..MATCH! You were not a TWO for me today. If you're not gonna be my TWO, not gonna match, not do as I say, then what? Yeah, punishment."

Jenny barely had time to understand what he meant when she felt the impact of the leather belt across her hips and pubic area.

## CHAPTER 26
## AUGUST 31, 2007, 9:18 P.M.
## TWO HIGH A PRICE

David sat on the couch in the living room with the Taylor twins on both sides. They were asleep, Penny's head in his lap and Jenny's head propped on his shoulders. Both girls were nude except for matching red cotton panties.

His eyes gazed at their stomachs and legs. The welts and bruises from their latest whippings a few days earlier were nearly gone. They had disobeyed him again. Earlier, a twin had one button undone on her shirt, the other had two undone. They didn't match. He'd beaten them, but not as severe as other times. He was too tired at the time and his heart just wasn't in it.

His birthday was a few days away. He'd never actually had a happy birthday but was looking forward to this one. It would be different this time, from now on.

His hands slid down to their breasts and pinched their nipples. The sisters groaned quietly in their stupor but otherwise didn't react. "Stupid-ass sluts," he said. He thrust himself up off the couch, and Penny rolled over and landed on her back on the floor. Jenny dropped her head down to where David had sat. He went into the kitchen to pour himself a glass of regular tea. He propped his hand on the kitchen wall, took a long drink, and stared at the almost-naked twins. "Worthless sluts," he said aloud. He walked back to the living room to where Penny lay on the floor. He kicked her in the ribs. "Get up, bitch. Time for you TWO to give me my birthday present."

Penny curled into a ball and groaned in pain. She tried to breathe in but could barely draw breath. "D-Davey, I don't feel so good," she stammered.

He felt Penny's body go limp, her arms and head lay motionless on the couch. He stopped himself and realized her ribs weren't moving; she wasn't breathing.

David turned to look at Jenny, still lying on the couch. Her breathing was slow and shallow as well.

Jenny tried to push herself up onto one elbow, but her body wouldn't obey the brain's command. She could only lie on the couch, barely breathing, and not feeling the pain from David's harsh rape. She tried to open one eye and saw a blurred David that stared down at her and hated him for what he'd done. She tried to speak but fell back into a drug-induced world of unconsciousness.

David's eyebrows crinkled as he stared at the twins. "Henri!" David bellowed as loud as he could. "Get down here!" Within a few seconds he heard Henri's bedroom door open. Annoyed, Henri had thrown on a pair of jeans and took a few steps down the staircase. He saw David standing in the living room with his hands on his hips and a scowl on his face. He looked at the twins on the floor and couch.

Without looking up the stairs David barked, "How strong was that last batch?" David withdrew from his pocket a small plastic bag that contained the heroin.

"Geez, David, I dunno. My guy said it was the purest he had, why?" Irritated, he added, "I'm kind of busy upstairs with Gwen, if you know what I mean."

David glared upwards and Henri, angered that his brother was so dismissive. "It's killed one of my TWO!" he yelled and threw the closed bag up the stairs at Henri. David shook his head and stared at the girls. Through gritted teeth he said, "I'm put out, brother. One's dead, the other's probably on her way out. I can't keep 'em! I can't have just a ONE! We have to get rid of these TWO and get compensation. Then get a fresh TWO."

Henri said again, "Brother, I'm really kind of busy upstairs right now."

"I DON'T GIVE A SHIT," David bellowed. "Get dressed, we have to clean up this crap now."

"Okay, David." Henri suddenly realized he needed to fall back into the quiet, submissive role that he'd always been in. Gwen would have to wait. He retreated to his room, got dressed and told the girl to stay in the room until he returned.

"But, Henri, you promised me a good time."

"Oh, I will, honey, you bet I will. Just be a good girl and lock the door, I gotta go help David with something important in the garage and I'll be back in just a bit. You know how David gets with his projects." It was an alibi, he knew. He threw a porno DVD at her from the stack on his dresser and told her, "Watch it while I'm gone, to get warmed up."

Her face lit up. "Hurry back then, I may have to start without you."

Henri groaned, exasperated, he didn't want to leave the cutie in the black bra and panties that sat on his bed. He peeked in on Elise in her room. She sat on her bed reading a book. He told her that he and David would be downstairs working on something. Another alibi. She heard him well thanks to her new hearing aids, though he did use sign language out of habit. "Wh'evr. Close ma door wen' 'ou leave."

"Okay, but don't come out. I'll have a surprise for you when I come back up. But you have to stay in your room, got it?"

Elise smiled and gave him a thumbs-up.

"Damn, I hate it when David does this crap," he mumbled to himself while he descended the stairs.

When he hit the last step, he saw David coming in the kitchen door. The Firebird was parked right outside. "I got the girls dressed and put Penny's body in the passenger seat. You gotta help me with Jenny, got it?"

Henri said nothing. He just stood and stared, almost panic stricken. David reached into Jenny's purse, his hands wearing gardening gloves, and retrieved her car keys and cell phone. He shook Jenny to wake her up. "Jenny, baby, I'm gonna call your parents, okay? You're gonna tell 'em you're both on your way home, okay, baby? Got it?" He shook her some more.

"S-sure, Davey," she said weakly, "whatever you say."

"Say what I told you," he ordered.

"We're on the way home," Jenny said aloud, sounding half-asleep.

"That's my good little TWO," David said. He pressed Call on the phone and held it to her mouth. He watched the display on the phone's screen and when the call connected pressed the mute button. "Say it again, baby," he ordered, then unmuted the phone.

"We're on the way home mom, bye." Jenny repeated obediently. David heard a voice on the other end start to say, "Ok, drive safe," and he closed the flip-phone and ended the call. He replaced her phone and handed both girls' purses to Henri.

"Let's put Jenny in the passenger seat on top of Penny, then you follow me in their car."

"David, what in the world?"

"Henri don't ask me anything! Put these gloves on and get in the Firebird and follow me! It's dark, no one will see us. Damn, you're gettin' on my nerves questioning me about everything! Just do what I say!" Henri nodded in response. They lifted the girl's almost-lifeless body out the door and into the car. David pulled the lever to let the back of the seat down, leaving both girls in a semi-prone position so they couldn't be seen. He handed Henri the keys and told him to follow.

He walked to his Hummer, a reflection to his right caught his attention. He couldn't tell what it was in the night, so he walked over for a closer look. It was one of Penny's shoes he had tossed away earlier. "Damn, I forgot. But there were TWO." He picked it up and looked around, finding the second a few feet away. "And the TWO in my car," he remembered. After retrieving Jenny's shoes from his back seat, he threw both pairs into the Firebird's passenger seat footwell.

Several miles out of town on River Road West they came to a stop, out of sight of any houses or other structures. David exited the Hummer, hurriedly placed Jenny in the Firebird's driver's seat, and lifted the lever on Penny's seat so she would be in an upright position. He buckled them both in and noticed Jenny's eyes were slightly open, and she was unaware of her surroundings. David started the engine, put the driver's window all the way down, and closed the driver's door.

Out of breath, David said, "Henri, I'm gonna drive down the road just a bit and turn around. When you see my headlights, you reach in and put this thing into 'drive', got it? Then get your ass the hell away from the car as fast as you can."

"Yeah, I guess. No, got it, brother, whatever you say." Henri shook his head, not really understanding what all was going on.

David hopped in the Hummer, drove west, turned around, and drove back as fast as he could. No tread marks, no evidence, just attempting to be the "drive-by shooter". Henri did as he was instructed. He reached in as far as he could, grabbed the automatic transmission gear handle, and put the Firebird into drive. He pulled himself back out of the window as it slowly started forward on its own. It picked up only a little speed, straight down the road. David's Hummer neared the Firebird and slowed. Gun in his gloved right hand, he aimed and fired six shots out his driver's-side window as he passed, bullets entering through the Firebird's driver's window, car door, and the edge of the windshield.

David came to a stop in the middle of the road, got out, and ran back a few feet to Henri's side. By then the Firebird had accelerated downhill, veered off the road in a slight curve, and crashed head-on into a tree. Henri flinched and stepped forward when he saw the car crash. David placed his hand across Henri's chest, "No, don't go close. No evidence. Just lemme' check it then we're outta here."

David ran forward just close enough to see both sisters slumped into the airbags. He stood and grinned when he saw the blood and large bullet wound in Jenny's head.

David hurried back to Henri and grabbed him by the arm. "Problem solved. Look around, make sure we didn't drop anything anywhere. Got a quick stop to make then on to the house to get rid of anything else those bitches left behind."

## 2s and 3s

In his bedroom, David woke to a constant banging noise at the front door the following morning. He'd been up late, getting rid of evidence, and slept in. In a haze David dragged himself to the door. He yawned and opened the front door to the house. Two men in suits stood before him, they held Detective badges out in front of David's face. "David DeVeaux?" one asked sharply.

David closed an eye, the sun shined in where he could barely see. A bit sleepy, and curt, he responded, "Yeah, I'm David DeVeaux. And how may I help you?"

"I'm Detective Davis, this is Detective Russell, Richmond PD." Davis, a tall balding middle-aged black man, held up a paper with two pictures on it. "You know these girls?"

David squinted at the pictures. He shuffled his feet and was elated to see his TWO. "Aw, yes, sir. Penny and Jenny. They're my girlfriends. They in trouble or somethin'?"

"Girlfriends?" Detective Russell raised an eyebrow. He made a statement more than a question. He was a younger man with soft reddish hair and matching moustache. He stared at David from head to foot and peered into the house without trying to be noticed.

David shrugged his shoulders and attempted a smile. "What can I say, I got lucky with twin sisters? We're having the best summer ever, and I mean 'best'."

"When's the last time you saw them?" Davis asked.

"Last night. Hope you don't mind if I don't get specific, don't want to say anything to embarrass my ladies."

"You might have to," said Russell. "They were found dead earlier this morning."

David pretended to go into shock. His eyes turned wild, and he stumbled back, off-balance into the living room. "Dead? DEAD? How? Henri! Get down here!"

Henri came running down the steps clad only in a pair of briefs. He was followed by his current girlfriend, dark-haired Gwen, wearing one of Henri's shirts. Elise followed them. "David, what is it? Oh, good morning, sirs," he said after seeing the men in the open door. Gwen backed away and held closed the unbuttoned shirt.

"You are…?" asked Russell. Introductions went around, with David helping translate Elise' answers.

David said, "Yeah, they were here last night. We all were. Kinda had a very romantic night. Well, our sister didn't, you know, she was in her room as usual. Had a little bit too much to drink, I'm afraid. Everyone was invited to stay here, but the twins insisted on going home. What happened?"

"What time was that?"

"Oh, around 9 p.m., maybe a little later. But please, WHAT happened to them?

"Neighbor said he saw you leave same time as them," said Davis.

Exasperated at not getting an answer, "Well, yeah, we-we went out, too, me and Henri," David said, trying to force tears to well up in his eyes. "We had a craving for ice cream and went out to get a box."

"May we come in, Mr. DeVeaux? Don't think you want neighbors staring at us."

"Oh, yeah, sorry, come on in." David closed the door behind them.

"Got any proof, Mr. DeVeaux? Things are looking a bit suspicious," Russell asked.

"What, suspicious? Good God, we went out for ice cream, the girls drove home! Here, come to the kitchen." David plucked a box of ice cream from the freezer, a receipt frozen to the side of the box. "I don't know what to say, but here's the box. Look, there's even a receipt stuck to it, see?" He handed the open container toward them.

The men noticed ice cream had been scooped out, and inspected the receipt on the side, verifying it was purchased the night before. "You always keep receipts handy like that, Mr. DeVeaux? That's awful convenient," asked Davis.

"What, no, it musta got stuck there, I didn't know. Look, what is going on? Where's my girls?"

Davis looked over at Russell and said, "Traffic accident, sir, that's all we can say for now. Their parents were already notified. They were the ones who told us that the sisters were with you last night."

David walked to the living room and sat on the couch, head in hands, forcing himself to cry.

The detectives went through their notes, and asked questions of everyone. Satisfied with their answers, Davis said, "Thank you for your time, our apologies and condolences." He handed each of them a business card. "Think of anything else that might help, give us a call. We may need to get back in touch with you later during the investigation anyway."

They all stared at the detectives as they opened the door and started to leave. David stopped and turned, "Son, aren't y'all a bit young to be drinking? Drinking and driving?

"It was already here," David answered innocently. "It used to belong to our father. He left a lot behind when he died. I guess we were curious. The twins didn't have any, they only had tea, it was just me and Henri."

"Well, I'll just warn you this time. No drinking and driving in the future. Can't give you a ticket after the fact, but you should be more careful next time. We may be back with more questions."

"Yes, sir," David replied as he nodded and closed the door behind the detectives. David looked at the girls. "Please go upstairs, I need to talk to Henri in private." Gwen led Elise by the hand up the staircase and into a bedroom and shut the door.

"Henri, your 'friend' cost me an incredibly good TWO. Time to pay him a visit."

**CHAPTER 27**
**SEPTEMBER 1, 2007**
**A SCORPION STUNG BY THE BIBLICAL BOMBER**

Henri and David stood in front of an apartment door in an upscale building in the suburbs. The quiet of the hallway echoed the series of knocks Henri made on the door. Three knocks, one knock, two knocks, wait for a five-count, then one knock. "Name," they heard from inside the door, as someone looked out the door's peephole.

"George Custer," Henri said.

The man inside unlocked the door, peered out briefly, and opened it just enough to let the two men in. Henri stepped in hurriedly, David right behind. The apartment was well-kept and looked typical of any common middle-class home. David glanced around casually but with intent stares. He took in every bit of the apartment.

A tall lean black man wearing a blue long-sleeve dress shirt and gray slacks slammed and locked the door behind them. He had cascading, thick dreadlocks and smelled of expensive cologne. The Jamaican man spoke, almost too sternly, "George," he said to Henri, "who dis?"

Henri never used his real name, selecting 'George Custer' as his alias. "He's cool," said Henri, hands raised in a calm posture. "This is my brother."

The man stared intently at David, then back at Henri. "He don' be lookin' like you."

"Adopted," said David with a smirk. His one-word answer was rewarded with a fist in David's stomach.

"You don' be talkin' here less I talk ta' ya' first." He turned to Henri, "So whatcha wan', George? Not time for you ta' be back so soon."

"We have," Henri started "a, um, complaint."

"'Complaint'?" he laughed incredulously. "You gonna complain to Scorpion 'bout his business?"

David was almost able to stand upright again, catching his breath. He was still slightly bent over, left hand on his left knee and right hand resting on the small of his back. "You damn straight we got a complaint," David snapped. The man saw the hate and meanness in David's eyes. The black man turned and walked away, staring back at David, sizing him up.

"My name Scorpion! What I say 'bout talkin to me?" he sneered at David. "Why you tink' they call me Scorpion? Huh? I can keel' ya' in one snap."

Scorpion sat in a plush purple leather chair. His right hand dropped down to the side, out of view. David realized the man was probably armed, perhaps a gun in a side pocket of the chair. He took heed of the situation and remained cautious.

"George, what makes you 'tink I run a money-back guarantee business? And why did you bring your broder into my home?"

Henri slowly stepped to the side. He pretended to walk toward a chair opposite Scorpion. Coughing, David said, "You've done us well, I admit." David coughed again, half contrived and half real from the punch he just took. Still tilted forward, he kept one hand on his back and the other arm up to his mouth to cover the cough. "My brother has always brought me what it took to keep my TWO happy and coming back."

"Your 'two'?" Scorpion interrupted. "What's a 'two'?" The man looked back and forth between David and Henri searching for an answer in their faces.

David ignored him and angrily continued. "My TWO girls were really happy with me, with your 'product'." Until last night, they stayed nice and happy with me. My dear brother always made sure my TWO were happy, even got his own ONE for himself. Our THREE girls were incredibly happy."

Scorpion put both hands on the chairs arms and sat forward, angry. "What you talkin' 'bout? Dis' Two and One and T'ree? This some kinda bullshit code?" Scorpion demanded.

Henri closed his eyes and shook his head in a calm postulation. "Not exactly, sir, it makes sense once you get to know him, you just don't know him yet. He's really a nice guy, he just rambles like that sometimes."

"I don' want ta' know 'im," Scorpion growled. "You and your one-two-t'ree brother get da' hell outta my home, now!" The man reached down for his gun and started to raise it. It never made it past the chair arm.

Faster than Henri could follow, David, still crouched, swung his right hand around from his back, a 9mm in his grasp, and fired two times at Scorpion's right hand. The shots were dead on target. Blood spurted outward from the dealer's hand and his Kel-Tec pistol fell to the floor. Scorpion yowled in pain and grabbed his mangled right hand with his left hand.

David stepped forward. Scorpion crouched back in his chair in excruciating pain, fearful now that David had the advantage. David held his gun up and gazed at it. "You know, I never knew how good Father was with this," David began. "I never even knew he had this 'til I was throwing out his damned furniture. Left lots of ammo. Left me the opportunity to practice, A LOT!" David pointed the gun at the dealer as he spoke. "I practiced twice a day because I want to protect my TWOs. Henri and Elise, they're my first TWO to protect. Jenny and Penny, they WERE my second TWO, no thanks to you."

David felt elated and walked around to the side of the dealer and nudged the man in the neck with his gun barrel. Scorpion held tight to his wounded hand but otherwise didn't move. "But then you sold my brother different stuff to keep my TWO girls happy. It was too much, and it killed one of my TWO girls, and I had to put the other out of her misery." Scorpion was in pain, and scared, and knew full well he had a lunatic in his apartment. His head remained stationary, but his eyes rolled sideways, trying to watch David.

David circled around Scorpion's chair and stood in front of him again. In a calm, nonchalant voice David spoke. "Yep, lost my TWO because of you. You, my friend, have earned the right to be a THREE, to be part of my own THREE. Don't you agree, brother?"

Henri nodded his head slowly. "Absolutely, brother. Makes more sense than anything."

"What da' hell you talkin' 'bout?" Scorpion spoke, in agony.

David knelt and looked him eye-to-eye. "You cost me my nice pretty TWO with your stuff. It was too potent, you dick-head! You're gonna join 'em, be a matching THREE. Doesn't that sound like an excellent arrangement?"

"You guys, you crazy!"

David raised his gun, about to fire. Henri crossed his arms and shrugged his shoulders. "No, he's not crazy. You've heard of him. They call him the Biblical Bomber."

**CHAPTER 28**
**APRIL 2008-FEBRUARY 2009**
**TAKING CARE OF FAMILY BUSINESS**

The coroner found high levels of heroin in the Taylor sisters' bodies. The police found no evidence of heroin in the DeVeaux home, nor any trace there ever was any. David, Henri, and Elise were written off as suspects in the girls' murder.

## 2s and 3s

Elise seemed happier now-a-days. Ever since the passing of their father and mother, David felt some obligation to help in all aspects of her life, mostly to keep the family his THREE. She was ecstatic at the sudden ability to hear and cherished every sound. Elise never asked why her father didn't take her to the doctor, she simply loved her brother more for taking her to get checked and fitted with state-of-the-market hearing aids. She was self-conscious, however, and started letting her hair hang free to cover her ears. The doctors suggested speech therapy to help her learn to speak better, but David let her decide for herself. Elise chose to stay home and enjoy "listening" rather than taking classes to speak clearly.

David and Henri were ready to move out of the house and leave behind a lifetime of abuse and terrible memories. Elise insisted she didn't want to move, that she was comfortable with the house she'd grown up in all her life. The brothers gave in to her pleas, resigned to live there a few more years. David and Henri figured they did, after all, completely remodel the house last fall. They agreed there was no reason to move all the furniture they'd just gotten into place.

The weeks and months passed quietly, though David had his normal outbursts that came out of the blue. Henri was happily dating Gwen. David got his brother and sister to fix a Thanksgiving dinner while their uncle and aunt visited (making a comfortable three-guys/two-gals group at the table for David), and then again at Christmas. When Henri got Gwen to join them so there would be three girls to balance out the men, David was content. His sense of order was balanced, because he had his TWO sets of THREE at his table: THREE men, and THREE women.

As Valentine's Day neared, Gwen dropped the news on Henri that her family was moving away. Her dad got a job promotion that would take them across the country. She invited Henri to go with, but he said he needed to stay to help David take care of Elise.

David demanded that Henri find nice things to give Elise for Valentine's Day. For the most part holidays didn't really matter to him, he just wanted to keep his THREE together. Their sister felt spoiled on February 14th.

After the Valentine's gifts were all accepted with gratitude, Elise and Henri went to their rooms for the night. David walked around the back yard in solitude, smoking a cigar lit with Father's lighter, drinking a tumbler of bourbon, and realized he felt comfortable for the very first time.

**CHAPTER 29**
**APRIL 2009**
**MESSAGE FROM HELL**

Elise just turned 18 and was elated that she was of legal age. Her brothers threw her a small party, just the THREE of them. The brothers bought presents, cake, and ice cream…and snow globes, her favorite collectable, along with some clothes and other small items. Later in the afternoon, their attorney showed up at the house. When he handed David sealed envelope. David looked at the front of the envelope, and regretfully recognized his father's handwriting. It read:

DAVID, HENRI, ELISE:
NOT TO BE OPENED UNTIL ALL THREE CHILDREN ARE
18 YEARS OF AGE AND WE TWO ARE DEAD

David looked up at the attorney in a momentary state of disbelief and stared at him with narrowed eyes. He opened the letter in disbelief, "Father and his damned TWOs and THREEs again," David fumed inside. He took a moment to read it silently.
*"My three children, if you're reading this, it*
*means I (and your annoying mother) have moved on*
*to be with God at His right hand, and the three of*

*you, my three, have received the results of MY efforts."*

David could almost hear his father's deep baritone voice echoing inside his head.

*"You truly don't deserve the compensation I've left you, but, as they say, the Good Shepherd must take care of his sheep. You don't deserve my money, my house, or possessions, but it seems I have no choice, as this is the way life goes. The Good die, and the Unworthy split the spoils. The people in MY church expect nothing less of me. There's no doubt in my mind you'll squander it and be left penniless in no time. You were mine in life, I needed the three of you to make my life complete, and now you're mine in death. I WILL be watching you, I always will. My eyes will follow you all the days of your life. I'll be holding the door open to hell's entrance for you."*

At this point Henri saw that David was getting angry at what he was reading. He'd learned in the past two years that whenever David got angry, bad things were going to happen. And he waited.

David's lips tightened, anger seared inside, and his hands began to shake. He folded the letter and placed it back inside the envelope.

The attorney was more than aware of David's sudden mood change. "You ok, son? Is there anything I can do?"

David shook his head and quickly escorted the man to the door, "Thank you, sir. Thank you very much." He all but pushed the man out the door, and he left perplexed at David's actions.

After he heard the car drive off, David stood in the living room and kicked the side table across the room. Henri flinched. Both the side table and his father's precious humidor fell at the foot of the stairs in pieces, and cigars rolled all about. David's mind reeled with anger, confusion, but worse, overwhelming paranoia. "He's back, Henri!" David roared. "He's come back from hell to persecute me!" He paced back and forth, thinking, "Obviously I wasn't thorough the first time. He thinks he's in Heaven, but I know where I sent him, I saw it on his face in the car! Somehow, he came back, Henri, I did something wrong the first time, so I have to do it again!"

He stared at this father's former bedroom door; his eyes then darted over to Henri. David pointed at the bedroom, "He knows, Henri. He knows what I did to his bedroom." David smiled. His mind suddenly warped into an obsessive belief that his father knew what was going on inside the house, what David was doing all the time, and what he'd done to the bedroom. In a giggly, almost girlish voice he said, "He hates the bedroom, because it's alive, I spent money on it, I 'wasted' his petty allotment and he wants to take everything away!"

Henri didn't believe that their father had come back, but knew to remain silent, to just listen. He'd already suffered the wrath of David on more than one occasion when he tried to reason with him.

David crumpled and threw the envelope; it sailed across the room. "I have to do everything over again, and again, until he can't come back!" He grabbed his leather bomber jacket from the chair beside the door. "I'm gonna kill you right this time, Father. You'll get yours for sure!" David shouted as he left the house.

## CHAPTER 30
## APRIL 2009
## FEELING BLUE

Over the next few days, the newspapers headlined three vehicle bombings in the city. The first bombing was a family car: a husband and wife were killed. An ambulance exploded later in the day on the east side of town, killing one paramedic. Lastly, and most painful for the community, was the bombing of a school bus. The driver and numerous children were killed just outside a school when leaving for the day. Again, local investigators were frustrated with the lack of evidence and the cause of the explosions. There were no fingerprints, no fibers, no hair, absolutely nothing to go on. It was as if a ghost had terrorized the city. Moreover, the lack of motive and witnesses was discouraging for the town's citizens and law enforcement. Again, the three bombings were accompanied by a Biblical quote found on a crumpled note at each scene. The media had a field day with "The Return of the Biblical Bomber."

The Task Force Agents from Washington were called in and returned to help in the investigation. Profilers and experts convened in the command room at the local police station to review notes, evidence, etc. They conducted daily briefings for all City and County Officers and other specialized law enforcement to keep everyone updated on their findings about the serial killer and to be vigilant in their patrols. A public information officer was assigned to handle the press, mostly to urge them to warn citizens to be wary, more than anything.

One of the newer Task Force Field Agents was on a separate investigation, however. Her name was Harri Lewis, but her agent name was Proteus, and her specialty was in disguise, camouflage, and misdirection. She was having trouble, however, masking the apprehension she felt on her first solo investigation. She'd always worked with a group or with other team members after she joined the Task Force field unit. She still couldn't believe she'd been hired on with this elite team, dressed in the strange form-fitting black uniform, and armed with more weaponry on her four-foot-eight body than she ever imagined she could carry. She especially found it hard her petite size was ignored for the position.

She waited in her Task Force car, a non-descript specialized black sports car with a sophisticated on-board computer and polarized windows. No one could see in from the outside. Proteus waited until all the investigators finally departed the taped-off scene surrounding the bus explosion. When no more people were around, she stepped out of her car and approached the area.

She didn't have to crouch much to go under the police tape, and as she rose, she donned her sophisticated cocoon glasses. The special lenses and microprocessors allowed her to see the entire area easily in the dark of night.

Proteus set her mind to the job at hand, to look without seeing, find without searching, to be one with the scene, as she was trained. There was so much carnage, pieces of bus all over the street and yards and inside buildings, the force of the explosion had propelled metal fragments through windows across the entire block. Crews had worked all through the day and partly into the night with the cleanup. All the human remains had been rapidly catalogued and removed, but the vehicle debris would take much longer. Distant hammering could still be heard from nearby business owners putting up plywood as a temporary fix. It was late, and now was the best time to investigate without interruption.

The blonde agent tapped at the Bluetooth in her right ear with her gloved forefinger. "Tactical, Proteus," she said softly. Though the Bluetooth was nothing more than a specialized cell phone, the transmission was plotted on a GPS and all conversations were recorded back at Command.

"Tactical, go for Proteus," she heard in her ear.

She smiled. "Tactical Nine, is that you?"

"Confirmed, Proteus," said the male voice in her ear.

"Nice to know I've got a friend on the other end of this channel," Proteus said.

"You always do," said Tactical Nine, her contact at Task Force Command in Washington, D. C. on this mission. "What's your status?"

Proteus stood in the middle of the destruction near what was left of the bus's rear axle. "I haven't seen anything like this since my last movie date," she joked, her natural protection from bad situations. She turned her head from side to side, taking in the whole view. "I don't see anything out of the ordinary, if you'd call any of this ordinary."

"What setting are you using?"

"What?" she asked. "Oh, right." She tapped a tiny control on her glasses' left wing and a digital display appeared in the upper area of her view field. "Standard night-vision, 0100 setting."

"Try switching to BL-A view," said Tactical Nine.

Proteus nodded, "Shoulda thoughta that myself," she chided herself. *Still learning.* She changed the settings with the control on the right wing. "Ah, much better. Wow, look at all the glowing blue." Her response was emphatic but whispered.

"That's blood you're seeing, Proteus," Nine reminded her.

"Yeah, I know. Oh my God, it's just everywhere." She looked down at her boots. Her feet were in a glowing spot bigger around than herself. "I'm standing in it, great." Proteus shuffled to her right to stand on the "un-glowing" sidewalk. "These boots are so gonna get burned when I'm done."

"They'll be coming out your salary," Nine teased her.

"I was standing in blood."

"You're wearing the black standard TF tactical boots. They're waterproof and chemical-proof."

"But they're not yech-proof, I'm so ditching these boots when I get—wait, what's that?" She stared at a section of grass far off in front of her, about twenty feet beyond the police tape beside the sidewalk.

"What is it, Proteus?"

"Something, wait." Proteus walked forward cautiously. "I see more glowing blue, but in a singular line pattern leading away from the main event. One dot after another, not following the random pattern that's everywhere else around here." She ducked under the tape and stopped at the first line of blue dots. She knelt and peered closer.

"Proteus, report."

"It's a piece of metal. Ragged edges." She used the controls on the glasses to switch to artificial-light view. "Traces of yellow paint, and red smudging. I think it's blood." She adjusted her lenses to magnification mode. "And it looks like there's traces of flesh, too." She changed the magnification in her lenses. "I see smudges in the blood, like from gloves. No discernible fingerprints on the top surface." She picked up the one nearest her with her gloved forefinger and thumb, turned it over to examine the other side. "Same on the reverse. Smudge, no fingerprint ridging."

"Bag and tag all items, Proteus, then return to Command."

"Copy, Tactical Nine, I'm on my way," she smiled. "Have another pair of boots waiting for me, and someone to scrub and decontaminate my floorboard and pedals."

◆

The Task Force took its time in reviewing the bombings from two years before and now the newest ones. The agents' day-to-day investigations lead to more growing frustration. They were left to study the mysterious notes and attempt to profile the bomber based on the notes content and the type of vehicles that

149

were bombed in the two-year timeframe. Their specialists still scoured the vehicles in the forensics garage area.

The evidence showed the Biblical quotes were printed on plain white copy paper, but there was nothing plain about the type of computer font chosen by the killer. The Cryptologists were immediately alerted to the text peculiarity, determining it was the common "Chiller" font that comes with most computer text programs. It had an alarming and undisciplined presence with shocking splatters that gave a dangerous, reckless look to them, but surprisingly legible. Agents believed it was obviously used to make a bold, blasphemous statement, a direct contradiction and mockery of the words in the notes. The profilers in the bombing cases reasoned that the font itself was calculated, much like that of the serial killer they now studied. The killer, most likely male, wanted to look dangerous and reckless, yet contrary, just like his font. They noted the "Chiller" font wasn't used in the first bombing, the DeVeaux murders. They decided that the initial killing might have been a first for him and he was learning, transforming, growing into the killer they now knew as the "Biblical Bomber".

The Task Force team looked at every angle and wondered if the person was perhaps a religious zealot with an agenda. They briefly considered it might be misdirection from a terrorist, but the quantity of deaths didn't add up. There was no doubt they'd be looking for a sociopath or someone with a psychotic personality disorder, detached from reality, and harboring a pervasive pattern of disregard for people, as was obvious by the ongoing violence.

◆

David rested in his chair and took an expensive Stradivarius cigar from the newly purchased humidor, one much larger than the dinky humidor his father owned. He took great delight in lighting it with his father's lighter. His bloody gloves from the bombing lay on the table next to his cigar ashtray.

Henri came from the downstairs bathroom with a first-aid kit. David was settling in now, taking deep swigs of whiskey to calm his nerves and trying to numb the ensuing pain in this left arm. Henri took a seat on the ottoman next to David. "You ready, David? Gonna hurt a bit. Don't want you snappin' my head off."

David took one long, deliberate gulp of whiskey straight from the bottle. He closed his eyes hard and puckered up his face while the alcohol burned its way down his gullet. Shaking his head rapidly, he opened his eyes and smiled wildly. "Go ahead, brother, do what ya gotta do, I'm ready now."

Henri began cleaning the cuts on David's arm. The bus bomb had gone off too soon, and pieces of glass and metal caught him in the arm. David had already pulled the larger quarter-size pieces out with his good hand and threw them on the ground when he fled the bus bombing. The smaller ones required another set of eyes and hands to remove. David trusted Henri far more than he trusted a hospital. The ambulance drivers were all the Good Father's followers, even from hell, he believed.

Henri had learned about stitching and butterfly bandaging in school and from the Internet. "How'd it go, Davey?" he asked carefully as he worked. He didn't want to upset David in any way. "Was this a successful THREE?" He wasn't as obsessive as David, but his years of learned behavior were greatly evident.

"Yep." David nodded his head, more exaggerated than normal. Henri realized the whiskey had obviously kicked in and raised an eyebrow when he looked up at him. David took a comforting drag on the cigar and blew out the blue-gray smoke. "How many are there, brother?" He stared down at the cuts on his arm.

Henri counted the nicks in David's arm after removing the last piece of glass. "Sixteen it would seem, including the ones you took out yourself. Some are pretty deep, need to keep an eye on 'em so they don't get infected."

David looked at him with narrowed angry eyes. He calmed down just as quickly as the anger came on. "Good. TWO sets of TWOs and THREEs. Yep, that's a just reward." Out of nowhere he roared in fury. "Damn him! Damn father for his curse of TWOs and THREES on me!"

Henri flinched at the sudden explosion. He gathered up the kit and headed to the kitchen to tidy up the contents and store them back away.

When David got this way, the best thing for anyone was to be out of the way.

**CHAPTER 31**
**APRIL 2011**
**"I AIN'T NO 'SIR'"**

"Mark WHO?" Sarge said aloud as he sat at his home desk reading a long list of daily emails. He'd received an odd one, something from Mark Jason, President of Jason Enterprises. He asked the retired Sergeant to come in for an interview. The email was brief, giving few details and left a lot to the imagination. He thought to delete it, but something in him said "No." It wasn't like sarge needed the income; he did well with his retirement and disability from the military. Sarge printed off the email, and thought he'd take it down to the local watering hole later in the evening. "Well, guess I'll see what the guys think about this," he thought.

◆

Taking his usual position at the Recovery Room bar, Sarge handed the JE email to his good friend Roger "Dodger" Ahrens. Roger hated that everyone called him "Roger-Dodger", but he put up with it. His buddies seemed to like the way it rhymed, as well as being a common cliché. Tall, almost lanky, Roger took the printout and hunched over the bar to read it.

Roger and Clarence "Sarge" Brunson, both Master Sergeants, US Army Retired, served three tours in Afghanistan and Iraq. Both were wounded in combat in the same final conflict. Best friends, they felt they were the "Mutt and Jeff" of their unit. Sarge was a mountain of a man, six-foot-six and 250 pounds of solid muscle but now with a small paunch beginning in his stomach. Roger was lean and less muscular but rock solid at just under six feet and 180 pounds. They wore matching crew cuts, Sarge's hair dark brown, and Roger's sandy blond, their temples powdered with areas of short gray bristles. They were admired by subordinates and respected by their commanding officers for heroism and selflessness in the field.

In their last conflict overseas, the two single-handedly took out nearly twenty al-Qaeda terrorists in an ambush before falling from multiple gunshot wounds. Sarge and Roger were only too obliged to send as many terrorists as possible to collect their 72 virgins. The encounter was fast and furious. Their fellow ground pounders came to the rescue, not realizing how bad the two sergeants' wounds were until after the fray. Their stoicism inspired the troops to push on just as hard. After all, if the old sergeants could take it and survive, so could they. Ultimately, their injuries proved numerous and debilitating, and the two soldiers were sent home with honorable medical retirements.

Their weekly meeting at the bar was the usual Friday night ritual, killing a whole squadron of enemy bourbon shots in The Recovery Room. It was aptly named since its greatest clientele was armed services veterans. Purple Heart recipients got cut prices on drinks. The establishment could occupy fifty or sixty people without feeling overcrowded. The L-shaped bar area itself sat twelve people on stools, and the wall behind was mirrored with shelf upon shelf of various forms of liquid anesthetics. Pool tables filled the middle of the room and a few old Sharkies played eight-ball. Booths lined the walls around the rest of the area, each labeled with a sign defining a different war malady such as "Amputee", "PTSD", "Bullet Wound", "Forrest Gump…Shot in the Ass", the labels went on and on. It provided a fun jest for the not-so-fun outcomes of war.

The art décor for the walls, military paraphernalia, unit flags, badges, bullets, etc., was provided by the patrons. A POW/MIA poster was prominently placed on one wall. The manager set a solitary plate with utensils, an empty glass and lone chair underneath the poster much like those at VFW lodges. Everyone knew not to sit there, in honor of the missing, prisoners, or those killed in action. Pictures of Veterans shaking hands with Presidents and Generals were displayed, along with Unit Citations and Commendations. It went on and on, looking much like the walls of a Cracker Barrel, but in military style.

Sarge and Roger received honorable discharges, along with Purple Hearts and Silver Stars when they retired. Sarge provided a Memorial Flag for the wall, given to him by the family of a wounded fellow soldier that Sarge rescued on the front line. The man died after returning stateside, his injuries too severe. The family gave Sarge the flag as their way of saying "thank you" for getting him home, at least for a last goodbye.

Sarge was way ahead of Roger in the shot drinking competition, brooding that they'd forgotten to keep count.

"Mark Jason," Roger read aloud the email that sat on the bar counter. Looking up at Sarge he said, "Strange for a guy to have two first names. His momma musta been confused, eh?"

Sarge kicked back the shot of bourbon that Al the barkeep just poured. "Anyone know this Jason guy? Not that I really care…urp…mind ju'."

Al said, "He was in the Navy for three stints. Took over the family company when his dad retired due to cancer, then his dad died a year later. His mom also died a few months after."

"Navy?" Roger questioned no one in particular. "Humph, bet he was a flyboy, shoulda stayed up in the air where he belonged, eh, Sarge?"

Ignoring Roger for the moment, "What did he do?" Sarge asked. Al looked Sarge in the eyes as a reply. "Oh, he was a SEAL, eh?" Al simply took an emptied glass from the bar to the rear for cleaning as his reply.

"Hey, Sarge," said Roger, "you remember that Navy flyboy over in Japan?"

"Which one?"

"The one," Roger said slowly, "who couldn't hold his Sake?"

Sarge thought for a moment, searching his slightly numb memory cells. "Ah, yeah, Mister 'Sad Sake'." Sarge flung an arm up in the air in remembrance. "Al, those blue flyboys got no bizness doin' anything on the ground, ya know. Keep 'em up in the air and outta our way, right, Dodger? Better yet, keep 'em out on the water in their boats."

The liquor was kicking nicely, giving the two the mellow reward they'd been looking for. Roger playfully punched Sarge in the arm, hard, momentarily forgetting that hitting Sarge was like pounding a live boulder. "Ow, dammit, Sarge." Roger grimaced and shook his hand up and down.

Sarge smiled triumphantly and pointed at Roger's shot glass, still full. "You're falling behind, Sergeant. Sounds like ya suddenly need that med'cine more'n ever now. Wonder whatever happened to 'Sad Sake' anyway? As I recall, th' wuss couldn't hold his Japanese booze, all I remember."

"Wha' wuz' his name, anyway?" asked Roger, now half-sloshed and not caring that much. "Samson? Simson? Like Homer? Why're we talking about him any-who?"

The bar assistant TJ shook her head and the men's rhetoric. She refilled the sergeants' glasses, and busily punched the keys on Al's register computer at the same time. The two barely even realized she was there. TJ was a tall brunette with a female military cut above the shoulders and a figure to die for. She carried herself with an attitude that said "you can look but don't think about touching" in her navy-blue shorts and American-flag-picture sleeveless T-shirt. She caught Al's attention and pointed at the monitor. Al nodded as she said, "Lieutenant Michael Covington, US Navy Air. According to some, shall we say, specialized records, he drunk you two under the bar at the Tokyo Teahouse."

The two turned to stare at TJ, momentarily quiet with mouths slightly opened. "Musta been a couple other pounders with single stripes," Sarge growled. The few other vets in the bar couldn't help but laugh. This was the banter they longed to put up with on Friday evenings. It was the hot young brunette taking out the rough-and-tumble sergeants with a punch of a digital button. The Sergeants loved it every time, and the Friday night regulars howled in delight. No one ever asked how she could find answers to random questions so quickly; it was part of the entertainment.

The laughter subsided, and Al took the email printout, slouched comfortably with elbows on the bar, and mused over the invitation. "Hmmm, the president of Jason Enterprises invites you specifically to come for an interview at his office tomorrow at noon." Rodger slid it back in front of Sarge. "Ya got anything better to do tomorrow at noontime, sir?"

Staring into his glass Sarge gave a friendly growl. "I ain't no 'sir'. I worked for a living. That sir-stuff is for the guys with the gold braid on their caps."

"Right," said Al, swiping at the bar with a towel, the one he always had over his shoulder. This was more of their traditional Friday night barb. "Odd that he wants to see you on a weekend though."

"So, what's 'Jason Enterprises' anyway?" Sarge asked, looking up at Al and TJ. "Never heard of it."

TJ smiled as she replied, "Jason Enterprises is an international corporation specializing in government contracts." She paused for effect. "Electronic and computer software development for the military, just to name a couple."

Sarge narrowed his eyes, wondering how she knew all that information off the top of her head. It seemed rehearsed.

"Of all people, why me?" asked Sarge. "I ain't nobody special."

"There's only one way to find out," said Al.

**CHAPTER 32**
**APRIL 2011, THE NEXT MORNING**
**BOURBON, NEAT**

Mark looked up from his desk as the weekend security guard escorted the visitor into his office. "Sergeant Brunson," he said as he stood, extending his right hand in greeting.

Sarge enveloped Mark Jason's hand, sizing up the corporate president at the same time. *The man's got good eye contact, well sized, obviously works out a lot. Could probably hold his own in a good brawl. Firm handshake, even if he is a deskbound paper-pusher,* Sarge thought.

"Call me Sarge, if you don't mind, sir," his deep baritone voice boomed throughout the room.

Mark raised an eyebrow in reply and motioned for him to take a seat in one of the chairs in front of the desk. Mark waited for Sarge to sit, then took a seat himself.

Fingers interlocked on the desk in front of him, "My name is Mark Jason," he began. "Thank you for coming in on a Saturday morning, Sarge."

"No problem, sir," Sarge replied.

"I thought we could have a, how should I say it, 'more pleasant' conversation without the normal hustle and bustle that's usually in here during the week." Mark abruptly got up from his chair and stepped over to the wet bar, set into the wall to Sarge's left. Sarge thought it was odd that Mark would just get up and walk away like that at the beginning of a conversation.

Sarge took the opportunity to look around the room while Mark was busy. Hearing clinking sounds from the bar area, he surmised that decanters were being moved around. With Mark's back to him, Sarge took in the lavish surroundings. The cherry wood executive desk and credenza spoke volumes about the man now tinkering with booze and glasses. Cream colored Berber carpeting, plush bronze calf-skin leather couches, high end paintings (originals no doubt), and an expansive library of books aligned on cherry wood bookcases. Technology guy too, lots of computers and plasma TVs scattered about. *Pretty swanky,* Sarge thought.

He heard a pouring action, and turned as Mark poured two drinks, one with a splash of water, one without.

He turned back around in his chair, as if he hadn't been watching. Sarge was presented with a crystal tumbler. "Kentucky's finest, neat."

Sarge raised a questioning eyebrow at Mark, acknowledging that Mark had done his homework. "Thank you, sir."

Mark sat in his chair again. "You're curious, Sarge. Wondering who I am, how I know about you, and how I know what you like to drink." Before Sarge could reply, "I know you won't touch a drop until after noon exactly, for example." Mark leaned forward in his chair, propped his forearms on the desk, fingers intertwined once more. "Right to the point. We have many government contracts in progress here. We have rocket targeting software development, weapons research, military computer software, satellite software and equipment, and occasionally the complete satellite, just to name a few off the top of my head. We take on projects internationally as well. My last head of security, recently retired. So, I asked one of my Fed contacts for a recommendation, and he gave me exactly one, he gave me this." He lifted a manila file folder from his desk. Without opening the folder, Mark continued. "Clarence Brunson, Master Sergeant, US

Army Retired. Three tours awarded the Purple Heart, Oak Leaf Clusters, Silver Star, and took out a whole encampment of insurgents, with your pal 'Roger Dodger'. Took out 52—"

"—48, sir," instantly regretting making the correction out loud.

"—52," Jason continued. "I included the ones who died after capture. A ruthless but efficient operator. Dedicated to the mission to the exclusion of all else. 'Failure is not an option' is your philosophy."

"And I don't take crap from anyone, sir!" Sarge added, "Um, sorry, sir. That was uncalled for."

"Quite alright, Sergeant."

Sarge realized he'd stepped in it for the second time in less than a minute. He decided to go on to third base and followed quickly with, "And I give back more than I take."

Mark smiled, "Interesting paradox. I want you to take over the Head of Security position here. You run the security department your way. Hire and fire at your discretion. Training and personnel fall under your control. You have full background check authority on all employees, prospective employees, sub-contractors, at my direction as warranted. The only employee files you will not have access to are mine and my wife's."

"I don't believe in exceptions, sir."

Mark leaned forward in his chair and lowered his interlaced hands on the desktop. "You see, veteran to veteran, I was a Lieutenant Commander in the SEALs (Sarge thought to himself, *Damn, I was right!*) and my military files are off limits. Checking on me or my wife might, well, bring up certain questions that I prefer not to have asked. A man in my position doesn't need uncontrolled questions, and you're the kind of guy who can stop or start any inquiry. So, I ask that of you as one vet to another, as a courtesy." Mark slid a piece of paper that had been resting under his hands, forward on the desk. Sarge picked it up. His eyebrows lifted involuntarily when he saw the dollar figure on the paper. Mark sat back in his chair, resting his hands behind his head. "That's your annual salary, to start, and," Mark added, "I'll authorize you to carry your personal sidearm when on the clock, which is pretty much 24/7 by the way. You'll have complete carry permits with the city and state, and if business takes you out of state those permits will be made available as needed. There's also a possibility you may need to work outside the country, so get your passport in order."

Still staring at the dollar figure, Sarge kicked back his tumbler in one swig. He showed no reaction. Mark noted Sarge's steel facade. Setting the glass down in his lap and clearing his throat he asked, "What do you want of me, sir?"

"I want you to protect this company, its employees, and me. The Feds will make sure you get certified, of course. So long as you stay within the boundaries of the law, I don't care how you solve any problems that come up."

"One condition, sir."

"What's that, Sergeant?"

"Sir, I know my business. There may be circumstances that come up when I, well, need the freedom to do what I feel necessary, without having to check with you first. I'll keep you informed, sir, but I need to be able to do the job first and answer questions after the dust has settled. Will you trust me to work and do the job without question, sir?"

Mark stood, buttoned his jacket as he rose, and extended his hand again. "Welcome to Jason Enterprises, Mr. Brunson…Sarge." He handed Sarge a key card with Sarge's photograph already embossed on it. "You're on the payroll as of now, with full access to the building. My assistant has already prepared the appropriate documentation for your signature." Waving a hand toward her office, "you'll find it on her desk as you leave."

*Well, I'll be damned, he was gonna hire me regardless*, Sarge thought.

**CHAPTER 33**
**APRIL 2011, MONDAY MORNING**
**"YOU CAN CALL ME SARGE"**

The security staff was called into the meeting hall on the second floor of Jason Enterprises the following Monday morning. Those assigned to high-risk posts couldn't attend but were tapped in via other secure Wi-Fi capabilities. A low rumble of chit-chat amongst the employees seemed lost in the large hall. Upon seeing the size of his new crew, Sarge began to feel a bit nervous. Commanding a squad of a dozen men into battle against snipers was one thing but seeing this crowd of people who weren't even born when he shot his first enemy was unnerving. *I'm going to be training and leading babies*, he thought.

Mark stood front and center and called the meeting to order. Talking went to whispering and then to full silence. Going through the general formalities of thanking the employees for their attendance and providing information as to why the meeting was called, Mark finally introduced the new Security Chief. Sarge felt extremely uncomfortable in a business suit, but he still presented an imposing figure standing before the numerous security staff members. Employees were slightly stunned to see his physical size greater than Mark's, and Mark had a powerful frame. He was given the floor and the microphone. The staff was about to learn very quickly that he didn't mince words and had no problem speaking his mind. Clearing his throat, Sarge began. "Thank you, Mr. Jason. Good morning, ladies and gentlemen. You probably think I'm gonna change things to run my way starting now. Well, you'd be wrong. We'll do that next week." Mark laughed, leading everyone else at Sarge's humor. Sarge continued, "But first I'm gonna learn everything you do and you're gonna tell me when I got it wrong and keep telling me until I know it as well as you. This man here," pointing at Mark, "thinks I'm the one to run this here department. And I'm gonna do it so he has one less thing to worry about the rest of his day. I already know you're the best at what you do. Otherwise, you wouldn't be working for him. But the best can always be improved. Like you being the best here, I was the best on the front line with a rifle in my hand and a terrorist in my scope. But we're here now, and we're gonna learn all about each other and be a better team. Yeah, I'm gonna learn your techy stuff, and you're gonna learn how to be better soldiers. And WE are gonna take exceptionally good care of this man and his company." Leaning too far into the microphone, Sarge asked, "Questions?"

A short young security PFC raised her hand. She stood when Sarge pointed at her. "Deborah O'Brien, welcome to Jason Enterprises, sir," she began.

Sarge leaned down into the microphone to speak, "I ain't no 'sir', young lady," Sarge interrupted with a straight face; Mark shook his head as he smiled. Sarge shot a thumb over his shoulder toward Mark. "He's your 'sir'. You can call me 'Sarge'." O'Brien's eyes darted left and right and wondered what she'd said wrong. "If you piss me off, you'll be callin' me Mr. Brunson. You piss me off twice, you'll be calling me from the unemployment line." The staff room was dead silent, until Sarge broke into a smile. "Just seein' if you're payin' attention."

Laughter and chuckles broke out, nervous at first but then more relaxed when Sarge turned toward Mark, who also smiled and gave Sarge a pat on the shoulder. Over the dwindled chuckles Sarge continued, "What's your question, O'Brien?"

"Sir, I mean Sarge. I'm the new kid here. What's your policy with someone hired right before you? I mean, I'm in a probationary timeframe right now."

Sarge crossed his arms, looking quite comfortable, and gave a big white toothy smile. "You're gonna start at the bottom, O'Brien, just like I did."

◆

Sarge knew from his interview that Jason Enterprises was a global operation, but when he saw the actual security operations center, he was taken aback. He watched as Mark keyed a ten-digit code into the keypad and the pocket door withdrew into the door frame. Mark explained that in the event of a power failure, or generator failure, both the keypad and the door were on independent battery backups, as was every door within the building. Sarge stepped into the giant room, and he felt as if he'd been transported to a different world. The equipment and technology were not only state of the art but seemed to be from a different dimension.

The overhead lights were turned off, as the light panels and computer monitors throughout the room created more than enough illumination. He could hardly count the rows of connected desk stations and pods, let alone the number of computer monitors scattered throughout the room. Enormous plasma screens covered the walls, each displaying a different image. Every station was staffed. A low hum of human voices could be heard, discussions on radios, phones, person to person, etc. It was a beehive of controlled activity. Keyboards created a constant, soft tap-tap-tap sound. If someone needed to leave a station, a replacement worker moved in and took over the station within seconds. He never saw where the replacement came from, however. Mark pointed out that the room was the size of a basketball court in square footage, taking up 90% of the building's second floor office space.

The OPS Center had radio, computer and telephone feeds or connections to numerous agencies including local emergency services, NCIC, NASA, NSA, Interpol, a variety of military establishments and finally certain agencies within the White House and Pentagon. Their contracts were wide and varied. International news broadcasts quietly streamed on separate monitor clusters in each corner.

"Wow," Sarge could only say as he took it all in. "You said you were international, sir, but this is like a government facility instead of a business."

"When you see what we do on the 14th, you'll understand why we're tied in so heavily to international security," Mark answered, "as a private company, of course." He offered an "I know something you don't" smile.

It was imperative to keep the operations center at an extreme low profile, hidden and as secure as possible. All the doors seen from the lobby were false entrances, opening to nowhere, helping to create an illusion should there be a security breach. There was only one true entrance and exit. The workstations were situated in seven groups, "One each dedicated to each continent," Mark said, making Sarge think back and count his geography lessons. "You telling me you have an outpost or something in Antarctica?" To which Mark replied, "I thought it was a cool idea, don't you?" Sarge couldn't help but grimace at the excruciatingly bad pun.

Mark pointed out specific pods that were set off separately from the rest, which exclusively tied to the building's security system of cameras, microphones, heat and weight sensors, after-hours laser grids, etc. He explained that the primary feeds could be sent to the Security Chief's desk in whatever order he preferred. The Chief's office was located on the second floor as well, in a room tucked away behind the expansive OPS room. A secret door was built into the wall in the Chief's office so he could access the OPS area anytime he wanted.

Unlike the OPS center, the Chief's office was drab. The prior Chief took all his personal possessions when he retired. There were no paintings or other art on the walls. A lone bookshelf sat in a corner, with only a few books leftover from the previous occupant. There was a coat hook on the back of the main door, a large desk with small monitors behind a front panel, and an executive chair. A couple of flags would most certainly be placed into the empty corner opposite the door for his initial furnishings. Any visitors were going to be reminded what country they were in, and Sarge didn't care if anyone was offended or not. He fought to defend the American flag, and he was going to display it with great pride.

Mark stepped up to the first bank of stations. A woman in front stood and came around to greet Mark and Sarge. She was as tall as Mark, nearly six feet, with short brunette hair and a light application of makeup. She wore a simple white blouse and gray skirt with matching gray flats. "Good morning, sir," she said, coming to a relaxed attention before him.

"Freeman, good morning," said Mark. "This is Sarge Brunson, your new Chief. Sarge, this is Sandra Freeman, she's in charge of the International Information Network. Please, give Sarge an overview."

Waving a hand toward the room Freeman responded. "All these stations receive reports from across the world 24 hours a day, 365 days a year. These are the primary stations which provide information to the you as the Security Chief. The amount of data we receive from across the world is immense in relation to all of Jason Enterprises' operations, so it comes to our primary team here and backup team below for dissemination. By working in pairs there's less chance of missing any key information. And by working in teams in slightly separate locations, a conversation won't interrupt anyone else's work."

"Ever been a security breach in here?

Freeman looked at Mark, who gave a small nod. "Like last month, we had one of our weekend staff substituted by a look-alike, someone surgically altered to look like him. None of us caught on at first."

Mark almost chuckled at Sarge's double take. "You're kidding, someone was physically operated on, optics, fingerprints, everything, and just walked right in?" Freeman nodded. "Anyone bother to check his pee for DNA?"

"That's on alternating months sir, it wasn't on the schedule," Freeman replied with a perfect poker face.

Sarge didn't know if she was joking or not, but he was leaning towards "not" judging by the way she looked him in the eye.

Freeman continued, "Since we change pass codes on a daily basis, he got it right the first day, but wrong the second day. The guy was fed bad info and thought the pass code was good for a month. When the workstation row went down, we knew we had a breech and we had him."

"So where was he taken?"

"Federal custody," said Mark. "Our employee was recovered from captivity by JE and Federal agents, and given three months' leave with pay, along with ordered counseling as a precaution. We take care of our people."

Sarge unbuttoned his jacket and put his hands on his hips, pushing back the jacket panels as he did. Freeman saw the large pistol his right hand rested on, and instinctively reacted. She reached forward with both hands, grabbed his upper right arm, pivoted, and tossed Sarge over her shoulder, removing his pistol from his belt holster while he was in mid-air.

Once the sparkling spots began clearing from his vision, he realized he was on his back and staring at the ceiling. It took a few seconds to figure out how he got there. *Right, Freeman, she got the drop on me. How the hell did she do that?* he thought. Once his vision cleared, he propped himself up on one elbow. He noticed that no one in the entire complex had moved to help him, never mind gawk at the new chief laid out by someone less than half his size. He hadn't been ready for her move on him, and his body was busy trying to remember how to return to an upright position. His face may have been a steel façade, but his body was howling in protest and demanding more time to recover.

Freeman extended a hand to help him back to his feet and guided him up gently but firmly. Mark was still standing in the same spot, hand over his mouth to hide his chuckling. Once Sarge was on his feet she reached up and straightened his tie, smoothed his jacket lapels, and finally returned his pistol butt-first. "My apologies, sir. Habit. I thought you were going to draw." She smiled apologetically.

Sarge ran his fingers through his short hair and straightened his jacket like any proud Army Sergeant would. "Damn, I like you, Freeman," Sarge smiled. "But you do that again, and I'll kick your ass across this room." He silently vowed to himself never to be caught off guard by her again.

"Just reflexes, don't like guns I can't control in my own space, sir," she replied, again ignoring his title preference. Freeman excused herself by adding, "With your permission?" She returned to her station but remained on her feet.

As he guided Sarge away, Mark smiled and whispered, "Former CIA, black belt in Karate. Twenty-three confirmed terrorist kills in Iraq and Afghanistan." He gave Sarge a stern look and spoke quietly. "You'll come to find that I have security personnel working undercover in every department of this building. She's one, and she'll be answering to you for security matters but answering to me on all else."

"Damn, sir, I think I'm in love," Sarge deadpanned.

"Not on company time mister," Mark said, smiling. "Let's get you settled into your new home."

Mark and Sarge left the OPS center. Once the door closed, Freeman grabbed the top of her station's terminal frame and told the young man beside her, "Get me some pain killers, and I mean get them yesterday." She put a hand on her back and said aloud, "He was a lot heavier than he looked."

**CHAPTER 34**
**APRIL 2011**
**MOVING IN TWOS AND THREES**

During the last two years Henri was seeking things to do in his spare time. In high school, he had a keen ability for mechanics and design. Now, he'd tinker in the garage out back and even designed a few items he'd submitted for patents. He knew the reply would take time and require patience. He started to develop a circle of friends for the first time, unsavory at best however, who liked to work with him. They did more grunt work for him than anything, helping with projects and hanging out. They needed the money and Henri found he needed a fan club of sorts.

David had been calm during the last two years, since the last series of vehicle explosions that "cleansed his soul", as David put it. He still had his share of temper tantrums daily, however. He'd get upset over normal small issues. To David there was no such thing as a small issue. If a piece of furniture was dusty, it was someone else's fault. If an item were moved, and he didn't remember moving it, he'd have a tantrum thinking someone was messing with him. Paranoia never really left his side. It was an ever-present sidekick. His mental illness was prevalent, and most people simply tried to stay out of his way.

David intentionally spent more time with Elise now, fixated on helping her with her disability, and reveling in his need to control his sister and her surroundings. She was needy and depended on him. He was controlling and needed someone to control. They made a great match for each other and fed off each other's needs.

Sick of his parent's home, he'd talked Elise and Henri into letting him sell the house and move out. He knew how Elise felt about the place she'd grown up in, her extreme hesitation to leave it. He recently made-up elaborate stories about it being infested with termites and was being eaten from the outside in. He told her the wood was rotting and at some point, very soon the walls and floorboards would start crumbling and there'd be no home left, and they needed to sell it before anyone found out. His fabrications paid off, scaring her into a mode of desperation, now afraid to even walk through the house for fear she'd fall through the floor.

On one chilly evening in April, David decided to build a bonfire in the backyard. Elise, Henri, and Henri's buddies were all at the house. David had been drinking for a good part of the afternoon, eliciting false bravado and discourse in his mind. The house and property had just been sold, but David felt a need to extinguish the memories of their father, once again. Months earlier, when he'd purchased new home furnishings, he'd taken all his parent's old furniture and temporarily stored it in the garage. In David's drunken stupor and wandering mind, he knew his father's presence was still around, mingled among the old furnishings stacked one on top of the other. "Time to burn it, Henri, burn it all!" David rambled as they all sat around the bonfire. Henri now had a taste for his father's alcohol as well as David, and they'd even persuaded Elise to try some of the milder liqueurs. She'd found it enticing to a point, laughing with the boys, though she had no idea what their conversation was even about.

"What, David? Burn what, the house?" Henri sat up straight in the folding chair. "No! We just sold it!"

"No, idiot," he replied, nodding back at the garage. "His furniture." David puffed on a cigar as he spoke. "He's in it, can chu feel 'em? His stench is in every damned piece of furniture, and it needs to go! We have to start over Henri, a new beginning. Boys, up!" he growled at Henri's friends.

They stared at each other and stood in silent obedience, and with a bit of deviant pleasure the four young men jumped at the opportunity for mischief and destruction. All the men headed for the garage, leaving Elise wondering what was happening. She didn't really care so much about their mischief, she discovered she rather enjoyed the liqueur and the way it warmed her belly, loosened her shoulder muscles, and really wasn't interested in whatever else was going on around her.

David opened the back door to the garage and with an exaggerated wave, implored all to enter. They retrieved one piece of furniture after another and at David's command placed them in "order" in the backyard. "Two pieces here, three pieces there," and so forth." He poured more drinks for everyone, and at his direction the men placed one furniture item after another on the bon-fire throughout the evening. He knew not to attract too much attention to their revelry, as the neighbors might call the police and report "something", so only one piece went on the fire at a time.

David sat in his chair and drank. The inferno blazed, and the fire snapped, bubbled, and popped throughout the night. The flames licked at every piece of furniture, and the reflection of hell's fire danced in his eyes.

## 2s and 3s

He'd been looking for a small house for Elise, something modest that was within walking distance of shopping and neighborhood businesses. The house he found was pale yellow with white trim, and a white wooden fence surrounded the yard. The yard was neat and well-manicured. The boxwoods out front were pretty much the selling point for David. The landscaper kept them perfectly trimmed and absolutely squared, not a leaf higher or lower than the others. David liked the precision of the bushes, the straight walkway, two steps up to the front porch, everything angled and squared just as he liked. It would be a refreshing change.

"No, no, NO!" David screamed. "I told you, all her skirts are hung first, then pants, then short sleeved shirts, then long-sleeved shirts. Each color will be lined up with each color. All white skirts together, all blue shirts together, all black pants together, got it!" It wasn't even a question, but more a command to the movers, designers, and interior decorators that David had setting up Elise's new house in the suburbs. He paced as they moved everything in, and their nerves were on edge, trying their best to appeal to his demands. After all, they were getting paid extremely well for their efforts. David purchased all new furniture for the house, except for the bedroom furniture, which they already had. He knew the colors and styles she liked. *She better like it,* he thought. *Spent all this damn money on her, she better not say a word except "thank you".*

He guided Elise by the hand to the front gate, his other hand over her eyes. Thankful that her hearing aids gave her near-normal hearing, he whispered, "Don't look now, but this is all yours, honey." He lowered his hand so she could see the front of the house and the tiny yard. Her smile turned into an open-mouthed silence. She wanted to speak but couldn't. Tears welled up in her eyes and ran down her cheeks. Her mind crashed backwards to years of neglect and abuse, even from David and Henri. The fact that someone did something for her was overwhelming. "What? Whoa, wait a minute," David began in frustration. "You don't like it?"

Elise looked up into her brother's blue eyes in disbelief and simply stared for a few seconds. "Da'id. It's bu'niful! I love you!" She wrapped her arms around his neck and hugged him and squealed in excitement. David had to bend forward, holding his cigar straight out and down with one hand, and wrapped his other arm around his sister. He was relieved. Despite his evil bravado, his love for his sister was undeniable.

The yard was about twenty feet from the door to the sidewalk on the south and east sides. Along the sidewalks on both sides, and the driveway up to the front concrete path, the landscaper had already planted a forsythia border. The yellow plants matched the house perfectly. "Those bushes," he told her, "will grow big and full and you'll have perfect privacy in your yard in just a few months. The only way into the yard will be this middle walkway here, and locked at that gate between the bushes there, and the walkway from the driveway." On the west side was a two-car driveway, and beyond that was another house. Both houses took up the entire short block.

She was ecstatic, ran through the house and checked all the rooms, and hugged him over and over. She stopped at one point in the living room and noticed David had already placed all her snow globes on shelves (in groups of twos and threes) throughout the house. She could see them no matter where she was. She'd fallen in love with various shopping channels on her TV and wanted to buy every snow globe or similar round object that came along. David and Henri gave in most of the time and helped her purchase them. She'd had no idea how to buy anything, so Henri took her shopping for clothes and groceries or for what was needed. She'd lived for eighteen years without a television, so it was her newfound livelihood. Thanks to the new hearing aids she got nearly four years ago, she spoke more from watching people on TV.

He walked her to her personal living room chair and eased her into it. "Every homeowner has to have a seat no one else is allowed to sit in, and this one is yours, little sister." He knelt beside her and held out his hand. "Now, let me hold that marble I gave you." She always carried it, either in a pocket or in her hand. No one else except David ever got to touch it, and she gave it to him without hesitation. He pointed to a small, round block of marble that sat on a side table. It had a concave cut in its center. He placed the clear glass marble down onto the concave block. "See, a place for the marble."

Elise smiled. "A ma'ble on a ma'ble!"

"Yeah, a marble on a marble. You're clever, you know." David was proud of himself, elated that he'd done all this for his sister. He loved her, but it really wasn't all about her. He needed control over her. "My young THREE is happy. We'll always be a THREE!"

**CHAPTER 35**
**APRIL 2011**
**REBORN**

David decided to treat himself to lunch and went down to the restaurant he liked by the Interstate exit. The cooks there made the best hash browns, smothered, and covered with cheese and mushrooms. He sat at a window booth, enjoying good food, reflecting on the blue sky and happy that Elise liked her new house. His day was nearly euphoric, one that was especially rare for him. Even his coffee, his second new favorite beverage now (bourbon remained first), caressed his taste buds. "Ah, yeah, Father," David mused in silence, his eyes closed taking in the moment, "you can't be in Heaven, 'cause this meal was from Heaven, and you never let us enjoy food like this."

He was jarred back to reality by the waitress. "Hey, you ok, David?" she asked. Tonya was a high-school senior, attractive, with a fabulous figure that was a little fuller than David liked. She found David intriguing since the first time he'd come in. He'd asked for two separate cups of coffee, not one. She'd remembered how quirky it was and was quick to bring him two every time. In turn, he was generous with his tips.

"Um, yeah," he answered as he looked up at the girl. "I was just talking with Father about this wonderful meal you brought me."

"Well, God Bless you, too, David," Tonya replied. "Wish more people prayed in here like you. Just let me know if I can get you anything else."

After she left, David looked down through comfortably narrowed eyes, and thought, "She blessed us TWO. Yeah, Father, sometimes TWOs are fairly good. Oh, no, she didn't mean you, my 'dear' departed Father, she meant us…she and me. I think she and I will become a new TWO. Wouldn't you just hate that, you self-righteous bastard? You'd hate to see me happy, wouldn't you? Happy that I'd be liked by a girl for the second time? Don't think I even have to fix her any of that tea, either."

David rested his head on the back of the adjoining bench tops. "Yep," he whispered to himself, "I won." He rolled his head slightly to the left to look out the restaurant window, and watched as insignificant little people walked by, caught up in their worthless lives, so unimportant to him.

A gray sedan pulled up just outside the window next to him, a car so like the one his mother and father owned. Panic jumped from his stomach to his throat at the sight of the old car. His vision blurred slightly, blood pressure made his ears turn red and pound as he watched the man and woman exit the car…his delusion took over and he saw his mother and father were back from hell.

He sat up straight, barely able to fathom the image. He was enveloped with a new wave of delirium, and his mind was crushed with blows of anxiety. *It's impossible! I destroyed you, I just saw you in hell!* David thought. *How can you be back?*

Panicked, he visually panned the restaurant, not seeing anything out of the ordinary. He hoped no one picked up on his anxiety. To David, the delusions of the older couple bore a striking resemblance to the long-dead DeVeaux couple.

Old memories of his tyrannical father resurfaced in full fury. The images flew through his brain like a film in fast forward. He swallowed hard and tried to think of what went wrong during the last "parent purging". He took a pair of sunglasses out of his shirt pocket, put them on, and quickly put on his leather jacket. He watched while the pair headed into the restaurant and passed by him, shading his face with his hands as best he could. They didn't seem to notice him, but his mind snapped into defense mode, looking for his next point of action.

He remembered the supply of improved explosive supplies and components that were kept in a locked duffle bag in the back of his Hummer. He'd put them there two years back as a precaution, in case his dead father decided to resurface again to seek him out. It also contained appropriate and well-thought-out Biblical quotes typed on paper, again, in case his father returned from hell. Months had passed, no one "reappeared" and he'd essentially forgotten they were back there, until now.

Any tranquility he'd relished earlier was banished in a matter of seconds. He remembered the duffle bag and knew what he needed to do. Sliding out of the booth he handed Tonya a twenty-dollar bill, telling her to keep the change. He left the restaurant and headed for the Hummer.

The incendiary devices he'd developed two years ago were much simpler to install in or on a vehicle. A simple, prepaid generic cell phone could be used as the trigger. It could be activated from another cell phone and the receiving one would read as a "blocked sender." The burner cell phone battery was always fully charged, thanks to the car adapter plug that came with the phone. The devices were indistinguishable from any other standard car part. David was sure that any investigations would again lead to nothing out of the ordinary. Everyone used cell phones. He thought if one was found in the wreckage, then no one would suspect it.

*Dammit! This time,* David thought as he left the restaurant, *I'll destroy you once and for all!* He quickly snapped on a pair of surgical gloves. He retrieved one of the small devices from the back area of the Hummer, unplugged the battery, and assembled it within seconds. He shuffled through the Bible verses, found an appropriate one, and brought it along.

Heading toward a newspaper stand on the sidewalk, he made a pretense of dropping coins on the ground next to the haunting car. While he stooped down, he quickly reached under the car and placed the device in the wheel well next to the engine block, affixing it with a strip of double-sided industrial tape.

"Okay, you piece of shit, this time I'll wait until you're back in your damned old car, and I'll make sure everyone sees you." He reflected briefly on everything. It occurred to him that TWO years had passed since he'd performed his last set of THREE "cleansings". "Oh no, I WON'T let you return again in TWO years. This is the THIRD time. There-will-be-no-more, damn you!"

He bought a newspaper and found an outdoor bench, a block from the sedan, to sit and pretend to read. He sat and read the verse on his sheet of paper to himself, then slowly crumpled it into a ball and dropped it on the ground beside him. Slowly he removed the surgical gloves and slipped them into one of the outer pockets of his bomber jacket, to dispose later when no one could watch. The cell phone detonator's number was long ago plugged into his own phone. He slipped a Bluetooth over his ear and waited. The woman and man finally left the restaurant and got into their car.

The couple left the parking lot and waited for a clear opening in traffic to the main road. David pushed the dial command on his Bluetooth. He turned the newspaper page and calmly said aloud, "Redial." His anxiety and excitement built, having a brief doubt that he'd dispatch his parents once and for all.

The car exploded seconds later. David was more than elated. Under pretense, he dropped the newspaper, and paused a few seconds to watch while the car burned in flames. He jumped up from the bench and screamed for someone to call 911.

In his delusion, he watched his parents die again. "For the THIRD time, to be complete there must be a THREE, or they'll come back again in TWO years. Damn, I've gotta stop them from coming back in TWO years!" His mind was overwhelmed by the thought that his father was a demon coming back to kill him. "Calm down, David, the police are coming. Make them happy so you can leave, so we can complete another THREE, and banish him forever."

A large crowd began to gather to observe the fiery spectacle, during which David slowly backed away from the area on foot. In his Hummer, he slowly left his parking space, keeping his license plate out of view from observing eyes. Fortunately for David, all the attention was on the exploded car, and not on someone leaving the restaurant's parking area. The note would be found and read, a small verse to sanctify his actions, just as his father did on his last day four years earlier.

He watched the ambulance arrive on the scene and took note of the vehicle number. He dialed the cell phone and called Henri. When the call was answered he said, "Brother, they came back again. It was TWO years…I should have known because it was TWO years, they'd be back…that HE would come back. But I did it. He was in his car, mother was with him, and I got rid of them for good, for the THIRD time." Henri said nothing, hearing a different tone in David's voice. He sounded more manic this time.

"I have to complete it again, Henri…or he'll come back again in TWO years. I have to do it today, the rest of it, this can't wait. I need your friends to help me. Tell them to meet me at the junk car yard at sunset. I have to follow that father-loving ambulance driver, he came back with father as his advocate and guide. I have to get rid of him once and for all. Then the children."

"No, David! No children this time, okay?"

"YES, the children that loved father, they have been sent away, Henri! For the last time! I gotta find 'em all…send them to hell once and for all."

## CHAPTER 36
## APRIL 2011
## THE SPY AND THE BIBLICAL BOMBER

Mid-morning news flashes online, on cell phones, and on the 24-hour news channels reported that a car exploded as it was driven out of a restaurant parking lot, killing a woman and her father. They were identified as the family of a prominent Senator, who demanded immediate action to bring the killer to justice. The fury in the Senator's voice on the TV news bytes was contrived, David believed, *it was a ruse to cover his grief.*

At a local hospital in Richmond, an ambulance exploded around noontime, killing only the driver. The local police and federal officials were stymied, again, at these two bombings. The investigators remembered the events two years before and began whispering about the return of "The Biblical Bomber."

The Senator's demand made its way quickly from the Justice Department to the Federal Task Force Division. The Task Force Director, Tom Michelson, called in the Field Team Leader, Marshall Gray, the agent code-named "Spy".

"The locals believe their 'Biblical Bomber' is back for another round," Tom said to his agent. "We've been notified by a Senator; the Richmond police haven't called us yet to help, and fail again," he said with some frustration. "I'd like to be proactive for a change. Get down to Richmond and find this 'Bomber'. Who do you want to take with?"

Proteus is on assignment in London, Seeker is having another tête-à-tête with FBI Special Agent Anderson."

"Again? I swear, Spy, you put Seeker and Anderson together for more than a minute and it's like gasoline on a fire." Michelson sat back in his chair and shook his head. "Gotta put some cold water on that one, soon."

Spy smiled. "I honestly believe it's their version of a mating ritual. Anyway, Hunter is off-duty."

"OK, so this is all yours. The Richmond office will be notified you're on the way, and highway patrol notified to leave you alone on the highway."

"Not that they could keep up with a Task Force car anyway," Spy said and left Tom's office.

◆

For the most part, the public liked this Senator. What was not public knowledge was that he was a member of a committee which provided the Task Force's off-book funding, and he could be very persuasive when he wanted something done. Spy had a particular distaste for politicians of any ilk but was well-aware of who controlled the Task Force purse strings. He made record time driving from Washington to Richmond down Interstate 95.

The latest version of the Task Force uniform had weapons, tools, and equipment hidden in the elbow-high leather gloves and knee-high leather boots, as well as canvas pouches along the leather belt attached by Velcro and held closed by magnets in the covers. Spy began his investigation. Despite his arrival at the ambulance bomb site after sunset, and long after all the other investigators had searched the area, he found a lone car key beside a parking space dozens of yards from the explosion site through the electronic metal detector readouts in his glasses' view.

The key was dirty and mostly covered by small trash debris from the explosion, easily overlooked by the earlier investigators. In his mind, Spy could envision the criminal set an explosive timer, ran for his car, reach for his keys, and retrieve one key too many from his pocket. The mobile data computer in his car had a direct link to headquarters. Jason Enterprises had been hired a year earlier to outfit the TF cars with numerous features to aid in crime scene efforts, although the name "Task Force" was never mentioned. The key was scanned, and the images sent via the remote link to the TF data center. Once the key cut was identified, it was quickly determined by the techs at headquarters that the key belonged to a vehicle located in a junkyard on the city's west side. Spy requested that local police be sent to the junk yard while he contemplated his next move. Spy jerked the car into gear and was enroute to the junkyard.

The police radio in Spy's car announced that the junk yard was unoccupied, although a police unit had just given chase to a vehicle driving away from the junkyard but lost it in the night. The city's Traffic Camera Division was on full alert, however, and technicians were able to find and follow the suspect vehicle using special low light enhancing lenses. It was a gray sedan.

By tapping into the city's camera system, the Task Force technicians followed the vehicle directly to the Jefferson Davis Performing Arts Center, where a special evening show by a local school's drama class was about to end. The driver and several other men calmly exited the vehicle near the building. However, the technicians lost view of the men after they exited the car and turned a corner behind the Arts Center. When the new information was relayed to Spy, he immediately changed directions and broke nearly every traffic law in the city to get to the arts center. "This case is becoming more complicated by the minute," the agent muttered to himself.

Camera views recorded several men moving out of the shadows, converging on a bus at various points, then returning to the shadows as people left the Arts Center's main entrance. Task Force tactical contact forwarded the information to Spy through his ear comm unit. Going into a five-against-one scenario he felt he probably could handle it, but extra help always made for better odds. He toggled the communications unit in his right ear to connect with headquarters. "Tactical, Spy."

"Tactical 3," he heard over his headset.

"Let's play this one safe and send some reinforcement down here. How long will it take?"

The reply was delayed only a few seconds. "Local law enforcement has been notified to diverge on a suspect bomb target, but you're several minutes ahead of them. Closest TF agent is Hunter, she's three minutes behind you."

Marshall's eyebrow went up. "Is she now? Guess she got antsy." He wondered why she was in Richmond, never mind that close to him. He swerved sharply to miss hitting a car in an intersection. He did run the red light, after all, but lives were at stake. "Well, relay to Hunter to haul her ass."

"Copy, Spy. Tactical out."

Children piled out of the Arts Center after the performance and boarded their school bus parked in front. Other children and parents headed for their cars in the adjacent parking lot.

Spy arrived and parked behind the gray sedan on the main road and got out to survey while he waited for his teammate to arrive. He'd just locked eyes on several shadows in motion around cars. The bus suddenly exploded into an enormous ball of flames. Metal fragments, wheels, body parts, all shot outwards and upwards, turning night into daytime, and changing the block into a conflagration of fire and smoke. Hot debris fell from the sky. Marshall instinctively covered his face with his arm and ducked down for cover behind his open car door. On the ground, he saw several men run from different directions toward their car. A quick count of legs told him there were at least three people right in front of him.

Spy drew his pistol, rose, saw the three men in front, all with guns drawn. He aimed over the top of his car, still shielded by the open door, and with three perfectly placed shots permanently took them out. A fourth man, closest to Spy, abruptly turned and charged. The agent back-stepped away from his car, ran around the rear of his car toward the shrubbery on the opposite side of the walkway to intercept. The fourth man was too fast and collided with him, and both fell over into a large bush. Spy landed with a thud on the other side, directly on his back. The attacker landed on top of him much like a football lineman would sack an opposing quarterback; the impact knocked the pistol out of Spy's hand and the comm unit out of his ear.

The burly attacker had two hands around the Spy's throat, executing an excellent job of choking him to death. The agent thrust his arms out to his side, palms flat, swung both arms up, and solidly slapped his choker's ears with all his might. The force of the impact made the attacker let loose and howl in pain. Spy forced his body to roll them both to the left so he would be on top, just long enough to reach to the sheath on his belt behind the empty holster, pull out a knife, and bury it deep in the attacker's gut just below his rib cage.

The agent got back to his feet, caught his breath, bent, and reached with his right hand for the pistol he had dropped. Despite his excellent physique, he was already getting tired. *Think I'm starting to get too old for this shit.*

He felt a lightning strike in his upper right arm, a gunshot which in turn sent spasms of pain throughout his body. The shock of the injury sent him back to the ground beside his now-dead former attacker. The stars in his vision swirled in multiple spirals, taking away his sense of balance. In fact, all his senses were momentarily turned off, as all he could see and experience were the spinning galaxies in his sight. After seeming an eternity, the stars began to recede, and a single sun began to rise in the horizon of his visual perception. By the time the single source of light finally dimmed, he remembered where he was and the battle in which he fought. He was aware that someone was standing next to him. His right hand moved slowly to his holster, but his gun wasn't there. He started to reach and look around him, but instead craned his head and looked up into the barrel of a different-model gun. "Well," Spy said, hiding the pain from his voice, "this is damn awkward."

David chuckled and smiled insincerely. "'Awkward,' you say? What is really awkward is why you're dressed like some movie superhero. Oh, my sister would just love to see you, yeah, she would. She loves hero movies because they're all so exciting!" The bomber stopped, taking a dramatic deep breath, and settled his excitement. "Just who are you, anyway?"

The Agent's glasses were still set to night-vision. He quickly formulated a defense and examined his surroundings behind lenses that hid his eyes from his opponent. "I'm just a guy trying to be a Good Samaritan."

"Oh, really? A Samaritan? You don't look like a Samaritan to me. You look like an idiot." The adversary wore slacks, shirt, sport coat, neatly combed blond hair, and sported the face of a male model. There was nothing unusual to associate him with any group. Anywhere else, he would be indistinguishable from any other guy on the street, except for the gun in his right hand, a .44 Magnum. Standing perfectly erect, he continued, "But, as 'FUN' as this was," again smiling that strange and insincere smile, "you're upsetting my routine; my finale to this year's THREE. I'm nearly done, it's all nearly done, and I'm content, I just have to leave my goodbye verse to Father, for the last time. But this was a particularly good day, I deserve a good dinner; BUT YOU'RE NOT INVITED," screamed the blond man, shaking the gun in Spy's face. "No, we're already a THREE, no, we're already THREE..."

Spy didn't react. *This guy's a fruitcake! I've got to stop him, NOW,* he thought. "So, now what?" he asked out loud, hesitating, giving himself time to think.

David clucked his tongue and kept smiling. "Now? What now? What now?" he said as he took a deep breath. "I have finished the THREE, it is done. Leave my letter." He waved his gun a bit more dramatically.

Watching the .44 wave in the air, time seemed to slow as Spy made his move. His right hand, only partly numb now despite the bullet wound, shot out for the knife in the dead attacker's chest beside him, grabbed it, and released it a split-second later. His aim was off, but close enough; it sliced open David's left cheek as it sailed past and hit the tree behind, the impact was muffled with a woody "thunk". David howled in pain and fired his gun, but Spy had already rolled and retrieved his once-again dropped pistol, this time with his good left hand.

Panicked and infuriated, he covered his left hand over the long deep cut in his face. Blood flowing out over his knuckles, David turned and ran, Spy following close behind him. The chase went past the burning bus, past the front of the Arts Center building with sirens getting louder as police cars neared. David turned at the back of the building and was out of sight by only a few steps. The sound of gunshots and then bullets ricocheting off the building stopped Spy from rounding the corner at first. With heart pounding, and breathing heavily, he allowed a second to pass then cautiously peered around the corner. He saw David trying to hide in an open garden shed behind the arts center.

From his vantage point he couldn't tell if there was another exit from the shed, but common sense told him there was not…he had never seen a garden shed with more than one entrance. There was at least twenty feet between the shed and him, no cover, and he was starting to feel wobbly from his wound because the bleeding wasn't stopping. He knew he was running out of time and needed to bring this to an end and call for help while he still could. He reached up to his ear but found his comm unit gone, and then reached for his cell phone in its pouch but discovered the pouch missing from his belt. It was apparently lost it in the fight. "Dammit, Hunter, where the hell are you?"

He holstered his pistol, pulled one of the pouches from his belt behind the gun holster and peeled open its Velcro tab. Inside were four small sonic grenades, effective only within a six-foot radius of their detonation. He palmed one into his numbed right hand and dropped the pouch to the ground as he withdrew his pistol from the holster with the other in preparation of his next assault.

He rested his right hand on his belt buckle, taking one brief second trying to clear his head and force as much feeling as possible into his injured arm. The blood-smeared sonic grenade was nestled between his still-functional right thumb and forefinger. Hoping he had enough strength in his wounded arm to make the throw, he rounded the corner and tossed the grenade ahead of him as he ran, pistol aimed forward in his left hand.

At that moment, David chose to step out of the shed and charge back. Unfortunately, the tossed sonic grenade was on target, and exploded behind him. The shockwave pushed David forward and the two men collided, HARD.

Spy again landed on his back with his enemy on top, sending another surge of pain through his body. Unbidden, his hand released its grip on his pistol. When his vision cleared enough for him to see his surroundings, he noticed the gunman was already standing over him, pointing his own pistol at his eyes. He spoke in a panicked tone, "Nice trick, my friend; you're good, incredibly good. Nothing's better than my sacred THREE, especially when it was the third THREE. But you are a threat to my THREE, so you must die…"

◆

She was only a couple minutes behind her partner when word of the bus explosion was on the police channel in her car.

"Hunter, this is Command," she heard over her comm.

"Hunter, go," she replied.

"Contact lost with Spy. Advise you proceed with extreme caution."

"Copy, Command."

She parked her own black sports car behind Spy's, just out of sight of the explosion scene on the opposite street from where the Spy parked his car. She positioned herself behind her open car door to survey the area, Glock drawn, and then stepped forward silently to investigate Spy's open car. It was empty. Leaving the cars, she stepped forward toward the shrubbery and trees. She had just entered the shadows beside the Arts Center when she heard the gunshot.

At the back corner she found a discarded belt pouch, like hers. She retrieved the pouch with her gloved fingers and examined it.

She saw through her own polarized lenses one of the four small sonic grenades was missing. She wedged the pouch under the metal buckle of her gun belt, as there was no room to add the abandoned pouch on her own and peered around the corner cautiously.

She saw a black body lying on the ground halfway to the garden shed, and plenty of blood on the ground. A rush of adrenalin flowed through her body, and she felt her heartbeat pounding in her ears. Looking around the area quickly, detecting no movement and hearing nothing, and no heat signatures visible in her glasses, she determined the area was safe, and approached carefully.

Spy lay in the grass, the bullet hole in the left sunglass lens answered her unasked question, and a closer look revealed a trail of blood flowed down his left cheek and temple. There was no movement in his chest, no respiration. She quickly took stock of the immediate area. His holster was empty, and his pistol was nowhere to be found, although she saw a .44 Magnum discarded nearby. Protruding out from under his blood-smeared buckle was a folded piece of paper. She carefully removed it and unfolded it. It looked like a Bible verse. When she spoke, the comm unit in her ear activated, and she said softly but firmly, "Command, this is Hunter. 10-100, agent down. Request cleaning crew and containment ASAP. Lock onto my phone's GPS." She ended the call and holstered her pistol, fighting to hold her emotions in check.

Hunter looked at the note again, trying to make sense of the strange message, then looked up and stared into the stars. She allowed one tear to fall as she knelt by her friend, then another, and more, until she cried openly while she was alone with him, holding his left hand in both of hers.

**CHAPTER 37**
**APRIL 2011**
**A TALE OF TWO AVATARS**
**A COUPLE MINUTES EARLIER…**

Outside lights from the arts center illuminated the area slightly, and David watched the smoke trickle upward in blue colored wisps in the cold night air. He pulled his coat collar up around his neck, shrugged his neck and shoulders, and stared down at the dead man. Waving the gun toward the body, David spoke, "One shot was wrong, there's gotta be TWO shots. THREE would even be better. I can't leave you dead from just ONE bullet, from your own gun." David pointed the gun at the man on the ground and fired.

The man was dead to David's final satisfaction. Wild-eyed and pumped with adrenaline, he looked around, but saw no one in sight. *Good. This should give me some time*, he thought, calming himself a bit, almost getting lost in time while he reveled in his success. He gazed at the gun intently, changed his grip from aiming to cradling it in his hands almost reverently, admiring its workmanship. Closing one eye, he bent slightly at the knees and extended the gun out in front of him as if to fire it, feeling the weight in his hand. Straightening, his eyebrows furrowed, he thought, *Balance feels a little off, powerful kick though. No serial number, not removed, just never there. Nice gun.* "A perfect trophy to celebrate this year's THREE," he whispered out loud. He flipped the gun around in his hand and noticed the unusual diamond outline on the butt of the handgrip, "A perfect diamond shape. Wait, the same shape on this guy's belt buckle. Maybe an emblem or symbol for some military unit?" He pondered the shapes while he rubbed the back of his neck. Kneeling beside the body, he tried removing the gun belt in hopes of examining its arsenal later, to claim more trophies. But couldn't figure out how to detach it. He placed the stolen pistol on the dead man's chest and began twisting and turning the belt. The lamp above the arts center door illuminated the buckle.

Flashes from the reflected light seemed to burst from the buckle into his eyes. David blinked hard and fast for a couple of heartbeats, exhaling, not realizing he'd been holding his breath. He shook his head to clear his mind, to break the spell of the lights in the buckle.

A sound from the shadows past the arts center sent David into a brief panic. He thought it was an unusual sound, almost like Velcro being ripped open, nevertheless he knew he was no longer alone. He was out of time and cursed himself for not finishing his three gunshots and his only trophy would have to be the pistol. He reached into his coat pocket, retrieved a folded piece of paper, and slipped it under the belt buckle. Looking behind him, he thought, "At least it's one more demand to Father to die and stay dead." David retrieved the gun from atop the body and sprinted into the shadows behind the arts center, disappeared as a new figure rounded the far corner.

David realized he didn't fully escape but hadn't been discovered either. He stopped and watched in silence as a new player entered the game. Even in the dim light, he could tell this was a woman, tall and slender. David was intrigued to see she was dressed the same as his opponent, all in black, with the gun belt and sunglasses. *TWO of 'em? What the hell? Why are TWO of them after me?* he thought.

David snuck his way around the far side of the arts center building, carefully avoiding contact with the gathering police and fire department personnel. He stuck to the shadows as best he could. He neared his own car and saw the bodies of his dead crew being examined by investigators. *Shit, can't get to my car!* he thought. He decided to keep walking, and intently watching, instead of trying to retrieve his vehicle. Everyone had convened in and around the arts center.

David noticed the two black cars parked a few blocks away from his car. "TWO matching sports cars? Together, here, now? What the hell?" Cautiously, he walked the tree line adjacent to the first one. Someone had left a driver's door open, obviously in too big of a hurry to close it. Looking around, he saw no one near and edged toward the car. He glanced inside and observed the near-futuristic digital computer displays everywhere. They were located where the normal speedometer, tachometer, and glove compartment would be. *Looks like a damn jet fighter cockpit or something,* he thought. There were a myriad of colored buttons, technical readouts and computer displays. Without breaking stride, he continued to the second car. Its door was open as well. *Stupid cops,* he thought. He peeked inside quickly, realizing it was a similar setup to the first. *Damn, Father's sent his own avatars, with their "super" cars. What the hell do I do with this? Hell. They've come from hell, he sent them.* David's mind crept into its own little world. He slipped back into the darkness and waited. He tried to process the new circumstances, the discovered information, and slipped into a world of darkness, overpowered by everything surrounding him.

## 2s and 3s

David showed up at a man's home office, a doctor, and pounded on his door despite the early hour. The man had been sued for medical malpractice and his license as a physician had been revoked. The Doc kept his skills honed by keeping up with the latest in new medicine and current procedures, making him an asset to the underground crowd, cash under the table. David knew the Doc would help clean up his face and nothing would be said about it.

"How'd this happen, David?" the doctor asked as he began cleaning the cheek, putting on his bifocals to get a better look. "Cut through almost to the bone here, David, good God!"

"Don't bother askin'." David tried his best to avoid the subject. "Let's just say it was from an argument I eventually won."

"Fair enough. This is gonna sting a bit…actually, it's gonna hurt like hell. Gonna give you some local anesthetic before I finish cleaning this out and sewing you up. Ready?"

"Fine, just get it over with." He laid his head back and closed his eyes. "Doc, do the stitches like TWO, THREE, TWO, THREE, you know what I mean."

Doc stared at David's closed eyes and shook his head. He had no idea what David was talking about but accepted the fact that the man was crazy enough to ramble on like that. *Better that you ramble on about your numbers, I've seen your temper when you start your crazy two and three crap.* "Sure, David, twos and threes, you got it."

David was exhausted and fell asleep in the chair, never feeling the sharp pain from the needle…

## 2s and 3s

*…sharp pain in his face where his father slapped him. "You're gonna behave, boy. You best start learnin' that. You learn by not putting your hand in your sister's face."*

*The dream switched to him and Henri as small children, playing marbles on the sidewalk outside of their tiny house. "Here, Elise, you take this one." David handed her a perfectly clear marble. She looked up at him. He was appalled to see that her smile was the same as Father's. He saw the anger and evil in her face and no joy in her grin. He suddenly realized she had their father's blood running through her veins and had the capacity to be just as evil as he.*

*She took the glass marble and squeezed it tight in both hands, and it melted down into a flat crystal. She parted her hands to show him a four-pointed diamond shaped crystal in each palm.*

*The dream turned into a nightmare as Elise stood, threw the left-hand diamond at his face, missing him completely. David panicked. She then threw the right-hand diamond, and it sailed at his face. He felt the razor-thin edge of the crystal diamond penetrate his cheek, embedded in flesh, muscle, and bone, just like the evil that was perpetually embedded in him.*

*David roared in pain, the agony of the tearing flesh and separating bone drove him into a fury. The diamond wedged deeper and deeper into his face, and he reached for the devil's daughter with both hands. He grabbed her by the lapels of her blouse, brought her smiling face to his so they looked eye-to-eye. "What are you gonna do, boy?" she said in Father's voice. "You're just a little baby, never amount to anything. You'll be wearing diapers all your life, always gonna need a mommy to take care of you."*

*David let out an animal-like growl and threw her against the side of the house. The impact was so solid that her tiny body crumpled to the ground, her limbs twisted like pretzels. Though she was dead, her eyes followed David. He watched in horror as blood oozed from Elise's mouth, and literally crept up his legs, torso, and shoulders, then dripped down his arms in rivulets. He realized the wickedness had engulfed him.*

*In the dream, Henri walked up to David and plucked the crystal diamond from his face. David felt the warm blood seep out of his cheek and watched as it cascaded down his shoulder and arm. The blood was black instead of red. He realized the black evil was trying to escape his body, and it gushed out to consume, take over, and control everything around. David felt a sudden pride in the very literal representation.*

*Henri looked at David's face, cocked his head to one side, and said as though nothing were amiss, "That looks like a nasty cut..."*

## 2s and 3s

"...nasty cut," said the doctor.

David jumped out of his seat, nearly knocking over the doctor and his surgical rolling table.

"David! It's ok! I'm all done. I've stitched it up as well as I can. Ten good stitches there, just like you wanted. It's gonna leave a scar. I'm sorry, David, the only way to get rid of it will be plastic surgery."

"That's ok, doc," David replied. He shook his head to clear his mind, remembering where he was and what was real, now realizing it was all just a dream. He sat slowly and settled himself and held onto the chair armrests. "Just finish up and I'll pay ya. I got a TWO ta' solve."

**CHAPTER 38**
**MAY 4, 2011**
**GOODBYE TO THE SPY**

A few family members attended the funeral for Marshall Gray, along with others who presented themselves as co-workers to his sister and his parents. The temperature was in the upper 40s and a light rain was falling, adding to the somber mood for the occasion. Thin pieces of ice still clung to the fallen leaves from the bitter cold the night before. Crunching sounds could be heard as everyone walked through the graveyard.

At the conclusion of the graveside service, an older gentleman, Marshall's father, stepped forward and removed a rose from the funeral display, and handed it to the woman beside him. He took her hand and turned to leave. Seeing Tom Michelson, the man stopped. He motioned for this wife to continue without him and waited for others to leave as well. Approaching Tom, he asked, "Is there anything more you can tell us about what happened to our son?"

Tom locked eyes with the older gentleman and tried to avoid the truth with a display of eye-to-eye contact. With brow slightly knitted, he answered with true compassion, "Nothing more than what we know so far, sir. Just the break-in at the office. The intruder had a gun, and he tried to stop him before anyone got hurt.

You have no idea how sorry we are for your loss, he was respected and admired by all of us. He can't be replaced, and he was a very brave man." Tom felt he had stumbled over his words. Maybe saying too much or not enough. It was nothing that helped Marshall's father feel any better or give any comfort. Marshall's parents would never know the truth behind their son's murder.

The older man stared at the ground, looking even older and paler than before. Holding back his tears, he took a deep breath and let it out slowly. Shaking his head in disbelief he said in a cracking voice, "Yes, he was. He always was very brave, it's just so hard." Tom reached to place a hand on his shoulder, but the man simply turned and walked away, making him feel even more awkward.

Once the man was gone, Hunter stepped forward and stood beside Tom. Like him, she was dressed all in black, but her clothing was her Task Force uniform. She wore her uniform without the gloves and gun belt but wore a gray Eisenhower jacket to conceal her upper uniform for the funeral. She wrapped her arms around herself but felt the cold despite her insulated attire. The umbrella in her hand remained shut. Light rain fell harder, wetting her hair and sending chills through her body. Large droplets hit the dried brown grass, only just starting to turn green for the spring, making a "tap, tap" noise on nearby leaves. With head hung low, she kicked at the ground angrily with the toe of her boot. "I still can't believe he got taken down by that mystery bastard. Marshall was the best. Kidnappers, extortionists, drug lords, no one ever came close to taking him. But some local punk with delusions of power was the one who did it." She looked away, a lone tear escaped her eye and slowly trickled down her cheek, more emotional than she wanted to let on. Tom noticed but pretended he didn't.

Tom knew how emotional it was for Hunter. After all, she had been engaged to Marshall. Tom was sympathetic but attempted his best to act businesslike. He knew that was how she wanted things to be. "Hunter, you know the incident is under review, and it's gonna take time. There's a lack of clear physical evidence and no surveillance video available. I can't order you to investigate his death. There is just nothing to support your contention of who did this, at least for the moment. But we must look ahead now. As much as I hate to say it, we have to replace him on your team." Tom offered a little emphasis on the words "your team" for her benefit.

Raising her umbrella, Hunter jerked her head sternly toward Tom. "His team, sir. We were HIS team." The word "his" almost came out in a harsh hissing sound, acknowledging her annoyance with the situation.

Tom crossed his arms and nodded gently. His head and eyes lowered downward. "Granted. So, let me ask it this way, Agent Hunter, knowing full well this will happen regardless of your answer. Are you ready for a new Spy on the Task Force?"

"Yes, sir," Hunter replied formally, hiding the hurt she really felt. "Do you have a candidate, sir?"

A small smile formed on Tom's face. "Oh, yes. Time to get everything started. Let Seeker know he's taking a test flight on the new bird and tell Proteus it's time to wrap up her assignment."

**CHAPTER 39**
**MAY 6, 2011, 7:30 P.M.**
**CHASING SHADOWS**

Though immense in size himself, Sarge Brunson looked perfectly comfortable behind his massive desk in the Security Chief's office in the Jason Enterprises building. He hadn't added any personal touches to the office, aside from his American and US Army flags. Anything that looked different from the day he assumed occupancy was due to the tech personnel updating and installing what he wanted. Hidden behind the elevated front panel were half a dozen monitors which only he could see. He normally had the desk monitors on rotating feeds throughout the building, but at the standard 8 a.m. and 5 p.m. workday start and stop times he locked them in place. This allowed him to view all the unsecured doors to the Jason Enterprises skyscraper when the most activity was occurring, especially at 5 p.m. while the security teams on the upper floors began their lockdown checks.

The door to the main walkway was open and Mark stepped in silently; Sarge never heard him come in. Lightly tapping the desk with his fingertips, Mark said, "You don't need to work double shifts every time I'm in the office late, y'know. So, do the accommodations suit you, Sarge?" He had ordered the IT department to completely redesign the office to whatever specifications Sarge wanted.

Not at all phased, and raising his head in response, "Yeah, the grunts did okay, sir," growled Sarge, with a slight smirk. He pointed at the wall behind Mark's head, by the office door. "I'd like a bigger screen up there, sir, and configured so I can put any security images up there that I want."

Mark turned around, looked up, cocked his head to one side, and narrowed his eyes. "Looks like a 52-inch screen would fit nicely. I'll tell IT to get one in here by tomorrow." He took the cell phone from inside his tuxedo breast pocket and speed-dialed, "Hito? Mark Jason. I need another full terminal install in Brunson's office by 6 a.m. Testing time is included on that... Yes, yes...Sarge will fill you in on what he specifically needs," Mark stopped himself as he looked at Sarge and smiled. "And Hito, failure is not an option." He hung up and returned his phone to his inside jacket pocket.

Sizing up Mark's formal attire, Sarge commented, "Special occasion, sir?"

Resting his arms on the counter, "Yes, Sarge, my wife and I are spearheading a charity event for the families devastated by the recent bombings across the city. JE is starting with a five-million-dollar contribution. That should put everyone else on a slight guilt-trip...make them want to match or beat us." Raising one finger in the air, he emphasized, "This is important..."

"Fine plan, sir," replied the security chief. Mark thought he heard a little softening in that gruff voice, even if only momentarily. Raising his immense body and rolling his chair backwards, Sarge ended the short meet. "Well, I best get to my final rounds, sir."

"Sarge, remember, you have a staff; you don't have to be here day and night."

The former soldier smiled down at Mark. "I'm not, sir, just need to double check the start of the weekend shift."

"Very well," finished Mark. "Conclude your duty and call it a shift, Sergeant."

"Yes, sir."

Half an hour later, Sarge was at the executive suite office level to start his own lockdown rounds, one floor below the penthouse that Mark Jason used only occasionally, and more often for casual office meetings rather than residing. Like Mark and Jan Jason's personnel files, the penthouse was one area that was forbidden access to Sarge under normal conditions. Sarge felt an officer earned his privileges and agreed not to pry at all except in dire emergency. He had agreed to leave the Jasons as exempt to his duties as part of his hiring agreement. Mark and Sarge agreed upon a new protocol, however: Code Black would give Sarge access to anything normally locked to everyone. If such a situation were ever to arise Sarge would do his best to contact Mark first, but situations would play out whatever way they did, and he might not have that opportunity. If Sarge ever had to invoke the Code Black security protocol that dropped all walls to his security access he would report to Mark as soon as possible; both men were satisfied with that arrangement.

As he checked each of the executive assistants' offices, he locked the doors behind him… then thought he saw a movement outside the window at the end of the hall. Could have been a bird, twenty stories up… but the bristles of hair at the nape of his neck wouldn't stop tingling in alert. He drew his Glock from his shoulder holster and held it by his leg as he advanced toward the window. This high up the window was sealed shut, but he checked the frame anyway.

The building across the street was glass-fronted, just like the Jason building. The light from the sunset reflected off the Jason building onto the glass across the street… and in that reflection Sarge could have sworn he saw a human figure climbing on the outside of the Jason building, near the window at which he now stood. All senses in full gear, Sarge took his cell phone from his pants pocket and speed-dialed, "Mr. Jason, this is Brunson. I'm on the executive floor, investigating what may be an intruder."

"Your discretion, Sarge. Proceed, and keep me apprised."

"Yes, sir," he replied. Ending the call, he drew his communications radio from his belt and signaled the rest of the security teams throughout the floors of intruder alert status.

Squinting at the figure, Sarge watched as it seemed to swing around the corner of the Jason building, out of his field of reflected view. Sarge was getting that pissed-off gut feeling he used to get over in Iraq. He darted quickly into one of the assistants' offices and peered out the plate glass window. There was no opposing building this time to provide a reflected view, Sarge only reacting to what he could detect.

He heard a sound at the other end of the hall...where Mark Jason's office suite complex was. Sarge quickly but quietly ran down the hall and crouched by the closed door to Mark's secretary's office. Again, he heard a sound, but this time muffled. He keyed his Code Black security override into the keypad beside the door, thinking all the while about Mark's reaction if this was "nothing." *Well, hell, a week on the job and I'm already violating privilege. Well, Sarge, you may as well go out with a bang... and maybe I'll get lucky and someone else will be on the other end of the bang besides me.* The lock silently disengaged, and the door swung open automatically.

Gun up and safety off, and in the ready position, Sarge stepped into Mark's secretary's office carefully. He advanced one step at a time, his stealthy silent movement in complete contrast to his physical size. He surveyed the dimly lit exterior office as though searching for hidden IEDs. He approached Mark's office door; again, after punching in his override code into the keypad, the door to the president's office slid open silently.

For only the second time, Sarge stepped into the huge room. Unlike the other offices on this floor, Mark's was the size of four offices combined, with areas for his desk and computer, bar, conversation seating area, and library. Gun at the ready, he visually took in every shadow created by the few mood lights in the office. Again, nothing attracted his attention...

...except this was the first time he noticed that Mark's office had a balcony outside, and there was a sliding glass door where every other office had sealed plate glass. He cursed himself for not noticing during his interview.

Approaching slowly, he focused his gaze on the door handle lock. It was unlocked. He pressed himself against the wall beside the sliding glass door frame and peered out onto the balcony. It was large enough to have an entire seating area, easily enough for a dozen people, and an outdoor bar that wasn't stocked at this time. A security fence ran the entire length of the balcony for safety reasons. Sarge figured there was a bit of floor out there beyond what he could see from the inside; he took a handkerchief from his pocket and used it to protect the door handle from his own fingerprints (just in case) and slowly slid the door open, a slight gust of wind blew inwards.

Cautiously he peered out from the door jamb onto the balcony. Over the slight whistling breeze, he heard a sound…

…raised his gun, ready to fire…

…Sarge's adrenalin-charged heart skipped a beat as a pigeon flew off the balcony. It blended and disappeared into the night sky, already full of stars.

Momentarily closing his eyes in disbelief of the pigeon, Sarge holstered his weapon, closed the balcony access, and slid the lock into place this time. He noted a small manila envelope on Mark's otherwise clean desk, probably left by the end-of-day courier and locked the internal and hallway doors to the offices.

He shook his head. "Helluva way to make a first impression, Brunson; first week on the job, seeing a Spider-Man climbing on the outside of the building, yeah that'll go over like shit hittin' a fan," he muttered as he redialed his boss' phone. "Jason," he heard when the call was received on the other end. "Mr. Jason, sir," said Sarge.

"Yes, Sarge?" came Mark's reply from the phone.

"Just wanted to pass on to you about the earlier security alert. We're sure it was a false alarm. All clear on the executive suite floor. We're still continuing with our checks, and not finding anything so far."

"Good job as always, Sarge. Lock up and go home."

"Yes, sir," said the security chief and he pressed the "end call" button on his phone. He sent the all-clear signal to his teams via his radio just as one pair came out of the stairwell at the opposite end of the hall, by the window where this all started. "Everything ok, sir?" asked one of the pair.

"All clear," said Sarge. "Pack it up and set up the automation." As they approached the elevator he added, "And I ain't no 'sir'. Our 'Sir' works in that office back there," he added as he jerked a thumb back at Mark's office. Sarge was beginning to suspect the staff was calling him "sir" on purpose, just to raise his hackles for some friendly fun.

The elevator doors opened, and the trio stepped inside. Seconds later the dual doors slid closed, and the floor indicator showed the elevator car going down.

Outside above the balcony, holding onto a narrow black nylon cord, Task Force Agent Seeker allowed himself a small smile before climbing back up to the penthouse patio of the Jason building, pulling the dangling rope up behind him. A few minutes later a black parachute with a human figure hanging below disappeared into the night…

**CHAPTER 40**
**MAY 5, 2011**
**ENCOUNTER**

The stars sparkled bright in the night sky, and a full moon cast a calm glow over the city streets of Richmond. Pedestrians were out in normal numbers for a cold Friday evening. Traffic was finally at the after-rush-hour calm. The Jason limousine made its way in the dark and the streetlights seemed to fly by one after another as the couple relaxed in the back seat of the car.

Despite the past decade working behind a desk, Mark remained strict and self-disciplined when it came to exercise. He got up every morning at five a.m. and worked out for at least two hours in their home gym. Tonight, depending on his posture, his tailored tuxedo occasionally appeared to want to burst at the seams. He was every bit a man one did not want to cross.

Jan looked younger than her 36 years. Aside from a couple lines around her eyes and at the corners of her lips, she appeared much the same as she did on their wedding day. She was now Executive Vice-President of Jason Enterprises, second-in-command only to Mark over the entire corporation. She had earned an MA in finance while studying corporate law, and effectively ran the day-to-day operations while Mark tended to the major executive duties. Jan adjusted an overhead mirror in the limo, checked her makeup and hair one last time before the upcoming event.

They were en route to a charity event to raise money for the families of those killed in the recent unsolved vehicle bombings. The community was emotionally savaged by the senseless killings, and Mark led the charge, along with other local corporations, for a massive city event to help the families in their time of need. Money certainly wouldn't bring the loved ones back, but it would help with funeral expenses, as well as ease the city's budget in the clean-up efforts and first responder operating costs. The worst part was so many parents were now without children, and there were no answers.

When the bombings happened, Mark and Jan were deeply concerned. They dwelt on what it would be like if their daughter Angela had been a victim in such brutal murders. They couldn't imagine what life would be like without her. Jason Enterprises had succeeded extremely well over the years, with profits well into the tens of billions. Mark felt it was their duty to spearhead this event, and he made it happen.

Concerned about Mark's previous phone call, Jan stared into Mark's face. "Everything ok?" Jan asked as he pocketed his phone.

"Yeah, just a false alarm," Mark said with a smile, squeezing Jan's hand. "Sarge just letting me know he's got it under control."

"Doesn't he always?" she smiled back. "He's done a great job getting security into a better shape in just a week."

A flash of headlights abruptly whizzed by from behind, too close to the driver's side of the limousine for Mark's preference. They were followed by a second flash of headlights that passed almost as close. The limo driver's adrenaline rushed, and his reflexes responded as trained. He swerved the vehicle sideways to a skidding halt. As soon as the vehicle stopped, Mark bolted out of his door to witness the action and help if necessary.

About a hundred yards ahead he watched as the lead car took a turn too fast and flipped over twice, crushing the car, and then burst into flames. Mark's mouth fell open, and he raised an arm to his face in reflex. The pursuing vehicle, a black sports car, stopped nearby. A man, dressed in full black attire, stepped out and approached the blaze in the intersection. Determined to help, Mark ran closer to the scene as the man in black turned around.

As part of his military training years ago, Mark was taught to be an exceptional observer. He saw in the light of the fire that the man had dark hair, and strangely enough wore what appeared to be black sunglasses at night. He also made a mental note that the man had a gun belt around his waist. He thought perhaps he was part of a SWAT Team, or some sort of law enforcement agency. Mark was about ten feet away when the man in black heard Mark's shoes on the pavement and turned around. He raised a gloved hand in a "stop" motion, and Mark did just that. They looked at each other for several seconds. The man turned back to the burning car, drew a weapon from his belt, aimed and fired at the trunk of the car. Mark took a few steps back, not knowing what to expect next.

The unknown man stepped forward, looked around, easily opened the trunk, calmly reached in through the flames and removed a small box. From where he stood Mark could tell it was a silver-colored box, ornately designed perhaps. He couldn't see its features from his distance though. The man returned to his car, lifted a hand to his ear with a tapping motion, and said something Mark couldn't hear. The man got back into his car and burned rubber as he sped off into the night.

Shaking his head in disbelief, Mark approached the burning vehicle again to render aid. He'd only taken a few steps, and another black vehicle abruptly arrived. It was a large van with tinted windows, from which several men in gray overalls emerged. They also wore the same style black glasses. One of them took a few steps toward Mark, pointed a finger, and stated authoritatively, "Sir, we have this under control, please return to your car and continue on."

Mark stopped, glanced around the scene one more time, nodded politely, and returned to the limo where his wife waited expectantly. After he was seated beside her, the limo driver closed the door, returned to the driver's seat, and the car once again rolled forward. Staring out the back window, Jan asked, "What happened?"

He answered honestly, "I have no idea."

**CHAPTER 41**
**MAY 6, 2011- 5:00 P.M.**
**SECOND SKIN**

Sarge Brunson was going over the day-end shutdown report as his last team checked in. The duo consisted of one experienced security agent (who proceeded to his own station in the lobby for the evening shift) and the new-hire, a petite younger woman with strawberry-blonde hair and a face that was pretty but not gorgeous. Deborah O'Brien, he remembered; she had been hired shortly before Sarge; he remembered her from her question at his introduction. He'd read in her file that she was in the middle of the class in averages, tests, grades, and physicals. Two years with the local PD, then wanted to try something new. *More kids need to stay in one job*, Sarge had thought. There was something about this girl that he wanted on his team…how she carried herself, presented herself. Greatly confident in bearing and performance, and a little out of character for someone "average"; nevertheless, he thought he'd give her a chance.

Deborah O'Brien knocked on Sarge's open office door and waited for him to bid her entry. Without looking up from his desk Sarge barked, "Come on in." Sarge had developed a habit of putting on a tough exterior, but on the inside, he was a teddy bear. Most of his employees figured him out quickly but remained aloof about the whole "tough guy" thing. She entered and handed him the team's shutdown report of the 1st and 2nd floors. (Sarge's new rule to the staff: "you have to work your way up to the top, figuratively and literally…so rookies start at the bottom floors", except himself, of course.) He took it from her, glanced through it quickly, and without looking up, and said "Looks good, Rookie. You keep up this level of work and you'll be running your own team soon. Thank you. Dismissed."

Deborah shuffled her feet and a tiny knowing smile crept across her face, trying not to acknowledge the teddy bear's assertiveness. "Yes, sir," she started, and then said, "I mean, Sarge."

◆

Deborah locked up her earpiece and wireless transmitter/receiver and other security equipment in her locker, along with the standard issue police .9mm semi-auto that all the security staff carried (except Sarge, who carried a Glock). On her way out of the front door she eyed her partner and waved at him. He was now at the lobby security desk for the evening shift. "Night, John… see you in the morning."

"Night," he waved back to her. "Be prepared for really strong coffee when you get in tomorrow morning. These occasional double-shifts aren't hard, just damn long!"

She smiled and stepped out of the front door, which automatically closed and locked behind her as she walked out into the building's front courtyard. Deborah unhurriedly proceeded down the steps to the sidewalk, then to the bus stop to the left of the building's front entrance (still in view of the security desk). The rapid transit bus arrived on schedule; she stepped up, paid her token, and went to the back of the bus. John had casually been watching from inside the lobby, and when the bus drove off, he set himself to the long evening hours ahead.

At the next bus stop, Deborah disembarked and stood at the bus stop kiosk until the bus drove off, not unusual for someone waiting to make a transfer. Gassy fumes from the bus wafted in the still night air. A black sports car, headlights off, drove up and downshifted…the passenger door opened by itself, as if alive. Looking left then right, she got in. Lights now on, the car pulled ahead at city traffic speed, disappearing into a sea of cars.

Inside the car, she looked at the black-haired driver… he was still wearing his black uniform and glasses. "Package delivered. How'd it go for you, Proteus?" he asked.

She had created a special silicone and latex life-cast face mask, in case a replacement recruitment order was ever issued, and she got to go undercover herself. It had taken weeks to mold and sculpt it into a life-like face, using rubber alginate, but she didn't expect to have to wear her latest masterpiece so soon. The light dusting of a few freckles and the tiny beauty mole under the left eye were indistinguishable from natural skin.

As Deborah began peeling off the mask, she said, "New security chief is excellent. Next DOD contract is in excellent hands. Brunson is one helluva stickler for detail and protocol. The JE work is in good hands while we take care of Mark Jason."

**CHAPTER 42**
**MAY 6, 2011**
**THE FAMILY THAT WORKS TOGETHER**

Mark and Jan decided to give Angela a chance to work as an intern at Jason Enterprises. Angela had begged for the prospect, and when she finally turned seventeen, her parents gave in to her pleas. Her first day had started in the mail room, where all new interns and service employees started. Jan joined Angela in the mail room to make her more comfortable, introduce her to the employees, and begin her training.

After a lengthy two-hour session on mail intake, sorting, workplace safety, protocol, chain of command, and confidentiality, the real lessons started next: suspicious packages.

"Angel, we must always be on the lookout for anything that seems out of place. Torn packages, boxes or manila envelopes with wires sticking out. White powder. You never know if crazies will try to send a bomb in the mail, or stuff an envelope with anthrax. They may just be hoaxes, but we must be vigilant for the safety of everyone who works here. It's that way in all large companies, especially with a company as important as Jason Enterprises. That's why the mail room isn't the lowly place that you may think it is; it's actually one of the most important places in a business…the beginning to the success of the company, if you will." Jan hoped that Angela was beginning to get the big picture, while at the same time promoting the importance of the mail room.

The fact was, since 9/11, businesses throughout the city had indeed experienced such threats, chicanery, and the real thing. Putting Angela in the mail room was a difficult chance for Mark and Jan, but it was vitally important to train her in all aspects of the business, even the unpleasant details, if she were to work her way up to the top.

"You'll be fine, dear; just do as I instructed and listen to your supervisor and the other workers. Never be afraid to ask questions. Always err on the side of caution." Jan smiled confidently at Angela as she walked toward the elevator, though the butterflies in her stomach danced about, warning her of their premonitions. Angela tentatively waved goodbye to her mother, forcing a tiny grin to reassure her mother that she would be fine. Jan's presence grew smaller and smaller as she walked farther away, her heels clicking a self-assured rhythm upon the concrete floor.

◆

The Jason's' large two-story home represented colonial architecture, with wide porches and tall white columns. They lived in an upper-middle-class subdivision, quiet, with green manicured lawns which steadily followed concrete driveways upwards toward houses on hills. Magnolias and white and lilac Crepe Myrtles enveloped the sidewalks; Live Oaks sprawled dreamily in the yards; Spanish Moss hung daintily from each tree.

Grace, the Jasons' housekeeper, walked down the long driveway to the mailbox. She enjoyed this moment out of the house, feeling the sun on her face and breathing in the fresh air. She enjoyed the difference in the feel between experiencing the sun and air here and in her hometown of London, England. After a short diversion from her otherwise structured job of keeping the Jason home in perfect order, Grace retrieved the mail from the box and sorted it by family member and junk mail as she returned to the house.

Jan and Angela arrived home at 6 pm, parked the car in the garage and strode inside, eager to see what Grace had prepared for dinner. Mark would follow shortly after; many times, he worked late into the night depending on the company's particular assignment, or issues that needed dealing with that were out of the ordinary.

The smell of beef stew and cherry cobbler assaulted their noses as soon as they entered from the garage. "Oh, Grace, you're the best!" squealed Angela, squeezing Grace around the waist. "You know cherry cobbler is my very favorite!"

Grace kissed Angela on the top of her head and whispered, "My sweet Angel, you know I'd do anything in the world for you. Besides, it's your father's fault... he's the one who introduced me to it in Savannah."

On her way upstairs to change clothes, Jan briefly stopped in the foyer to check the mail that Grace left on the entry table. She smiled as she thought about Angela's first job in the mailroom, and here she was going through the sorted mail at home.

◆

Seventeen-year-old Angela came down the steps first the next morning, anxious to start another day at work with her parents. She remembered the story her dad had talked about how he took his business degree courses while stationed overseas or stateside when her mom and she could stay with him at his duty station. It was an impressive task in the early-Internet days, and she was bound and determined to be just as dedicated and professional as he in her training to eventually assume the mantle of Jason Enterprises President. It would be many years down the road, however, and she had to work her way up from the bottom like grandpa required of her dad. Angela was also working on obtaining her driver's license when she turned eighteen in a couple months and hoped of owning her own car soon after.

During her new internship she rode to work every day with one of her parents. She privately relished the days when she got to ride with her dad; he always drove his car with the top down, and she loved the feel of her long black hair flowing around her face in the air at highway speeds, even though her hair was a tangled mess by the end of the trip.

As she waited for them to come downstairs, she glanced at the prior day's mail which was still on the foyer table. Casually she looked through them, keeping the mail in their respective stacks.

Mark came down the stairs dressed in his brown three-piece suit. After watching her parents and listening to their conversations her entire life, Angela had become quite astute and intuitive in reading her parents, based solely on their attire. A three-piece suit meant he had a meeting first thing this morning. A brown suit meant today's meeting was likely with a new client, so he wanted to appear relaxed and inviting instead of the stuffy executive in a traditional dark suit. *Probably means dining in the penthouse or at the club,* Angela thought. She looked at the way his hair was brushed: sideburns brushed down instead of back over his ears, covering his first gray hairs from the temples. The meeting was with a lady? Hair over his forehead was brushed more to the side from the part on his right side rather than his normal left, which made his hair look fuller, so probably with more than one female client. She looked at his hands on the normal morning pretext to "make sure his hands were clean", saw he wore the black onyx on his right ring finger. So today was a purchase or takeover meeting, and meeting with ladies meant a comfortable offer. "What?" Mark said, with hands gesturing upward. "You're eyeballing me like an X-ray machine." Angela smiled an innocent "I don't know what you're talking about" smile at him. He knew that she knew exactly what was on his agenda this morning without her ever saying a word.

Jan followed her family down to the base of the steps. She was wearing her dark green dress suit, white silk blouse, black strap open-toe pumps, red toenail polish, no stockings, and hair pulled back in a ponytail. *Mom's in her executive-nanny outfit. It's a friendly takeover for sure.*

"How's the future company president?" asked Mark as he gave Angela a big bear hug. She loved the feel of his well-muscled, powerful arms engulfing her, and his beard tickled her forehead.

"Feeling like making executive decisions," she purred in his arms. She left his embrace and stepped back. "How do I look today?" she asked.

Holding her hands, Mark stretched Angela's arms outwards and gave her a good once-over as well. She looked so much like Jan did at 17, long hair (black as opposed to Jan's red) flowing freely over her shoulders, powder blue blouse, black slacks, black stockings, and flat shoes. She wore simple earrings in her ears and no other jewelry. "Very official," he replied with a smile.

Jan said, "Meeting is at 9:00. You decide what you want to do?"

Angela resisted the urge to raise her hand and give Dad's answer for him.

Exhaling confidently, Mark replied, "I'm going to offer compassionate acquisition; she keeps control of the company as a subsidiary of JE. We get the benefit of a new technological source while she gets much-needed revenue to continue her research and development. No one loses a job. And you—" he pointed at Angela "—will be attending this meeting."

Angela's eyes widened to saucer-proportions. "Me? I'm supposed to be in this morning's mailroom staff meeting!"

"You're already talking back to your boss on your second day?" Mark smiled as he took the car keys from the key hook and silently bade the ladies to follow him to the garage. Jan and Mark accepted the coffee-filled travel mugs from Grace as they stepped through the kitchen and out the back door. They entered the multi-car garage and walked to the silver Lincoln Continental at the far end. Mark said, "Your grandfather had me attend my first merger meeting a month before I was to leave for navy boot camp," he said, "and gave me a week in advance to research the other company. Then I had to present my recommendation an hour before the meeting. I recommended passing. He passed. A month later the CEO of the other company was arrested for embezzlement and that company went belly-up. I know you're working in the mailroom now, but you won't be in the end. I just want you to experience what can happen."

The trip to the Jason building was filled with casual conversation of little importance. Jan did keep asking if Angela had any intention of finally telling the Jurgens boy "yes" to his regular date invitations, which Angela always answered with, "Oh, MOM!" and rolled her eyes with impatience.

Inside the Jason building garage, there was one private ramp that no other vehicles were allowed to use; this was for Mark and Jan's cars only. The ramp was located right behind the guard station which took them to a sealed-off parking level with room for five cars. Mark parked in the second slot of five parking spots near the private elevator to the executive suite. The first slot was his father's space, and he just didn't feel ready to start parking in Dad's place. The third slot was where Jan parked. The fourth slot would be for Angela's car, once she got her license…and that surprise of a car they were planning for her eighteenth birthday. The final spot would be for another Jason family member, either not yet born or not yet married into the family. Mark smiled to himself, thinking of surprising her with that convertible, listening to her squeals of happiness. He dearly loved spoiling his family.

Some days Mark would walk back down the ramp to greet the guards in person, say hello to the front door receptionist and the guards stationed in the lobby that monitored the courtyard outside. Today the Jason family took the retina-scanner access elevator car from the private garage to the top floor below the penthouse.

On the executive floor they stepped out of the elevator and across the hallway into Mark's office suite. His secretary Eleanor Worthington rose from her desk as the Jason family entered. The Franklin-style glasses on the bridge of her nose gave her an aristocratic presence. In her inviting English accent Eleanor greeted her boss, "Good morning, sir, ladies," as she presented his coffee as her preferred courtesy; she had simply assumed the habit when hired, never being asked to do so. Over the past few years, he had given up asking her to stop, and when she began providing his morning binders or notes before asking for them, he decided to increase her responsibilities by coordinating all executive activities for the company's Vice Presidents for Jan's review. Eleanor expertly coordinated all scheduling and interoffice meetings via her computer. She also had a direct link to Sarge's office, eighteen floors below.

She followed Mark into his office, and both were followed by Jan and Angela. Mark's desk dominated the room. The private balcony and cityscape sat invitingly behind the massive desk.

Today, Angela would be taking a seat in the conversation area to watch and learn.

As Mark rounded his desk to sit, he noticed a manila envelope placed perfectly centered right in front of him. It was addressed to him, and the sender was identified as "United States Justice Department." He noticed that there was no postmark on the envelope. Looking up, "Ellie," he asked pointedly, "when was this delivered?"

Eleanor, who was ten years older than Mark and allowed only him to address her as "Ellie", took the envelope from his hand and examined it. In the privacy of his office was the only time she addressed him by his first name, and only in the presence of his family at most. A worried look crossed her face. "I don't know, Mark. This was not here when I locked the office last night."

Mark began to get an uncomfortable feeling. He pressed the direct connect line to the Security Chief's office. "Yes, sir," came Sarge's gruff voice over the speaker. "Up here now, Sarge, and don't spare the horses." And he depressed the same button to end the call before Sarge could answer.

Sarge Brunson bounded into Mark's office without knocking. He was about to speak when he saw that envelope in Mark's hand. "I think we may have a problem sir," began Sarge.

**CHAPTER 43**
**MAY 6, 2011**
**FINDING SHADOWS**

Sarge was reviewing the night surveillance videos and reports when his eye caught something strange on one of the video feeds. Not sure of what he saw, he reset the video time back several minutes and redirected it to the new large monitor Mark ordered installed on the opposite wall. He watched the same footage again, and a third time. He reached to call Mr. Jason's office when the phone rang; it was Mark calling him first.

"Yes, sir," answered Sarge in his standard gruff tone.

"Up here now, Sarge, and don't spare the horses," he heard Jason say from the speaker. The line was cut off before he could report on the video finding.

By the time he got to the top, Sarge decided to charge ahead with his report first. "We have a problem, sir," he announced as he walked through Eleanor's office and into Mark's office without knocking.

That threw Mark off his train of thought. "What kind of problem?"

"An intruder," said Sarge.

Mark looked at him with a furrowed brow. "What intruder???"

"Last night, when I reported I thought we had an intruder and then said all was clear…" Sarge rumbled in his throat, "I was wrong."

Mark saw Angela start to say something, but he gently waved his right index finger her way from his waist and she held her voice. Jan saw the deft movement and motioned Angela to join her to the conversation area of the massive office. "OK, Sarge, how the hell did we miss an intruder? I'm not aware of any alarms going off, I got no calls or emails or other such damn thing…"

"Sir," said Sarge, "all standard protocols and procedures showed clear. But we did have a break-in."

Mark's temper was starting to rise. To everyone else, his facial expression did not change, but Jan could tell he was nearing explosion. "Talk to me, nice and clear, mister. I do not like mysteries."

"May I show you, sir?" When Mark nodded wordlessly, Sarge walked to the computer console in the conversation area and keyed in his security access to send a video file to the plasma screen on the wall between the bookcases. Mark and Eleanor joined him to see the footage. "This is last night; time index matches when I called you the second time." The view was of the balcony outside Mark's office from the perspective of a bird between the skyscrapers.

"Now just how the hell did you get this angle?" Mark demanded, the irritation growing in his voice. "We don't have a building camera there—"

"No, sir, we don't, but the building across the street has external cameras that focus on this building on occasional sweeps. Before Mark could respond Sarge said, "But, the guy across the street in security is an ol' front liner who served with me. Reminded him of a little ass-saving I did in Iraq, so he does some favors for me…we go back and forth with this, sir. He checked his system's roving surveillance this morning and caught this little snippet." The footage showed Sarge checking the balcony with his gun in hand, then closing the sliding door back and locking it in place. Then from the shadows above the balcony emerged a dark human figure, with brown skin and black hair. The footage showed him climbing up away from the balcony to the penthouse level, donning a parachute pack, then jumping off the roof into the air and disappearing from the camera's view.

"That looks a lot like a guy I met on the road, on the way to the benefit. Sarge, get a security team to the penthouse. I want that entire floor swept to within an inch of its life, and I mean yesterday."

"Aye, sir!" said Sarge like the Army man he was. He spun smartly on his heel and departed the office at double march.

"Ellie," said Mark as he sat down in his desk chair, "we've got three buildings with a view of this balcony. We've already seen one recorded view. Get with Sarge, contact the other two buildings' security and see if they have any more views of last evening."

"Yes, sir," she said and departed his office for hers outside.

There had been nothing for Jan to do to this point but stay out of the way, but now she joined him at his desk. Angela remained seated in the conversation area. "What can I do?" Jan asked.

Mark looked Jan in the eyes, took a deep breath, and picked up a pen from his desktop set. "Get the checkbook. We have a business to buy."

**CHAPTER 44**
**MAY 6, 2011- 5 P.M.**
**SEARCHING FOR ANSWERS**

Tall trees behind the Arts Center cast long shadows onto the ground. The darkened mirages gave an illusion of fingers slowly reaching out, stretching with the setting sun. Streetlights along the back of the building hadn't yet lit with the oncoming darkness.

Task Force Agent Hunter moved invisibly amongst the dim trees. The agent was furtive, almost like a stalking cheetah. She wore her black operations uniform, helping her meld in with the environment. Squatting, she took a few minutes to adjust to her surroundings.

*Why did you have to die?* she thought to herself. *You're the one who knows how to do this the best.* A dove flew about in the trees above her head after hearing her slight approach, cooing, calling for its lifelong mate. Within a moment, the female dove returned his call. The sounds saddened Hunter. The fact that the pair were mates for life pained her even more.

The cleaner crew executed its job perfectly as always. The scene had been cleaned over a week ago, and nothing seemed out of place or even gave a hint that a murder had occurred.

Hunter solemnly recalled the night of Marshall's murder and remembered the police that investigated the explosion. The cleaner crew arrived in identical police uniforms, and the crew leader barked orders like a police sergeant. Her memory stopped as she stared at the ground, remembered the sergeant's insignia on his collar and how he ordered his officers around to the back. That night seemed surreal to her now, memories fading into a blur of lights and sirens, men's voices echoing into the night and in her brain. Again, she realized her Marshall was now gone.

She snapped out of her brief fog, and finally recalled Spy's concussion capsule had gone off and imploded all that was around. Within minutes the crew had the area behind and inside the shed completely cleaned and straightened, as if nothing were amiss.

Hunter was informed the inside crewmen hurried to the top of the Arts Center, lowered a grappling hook and harness to the ground where it was affixed to Spy's bagged body, and he was hoisted up to the roof in less than sixty seconds. They placed Spy's body on the roof, the crew sealed the roof door with an alarm-rigged lock and left. The "sergeant" reported back to the command post and advised the roof was clear. The cleaner crew departed as inconspicuously as they'd arrived. Once the scene was fully cleared, a Task Force helicopter was dispatched to the Arts Center. It hovered on "silent run" long enough to retrieve the dead agent.

All that was over now, and Hunter was back at the Arts Center, looking for something, she just didn't know what.

She'd worked with him for years and was always amazed by his uncanny ability to spot clues that others missed. Again, Hunter was lulled into a momentary resignation of him being gone forever. She'd never work with him again. Jerked back to reality, something spoke almost audibly. It was her subconscious yelling, insisting she'd missed something that night.

Working her way alongside the building and to the front sidewalk, she watched as pedestrians still walked about in the near dusk-hours.

Glancing down to avoid eye contact with a passerby, she saw it. Hunter looked around to make sure no one watched. Squinting at the specimen below, she knelt to the ground. She adjusted a knob on her glasses to change her view to black-light mode. The minicomputer in her glasses surveyed the area as she looked at the shrubbery edged along the sidewalk. She observed two-minute droplets of what looked to be blood on the very edge of the sidewalk. The microprocessor performed an optical zoom on the stains and conducted an analysis of the substance. It separated parts and elements and was finished within seconds. It displayed a code inside one of the lenses for Hunter to read. The code showed a red-colored tear drop shape: blood. She took a swab from a pouch on her belt, swabbed the area, then placed it in an evidence bag, zipped and tagged it to be tested back at the office.

Hunter remembered the traces of blood that streaked down Spy's right arm and hand. He'd been shot in the arm, then the fatal shot to the eye. Her stomach knotted as she thought about him, motionless, the finality of it all. *Stop the damn remembering, Mae-Lei,* she scolded herself in her mind. She shook the memory off and decided to backtrack to where the trail started.

She took a mini flashlight from another canvas pouch. Clicking it on, Hunter began shining the light beam across the grounds, being careful not to attract attention. The special lenses aided in detecting light blue drops that dripped over the hedge and into a garden area, one well hidden from the street by overgrown shrubbery. She wiggled her way through the hedge and followed the trail to the garden area next to the Arts Center. "I'll be damned," she muttered out loud. The tiny blue drops turned into a massive blob of blue, and ultimately formed the shape of a human torso, one much bigger than Marshall. The sensor in her glasses was blinking on and off like mad, almost screaming at Hunter that massive amounts of blood were everywhere. Taking off her glasses for just a moment, she saw nothing, as it was so thoroughly washed by the cleaner crew, nothing could be detected with the naked eye.

She stood next to the shrubbery, Hunter's adrenaline flowed, and her heart stepped up a beat and knew she was onto something. She scanned the entire area, grass, trees, and bushes. Not far from the body outline, she homed in on a spatter pattern, deducing it was probably where Spy had been shot in the arm. She could envision him as he was shot, probably flinging his body around to where the shooter stood. Hunter tried to duplicate the same, reenacting what may have been Spy's final moments. Flashlight in hand, her glasses blinked at more blue droplets off in the distance on a tree. This time, the inside of the lenses danced with two codes. She saw the red teardrop and a second as a white teardrop, indicating body fluid of some sort. Hunter walked closer to the tree and looked up as she followed the blue spots. More tiny blue spots appeared in her lenses. A black handled knife was wedged in the tree trunk behind two low-hanging branches. "Gotcha," she whispered.

She remembered Spy's knife sheath was empty. She made a mental note to advise Tom later that the cleaner crew screwed up by missing this key piece of evidence but was also thankful for their lapse.

She retrieved another evidence bag from the pouch on her gun belt. Hunter placed it over the knife, carefully extracted it, sealed, and labeled the bag. Waiting for a break in the pedestrian traffic, she stood silently until there was an opening, then stepped briskly to her car, got in, fired up the engine, and took off into the night.

**CHAPTER 45**
**MAY 7, 2011**
**DIAMOND IS FOREVER**

David kept his small apartment immaculate and vacuumed it every morning. He made sure the vacuum cleaner tire tracks formed straight lines, one next to the other, and never deviated into a zig-zag effect. If it did, he'd have to start over, as he often did, over and over.

He'd collected a variety of extravagant nick-knacks over the years. His favorite was the collection of old-fashioned cigar lighter boxes, popular in the early 1900's. Some were 24 karat double gold plated, his favorite being the box made with brass. The money from his natural parents' trust fund assured he'd live in comfort, and money from Father DeVeaux's pittance of an inheritance he spent on things Father would have hated. He bought a curio cabinet for their display, placing two items on the first shelf, three on the second shelf, two on the third shelf, and lastly three on the fourth shelf. Everything had to be grouped in TWOs and THREEs as they were meant to be, as his hated adoptive father had taught him. "Ass-wipe," David said aloud as he stared at the curio and recalled his father and now his "damned TWOs and THREEs" yet again.

His father's lighter sat alone in the middle of the kitchen table, and he stared at it. "Adopted father, you son-of-a-bitch," David sarcastically thought to himself. The lighter was the one possession he'd kept when all the rest of his father's personal effects were taken out of the house. He felt compelled to keep it as a reminder, a prize, the first thing he claimed after he rid himself and his siblings of their tyrant. He was thankful it was old and refillable. David kept it always filled with lighter fluid and used it to light his own cigars now. It was old, square, made of silver metal. He flicked the lid open with one hand and stared at the wick and thumbed the old flint wheel. He ignited it on and off, on and off, fixated at the flame that jumped up each time. Eleven short days had passed since he'd shot the man in black. Engrossed with the flame, he reflected on the fight, how good it felt to be in control. The sound of the final gunshot reverberated in his head and echoed silently in his brain. He smiled.

A cigar dangled from his teeth; smoke encircled his head. David picked up the pistol, "Yeah, you got yours," he mumbled as the cigar bobbled up and down. Cradling the gun in his hands, he gently ran a polishing cloth over it, almost caressing the new prize. He'd come to love and understand guns over the past few years, and he was especially enamored with the dead man's gun. The weapon seemed well-balanced, though the grip felt slightly off as he aimed it toward the apartment's French doors. David examined the bullets again. It was something he'd done numerous times over the past week, one of his many OCD habits. *Normal baby bombs, nothing different,* he thought to himself. Getting matching ammo wouldn't be a problem. The engraving on the butt of the gun, that was a different story entirely: that diamond shape. The perfect engraved four-sided diamond.

David remained confused with the gun, the diamond shape, not knowing who the man in black was. Somehow, he felt comforted by the weapon, its configuration, and the special emblems. His real frustration now was with the woman, the one dressed in black, just like the man he'd killed. The "not knowing" infuriated him. The whiskey was settling in, doing its job. The fury made his face itch, his cheek twitched involuntarily. The stitches were still healing, and flesh was binding back together, attempting to repair itself under a large bandage. Resisting the urge to scratch at the wound, he set the pistol down and picked up the lighter, flicking it once more…

*…flicking it once more. The flame burst forth from the lighter just inches from his eyes.*

*Father pulled the lighter back and lit his cigar. "What did I tell you before, David?" he growled.*

*"Not to go out," David said tentatively, trying to be brave, knowing it would be futile.*

*Father puffed in, and then blew smoke out.*

*"But it was only in the backyard, Father!"*

*"Don't matter. 'Do not go out' does not mean 'except in the back yard.' Henri, get your ass in here!" Henri had been listening and knew what was coming. He ran in, with full knowledge to bring a leather belt, the big leather belt. "You WILL learn if I have to beat it into you and through you. Drop 'em." David and his brother obediently turned, dropped their pants and underwear, and waited for the beating…*

*…beating his eyes open and closed as the memory rose and fell…*

*…and as the boys pulled their clothes back on delicately over hurting and welted buttock cheeks, their father sat back in his chair, flicked his lighter to reignite his cigar, and said, "Now what do you say boys?"*

*"Thank you, Father."*

*"Done. Go to your room—"*

"—rooms. "These are MY rooms, damn you," David said. "This is MY home. You don't tell me what to do in MY home, you dead bastard."

He recalled the man in black who killed his crew. David completed his mission of fiery cleansing, but this stranger kept him from feeling released for good.

The ONE lighter and the ONE gun, each unique, but together they made TWO. It was comforting to David.

There was a knock at the door. David went to the apartment door and looked out the peephole. His brother Henri was alone outside. David opened the door to let Henri in.

The brothers sat opposite each other at the table. Henri saw the pistol in front of David. "Still puzzled over that, Davey?" he asked.

"No. Yeah. I don't know," David replied calmly. He lifted the gun by the cloth, rotated it so the butt faced Henri. "You sure you've never seen this symbol before?" David asked again, the frustration clear in his voice.

"Never," said Henri as he shook his head. "Checked the Internet, called some friends, hell, I even called some rivals, no one knows what that means."

"I hate it," said David. "I hate not knowing!" His cheeks were flushed red by the whiskey as well as his scrambled thoughts. He almost slammed the gun on the table but stopped himself. Instead, he set the pistol down gently, rose from his chair again and walked to the bookshelves in his living room, shoving his hands in his pants pockets. He stared at the first row of books, sorted alphabetically-by-title and absolutely in a straight line. David loved to stand before his bookshelf, his own perfectly organized display. Everything was in place. It was a comfortable place for him to stand. "Henri, I HAVE to find out who he is. What that symbol means. He picked such a damned perfect symbol! He was an absolute enemy for a fool, and it was my destiny to kill him and keep his trophy, to make me discover his secrets." Satisfied his books couldn't answer his questions, he returned to the table and picked up the pistol, this time with his hand.

Henri sat in his chair and watched as David played with the pistol, pretending to draw it and fire, twirling the trigger guard before he put it in his imaginary holster, and drew again and aimed at some enemy in the distance. "How you feeling, Davey?" Henri squinted his eyes watching David play with the gun. "That's not loaded is it?"

"Not right now. I only load it for target practice. Got real good since I sent Scorpion to hell to join Father."

"I know, Davey," said Henri.

He rotated the pistol in his hand, smiled and showed it to Henri in the palm of his hand. "From hell itself this man persecutes me; demands I find out who he is and why he chased me. It was a perfect THREE, Henri. I know this time I sent our father back to hell once and for all, but he tortures me by leaving a mystery at the end of this THREE. Just to keep me from finally being free, he tests me, and taunts me again. This mysterious avatar, this Diamond Man, he's dead without a doubt. No way in hell can you survive a bullet through your brain. Diamond Man paid for intruding on my THREE by going to hell, and now Diamond Man taunts me by having a TWO, just like him. I don't like knowing who they are, these TWO." David placed the gun down and put his hands flat on the table and stared at Henri. "How dare they be a TWO! But, what if they're not a TWO? What if they're a THREE?"

Henri knew better than to argue. "Davey, you know we lost everyone on the last job. We have no one to help us, to help YOU, answer your mystery."

"Yep, a new crew. A better crew. They need to know how to fight, not just arm and plant. We have to find this TWO, kill her, send her to join her other half."

"It will be expensive."

David narrowed his eyes and smiled. "We've got the money. Hell's waiting to be paid once more. Let's make it for the last time."

## CHAPTER 46
## MAY 7, 2011
## "IT MEANS I'M DRIVING"

A stern expression was frozen on Mark's face as he hit the pause button on the remote control yet again. He sat in his office, feet atop his desk. His head was slightly lowered as he scowled at the plasma screen in front him. "Dammit, Sarge, this is all pissing me off!"

The 60-inch plasma was always on. It usually displayed a constant crawler of stock market figures and split into a second screen that had world news playing quietly in the background. Today was different though. Today nothing else seemed to matter but the security concerns at hand.

Sarge sat on the leather couch to the left of Mark. His hand knotted into a fist under his nose, his elbow on the arm of the couch. His brows were furrowed, and he remained silent as they both watched the images play over and over on the big screen.

Security cameras from the JE building and nearby buildings had captured footage of the intruder. Ellie called in a few favors to get the delivery of the footage expedited, not that it was much of a problem for her. What Ellie wanted, Ellie had a way of getting it, most efficiently.

The IT Department collected the footage, split the monitor into three separate images, and now the disgruntled men watched and studied. The view of the balcony outside Mark's office was captured from three different angles. They watched as a man in head-to-foot black clothing approached the glass doors. As they zoomed in, they were perplexed at the uniform the man wore, form-fitting, obviously easy to move around in. "This is the second time recently I've seen some mystery guy dressed like that." The cameras were too far away to get a clear enough picture to run through facial recognition.

"What the hell?" Sarge finally voiced his opinion toward the screen. Mark eye balled Sarge, irritated with everything now.

Mark continued to adjust the remote. He angled in and they watched in amazement as a black helicopter steadily hovered over the penthouse level. "And none of our security systems detected THAT over my building?" Mark said as calmly as he could. Sarge was angered that cameras and motion detectors hadn't been stationed on the roof before he was hired and especially after he was already on the job. The man in black jumped from the helicopter and onto the roof. From there, he tied off a thin black rope, dropped it to the balcony level, and slid down just outside Mark's office.

Mark leapt to his feet, shaking his index finger at the screen, staring at the helicopter. "Sarge look, that's the chopper we've been looking to purchase, recognize it? The NOTAR."

Sarge leaned forward, squinting at the screen. "Yes, sir, you're right, damn. Sumbitches got it before we could. But who are they?"

Both admiring and hating the object holding their attention. Mark had been intrigued with the NOTAR (No Tail Rotor) chopper for years and researched it for Jason Enterprises' own use, especially when various special projects on the top floor had to be delivered with extreme discretion. He'd learned it was developed by McDonald Douglas a while back and proved to be safe, quiet, and extremely responsive, everything the company needed. He'd flown choppers when overseas with the SEALs and had a rare moment of envy as he watched it hover effortlessly in place over the penthouse.

With no tail rotor, Mark knew the chopper's noise factor was reduced by up to 70%, and the FOD (foreign object damage) factor proved to be exceptional. It could barely be heard on the security footage. He recalled flying one over Tehran before being ordered stateside, its ability to take gunfire and keep going made that mission a success instead of a failure with no loss of the chopper or his squad. Captivated with this new enemy's sophistication, and obvious wealth, Mark sat back to view the rest of the footage.

The intruder slid down the rope as the NOTAR flew off out of camera view. When his feet were just above the patio deck, he pulled a black device from his belt, thumbed it, and then safely landed on the patio. "Remote bypass of the sensor system. The main computers thought the field was active. Very nice," Mark admired. "JE does have exclusive contracts with the government. I wonder if this is something we developed."

"Does seem like a 14th technology, based on what I've learned so far," said Sarge.

"Indeed."

All three camera angles witnessed the man in black easily pick the balcony's sliding glass door lock to Mark's office. He retrieved a manila envelope from his backpack, disappeared for a moment, exited and hid momentarily behind a hedge on the balcony. The footage showed Sarge step into view with a gun drawn, glance about, return inside the office and lock the balcony door.

The final few seconds revealed the man shinnying back up the rope to the penthouse, pulled the rope up behind him and literally dove off the top of the penthouse level. Both Mark and Sarge inhaled as they watched the infiltrator jump from the JE tower. Toggling the camera angle again, they saw a black parachute erupt from the man's backpack, and he disappeared between the buildings then out of range of the available footage.

"If you want, sir, I can check with the buildings further on, try to find a flight pattern for this guy and see where he landed," offered Sarge.

Mark sat next to Sarge on the couch, took his Scotch from the end table and took a sip. Swirling the drink gingerly he stared down into it. "No, Sarge, I've seen enough. We've been made a fool of, my friend."

"Sir? Whatcha mean?"

"Think about it, there's a hundred different ways to sneak something in my office. Why go through that elaborate rigmarole, helicopter, and parachute, just to put something on my desk?" Mark tossed back the rest of his Scotch, crossed his legs, and grinned. "Nope, something's up, we're being tested."

"Tested? What the hell, sir?" Sarge wasn't amused that Mark smiled about the incident.

"Wrap it up, Sarge, file all the incident reports and put all that footage on a DVD for me. Have a nice, tidy package ready so I can take it with me. I'll be gone for a few days."

"Gone, sir? I don't have anything on the calendar for you."

Mark gave Sarge a confident slap on the shoulder, "Going to D.C. Invited to meet with the A.G. on something or other."

Sarge bounded from the couch, staring at Mark. "The envelope, from the intruder. He left it on your desk; it was an invitation? I noticed it when I was doing the security check of your office. Is that who it was from? The Attorney General?"

"Well, that's what the envelope says, and that's what the letter inside says. But this unusual courier tells me the opposite. Besides," Mark narrowed his eyes, "I get the feeling we were supposed to figure this whole thing out."

"You do?"

"Mm hmm," said Mark. "But the overall question is, why? And then, what does all this mean?"

"A trick? Or a Trap?"

"Both."

Sarge sat back onto the soft couch, the luxury was against his nature to enjoy, admitting only to himself that his boss had excellent taste in comfortable furniture. He picked up the bourbon Mark served him earlier. "Math was never my strong suit, sir, but A and B isn't equaling C here." As he downed his drink he mumbled, "Or something like that." Mark smiled. "So, sir, what does it all mean?"

Turning back, he smiled at Sarge, "It means I'm driving."

**CHAPTER 47**
**MAY 9, 2011**
**FOR YOUR EYES ONLY**

Mark arrived at the Department of Justice in Washington, D.C. He parked his car, got out with his briefcase in hand, locked it, clicked the remote a second time to hear a confirmation "beep" from the car. He stepped to the main entrance. On his way into the building, he was stopped by a stunningly attractive woman. The first thing he noticed was her dark eyes and waist-length black hair. He placed her as Polynesian because of her soft tan complexion and exotic Pacifica facial structure. The second thing he noticed, and it jumped out at him, was that she was clad in black from head to toe, slacks, leather jacket, glasses in hand and boots. She was beautiful and looked deadly. "Mr. Jason," she addressed him on the sidewalk just before they passed each other.

"Depends," he replied. "And you are…?"

"We were awaiting your arrival. Please join me, will you?" she said, and she motioned him to a waiting black limousine.

Staring at her, Mark's eyes narrowed momentarily and looked over at the limousine. Prior to his arrival, he expected something to happen to keep him from entering the Justice building, a gut feeling had told him. He looked around, observed nothing suspicious or out of the ordinary. He followed the woman to the waiting vehicle. The back door was already open awaiting his entrance. A polite smile crossed his face as the mystery woman donned her glasses and motioned for him to enter the vehicle.

Mark unbuttoned his suit coat and slid inside, ready for his covert adventure. He made himself comfortable in the cushioned seat. The woman joined him in the back compartment, and he got a whiff of a familiar fragrance as she moved past him to sit. She faced him from the opposite seat. He mulled in his head whether to say anything about her perfume as he tried to read her eyes. Her glasses were so dark that he didn't even have a chance. It grated on his memory for not remembering where he'd smelled the fragrance before, and his intuition told him to say nothing.

"I won't ask you to surrender the weapons you have on you," she said calmly. "Just resist the urge to draw them." Then the woman reached into a section in the door panel beside her. She retrieved a pair of dark glasses like hers. "Please put these on," she requested as she handed him the glasses.

He accepted the glasses and examined them for a moment. They were completely blacked out, and cocoon-shaped like hers to completely blind him, even peripherally. Without a word, he gave in to the adventure once again, and placed them over his eyes. Except for glimpses of light from where the frames rested against his face, he couldn't see anything. Once they were in place he sat back and nodded his head. He knew this woman was watching him. Seconds later he felt the vehicle moving forward.

Sometime later, after many turns and speed changes, the car came to a stop. The door to his left was opened, and sounds echoed with volume. *Some sort of large garage area,* he wondered. He heard the lady in black move and felt the car jostle slightly as she stepped out. Someone leaned in and politely grasped his left arm and guided him out of the limousine. They walked a few steps, and he heard a door open, was guided forward, and a few steps later he heard the door close behind them. He was led down a long hallway, stopped, and was pulled to turn to his left. Another door was opened, and he was steered in.

"You may take off the glasses for now," he heard the woman say. He removed them, turned around, and immediately took in his surroundings. He noted that the office area was casually decorated. A desk, chair, guest chair, potted plant, filing cabinet, computer on the desk, coffee pot and cups on the side table. No windows. "Please, make yourself comfortable, Mr. Jason," she said. She backed out of the office and closed the door as she went.

Mark looked around the room a second time and took in more details. *No sense in checking drawers or the computer. Everything is either locked or empty or doesn't work. It's a presentation room, not functional at all,* he surmised. *Worked a few of these myself.* He retrieved his cell phone from his coat pocket. No signal, no surprise. So, he stood and waited patiently.

A few minutes later Mark turned around as the faux-office door opened again, and a gentleman stepped inside. Unlike the guide, this man wore a blue suit with a white shirt and black tie. He set a briefcase on the desk, extended his hand, and smiled. "Hi, my name is Tom Michelson. You must be Mr. Jason; may I call you Mark?" Mark nodded one time to grant permission. "I thank you for coming up here to the Nation's Capital today. Please, be seated and make yourself comfortable. I'm sure you have many questions, but if you'll allow me, I can give you the answers you seek."

Tom seated himself behind the desk. "You were invited today because you have natural, innate skills and talents which could serve your country uniquely."

"In case you're not aware, Tom," Mark interrupted, "but I've already served."

"You still do, Mark. On your reserve weekends," Tom replied. "And for that we owe you a debt of gratitude. I was a career man myself, retired Marine." Mark bowed his head in mutual respect.

"And you still do as a select provider of tech to the military and federal government. Now, before I continue on, I must add this disclaimer. You are under no obligation to stay here. You weren't even asked to surrender your hidden guns."

"I figure there are already plenty of targets on me right now, so why would I even try?"

Tom smiled and nodded. "You may walk out that door and be returned to where you were picked up with no questions asked. Of course, you will have to be blinded with the glasses again to keep this facility unidentified. But otherwise, you will have lost only a couple hours or so of your day today, and we will not bother or contact you in any fashion again.

"On the other hand, if you choose to stay, you may, no, you will, find yourself in the most challenging opportunity of your life. Resources available to you for tasks presented or assigned to you. There will be risks and dangers with the job we are offering, but we feel you are among the possible best for what we have to offer. And," Tom said as he retrieved papers from his briefcase, "this is the job description and what you'll be paid per assignment."

Mark took the paper, looked at the dollar figure but giving no reaction, and read the cursory agreement labeled "FOR YOUR EYES ONLY."

"But you have to choose now. You may speak with your wife, and her only about this…though I know you'll talk with your daughter, also." Tom reached into his pocket, pulled out a cell phone connected to a private network, and handed it to Mark. "Call her, sir. And if you say 'yes', you cannot tell anyone else."

Ignoring the phone offer, Mark read the agreement completely, then set it on the desk across from Tom and looked at him with an expressionless stare…

**CHAPTER 48**
**MAY 9, 2011**
**NEW FOLLOWERS**

At David's demand, Henri made phone calls to nine of his friends and contacts around the city, asking them to meet at David's apartment ASAP. Since money was involved, they had no problem, and each rushed over without delay.

David anticipated their arrival. He was tense and agitated for several reasons. While the men were enroute, he obsessed over where they would sit in his small apartment as he gave his lecture and instructions. "Eleven men total, not an even number, crap. Three can sit on the couch, two on the loveseat, I'll bring in the dining room chairs. Two in that corner and another two in that corner. Henri and I will stand. Now there's a plan! That'll work for me." David reflected as his number's obsession kicked into high gear. Henri leaned against a wall and watched on as David fidgeted, somewhat amused at his brother's turmoil.

One by one, the men arrived. They looked scraggly, unkempt. For the most part, all had arrest records and were pretty much the low-life type David needed. David's persona turned from one of anxiety to a stern calm, assertive. Henri opened the door for each while David sat at the dining room table. With a finger pointed toward the living room, he'd direct each, "Have a seat in there."

Once all were in place, David walked to the living room and placed a black pistol on the coffee table atop a small towel. He didn't want to mar the gun in any manner. The men were caught off guard, and silently eye-balled each other. Most carried their own weapons, and the fact that another man set a weapon in front of them got their dander up.

In a hardened voice David spoke. "I need something from all of you. I have many needs actually." He picked up the trophy gun and rotated it, so the grip butt faced the new recruits, his crew. "Do any of you recognize this symbol?" he asked, pointing at the diamond etching on the bottom.

The men stared at the gun butt, then looked at each other. One by one, all shook their heads in the negative.

"Um, sir?" one man on the couch asked politely as he raised his hand.

The courtesy caught David off-guard, and his eyes narrowed. "What?"

"If I may say, sir, are you ok?" He gently patted his own cheek like a living mirror.

David reached up to his bandaged cheek out of reflex. "Why do you ask?" David growled. This discussion wasn't on his itinerary for the day.

The scrawny man with geeky glasses spoke. "Your cheek, it looks infected. I can see the red around the bandage. See, I was a medic overseas, before I got out that is. I'd be happy to help, it really needs tending to. It's only gonna get worse, I mean if you want, after you're done talking." The man seemed to ramble on.

David sized him up with a silent, hard stare. The man swallowed, almost regretting that he spoke so soon. David stared at the floor and thought for a few moments. Looking back up at the man, he retorted, "We'll talk. Later." David then changed his tone again. "Nobody interrupts me again! You wanna work for me, you'll be paid well, very well. You do exactly as I say, when I say, without question. Otherwise, there's the door." David pointed an index finger at the apartment entrance.

He held the trophy pistol by the grip, no finger in the trigger ring. "I completed my cleansing THREE last month, but an Avatar from HELL was sent to me in return. I disposed of him, but he doesn't want me to live in peace!"

The group of thugs' eye-balled each other, nervously, realizing they'd be working for a nutcase. But they remained silent. Money spoke louder than insanity.

Holding the gun in the air, David continued. "I killed his Avatar, this Diamond Man, this black demon from hell, with his own weapon. THIS weapon." He waved it in front of the men, then set it back down. "Then there was a second."

David pointed to the three men on the couch. "You're a THREE now. Always work together no matter what." Pointing to the men on the loveseat, he directed, "You're a TWO, same thing, always work together. Same for you over here to my left, and same for you TWO over here to my right. But you on my right, yeah, you'll always be in front. You look like you can handle it." Henri handed each man a wad of cash, rolled up in rubber bands. The men smiled, mumbling amongst themselves, happy to get the money.

"Shut up!" David paced back and forth in front of them. "Look at this gun, take a close look. The man that had this wore a black uniform, boots, gloves, sunglasses. Wore a belt with a holster. The flat metal belt buckle had this SAME diamond symbol engraved in it. Sunglasses, at night! Then another one showed up, a woman, dressed just like him. I need you to find her!" David spoke methodically, robot like. "Bring 'er to me. Got it?"

"Sir," began one man. David swung around and pointed the pistol at him. The man blinked hard and held a hand in front of him. Nervous, he continued. "No, sorry, see, it would help if we knew what she drove, where she might be, what she looks other than that uniform and all. We might find 'er and she won't be wearin' that stuff."

David lowered the gun and narrowed his eyes. He was pensive in his thoughts as he rubbed the bristles of unshaven blond hair on his chin. "Yeah, okay, good point, lemme think. She has long black hair, it was dark, but looked like she had a dark tan, maybe foreign or something. She drives a fancy black car; I got a quick look inside. Computer screen on the dashboard. The good father gave his Avatars some sort of 'super' cars. She wore the same uniform, I guess she's also got this diamond shape engraving on her belt, probably on her gun, too." David pointed to his cheek. "See this? Her fellow Avatar did this to me. You find her! Search every street and building. And when you find her, you call Henri. Whoever finds her gets paid a second time. Whoever finds her and holds onto her for me gets paid a third time. Then I personally can kill the bitch. Got it? You, Doc, stand up." The disheveled medic stood while David looked him up and down. The man was about the same build as Henri. "You're filthy, clothes dirty, you stink. Yeah, I want you to look at my wound, but you're gonna clean up first. Henri take him to the second bathroom. You take a hot shower, scrub down your whole body, THREE times. I won't have you touchin' me looking like that. Henri give him some of your clean clothes. The rest of you, get outta here."

After the last man left, he closed the door and stepped to David's side. "We'll find her Davey," he said sympathetically.

Henri motioned the medic to follow him down the hallway. "What's your name?"

"Eric. Eric Vaughn."

"So, where'd you serve?"

David sat back at the dining room table with the pistol and talked aloud to himself. "I can't let an unknown TWO be out there, tormenting me. Gotta get rid of her, before Father comes back again."

## 2s and 3s

Eric returned to the dining room where David sat. He was still holding his trophy gun. "Well, you look and smell a hell of a lot better. Henri threw your clothes away, I'm sure you won't mind. Take a seat." David was calmer now, almost serene in his thoughts. "Medic, huh? Yeah, Henri checked your duty claim while you were in the back. Good thing you were tellin' the truth." The man sat beside David; Henri took a third chair. "Say you can treat me. How do you know anything's wrong with me anyway?"

"Well, I first noticed the swelling. There's an infection, it's causing the left side of your face to puff out and your left eye is more closed than your right. Redness from your nose to your left ear. Bet it doesn't feel so good either."

"Alright, go ahead, Henri's got one of his crazy medical kits. He tinkers with all this stuff anyway, his experiments and all. But Henri's right here the whole time, watchin' in case you decide to do something stupid."

"No, sir, nothing stupid."

Eric opened the silver medical kit, took out what he needed and donned a pair of surgical gloves. Carefully he removed the bandage from David's face. He studied the laceration, taking a closer look with a magnifying glass from the medical kit. "Yes, sir, the Doctor that did this did an excellent job. Deep cut to the Zygomatic process of the frontal bone, the maxilla, temporal bone."

"Yeah, yeah, I get it. It's a hell of a cut, get on with it."

"I've never seen stitching like this sir, fifteen stitches, but grouped in sets of two and three."

David smiled, "Very observant, Eric. Just the way I like it."

"Yes, sir. From the looks of it the cut went all the way to the bone. The infection probably occurred post-treatment. Doesn't appear to need lancing but looks like you've been rubbing it through the bandage."

"What do you think? It itches!"

"Yes, it itches because it's trying to heal. The tissue underneath is now infected and swollen. You have to resist the urge to scratch it." Eric found what he needed in the case, cleaned the wound, and applied lidocaine to help stop the itching and an anti-bacterial to the incision line to fight the infection. "I'd recommend cleaning and retreating two or three times per day sir."

David laughed. "TWO or THREE times, you say. Yeah, suits me fine. Hey, and it doesn't itch now."

Half an hour later Eric had re-bandaged the cut. He piled up the used bandages, gauze, sterile paper, and any other items that needed disposal. Henri provided a small trash bag and Eric put everything in it. "If you'll permit, I'll go out to the trash bin and dispose of this and come back and put the kit back together for you."

David just nodded, and Henri said, "Go ahead, I'll wait for you at the door."

On his way down the stairs, Eric stopped at the mid-junction and removed the voice recorder he had taped under his shirt when he arrived earlier and had successfully hidden from Henri when he showered. "Found a missing item from TF, a gang of ten males, all well-armed. Two leaders, male, early twenties. Main leader with laceration to left cheek. Other leader, Henri." He cut off the recorder, activated a GPS signal on it, and dropped it in the trash bag. Tying it off, he threw it in the dumpster and headed back upstairs.

Henri opened the door just as Eric started to knock on the door. Eric looked surprised. David appeared in the doorway, "Who were you talking to, Eric?"

Eric was caught off guard for a moment. He nervously laughed. "No one, sir. I often speak to myself, you know, kind of mentally review my steps, make sure I've made no mistakes."

"Does your mental reviews include describing everything you saw here?"

*Damn, they had the stairs wired for audio.* Eric began to calculate his options.

David pointed a gun at Eric's forehead. Before Eric fell to his death, he realized it wasn't the trophy gun, but a different one, with a silencer.

A thumping sound outside caught David's attention. He went to his apartment window and looked out and down. He watched as the contents of the apartment complex dumpster were dumped into a garbage truck. "Go, stop that truck!"

Henri leaped over Eric's body, headed down the stairs and outside. He was too late; the truck was gone.

**CHAPTER 49**
**MAY 9, 2011**
**"YOU'RE A HERO"**

Dinner was finished, Jan and Angela cleared the table, cleaned the kitchen, and joined Mark in the living room with filled wine glasses. He sat in his favorite chair, a cushioned Victorian armchair with gold thread fabric and oak wood trim and legs. Jan had a matching chair. They were purchased in England when Mark had been there on business many years ago. The ladies sat together on the plush, burgundy-colored sofa, a coaster already on the small tables on either end for their wine glasses. Angela enjoyed finally being old enough to join her parents in their evening cocktail, even though she was limited to one glass of wine.

"You're going to do it?" Jan asked. "You're going to go back into the service?"

"It's not one of the 'regular' military branches," Mark corrected, not for the first time during the evening. "At first, I thought they'd made a mistake, offering someone my age a job best offered to someone at least ten years younger. But I've found that I can make this work quite easily. With the work that JE already does with the secret government contracts, and I've seen where some of the JE research from the 14th floor has ended up, this could be a great way to control the new weapons tests before they're turned over to the government or military for practical application."

"That's my Mark, always the logician." Jan reached over and took Angela's hand in hers. "Doesn't mean I have to like it. Damn it, Mark, you're putting yourself back in danger!"

"Did I mention the tax-free income?"

Jan growled in frustration. "URGH! Mark, it's not like we need the money! So why?"

"No, it's not the money," he agreed. "I was told I was a candidate for this special team a decade ago, but I wasn't selected because of you and Angel. The officer who was selected was recently killed on an assignment, and I was approached to take over. It does explain the extra training I've had to do on my monthly reserve duty weekends though, keeping me proficient physically and militarily."

"I still don't like it," Jan said sternly. "You're at the age now where you would be at a desk or committee room making the decisions and sending the younger military into the field. Never mind that you are in really, REALLY great shape, love."

Angela closed her eyes and tried to purge the sudden image of her parents making out naked.

Mark realized he was out of arguments for the job. They hadn't argued so much as discussed it in detail before and during dinner and finishing now during after-dinner drinks. Mark knew it would also affect Angela, so he included her in the whole discussion, Tom's order be damned.

A peaceful silence fell over the living room for a few minutes, interrupted only when Angela rose from the couch and walked to one of the display bookshelves, and looked for one book. She found it, took the large volume in her arms, and returned to her seat beside her mother.

She opened the photo album on the coffee table before them. She began looking at the pictures of her father in uniform in different places across the globe. They were pictures Mark was allowed to keep after naval security determined they didn't show anything that would be deemed an information risk. Without a word she slowly turned the pages to look at each picture. Jan finally leaned forward to look closer with her daughter. With each turning page Jan realized how much she loved Mark and was proud of the courage he showed doing his secret missions in different countries, helping so many others without asking anything in return.

Finally, Angela flipped to the last page. It was a picture of Mark receiving a Purple Heart, Medal of Valor, and Medal of Honor from the President. She flipped the back cover over and closed the volume. Still without a word, Angela picked up her wine glass and sat back on the sofa.

"Mark, we have a very wise daughter."

He just looked at her with one eyebrow raised. "I remember something Dad told me a long time ago: 'You may find yourself having to protect your JE family one day, without benefit of law enforcement, in public, or away from the limelight.' Do you think he knew way back then that this day would? He always had that mysterious side…"

Jan walked over to Mark, sat seductively in his lap, and wrapped her arms around his neck. "You're a hero, big boy. You'd never say it, you'd never admit it, but you, Mark Jason, are an American hero. You're right, you can't say no. Your dad knew you could never say 'no' to such an invitation. That's just one reason why I love you so much!"

He took a deep breath and let it out slowly, then smiled. "I love you right back," he said.

"Speaking of heroes, does this family have room for another hero?" asked Angela.

Mark and Jan looked at each other, then over to her. "Oh, no, Angel, I'm not joining any such secret team," said Jan, shaking her head. "Someone's got to run the company while your daddy is saving the world, AGAIN." She elbowed Mark in the ribs.

"No," Angela said, "I meant ME." She pulled a folded letter from her back pants pocket and showed it to her parents. "I'm gonna follow family tradition! I've been accepted into the Navy!"

Instead of the expected "are you sure" speeches from her parents, they jumped up and gave her big hugs and congratulations. "You're not angry?"

Mark smiled. "Angel, when you're the head of Jason Enterprises you'll learn that you know what everyone is going to do before they know they're going to do it themselves. And I've got quite a number of military contacts. So, of course we knew. We just waited for you to tell us when you were ready. is all. And of course, this means a celebration!"

Angela asked, "Does this mean we're having champagne tonight? I've even rented a movie for us to watch! You ever seen 'Indecent Proposal'? It's got a real young Robert Redford in it!"

She couldn't understand why her parents started laughing.

◆

Mark drove to the Justice Department meeting spot the next day. The woman agent was there with the same limousine, dressed the same as the day before, but with a second pair of black glasses in her left hand. Her right hand rested on the top of the open back door. Mark locked his car and walked over to her. She was wearing the same perfume, the one he couldn't place. "Blindfold again?" he asked almost sarcastically.

"Depends on if you're saying, 'yes' or 'no'," she said without expression.

"What do you think?" Mark replied, this time with a straight face and tone.

She eyed him for a few moments, trying to read his expression. He had an unflinching poker face. Finally, she put the spare glasses in her shirt pocket and motioned for him to get in first. He did so, and she followed. Once they were settled in their respective seats the limo pulled forward, and Mark noticed immediately that it turned a different direction than before.

"Is this a good time for idle chatter while I try to figure out who you are?" Mark chided.

For the first time the woman smiled but kept her large cocoon glasses on. "Oh, let me enjoy a few more minutes of mysterious anonymity, sir," she said. "We'll be bosom buddies soon enough."

"I hope you realize I need several drinks before I get bosomy," Mark replied.

"Don't you think your wife would object?"

"With a devastating right hook." Mark looked at the passing buildings, memorizing the route. "So, you work for Tom Michelson?"

"Yes, sir," she acknowledged, "but after you're signed on, I'll actually be answering to you."

"So, you're a member of this 'Task Force'?"

She smiled again. "Let's let Tom answer all your questions." As if on cue the limo pulled to a stop in front of a brownstone in the outskirts of Washington. She stepped out first and Mark followed.

"Headquarters?"

"No, just another meeting spot," she said.

"You've got quite a number of them."

"You've no idea."

They went up the steps together and once inside she led him down the main foyer. The decorations were all early twentieth century American, the paintings in the hallway were scenes of the American southwest during the cowboy era post-Civil War. They stopped at the last door on the right. The woman opened it and bade him enter first.

Mark was greeted by three people in the room. There were four chairs in the room and one desk, behind which sat Tom Michelson. The other two, a short blonde woman and a tall, brown-skinned man, were seated. Tom wore a blue suit, the woman a one-piece red dress and matching pumps, and the man wore a tan sports coat over gold shirt and black slacks.

"Glad to see you, Mark," said Tom. "Please, have a seat." Mark sat down in the chair across the desk from Tom while his lady guide took the last seat in the room. Mark crossed his legs, intertwined his fingers in his lap, and waited.

"Mark," Tom began, "these folks are the Task Force field team. You've met Mae-Lei Komala, our agent 'Hunter'." He motioned at the woman who had been Mark's guide the past two limo trips. Mark and Mae-Lei exchanged nods. "This is Harriet Lewis, our agent 'Proteus'."

"You can call me 'Harri'," said the petite blonde as she stood and shook hands with Mark.

"And this is Calvin Geffers, agent 'Seeker'." Mark and the last man shook hands and said "hi" to each other.

"Interesting agent code-names," Mark noted after the introductions were completed. "I believe we've met indirectly a couple times, Mr. Geffers." Calvin smiled and nodded. "So, what am I supposed to be?"

"Your agent name will be 'Spy'. And you'll be the new leader of this team."

"Really? No insult intended, but do you really expect me to walk in off the street and suddenly become their boss?" He turned to the three agents. "Why weren't one of you selected for advancement?"

"Very simple," said Mae-Lei. "We're not line officers."

"As I told you yesterday," Tom continued, "you were on our shortlist when the Task Force Division was conceived. All the members of this team, past and present, are military personnel who've seen combat training and know how to survive. But you were one of only two who was a highly trained and experienced tactician and commander of a unit. Officers all, here, and the chain of command is still recognized. By rank, you are the senior officer here as well."

"If we were all still in uniform," Mark said.

"In a sense, you will be. Follow me, please." Tom got up from his desk and led everyone to the door and the foyer. While Mark followed Tom to the left, the Task Force agents walked across the hall into another room and closed the door. In the den beside the front door Tom stopped and poured two tumblers of whiskey and handed one to Mark. "Here's how it works, Mark. You're the leader of the Task Force field team, with authority also over the tactical and other support departments. You'll receive assignments from me, and it will be your determination which of your team, either individually or paired or teamed however you choose, will be given the mission. Just like in the SEALs, Mark. Now, let me explain the code names: Hunter is the tracker of the team, best trained in the Army. Seeker is your explorer, in his years in Special Forces he's been all over the world and is your get-you-there guy. Proteus is an expert in camouflage, misdirection, and makeup disguise. She can make you look like anyone else in noticeably short order and has the tech to even change your voice. Your time in the SEALs gave you skills of detection and observation, and your leadership ability comes from both the Navy and Jason Enterprises. Your reserve training was designed to keep you in shape should we ever have to 'activate' you. Frankly, in another couple years you would have been dropped off the rolls."

"Thanks, I think," Mark said with a smile.

"Good thing you're in good shape. You'll look great in your new uniform." The Task Force agents walked in. All three wore the standard Task Force uniforms and weapons belts. The gun belts' buckles were flat non-reflective metal, and there was a different geometric shape in the center of each: Mae-Lei's was an isosceles triangle, Calvin's was a circle-in-a-circle, and Harri's was two triangles upside-down, creating the illusion of five triangles.

"What's with the buckle designs?" Mark asked.

"It distinguishes between agents in the field. All your equipment will be coded with your symbol, as will your assigned vehicle. Plus, a few other things we'll tell you about later.

"When on assignment you don't go by your civilian name, only your agent name, and that holds true anytime you're in uniform, except for right now. Despite how secure our communications system is, there's always the chance someone could hack our wireless network while you're in the field, so never refer to yourself or any other agent by anything except the field name. From here we'll get you fitted for your uniforms and armaments. Your weapons will be measured to fit your hands and weighted for your optimum efficiency. And, if someone were to get their hands on your weapons, they'll never aim right because of the special balancing. So, let's go get started."

Over the next few hours support staff took measurements of Mark's body, and Tom briefed him on Task Force history. Late in the afternoon Mark and Tom were seated in the den once more, having another drink. They sat, and Mark opened the brief case he'd carried with him on both trips to see Tom. He tossed the envelope with the DVD and other reports his own people had assembled from the night the invitation was put on his desk. "We are so going to work on stealth, inexcusable for an agent to have been photographed so easily."

Tom smiled and nodded when a female support staff member came in with a box in her arms. "Ah, good," said Tom as he set down his glass and walked to her. He opened the box top and took out a black gun belt. "You never asked what your agent symbol was."

"I figured you'd get around to it sooner or later."

"Well, here you go. Try it on for size." Tom handed him the empty belt.

Mark looked at the flat metal buckle and the diamond symbol engraved in its center. He wrapped it around his waist and looked at the clasp on one end but saw no way to attach it at the buckle. "Press in the top and bottom edges of the buckle to attach and detach," Tom told him.

Mark did as instructed, and when he did, he saw the open-end swivel out and withdraw into the buckle plate, leaving matched openings for the clasp to be inserted. With a gentle click the buckle was locked. Mark looked at himself in the hallway mirror. "Fits perfect, looks good."

"Your weapons and uniforms will be delivered after they're all manufactured. But there's going to be one difference."

"And that is?"

Tom smiled. "Well, seeing as how you're a bit on the famous side we're concerned that the standard cocoon glasses won't totally keep you unrecognized. When you're in the field you'll be wearing this." He handed Mark a piece of fabric. Mark unfurled it and saw a full head hood with holes only for the eyes. "That's a prototype, but your actual hood will be wired with a full audio feed and automatic network accessibility, which are accessed by controls on the side of the hood. The eyeholes will actually be framed so you can put in different special lenses. You'll be shown how to work it all when it's assembled for you."

Mark set the mask and belt back in the box. "I think you forgot something."

"What's that?"

"The long scalloped black cape, pointed ears, a bat on the chest…"

**CHAPTER 50**
**OCTOBER 3, 2011**
**THE FIRST TWO PUZZLE PIECES**

Most everyone had gone home, and Tom Michelson settled at his desk at the end of another long day. Staying late was normal. He got more work accomplished without all the interruptions. The Task Force administrative work seemed to never end. There were reports and evaluations from everyone in tactical operations, paperwork from the support staff in the Division. Then there was the multitude of relayed intelligence to review. It alone consisted of information from confidential informants on the street all the way up to relayed intelligence from other Federal Departments. He studied them all and made notes on each, should any of them need to be assigned to the Task Force for implementation. Michelson's people were the absolute best-of-the-best, and it was his job to keep them that way. He made sure they were in constant training mode, in the best possible physical condition they could be in, and always prepared at a moment's notice. It was a job one hated to love, or perhaps loved to hate depending on the day of the week.

In the months since Mark Jason accepted the position with the Task Force, he had concentrated heavily on department operations. He found it normal for the most part and a bit on the mundane side. *Lots of paperwork, the government can't survive without lots and lots of paperwork,* he'd thought more than once. Michelson had told him to take everything nice and slow, take it all in, and observe. That was exactly what he did. For the first few weeks he met on a regular basis with the other team members and attended all meetings they held, whether it be full staff or with just a few. He talked, asked questions, discussed assignment duties, and learned of the team's history within the Task Force Division. The most interesting learning opportunities were the team member's individual specialties. Certainly, they were special operatives, but he was learning quickly just how specialized they were. Mark followed along on a few minor assignments, just to see how they operated in the field. He was fascinated by the superior technology, their knowledge, and what seemed to be an innate intuitiveness that most people would never know. Michelson knew what he was going through and approved of every step mark took in the process. He was waiting until the right time to let him take over.

One of the Lab Technicians walked into Michelson's office, not bothering to knock. "Test results on the knife," she said in a matter-of-fact manner and placed a folder in front of Michelson on his desk. He removed his reading glasses and stared at the woman. She turned and left without another word as he set down the paperwork he'd been working on, opened the file folder and put his glasses back on. He thought, *Let's see what had to be delivered now instead of in the morning.* He began to read the report. His eyes widened. He punched a speed dial number on his desk phone. "Good, Hunter, you're still here. Please come to my office."

Out of breath from her fast trip through the building, she sat and read the report Tom handed her. Fortunately, Hunter knew how to speed-read and flew through the data in no time. Her mouth fell open slightly and looked up at Michelson. "The Biblical Bomber? They sure? At that retirement party we had a while back, for who, Oscar, he said that was the ONE case we never solved."

"With the little we know about this 'Biblical Bomber' after four years? We're as sure as anyone can be," Michelson said. Standing, he took off his glasses and leaned forward on the desk. "Hunter, the only physical evidence of him is from an event from two years ago. A bus bombing. Proteus found fragments of bus metal with blood on them near the scene, but the DNA matched no one on file anywhere. He's more like a legend or myth than a real person if you believe the stories on the street. Undercover agents from other agencies have heard about this 'Biblical Bomber,' but no trail ever led anywhere. The blood on this knife is the first lead we've had since then. Two years later we finally recovered a second piece of evidence." Michelson pointed at the folder, "Next page."

Hunter turned the page in the file. "A Richmond undercover officer apparently infiltrated an unknown gang forming in the city. He had time to record a few notes about what he saw before he disposed of the bag, which contained some medical items, including a used bandage, and visual verification of Marshall's gun. The bandage had clean DNA, epithelial on them. The undercover was later found dead, shot in the left eye." Hunter looked up. "Oh, my, God, the same as Marshall." She continued to read, "The DNA on the bandage matches the DNA on Spy's recovered knife." Hunter asked, "Why can't the DNA lead us to him then?"

"Hunter, it looks like this 'Bomber' has never been arrested or caught or anything. Not even a doctor's visit we can find. No fingerprints on file. Not in any database. It's like he only exists when something's blown up, or now when an undercover cop's body is found. Not even sure if this DNA match actually tells us anything."

Hunter read a little further. "Okay, well, this says we're looking for someone with a knife injury."

"This knife incident was almost six months ago. This guy could be fully healed by now with little more than a scar!"

Michelson reached at the base of his desk lamp, picked up the black cocoon glasses that rested there. It was the pair with one bullet hole in the left eye. He also picked up a small plastic bag that contained a folded piece of paper. He handed both items to Hunter. A long exhale escaped from his lungs. "Okay, it's time. Go talk to Jason. Tell him about his predecessor. Tell him everything we have on that mission, and what we have on this 'Biblical Bomber,' whoever the hell he really is. At least DNA gives us the sex of the perp, so we've eliminated half the people in the area. Tell him to look at everything we have, to see if there's any way in hell he can figure out who this ass-wipe is. Ask him if he's ready for justice. Ask him to finish Spy's last mission."

**CHAPTER 51**
**OCTOBER 3, 2011**
**A TALE OF TWO SPIES**

Mark Jason worked at his desk in the Task Force Division Office in Washington, D.C. The database setup he'd asked for was not only exactly what he needed but had more bells and whistles than he'd requested and hadn't yet had time to figure out. The computers not only gave him access to TF but to his Jason Enterprises office in Richmond, Virginia.

In the Task Force building, the actual Field Team Agents' offices were considerably larger than a standard office. The reason, he'd learned, was based on their individual specialties. Some simply needed more room than others, more like unique workshops and laboratories. Jason's office was slightly larger than the average-size office, big enough for his desk, computers, and conference table with chairs. There were flat-screen monitors on the walls, a refreshment area, plus a comfortable sitting area like his Jason Enterprises office back home. The one device he liked best was the giant integrated touch screen wall-mounted computer.

He was extremely impressed with Seeker's office and all the treasures and secrets it held within. He visited that office more often than necessary just to study the rare collectables from around the world. There were shelves upon shelves of items like golden idols from South American excavations, ivory carvings from the Far East, gifts he'd received from African tribes, and so on. It was a veritable museum all its own. Mark was impressed with Seeker's work, his adventurous nature, and his vast amount of knowledge. The decor reflected a long career as a Task Force agent.

He was reading through some of Task Force's prior assignments, "light reading" as he liked to call it. A knock on the door brought his history lesson to a stop. "Come on in, Hunter." He knew it was her by a subtle but distinctive rapping pattern that he'd learned.

Hunter crinkled her eyes and wondered how he always knew it was her. She opened the door and went inside. Pointing at the door, she started to say, "How did you know—" but was cut off by Mark.

"Pays to know these things, don't worry about it," he said with a sheepish grin. "What can I do for you, Mae-Lei?"

This was the first time he'd seen her dressed in anything besides their black uniform. She wore a light blue blouse, navy blue slacks with black flats, and no jewelry. Her waist-length black hair was hanging free over her shoulders. She sat in one of the two chairs across the desk from Jason and crossed her legs. "So, Mark, all settled in?" Her question came out softer, almost not wanting to hear his answer.

He picked up on her shy tone and leaned back in his chair, "Yeah, pretty much." He stared at her, trying to read her expression. "So, seems to me like you've done this before. Train a new agent to join the field team."

Hunter looked down at her lap, "A couple times. Harri is the third Proteus I've known, and by far the youngest, she just turned thirty. And I'm aware of five 'Hunters' before me." She looked up, "But as far as I know, there's only been one Seeker."

"Interesting, I hadn't found anything in the team logs to indicate that."

Pointing a carefully manicured finger at him, "And you," she finished, "are only the second team leader, the second Spy."

"Indeed? I'll try to not have you welcome a third any time soon then."

Hunter smiled, "I'd appreciate that. But that's sort of why I'm here. Do you have a little time?" Again, Hunter felt slightly awkward and uncomfortable. She knew Mark Jason was picking up on the vibes.

Mark looked at his watch, "Well, I did want to be back home this evening. Feel like taking a drive down the interstate? If you've got no other plans, that is."

"I hear you have a nice house down there, and I always keep a travel bag packed."

"Not a surprise at all," he said emphatically as he stood. He retrieved his cell phone from his pocket and dialed his wife. "Jan, hon! Yeah, doing fine, wrapping up here in D.C. shortly and heading home. Would you mind asking Grace to set another place for dinner and prepare one of the guest rooms? Bringing a coworker to dine and stay the weekend. Thanks, see you in a couple hours. I love you, too. Bye." He hung up and returned his phone to its pocket.

Hunter looked at him, eyebrows raised. "Wow, that went well. Your wife gonna be upset when you show up with me?"

"Hardly," Jason replied. "This is the nature of being an international businessman. Let's go, Peppermint Patti."

All Hunter could do was look at him quizzically.

◆

Half an hour later they were traveling south on Interstate 95 to Richmond. The top was down on the Mercedes, so Mei-Lea tied her hair in a ponytail and tucked it inside the back of her shirt so it wouldn't fly all over the place. The weather was perfect for traveling with the car top down. "The autumn air, it's invigorating, I like it." She spoke louder than normal, the wind drowning out some of the conversation. "Well, I guess it's story time," she said at last.

Mark nodded. "Been waitin' on it, Mei-Lea. Ready any time you are."

She stared at him with a perplexed look. *He's always one step ahead,* she thought. "It's about your, well, about the first Spy."

Her voice cracked at the end of her sentence, and Mark realized there was a connection between her and the first Spy agent. His mind went into full throttle. "Was there a romance?" he asked.

"Well, I guess I should start by saying that he and I had a relationship." She looked at him for a reaction. He simply looked at her. *He knew,* she thought. *How did he already know?* She continued, "We worked several missions together over a few years. There was one where he and I had to play a married couple, knowing that every room we were in had cameras. So, we had to act like, well, a married couple doing, you know, married couple stuff." Hunter realized she was rambling and stopped herself.

"And the chemistry mixed perfectly, and you couldn't turn it off," Mark concluded.

"Exactly," she admitted. Her emotions were turning heavy. "We behaved professionally at the office and out in the field, well, unless undercover work required it, you know; but on our time off, that was different."

"Yeah, I kinda figured," Marked glanced over with a knowing smile. "What was his name, if I may ask?"

"Marshall. Marshall Gray. Recognize it?"

Mark nodded his head. "Yeah, been seeing his name in the various TF reports over the past several weeks."

"So anyway, a year ago he mentioned he wanted to retire, after a career in the military then ten years with the Task Force. Tom revealed your name to Marshall, and me, and the team, as Marshall's potential replacement. Tom said you both were in equal contention for the position when the Task Force was developed. Marshall was overly impressed that you were in great shape for a man nearly 40 years old."

"I'll try not to take that personally," Mark smiled.

She smiled back. "So, Marshall read your file and asked Tom why you weren't picked over him in the first place. Tom never answered, probably a top secret in the decision-making process.

But Marshall liked what he read and said you should definitely be contacted."

"So, consider me 'contacted'."

Mae-Lei smiled momentarily before continuing. "He was killed on what should have been a routine assignment." She shook her head, squeezing lightly at her eyelids with the edge of her thumb and forefinger. "I still can't believe he's gone."

"What was the assignment?"

"There were a couple of bombings in your town, Richmond. There was a car in a residential neighborhood, and an ambulance in a hospital lot, both the same day. Forensics, well, nobody ever figured out what kind of bomb it was or who the guy was. It was like both spontaneously exploded. The car bombing killed a Senator's family, which is how the Task Force got the order.

"Tom assigned the case to Marshall, and he took it by himself. When he realized he was in over his head he called for backup, but it was too late. Nothing I read in the post-investigation file indicated any significant danger of terrorism or such, which is probably why he took it alone. Well, he called me on the way to his first investigation site to let me know he was going to be late for, uh, our evening off. He said it was an easy job, just track and report. But I knew him better than that, so I got suited up and had tactical forward his GPS coordinates to my car's system, and I went out to follow him. When his car's signal stopped moving, I went in to assist." Mae-Lei let out a long sigh.

"Keep going, you're doing okay."

"So, I got there right after the bus exploded. My God, there were body parts all over the place, fire and smoke, and the stench. Then I heard a gunshot from behind the building, the Arts Center. I went back around and found him, just lying there." She reached for the sunglasses from her jacket pocket. "These were his," she said sadly, showing Mark the cocoon glasses with the bullet hole in the left lens. "The last thing he saw." Tears started to flow, and Mae-Lei tried hard to pull herself together.

They drove in silence for a minute or two.

"Was the killer ever caught?"

Mae-Lei looked out her side of the open car for a moment, and wiped tears away with both hands. "No. The only thing I found was Marshall's knife. Had enough blood on it to possibly identify the killer. It's Richmond's 'Biblical Bomber.' The other thing is this note found on the body of an undercover agent who may have infiltrated his gang, but it doesn't fit the pattern."

"What note?"

"Tom signed this out to me. It's a note in an evidence bag." It had been unfolded and sealed so it could easily be read. She held it securely in the windy open-top car, and read aloud, "'As it is said, third time's the charm. But still you tried to stay, by leaving your Avatar behind to torment me. I killed him, and you sent another. I will not stop until they are all dead and you can never come back.'"

"Sounds like a line from a bad movie."

"It's hand-written, though. Everything about the under-cover's death doesn't match the pattern of The Biblical Bomber, despite the under cover's recorded report."

"What 'under-cover's' report?"

"A street cop found himself invited, along with a bunch of other street-wise guys, to join a mystery gang. He found himself taken to a place where he treated one of the gang leaders for an infected cut. Under the pretense of disposing of blood and medical items, he gave a quick description of the gang and found Marshall's gun before dropping the bag in the trash. It was the last thing he ever did."

"So then, how do you know this 'Bomber' is who you're looking for?"

"We don't." She turned to him, taking off her glasses. She pointed at him. "But maybe The Spy can."

**CHAPTER 52**
**OCTOBER 4, 2011**
**VERY GOOD BEDFELLOWS**

*POP! The champagne cork flew out of the bottle and bounced off the bedroom dresser, then ricocheted off the mirror frame. "Hum, missed it by 'THAT MUCH'," he said, sounding badly like Maxwell Smart.*

*Mei-Lea smiled and giggled at the same time. There was the lovely feeling of too much bubbly already, with much more to come. She rolled from her side onto her back. The bed sheet fell off as she moved. Her petite breasts and erect nipples were revealed, and her long black hair flowed about her shoulders like a living cloak. She grasped her wine glass and rolled forward to present it for a refill.*

*Marshall sat beside her on the bed. The sheet still covered him below the waist, although one bare knee was exposed. He filled her glass halfway then did the same for his. "A toast," he said, raising his glass, "to the newly-engaged couple."*

*She sat up as steady as she could after already emptying nearly two bottles between them, and lightly clinked her glass with his. The last part of her sheet fell free, revealing everything. "To the best undercover couple ever!" she toasted back.*

*They drank, and both sighed almost simultaneously. His eyes grazed over her body. "You look magnificent wearing only a diamond ring," he grinned.*

*"You look even more magnificent," she slurred slightly, "or would if you didn't have that sheet in the way." She winked. She laid back, not spilling a drop as she did. "Oh, my, God, I never would have believed that after the Paris job we'd be like this again, but FOR REAL!" She lifted her hand up over her face to look at the sparkling jewel on her ring finger. "Just too bad I can't wear this at work."*

*Rolling over onto his elbows they were nearly face-to-face, demonstrating his own incredible prowess by keeping his drink from spilling. "Do you really think anyone at Task Force doesn't already know or suspect?"*

*Setting her glass on the bedside table, "Well, there's that analyst on the third floor who always watches me when I walk by," she said with a daring, teasing smile.*

*Also setting his glass down, Marshall teased, "When you're in uniform, EVERYONE watches you when you walk by!" His price was a solid punch in the arm from his new fiancé. "Hey, do that again; that made your hair fly around like a cape!" That got him a playful slap in the same spot.*

*She closed her eyes and said, "We gotta work on the wedding list, the location, my dress."*

*"Hum, first time I'll see you in anything white, besides your undies, that is."*

*She felt him move his body on top of hers. His well-muscled legs parted hers, and she responded by letting him move her wherever he wanted. She opened her eyes slightly to take in the face of the man she wanted more than anyone in the world.*

*She saw his face, dirt-smudged, wearing his regulation black cocoon glasses. His left lens had a bullet hole in the middle, and blood was streaming down his cheek and onto her face...*

◆

Mae-Lei sat up in the bed screaming. Moments later the bedroom door swung open, and the light was flicked on. Mark stood there with a weapon in hand, instinctively. Mark and Jan Jason were awakened by her cries. Mark ran in, once he realized there was no intruder, and Jan raced in on his heels. Angela arrived at the door moments later. Jan sat on the bed and wrapped her arms around Mae-Lei. Mark knelt and held her hands. "Mae-Lei," Jan said softly, "it was a dream, just a dream. You're safe. What was it?"

After a moment Mae-Lei said quietly, "My fiancé. He was Spy before Mark." Jan looked at Mark, who gave a slight head shake with eyes closed to indicate her fiancé was no longer alive. Jan hugged her tighter.

Mark said to her in a powerful whisper, "We will get him. Spy is going to finish his mission. That's a promise."

Through the tears, Mae-Lei looked up at Mark. Her eyes widened. In all the months she'd worked with him in training, she had seen him express a full range of emotions and had grown to like him.

But what she saw in his eyes now was an expression she never saw before.

His gaze filled her with terror, and, for the first time, hope.

**CHAPTER 53**
**OCTOBER 15, 2011**
**SECOND ENCOUNTER**

Friday evening found Sarge Brunson at his usual stool in the Recovery Room bar. "Roger Dodger'''" couldn't join him because of rare after-hours work commitments. Sarge settled in without him for a couple rounds before he headed home. He never admitted it, and no one knew his little secret, but when the rough-and-tumble Sarge returned home at night, his Persian cat settled in his lap and purred all evening. The two softies were content with each other's company in his armchair while they nodded off to reruns of M*A*S*H on the living room TV.

Al made his normal rounds from one end of the expansive bar to the other. Vets were usually seated in pairs or trios, and talked about the weather, baseball, or politics. Whatever the topic of the evening suited everyone the best.

Sarge noticed "That Lady Sergeant", as he referred to her, in the far corner. He'd lost a bar bet with her about six months before and had to pay her tab for a month. She was talking with another guy he'd seen in the bar occasionally, a non-com. Sarge claimed he could tell them apart just by smell and asserted "they smelled like they'd never seen combat".

His musings didn't turn off his own senses, however. A slap on his shoulder caused him to spin on his barstool and reflexively swing his massive fist up in defense. The hand that stopped his juggernaut attack was slightly smaller than his own, but surprisingly much stronger. Mark Jason released his grip on Sarge's hand once he felt the momentum fully stop. "Not bad for an old man," Mark smiled as he took the stool to Sarge's left. Immediately Al approached Mark with a drink already prepared: Scotch, neat.

"Didn't know you were a regular, sir," Sarge said, slightly nodding at the drink in front of Mark.

"Not so much a regular," Mark shrugged, "as a frequent stop-inner. I'd heard about this place from my teammates while I was still overseas. So, when I came home, I stopped by. Al here," pointing at the bartender, "bet me the moment I sat down that he knew exactly what my favorite drink was. Never saw him before, mind you. So, I said, 'Fine'."

Al came into the conversation. "Aye, you did that, sir," he said with a stolid straight face. Al pointed at Mark and said to Sarge, "He decided to stake that if I was wrong, he'd have free drinks in here from then on. But if I were right, I'd serve a house-round on him whenever he walked in the door."

Sarge looked around the bar at the customers at the tables and in booths. He didn't notice any extra drink glasses being paraded out by the cute waitresses Al had on staff. He turned back to Al. "And?"

"The honest men that we are, he lost. Haven't paid for a drink here in what, eight years?" Mark answered.

"Almost nine," Al said with a big smile. He explained to Sarge, "The Jason family's been well known in the area's catering circles, even our little hole in the wall, and they've had a fairly consistent set of menus for their events. We're sometimes called on to supply the open-bar supplies at social events. Never met Mark here before that day, but I knew what he liked based on his family's catering records. Had no idea he'd upped his pallet while overseas. Learned my lesson quite fast with him."

"He's never made even a game bet with me since," Mark said, his eyebrows going up and down a couple times in good humor.

"Don't get in a poker game with him, either," Al said to Sarge. "Best game face I ever saw. Gents, I have rounds to make and a break to take, if you need anything just give TJ a yell. TJ!" he called across the bar to the tall, short-haired brunette in the tight Navy T-shirt and white shorty-shorts. "Take care of my guys here for a bit."

"Copy that, Al," she saluted back. She finished delivering her order to the Lady Sergeant then entered the bar area to be at Mark and Sarge's call. Al washed his hands in the sink behind the bar near the two men, dried them with his towel and tossed it back over his shoulder as he left the bar area to the offices in the back.

They were relatively alone at the bar but kept their voices down. "So," said Mark, "how's the new job going?"

"All due respect, sir, but that line is worse than 'how's the weather?'."

Mark smiled and motioned at TJ for a second one for himself. "Just wanted to let you know I'll be out of the office for a few days. No, you can't ask why or where I'm going. Just a private matter." TJ delivered their drinks and left. Both men noticed the bar door opened and a man entered. He stepped quietly to the far end of the bar, hands shoved in his pockets and head down. He walked past several groups of men and sat on the last barstool. Mark watched as Sarge secretly eyed the man. "Know him?" Mark whispered without looking up from his drink.

Sarge whispered back, "Nope. Comes in on occasion. Figure he's in his early 20's. Fresh facial scar consistent with combat blade injury. Looks like he's got PTSD but doesn't completely act it. Probably fresh out, just getting his civvy legs back. But I dunno, got a funny feelin' about him."

"TJ," Mark said to the brunette, just as Al returned to the bar, "whatever our new friend over there is having, it's on me."

"You got it, MJ," she said with a charming grin, and strode over to take the new customer's order.

Sarge turned to face Mark. "'TJ'? 'MJ'? What's the deal here?"

"That's my cousin, Tamra Jason. Dad's brother's little girl."

"'Little' you say? Didn't know you had Hollywood stars in your family, sir."

Mark rose from his seat to leave and bent slightly forward so he was face to face with Sarge. "Bit of advice don't let appearances fool you. When she said she was taking a job here, I taught her everything she knows about Martial Arts. She can drop you and you'd never see it coming."

"Does every woman you know have the talent to put me on the floor?" he asked with wide eyes. Sarge stared at TJ, attempting to envision her karate chopping someone. "Must make the bouncer's job easier when it gets busy here late at night."

"Ah, Sarge, she IS the bouncer."

**CHAPTER 54**
**OCTOBER 29, 2011, 7 A.M.**
**MEETING OF THE TASK FORCE**

"Sorry for calling everyone in on a Saturday morning," Mark Jason, the new "Spy" and new team leader, said as the Task Force team members settled themselves into chairs in his office at Task Force Command. "Proteus will be joining us later. She's on a short detail assignment," he announced. "This may take a little while, so everyone get comfortable."

The team was told to dress in civilian clothes rather than their black field uniforms. The IT Department had set up four computer stations on the conference table prior to the meeting, interfacing with the pre-wired connections to the 65" wall mounted touch screen computer. The IT geeks had a field day with all the latest technologies, secret or otherwise, and made sure Mark Jason, and the other Agents had whatever they needed at their disposal. The Federal Government saw to it they had instant gateways to normally closed accesses, such as DMVs, banks, cellular service, and countless other places where tracking capabilities were needed.

The agents chatted amongst themselves while a small wait staff from the Task Force commissary brought in drinks and various pastry foods and fruits. "Apparently we're not the only ones working today," Calvin said under his breath.

"Heard that, Geffers," Mark said as he smiled and looked up from his notes. "Trust me, it's important."

The door to Mark's office flew open, and Proteus stood there decked out in full uniform and out of breath. Mark couldn't help but smile. She was the smallest team member and the semi-auto on her hip made her look like she could tip over at any time. "Sorry I'm late, guys. That was a killer all-night assignment. Just finished debrief in Admin." She closed the door and flopped into a chair, totally spent.

"Now that our last team member is here, more or less, let's get started." Mark's statement elicited smiles from the team members. "I was recently asked to solve the murder of my predecessor." His elbows rested on the table, hands together in a prayer-like posture on his chin. He intentionally spoke slow and methodical. "As you remember, Marshall Gray died the same night as the bus bombing at the Jefferson Davis Arts Center. Extensive forensic studies by the police, FBI and Task Force could find no explosive device in the bus remains. A very strange mystery. Earlier in the day an ambulance exploded as did a passenger vehicle, same lack of explosive detonator evidence. The only thing to tie the three together was an odd, crumpled note found at each scene, far enough away that it didn't burn: a random Biblical quotation."

"We know that," said Calvin. "As everyone remembers, the media never got wind of the note that Hunter found on Marshall's body though, or of Marshall's murder. The note was folded and neatly tucked under his buckle, instead of just crumpled and dropped somewhere at the scene. Actually, Task Force Division was requested to assist in similar bombings two and four years ago."

"Technically, the field team…us…wasn't involved in any of those investigations," said Mae-Lei. "The investigative division of the Task Force was assigned to assist but could never deduce who was behind them all. But, Proteus' first solo job, as a 'trial-by-fire' test, was to investigate the last bombing two years ago, and found some blood samples and evidence that were inconsistent with the rest of the scene."

"Yes," said Mark, "the path of shrapnel led off in a distinct trail away from the scene. Then there was this," he said as he took a bagged knife and held it up, "Gray's knife that Mae-Lei found imbedded and hidden in a tree at his murder scene. DNA testing confirmed that the blood and tissue residue on the knife was the same as the shrapnel two years ago, so it's the same person. Then, an undercover cop luckily infiltrated a gang being formed by this 'Biblical Bomber', confirmed discovery of Marshall's missing weapon, and managed to pass on more DNA samples. We lost the cop, sadly, but we were able to assume confirmation that this Bomber is assembling another gang for who knows what purpose." Jason turned his notes pages. "The cop's bag was recovered from a city garbage truck via GPS tracker in the bag, but by the time it was recovered the truck had already made several other stops, so we don't know which of a few dozen locations it originated."

"So," added Mae-Lei, "we have three separate DNA confirmations we're dealing with the same person. This 'Biblical Bomber' serial killer murdered dozens of people over the past five years, including Marshall and an undercover. But we don't know who this 'Bomber' really is."

Jason sat back in his chair and crossed his arms. "By the time we leave here today, we will."

## CHAPTER 55
## OCTOBER 29, 2011, 7:52 A.M.
## ASSEMBLING THE PUZZLE

"Note the pattern, I've studied it a good bit," Mark said. "A sedan, an ambulance, and a bus. Same cycle every two years, and always just those three."

At one of the computers on the conference table, Proteus said, "Well, I'd look at it this way. Force profilers have always said we're dealing with a young man with a grudge or something to prove. But there was no other specific description to identify him. This is no different than creating an alien face on an actor for a movie. We start at the beginning literally at face value."

Mae-Lei joined in from another terminal. After she opened her desktop file, "So it all began four years ago with a car exploding outside Richmond. The victims were a reverend and his wife. They left behind three teenage children: two boys and a girl."

"Hey, that's interesting," Proteus noted.

"What's interesting?" Mark asked.

"Three bombings every two years. There were two victims that left behind three children in the first bombing. Repetition of two and three."

"Interesting indeed!" Calvin agreed. "What do we have on the children?"

Proteus answered, "David is the eldest. Age 18 at the time the parents died. Henri, pronounced the French version, 'on-re' is the middle, was 17. Elise, also pronounced the French version, 'a-leese', the youngest, was 16."

Mae-Lei said, "'David', 'Henri', and 'Elise'? The eldest has an Anglican name, the other two have French? So was David born to a different mother?"

"'David' is spelled the same in English as it is in French," Calvin amended, "but pronounced 'Dah-veed'."

"No," said Proteus. "Records show that the Reverend DeVeaux was married only once, to Abigail Schuster."

"OK, so our very first victim of 'Mr. Biblical' was the reverend and his wife. There is absolutely nothing else on this serial killer prior to the 2007 events?" Mark prodded.

"No, sir. No patterns of violence match, no signatory notes."

"Proteus, get details on the kids," Jason instructed. "Calvin, find out if the reverend ever traveled anywhere, could he have made an enemy somewhere whether he knew it or not. Some religious crazy perhaps. Mae-Lei, what kind of person could we be looking for? Research the cars and ambulances and buses. What is the connection, why these three types of vehicles each time?"

Jason sat back at his computer station at the conference table and stared at the note in the evidence bag. "What's meant by an 'Avatar'?" he thought. "And 'third time.' Third bombing? Third year? He wouldn't mean the undercover. An Avatar is a symbol, a representation." He looked at his team working at the conference table and his eyes stopped at Proteus. "She's in uniform. That would be a symbol, an Avatar, someone in a uniform." He looked up at Mae-Lei, who was busily doing research on her computer. "He wrote that he killed the 'first Avatar,' then accused him of sending a second. He killed Marshall, then Marshall was found by Mae-Lei." Mark paused to tie it together before concluding. "Marshall is the first Avatar, and Mae-Lei is the next Avatar."

She looked up first. "What?"

"According to your own report, you found the last note under his buckle. From his note found on the undercover agent's body, he's doing these bombings to stop someone, he thinks he's finally succeeded, and then Marshall shows up in his uniform to stop him. Mr. Bomber manages to kill him, tries to get away, but he's not able to. So, he sees you in a matching uniform when you arrive at Marshall's body. He was the first Avatar, and you're the second."

"You're assuming he even saw me."

"True. But logical, based on the language."

"But Avatar for what?"

"Research on the children is complete," Proteus interrupted. She activated a relay command on her computer display and took over the plasma screen on the wall. She stood next to the screen, and using a laser pointer, she aimed it at the various children as she spoke. "David, age 18 at the time of the bombing that killed their parents. School records show he had high grades and aptitude in science and chemistry. Henri, age 17 at the time, graduated with high grades in engineering a year later. Elise, age 16, was treated as special needs throughout school. Never talked much, never paid attention in school, according to the teachers. Finally, at the mother's request she was taken out of public school and went into home-schooling. She never graduated high school or got a GED."

She moved the pointer to an icon on the screen, and the information page shifted. "Each of the children received one-third of the DeVeaux estate at their eighteenth birthdays. Elise turned eighteen this past spring. David, however, got the courts to grant him custodial control over her affairs due to her limited abilities. Their attorney took care of all the inheritance taxes, but otherwise there's been no recorded activity since the last payment was delivered."

Mark mused, "Easy enough to drop out of sight, provided there was enough. And interesting that her birthday was only days before the first bombing of this year's cycle by 'Mr. Bomber'."

"One out of three-hundred-sixty-five days," said Proteus. "I chalk it up to coincidence."

"So noted. Anything else?"

"Neither David nor Henri went on to college. It appears that after the sister received her inheritance, they all dropped off the grid, sir."

"We got any pictures of these kids?"

"No, sir. Figured obviously there would at least be pictures in the high school yearbooks, but none of the children ever appeared in their class listings. None of them have social media pages that I can find."

"Interesting. Anyone else have anything yet?"

"I'd say yes, in that I have a great big goose egg," Calvin reported. "This reverend, as far as I can tell, never left the city for any reason. I went so far as to run searches on his congregation, the cleanest bunch of sheep I've ever seen. Of course, he had a small church so not that many people to check. No one I could find who had any beef with the reverend. In fact, what I did find was a lot of social network commentary on how wonderful his sermons were, how much people felt moved by his words. A pillar of his community, loved by all. Wife Abigail, seen as totally devoted to her husband and children, always volunteered to help at their church. She was also very protective of their children."

"Any other reason why the kids would just disappear after the last inheritance payment?" Jason asked.

"It would make sense that they would want to disappear, in case they thought they were in any danger from whoever killed their parents," said Proteus.

"That makes sense," said Mae-Lei. "I have an idea. Whoever this is has a thing for 'twos and threes', as Proteus noted. Three vehicle bombings every two years. Nothing in this pattern in the odd years. And in his new note, complains about a second Avatar, he won't rest until he's killed them all. He killed Marshall, he's seen me, that's two. If we are indeed his 'Avatars'. He may be looking to kill me and possibly one other."

Mark sat back; arms crossed. "Is that the key? Is it really that simple? This 'Biblical Bomber' had a 'tell' all along that everyone missed. Everything was combined in some series or sets of two-

and-three. No wonder it was missed, everyone was overthinking this damn thing. But how does this help us now?"

"Still working on that, sir," Mae-Lei said. "But I do have this: I went back in the online archives to the stories following that very first bombing, the one that killed the DeVeauxs. I found one article from a few months ago that mentioned the ambulance that was blown up this year was the same one that had been sent to the car bombing at the restaurant earlier, the one that killed the Senator's family. So, on a pure hunch I checked with the log records of the prior two years, both those ambulances also were dispatched to their respective earlier car explosions. But the drivers for both years had no connection to the DeVeaux family. Since I found that connection to the ambulances, I figured there may be some other strange relationship between the buses and the others. I found several pictures in an article on the DeVeaux funeral, including this one." She clicked her own screen command, and her display took over the touchscreen. "There in the background of this newspaper article on the DeVeaux funeral, on the bus, a banner saying, 'We love you, Mr. & Mrs. DeVeaux'. I was able to get the bus number from the photograph. That was the bus blown up that night."

Mae-Lei went up to the screen, put her hands on her hips. "So, this Mr. Bomber killed the DeVeauxs, then destroyed the ambulance sent to render aid, then blew up the bus that ferried their friends or parishioners. It was all about killing the parents and anyone who tried to help them, maybe even admired or followed them."

"And still we don't know anything about why they were targeted?" said Mark. The team members could only just shake their heads "no". He cupped his chin with his thumb and forefinger and stared at the screen. The team members took their seats again. All fell quiet in thought.

"What if," Proteus offered, "what if what we're looking for isn't online? What if the answer isn't in a database, but maybe an old newspaper or magazine or other publication?"

"Makes sense," said Calvin. "Most newspapers and publications are years from getting all their decades' worth of copies digitized and posted online."

"Proteus, off to Richmond. Check the libraries. If this all started with the killing of Father DeVeaux, then find out if there's anything in the papers or such about our Reverend that would have made someone develop a grudge. One that festered for years until it was time to let it all out."

◆

They went to their individual offices to continue research, and Proteus got a jet-copter lift to Richmond to search print archives. Hours passed.

Mark Jason sat at his desk and activated his primary computer screen from its sleep mode after completing another database search on the second terminal. Before he could type anything Mae-Lei came in without knocking. "Got Proteus on the phone, boss."

He motioned for her to come in.

She pressed an icon on the lower left corner on the touch screen and Proteus' image filled the display. "Boss, you won't believe this. I found birth records of Henri DeVeaux in Richmond, Virginia, and a birth record for a sister named Elise. There is no birth record of a boy named David DeVeaux. However, the DeVeaux family adopted a boy named David when he lost his parents in a bus explosion."

Mark sat up straight. "Bus explosion?"

"You heard right. David was five years old, was the only survivor of a bus explosion in downtown Richmond. He was found with his dead parents on top of him, a total miracle that he survived. Reverend DeVeaux learned that he was the only survivor, and when no family came forward to claim David, he took him under his wing to give him a home. David came with a huge trust fund."

"How much?" asked Mae-Lei.

"Several million dollars," said Proteus. "The Reverend was granted three million cash immediately, and the rest went into a trust, payable when David turned 18."

"'Three' again," Mae-Lei said under her breath.

Jason asked, "So the bus explosion that killed David's parents, what was the cause?"

"It was a terrorist," said Proteus. "According to police records the guy wanted two million dollars or he'd blow up the bus. Then when police charged the bus, he blew it up. Incredibly he escaped just as the bus exploded."

"And another 'two'," Mae-Lei added.

"No idea of the terrorist's name?"

"No, sir," said Proteus. "But a police photographer did get a zoom image of the guy from a distance. The picture was never released to the media but was kept in local police files." She punched a couple keys on her end and a photograph filled the left half of the screen.

"Oh, shit!" said Calvin from the doorway. "That's Reverend DeVeaux!"

"What?" said Mark. "Are you sure?"

"Absolutely!" Calvin took control of a keyboard to access his files and put a second picture on the screen. It was a picture of Reverend DeVeaux that one of his parishioners had taken during a church service and posted to his social network page.

"'Oh, shit' is right," said Jason. Despite the age of the 1993 bombing picture and the distant digital image there was no doubt, the bus bomber was Father DeVeaux. Check DeVeaux's finances before and after David's adoption."

There was a flurry of keystrokes both beside him and from Proteus on the terminal screen. Geffers piped up first. "Let's hear it for banks, being more thorough about digitizing older records for their archives. DeVeaux was on the verge of bankruptcy in 1993, about to lose his house and his church, an independent Christian church that followed the Episcopalian doctrine. Suddenly he got three million dollars and just as suddenly his house was paid off and his church was solvent again."

"Okay," said Mark as he stepped to his private wet bar. He poured himself a glass of iced water. "Father DeVeaux took a bus hostage, for money, somehow screwed everything and blew up the bus and who knows how many people on it. Then he adopts the sole survivor of that hijacking, and the kid turns out to have a lot of money coming with him. Then, the good reverend takes that money to improve his own lot in life, as he was trying to do with the hijacking. But no one knew it was him, and he died a respected man. Nearly eighteen years later we discover what he really was…a killer." Mark suddenly stopped, turned to his team. "That's it!"

Everybody replied in unison, "What?"

"It's so obvious! If we figured out who Father DeVeaux really was, why couldn't David? How ridiculous would it be for David to be the one who killed his adoptive daddy, if he figured he was the one who killed his real parents? And what if something in his life caused him to snap in 2007 and kill his parents?"

"There's so much we don't know about their private life," said Mae-Lei. "Practically nothing, actually."

"But a hidden life at home," Mark continued. "Your own reports indicate that the children went to school then home, no social life. He kept a tight leash on his family."

Mae-Lei continued with Mark's logic. "What if this reverend was two-faced? What if everyone saw him publicly as this wonderful holy servant, but at home he ruled with an iron fist, letting his children out only as required by law to go to school, but otherwise controlling them completely inside the house? It would explain the lack of social records. And if David, if he somehow knew or realized that his adoptive father killed his parents, then he would naturally seek revenge. His education shows his aptitude in science, he could conceivably design a bomb that wouldn't be discovered by forensics investigators."

"Speaking of missing," said Calvin, "we still don't know where to start looking for them."

From the monitor, Proteus said, "Well, I was thinking about that on the trip down. No matter where they live, using cash or checks to pay for everything, they have to have utility accounts and such. But believe it or not there's no accounts with any of their names. So, they're operating under assumed names or someone else is making their payments."

"Payments," Mae-Lei interrupted. "It's not impossible that wherever they're living that they could have utility accounts under assumed names, or even under a company name, fictitious or not. Regular monthly payments would remain under the application's name, never changing. Is it possible that one of them could have slipped up, used a real name for a one-time transaction?"

"Like a mail order, or a package, or a registered letter," suggested Mark. "Folks, access all the Richmond delivery services' databases. Find something under any of their names."

Proteus worked on the monitor from Richmond, and Calvin and Mae-Lei worked on the computers while Mark let his mind try to find links to all the information. Finally, Calvin spoke up. "There was a package delivery to one 'Lisa Deever' a couple weeks ago."

Mark looked at him. "Phonetically, it's close to 'Elise DeVeaux'. You got an address?"

Calvin nodded. "Doing reverse search. See if I can verify the address to the name." He researched further. "According to the property tax rolls, the house is owned by one 'David Henry'!"

"Back search the delivery."

"Already got it, boss," said Calvin. "It was shipped from one of those television retail programs, it was a snow globe purchased across a toll-free number and payment was cash-on-delivery."

"Access the recording of the call," Mark ordered. "Just the information confirmation part at the end."

"How do you know there was one?" asked Proteus.

"There always is," said Mark.

A couple minutes passed. "Got it," said Calvin. "Playing now."

Over the office's stereo speakers, everyone heard the voice of a young woman, with an obvious speech impediment. "Muh' name ith Aileeth, uh--- Deevoeh--- addreth ith—"

"Stop!" said Jason. "The customer service rep heard 'Lisa Deever', I bet. But I heard it, 'Elise DeVeaux'. We have an address and confirmed sibling. We find David through her." Mark turned to the monitor.

"I found a car insurance policy," Proteus said from the screen, "still active under Reverend DeVeaux, even after all these years. The automobile policy for the family car paid out for the car's destruction in 2007, then another vehicle was added shortly after, a 2007 Red Hummer, followed by a 2007 gray Mercury."

"There had to be an ID presented along with proof of insurance when those vehicles were bought," said Mark. "Locate!"

Proteus was the first one to locate a digital scan of the driver's license provided at the time of purchase. She transferred the image to the main screen, then went to the screen herself to look closely.

"Report," Mark ordered.

Proteus looked at the image detail. "Oh, this is good, very good." She brought up a menu on the touch-screen's lower left corner and a couple finger stabs later the license image was increased to where the letters were each six inches high.

"Anytime, Harri," chided Mark, in a little jest.

"Working on it, boss," Proteus replied in little more than a whisper. "It would be easier with the original in front of me, but it looks like…"

The rest of the team waited quietly for the resident expert in deception and forgery to study the image silently, running her hands over the screen to move the image left and right and up and down.

"It's a fake. Good, but still a fake." She reduced the size of the image until the entire license was visible and filled nearly the entire screen. "The picture of the young man was digitally superimposed over top of another picture. At 1000 magnification there is an exceedingly small pixilation overlap to show that. The rest of the license is genuine, with only the birth year changed. Reverend DeVeaux's license was altered. I can't believe the car salesmen missed it."

"I know that face," Mark said, almost to himself.

"Well, if it was that good," said Mae-Lei, "maybe the salesmen didn't see that it was a fake or didn't know how to recognize a fake."

"At any rate," Proteus finished, "I think this could be David DeVeaux."

"And one more thing, remember," Mae-Lei interjected. "Our Mr. Bomber is sporting a knife scar, may be visible, may not."

"THAT'S IT!" Mark shouted. "Oh, hell, I've seen him!"

## CHAPTER 56
## OCTOBER 30, 2011, JUST BEFORE SUNSET
## A LITTLE GIRL TIME

Hunter brought her car to a stop in front of a small house in a mixed-use development within the city. She sat in her car, taking in the surroundings. Once the car was in park, the tactician in her began to develop scenarios in her head in case anyone showed up unexpectedly. She thought to herself, *Quaint little neighborhood, quiet, houses and businesses mixed, roads clear all the way around the house. The fence could be an obstacle, but the shrubs could actually help. Easy to surround.*

Hunter was dressed in her standard uniform, but with her gray Eisenhower jacket over top and the front unzipped. Her choice of a sidearm tonight was a Glock from her TF arsenal. Proteus, on the other hand, wore a black miniskirt that stopped just below her thighs and was slit almost to the hip on the left side. Strapped to her opposite thigh was a holster containing a custom .380 pocket pistol, undetectable from beneath her skirt. She'd requested the TF Procurement to supply her with a special-made little PT111, denoting it was very concealable for operations such as this. She wore a white blouse unbuttoned halfway down and no bra. Her shoes were black strap stiletto pumps. Built into the left heel was a tiny microphone, connected to a recorder inside the heel. Her makeup was heavily overdone on her eyes, cheeks, and far too much red lipstick. The long blond wig she wore as part of the disguise had a couple of loose braids on the sides but otherwise hung free.

"You got the drill. Go on up and pretend you're a hooker looking for her client and you've got the wrong address. You want Mr. Kanard, who actually lives ten blocks away on the same street, same last three digits as here but different first digit. This is information-only reconnaissance, Proteus. Avoid confrontation."

"Got it covered, Hunter."

Hunter gave her a warm smile. "I'll pull up a couple blocks out of sight," she pointed straight ahead. "And I'll be keeping an ear out."

"You're welcome to take notes on how to pick up a lady," Proteus smiled back, and got out of the car. She popped a piece of gum in her mouth as she started lazily up the walkway to the front door. She started popping her gum as she stopped at the door and rang the bell. Hunter guided her car a couple hundred feet away. Elise DeVeaux hesitantly opened the door and peered out. Remembering her character, Proteus asked in a lilting voice, "I'm lookin' for Mr. Kanard, is he home?" Proteus gave the girl a quick once over, taking in her appearance and clothing. *Slender, probably early twenties. No makeup, but pretty. Shoulder length sandy blonde hair, a little curl and wave. Dresses conservatively, blue polo shirt, black jeans, no shoes. I'm as tall as she is in these high heels.*

The woman replied softly, her speech sounding like she had a large wad of gum in her mouth also, "Dis is not da Ku-nod houth, no."

*Speech impediment, it's her,* Proteus noted. *Not too bad, I can still understand her. Wonder what caused it?*

"Push it," Hunter said through Proteus' ear comm.

"You sure?" Proteus pressed, smacking her gum with her mouth open. "This was the address I got—"

"I'm thure," Elise replied.

Proteus peered into the room, from what she could see beyond the door. She looked for something, anything to make a connection between her hooker persona and Elise. She saw books, pictures, snow globes all around the room. "Oh!" she exclaimed, remembering the shipment item that allowed the team to find Elise's address, "do you collect snow globes, too?"

Elise turned around to see what had caught Proteus' eye. The snow globes on her table, the ones she looked at every evening. She turned back, looked at Proteus, and smiled, "Yeth, I do. You collect thnow globth?" Elise had collected snow globes for a couple years, ever since Father and Mother passed away and David started taking care of her. The perfect spheres with their little buildings inside brought her comfort, almost as much as her special marble from David.

Proteus scored. "Oh, yeah! Well, yeah, when I have a few bucks leftover after bills and, you know, after I get to keep my cut and all."

"Your 'cut'?" Elise asked. "I don' underthand." Elise honestly had no idea what she was talking about.

"You know, my johns?"

Elise shook her head.

"My tricks? You know, guys who pay to have private time with me?"

Elise still shook her head.

"Sex? They pay me to have sex with them?"

Elise stopped shaking her head, finally understanding what Proteus had been trying to get across.

"Oh, please, she can't be THAT naïve," Hunter commented.

Elise lowered her head and dropped her voice, asking shyly, "Do you lite bein', um—?"

Proteus played her character, trying to make the bond with Elise to get invited inside. Smacking her gum loud again, she replied, "A hooker? Well, sometimes it's ok when I got a really nice guy to be with, but a lot are just pervs lookin' for a quickie. But y'know, got no other job and just a one-room place to sleep, no fancy degree or shit like that…hard to find banker's hours jobs in this economy. I do what I can…what I have ta.” She blew her gum into a bubble until it popped, then sucked it back into her mouth and chewed again.

Elise asked, voice still low, “Duth it hurt? I mean, the men an’ women doin’ thuff on TV thumtime, and dare tho much, well, I thop watching.”

“OH! Hey,” Proteus said upbeat. “The first time, yeah. I mean, after all, they’re all different sizes, y’know. Some need a lotta help, if ya know what I mean.”

“Yeah, known a few like that myself,” said Hunter. Proteus couldn’t stop her smile.

“Not really,” Elise whispered. When she was relaxed, her words were much clearer. “I don’t know any boyth thept’ my brotherth. I thay home here where it thafe, David thed he’d know if thumone bothered me and he’d take care of them, no one hurth me here. I’m not hurth anymore.”

Proteus noted that comment, more verification of Hunter’s profile of the children.

“You can leave your house,” said Proteus, now sounding more sympathetic. “Go out and see everything for yourself. See the real things, not just the miniature copies, although they’re all beautiful. There’s nothing to be scared of out here. Well, except maybe those guys on the north side.” She saw Elise’s eyes shoot up. Proteus put both hands up, palms facing Elise. “Kidding, just kidding! You really don’t get out at all, do you?”

“No. David and Henri thay it too dangerouth, not thafe for a girl.”

“Try to find out why they don’t want her to leave,” said Hunter.

Proteus posed, arms akimbo, with one leg stretched to the side, and balanced on the other. “Do I look like I’m dangerous? Ya think this dangerous world has beat me?”

“Well, no, I don’t think tho.”

“Until I grew these,” Proteus said, pointing at her breasts, “no one looked at me. Once these girls grew up and said hello, well, lemme tell ya, I got real popular. Never ended up any place dangerous with The Girls, if ya know what I mean."

"I really don't," said Elise.

Proteus looked left and right to the streets. "Hey, you remember how to play dress-up?"

"Where are you going with this?" Hunter said in exasperation.

Elise shook her head side to side slowly.

"Aw, man! You never pretended you were a movie star or fashion model or astronaut or stuff?"

Elise gave another wordless shaken-head reply.

"Proteus, get back on task. This is not playtime. Get info and get out."

Proteus cocked one eyebrow up. "You wanna play dress-up? I can make you look like a movie star! You know what movie stars look like, right?"

"I watch movieth," said Elise. "I like all kinda movieth. I really like movieth where the women are in charge, becauth they're all pretend. Father wath alwayth in charge, and David in charge of the three of us. Father thed women can't be in charge. But I like to pretend I am in charge."

"Well, I'd be happy to get you all dressed up like your favorite movie stars, if you're game."

"I don't know. David and Henri might not approve."

Proteus stuck her head in the door opening and did a dramatic side-to-side look. "I don't see anyone else. Aw, come on, let's have some fun!"

"What about your Mithter Kanard?"

"Oh, he can find someone else to screw tonight. I'd rather be with you!"

"What the hell are you doing, Proteus? We don't know when the brothers may show up! Find out where they are and get out!"

"Really?" This was the first time Elise sounded interested in the whole conversation. The woman extended her hand. "I'm Aileeth."

"Elise, I'm pleased to meet you, you can call me Harri."

"Would you like to thee my globth, Harri?"

Staying in character, Proteus looked at Elise's breasts. "I'd love to see your globes, Elise, kinda like what I see already."

Elise blushed. "N-n-no," she stammered, "I mean my collecthion."

"Oh, oh, yeah! Sure, love to see 'em. Then we get you out of those clothes." Elise' eyes widened in shock. And into some cute stuff!"

"Well, I geth it all right for you to come in then." She closed the door after Proteus was inside.

"Well! It's about damn time!"

Elise led her to a chair at the dining room table where a few of her snow globes stood, surrounding a single clear marble in their exact center. There was a dinner plate and water glass between the chair and the globes, as Elise had just eaten. She began, "Thith one my favorite, the Wathington Monument. David thed it in honor of our furth Prethident. I never got to learn about it when I wath in thchool, becauth I couldn't hear the teacher."

"Why is it your favorite?"

"It hath perfect, thimple thideth," said Elise as her gaze softened on it. "Thmooth, flat thideth. Perfect pyramid on top. I like looking at it. David bought moth of theeth," she said, pointing at them all around the living room. "Have you ever theen them, Harri?"

"Yeah, I been around. Hey, I got one of the IF-fell Tower," Proteus offered.

"Proteus, move it along. Ask about David. And you are so buying me drinks after this."

"Eiffel," Elise corrected the intentional mispronunciation. Proteus was impressed with her reaction.

Proteus sat back seductively, raising one arm over her head, and putting her hand behind her hair. Her half-buttoned blouse billowed to reveal more of her bust. "So, you live here alone?" she asked softly, looking around.

"Mothly," Elise said, "Although my brotherth come by often to check on me."

"You have brothers? Is that the Henry and Davey you mentioned?" Proteus played it up.

"FINALLY!"

"Yeth, David and Henri---not 'Hen-ree', but 'ahn-ree'. David my thtep-brother but we all grew up together. David been here for me ever thinth mother and father died. Henri hepth, too, but David ith really in charge."

"They as handsome as you are gorgeous?"

Elise blushed again. "I not the gorgeouth type, Father alwayth thed. Never let me wear nithe makeup like you do, or dreth up in nithe clothe."

"Aw, thanks! Tho, this is my nighttime makeup. Honey, you should see what I usually wear for my daytime job." Both women chuckled softly. "Speaking of 'wear,' I promised to make you look like a movie star. Let's go check out your makeup."

◆

Hunter had been listening to Proteus and Elise via the shoe microphone as they were being recorded. She didn't remember Marshall taking this long to get into someone's house, but then he was good at seducing women within a matter of minutes. *Not that it ever made me jealous,* she thought to herself with a smile. *He sure did a great job seducing me...mission after mission.* She looked at the clock on the dashboard and shook her head. "You can finish up anytime, Proteus," she said into her comm. "Get info on David and get out."

A major cramp developed in her right leg, and she got out of her car to stretch her legs. It was nighttime now, so she didn't worry about being seen in her uniform and armed. *Just for a minute or two, work out this damn Charlie Horse. Sure as hell can't drive with a Charlie, dammit,* she thought as she walked around to the passenger side and the sidewalk.

While she massaged her leg, she noticed a man walking toward her, with a dog at the end of a leash. He slowed to a stop several steps away. She noticed he looked at her intently. "Costume party," she smiled sweetly.

He thought for a moment, and then did a frown-smile and nodded his head. "Good evening," he said and began walking again. "Nice costume. Which movie character are you? One of the X-Men?"

Hunter gave him a big smile, realizing she had on her black cocoons. "Yeah, relative of Cyclops. Cute dog, Yorkie?"

"Yes, she is," he said. "Let's go, Lucy, time to finish up and go home." The man smiled back and moved on. "Enjoy your party!"

Hunter finished massaging out her cramp and got back in the driver's seat. "Geek!"

◆

"I don't have any makeup," said Elise.

Proteus feigned shock. "NO MAKEUP? O-EM-GEE, girl! That is just EVIL! I mean, come on a little shadow over your eyes, some liner for your brows, never mind what a little blush can do! You've got such great bone structure, God! You are SO LUCKY to have such great bone structure! Wow, I LOVE your hair! Nice and thick, can do lotsa gorgeous things with your hair! OK, tell you what we're gonna do, we're gonna have ourselves a girls' day out, just you and me! Go to the mall, sit at a makeup counter, and let the pro do you good, some nice lunch somewhere, and SHOP! O, girl, we gonna shop 'til we drop!"

"We didn't train you to be a hairdresser, Proteus. Get a move on."

"Oh, please, don't say no! I don't have a girlfriend to go shopping with!" Proteus was going for broke.

"WHAT THE HELL?"

Elise looked up; a smile formed on her face. "I…I'm your girlfriend?"

Proteus nodded her head with a tilt. "Shore! Well, not THAT kinda girlfriend, unless you wanna be THAT kinda girlfriend?"

Elise smiled wide, a smile of perfect teeth. "Um, maybe thumtime you can, um, teach me about it?"

"It's a date," said Proteus. She looked around the room. "Hey, got any pictures of your brothers? I'd love to meet them sometime."

"Well, it's about damn time!"

"No," said Elise, "they're not fond of having picthurth'. But if you really like, I could get them to call you thumtime when they're back over here for a vithit."

"Why, thanks, that'd be fun! You got pen and paper? I'll write my number down for ya." Elise retrieved a notepad and pen from beside a phone, and Proteus wrote down one of the "agent character" contact lines for her Task Force office. "I'm out a lot, you understand, so just leave a message, ok?"

"Thure," said Elise. She put the number on the table beside her chair, in front of the TDD device. Both ladies got to their feet and Elise led Proteus back to the door. "I had a very good time with you," she said as she opened the door.

"My pleasure," said Proteus. "Remember now, girls' day. Oh, I need your number so I can call you after I check my calendar, too!" Proteus waited while Elise wrote her phone number down and gave it to her. "Thanks, dear! My first opening is all yours!" She leaned forward and gave Elise a light kiss on the cheek.

"Oh, geez, I heard that."

"When your Mithter Kanard duthn't' already have you hired for thumthing," Elise said, her hand touching where she just got kissed.

"Yeah," smiled Proteus, and headed down the street. She waited until she heard the door close, watched the front windows, and walked to Hunter's car.

"That has to be the craziest infiltration I've ever heard," said Hunter.

"You weren't exactly helping, Statler. Hey, I was trying to get inside, figured I may as well and take my character to the extreme. I got inside, didn't I? And made solid contact and relation with her?"

"A little more relation than I'm comfortable hearing. We don't need to be paying for her psychotherapy when 'Harri' breaks her heart later on."

Hunter started her car's powerful engine. The digital display flared to life, with tactical displays glowing from Task Force Command's satellite relay. She gently accelerated the car. "Got anything else to add, that you couldn't say at the time?"

"First, I don't think she has any idea what's going on outside the world of her house," she said. "Second, she's deep down beautiful."

**CHAPTER 57**
**OCTOBER 30, 2011, JUST BEFORE SUNSET**
**THIRD ENCOUNTER**

"Evening, Al," Mark said as he opened the door to "The Recovery Room."

"Evening, Mark," Al greeted back from the far side of the seating area. "Hey, TJ, your cousin's here and lookin' thirsty." TJ hurried from the back office and ran to the serving side of the bar just as Mark sat on a stool. She took a cut crystal class from the shelf, poured, and set his drink on the counter.

"There ya go. Scotch, neat! On the house as usual, old man." TJ rested her arms on the bar, chin in hand.

"Six years older doesn't make me an old man, you young whippersnapper," he teased back. "Seen Sarge yet?" he asked her.

"Nope, not yet, cuz," she replied. She took down another glass and prepared Sarge's bourbon, taking Mark's question as a cue that the gruff retired ground-pounder would be in soon.

"Hey, TJ, you remember that guy I bought the drink for some time back? Sat over at that end. Blond hair, scar on one cheek, never said thanks that I know of?"

"Yeah, I know him," she replied. "Strange guy, must not like girls. I'm not bashful about being noticed, ya know? Guys drink more if they like the decorations. He's never once looked at my decorations. He got a problem?"

"Aside from ignoring you? Yeah, I think there is. I need you to do me a favor, no questions asked." He stared at TJ eye to eye.

TJ leaned in, her face inches from Mark's, and whispered, "We doin' spy-stuff now?" Mark couldn't stop the momentary surprise on his face. She continued, "Cuz, I was interviewed by suits about you, like, half a year ago. Then outa the blue you start askin' questions about a stranger here in the bar. Doesn't take a rocket scientist to figure out something's up." She winked at him.

"That's what I get for not taking Rocket A-School," he sighed and took a deep swig.

TJ stood straight, "Nah, it's the sexy white lines on the temples you got. Bet it makes Jan get really hot." She winked again, this time with a seductive open mouth. Both palms on the counter she stated, "OK, so what 'cha want me to do?"

Mark removed from his wallet a folded ten-dollar bill. Motioning like he was paying for his drink, he whispered back, "Inside the fold is a small GPS transmitter, one surface adheres to anything it touches. The inside of the paper is treated to not bond with it. Hold it by the edges, the side with the tiny diamond symbol is the non-stick side. I need you to put this on that blond guy next time you see him, somehow, where he won't suspect it. You expect him tonight?"

"Well, he seems to come in every other night like clockwork." *Another of Hunter's "twos",* Mark thought. TJ continued, "So, um, yeah he should be in tonight, probably most any time actually. Should be pretty easy, don't worry." She lowered the folded bill behind the counter to look at the nail-head sized transmitter. "Wow, that's small!" she whispered.

"Works better than you can imagine," Mark whispered back. "Well, I'll wait for a bit, see if he comes in tonight. Do you need any kind of distraction?"

"I'm insulted!" she teased back and slipped the special ten-dollar bill in her back pocket, folded down.

Mark smiled and went back to his drink just as Sarge came in and sat beside him. "Evening, Mr. Jason." He made a rare smile when he saw his drink was already waiting for him. Looking up, he said politely with a smile, "Aw, that TJ, she's the best."

"Good genes," Mark said proudly." Your pal Roger not coming tonight?"

"Nah, he's pulling a double tonight, covering for a guy who's wife's in labor."

"Hope I can be an adequate replacement for the evening," Mark said as he made a subtle gesture with his hand to keep voices low, then ended the motion by picking up his drink for another swig. He said quietly, "Remember few months back, those three vehicle bombings in one day? About a week after I hired you."

Sarge took a good sip and thought. "Yeah, I think I remember something about that. Some politician lost his family in one of 'em."

"Exactly," Mark confirmed. "And we believe our new friend, David, with the scar face is the one who did it."

Sarge was rarely surprised, but this pronouncement took him aback. Lowering his head and staring at Mark, he stated, "You serious? He don't look old enough to shave, much less be a mass bomber! So, what's your interest in him?"

"Don't let age deceive you," Mark said, ignoring the last question. "After all, Billy the Kid wasn't called 'Billy the Middle-Ager'. I just like to stay current on people around me, is all."

Ironically, David DeVeaux entered the bar while they talked about him. He went to the far end of the bar as usual and sat on the last bar stool. Mark nodded at TJ as she finished up at a table. She nodded back.

She casually worked her way across the floor and checked with other guests at their tables as she neared the bar. Within moments she reached the far end, which was also the only way behind the bar, where David sat in silence. TJ slid her thumb and forefinger into her back pocket, nabbed the tiny tracker between her fingers. She placed it under David's well-worn collar of his bomber jacket as she gave him a friendly shoulder rub and stepped behind the bar in one smooth move. "Hey, good lookin'," she smiled at him. "What'll it be tonight?"

"Um," he said. "What do you suggest tonight?"

TJ crossed her arms on the bar and shrugged her shoulders, making sure she bent forward. She was daring him to look at her cleavage, and he still refused to bite. "You ever have a Long Island Iced Tea?" she asked.

David's interest was piqued at the mention of iced tea. His eyes fell to her bust. She saw him smile for the first time. "No, don't think I have, but I'll try it."

He waited for her to prepare the drink and set the glass on the counter. He lifted the glass, sniffed it, did a stiff nod of approval, and took a sip, and after a few moments, a second sip. He gave her a bigger smile, and without finishing the first drink said, "I'll have TWO. Just TWO."

"You got it, love," said TJ. She prepared a second glass and set it on the counter beside the unfinished first drink. She looked over, saw Mark signal for a refill, and went to his place and prepared a fresh serving. "Gotta check on another customer, hon, check back with you in a minute."

Mark's hand was held casually over his mouth. He spoke low without moving his jaw. "Done?"

She took Mark's empty glass and made sure her back was turned to David. She bent forward and whispered, "Yep, under his collar, he never felt it. He always comes in wearing that same coat, bet he never goes anywhere without it."

"You're good, cousin. You know what he drives?"

"You think the only thing I'm supposed to do is give you drinks and information?" she said in mock disdain. Seeing Sarge's glass almost empty, she fixed him a fresh drink and set a new drink in front of Mark as well. "Think I've seen him in a big red SUV or something."

Mark casually looked around the bar as TJ left to do her rounds. "I'll be right back, Sarge." Mark observed David leave the bar and head toward the men's room. Mark stepped out the front door and looked in the parking lot.

He saw a red Hummer parked to his left, taking up the second and third spaces. Not seeing any other large red vehicles around, he walked casually toward it. He stopped beside it and looked at his watch. Pretending to check the time, Mark pressed a button on the side of the watch and the glass cover and watch face sprung open. He removed another tiny GPS transmitter from within the watch body and attached it to the underside of the back bumper. He withdrew his Task Force cell phone as he walked, stopped a few cars past the Hummer, and pretended to make a call. He watched David come out the front door, get into his Hummer, and drive off.

Marked activated one of the programs on the cell phone screen. A map of the area replaced the screen icons. He watched two blinking lights on the map, one light for each bug planted. They moved up the street away from the bar's location. He went back inside quickly to give TJ a twenty-dollar bill for the drinks and say "goodnight" to Sarge.

TJ said, "Cousin, you're a free drinker here."

Mark replied, "Let's call it a 'confidential informants' fee."

TJ answered, "You're gonna be some easy money, cuz."

He turned to leave, and his eyes gazed upward at the glass above the door. There, in reverse, he read the street address numbers; he had never thought about The Recovery Room's address. "222? Three twos? You gotta be kidding me," he said aloud. He turned back to TJ. "He said he wanted just two drinks, didn't he?"

"Yeah," she said. "That's what he always has. Two, no more, no less. Why?"

"I know a particular agent who's gonna to threaten me with, 'I told you so'."

## CHAPTER 58
## OCTOBER 31, 2011, NOON
## OF DIAMONDS AND TRIANGLES

Four months had passed since David gave his new crew their order: find the woman in black with that diamond-symbol belt buckle. *How hard could it be to find a woman like that?* David fumed over and over in his head. *Just find a woman in black with a gun on her hip!*

He sat in his apartment looking at his trophy gun. The symbol on the bottom of the grip was driving him crazy. Henri was the research expert and said there was still no listing anywhere on the Internet about any black-uniformed police teams.

David's only relief from the anxiety was his every other trip to The Recovery Room bar. Originally, he thought the waitress was his mystifying woman in black. He'd first seen her walking down the sidewalk near his apartment on her way to work several weeks prior. He'd since convinced himself that she was not his quarry but enjoyed the way she tempted him whenever he went into the bar. His warped mind thought she recognized his divinity and was attracted to that quality. He thought it was beneath him to acknowledge her advances, but he certainly did enjoy it.

Tonight was not a Recovery Room night, however. At home he placed a piece of paper and pen on the table in front of him, hoping the crew would call with information. Absentmindedly he picked up the pen and began drawing a diamond symbol numerous times. Fatigue finally took over. He moved to the couch and closed his eyes for just a minute. Within seconds, he was in a light sleep.

The knock at the door startled him and he reached to the coffee table for the trophy gun and pocketed an autoloader that contained more bullets. "Come!" he said loudly.

One of his crewmen entered cautiously, hesitant because he didn't see David seated at the table as usual and was very much afraid of David. "Mr. DeVeaux, sir," he said almost as a question. "I have news, sir!"

David stood and glared at the man. His finger was on the trigger, but the gun was pointed down. "Speak," ordered David.

"I saw her!" said the man. "The woman in black, I saw her!"

"WHERE?" growled David, his eyes suddenly wide in both excitement and fury. He waved the gun at his man.

The crew member stared at the gun, panicked, "YOUR SISTER'S HOUSE!" his voice cracked.

David's mouth fell open, and his gun hand slowly lowered. "Elise? She's with Elise?"

The man breathed in and out long and slow, to calm himself now that the gun was lowered. "Not with her, sir," he gulped. "She was outside her house, in a black car."

"Outside?" David asked, almost in a whisper. "How do you know it was her?"

The man raised his hands slowly, the "calm down" posture. "I was making a pass by the house around dusk just like Mister Henri ordered us to do, check on her, pretending to take an evening walk like the neighbors do, and I saw her standing beside the black car. Just like you described: black uniform, boots, gloves, belt, but she had on a gray jacket, and the metal buckle, sir. I was nice, sir. I said 'Hi' just like a neighbor would. I saw her buckle, sir; it wasn't a diamond, it was a triangle."

"Not a diamond? A triangle?" David was so dazed by the news that he dropped the pistol without realizing it. He stared down at the gun. "A triangle, three-sided. So, of the TWO of them, she is a THREE. No, she's a TWO and a THREE." David began pacing the living/dining area of the apartment, his personal logic trying to make sense of the contradiction. He turned to the man and took a deep breath. "After all those years of Father and his damn TWOs and THREEs, and his final Avatar to torment me is a TWO and a THREE herself."

The crew member stood very still, following David with his eyes as David rambled on.

David stood with his mouth open again, slowly closed it, his brow furrowed. "No, not good. She knows where Elise lives. Elise is our THREE. We gotta protect her. Call my brother, everyone here, NOW!"

"Yes, sir," he replied, and reached for his cell phone to dial Henri.

**CHAPTER 59**
**OCTOBER 31, 2011, 2:00 P.M.**
**DRESSING UP FOR TRICKS AND TREATS**

"I want to take her out."

Mark Jason looked at Proteus, seated in one of the chairs opposite him in his office. "Who?"

"Elise DeVeaux."

Mark laid the report folder on the tabletop and sat back in his chair. "Explain."

"I don't believe she has any idea what her brothers are up to," she answered. "She exhibits solid signs of severe introversion. Her only view of the world is what she sees on TV. She knows there's a world out there beyond her home but has no desire to experience it because she relies on her brothers to care for her. She has a fixation on spherical objects: marbles, snow globes, from what I saw. And is comforted somehow if she's near them or better yet, holding or touching them. I don't know if it's an illness or conditioning, but that's my take on her. She's companion-deficient, and after a little work jumped at the chance to experience some girls' time. In my opinion, if you're planning to get the brothers, she needs to be out of the picture, or she'll become a casualty."

Mark brought his hand up to his jaw, stroking at his beard in thought. He narrowed his eyes as he prepared his next question. Before he could, she handed him an SD card and her action report. "Got the whole conversation recorded. I asked one of the TF docs to take a listen, and that was his diagnosis. Elise mentioned that her brother David would know if she was in trouble, but I couldn't find any internal surveillance equipment during my visit, so I don't quite know what she meant by that."

"Excellent work. So, explain 'take her out'."

"I'll take her shopping, like I promised."

◆

Proteus was again dressed in one of her call-girl finest outfits and knocked on Elise' front door. This time Proteus wore tight leather pants, knee-high boots, and a light pink blouse, again opened halfway to her waist, and no bra. Over her blouse she wore a light-weight black leather jacket, which hid the shoulder holster and PPK under her left arm. She wore black stiletto pumps to keep her eyes level with Elise'. Her makeup was lighter and more natural for the daytime than what she wore last night.

Elise opened the door slowly, same as before, and her face lit up when she saw Proteus. "Harri? Hi!" Elise was excited. Elise wore a pair of blue jeans, brown loafers, and a tan long-sleeve shirt.

Proteus leaned forward and gave Elise another kiss on the cheek, eliciting a second blush from the shy girl. "Hiya, baby. Ready to go out and have some fun?"

"Um, I—she started.

"What's the matter, honey?" Proteus asked. "Not getting cold feet on me, are ya?"

"Well, my bruderth are coming over tonight. I haveta be here when they get here. I forgot to tell you when you call me thith morning."

"That's ok, honey, they'll never know you were gone. So, what say you grab your purse."

"I don't have a purth."

Proteus rolled her eyes. "O, my GOD, we've SO gotta get you caught up with the world, baby! Can't let my girlfriend look out of place in public now, right?"

Elise smiled sheepishly and slowly nodded. "I, um, juth need to make thure the doorth are lock, ok?" She stepped away to the kitchen and wiggled the doorknob to make sure it was locked. Proteus took a few steps inside, just to take another quick look around. Elise came back from the rear entrance, stopped beside her chair, picked up the clear marble from its base and put it in her pocket. Elise made sure the front door was locked before heading out. Elise sought approval from Proteus. "Are you thure thith ok?"

Harri knuckled her fists on her hips. "Are you kiddin'? We're gonna have a blast! So, what time do I gotta get you home?"

Elise looked down at her watch. "They'll be here at nine, David thed. I have to have dinner ready for them and their friendth. I got good at makin' dinnerth for my broderth!"

"OH! Your bros are having a party? Can I come and play with everyone?"

Elise blushed again. "I don't think ith a party. Bidneth, he thed. Told me to have dinner ready for everyone and then go to my room."

"Well that just sucks ass," Proteus pouted. "Oh, well, their loss, let's go baby, you and I have the rest of the day to get SEXY!" Elise's stomach did a little flip when she heard the word "sexy."

Proteus took Elise by the arm. She walked Elise down the sidewalk to her black Task Force car, and then slowly slid her hand down Elise's arm until their hands were together. By then she'd walked Elise to the passenger door and guided her into the seat. While Proteus walked around the back of the car, she said into her earpiece comm unit, "House is secure. You heard the conversation?"

"Affirmative, Proteus," she heard Spy's voice in her ear. "Returning to base?"

She stopped before she opened the driver's door. "Affirmative, Spy. But first, we're going to the mall before we take the trip to base." Proteus got in the driver's seat, buckled up, and started the engine.

"I really like your car," Elise said. Her eyes went to every digital control and readout on the custom dashboard, some areas completely black so as not to reveal the true functions of the car. Her amazement at the LCD panels and readouts slowed her speech to express her awe. "Wow, where did you get it?

"You've never been in a car like this, honey?"

"No, my broderth juth have regular carth."

Proteus smiled, happy to genuinely brag. "Well, love, this is a state-of-the-art supercar. There are some perks to my job, honey, and one of those perks is being able to afford a hot ride. And we're gonna go have a RIDE!" Proteus floored the accelerator and left smoking rubber in the air as the car rocketed down the street away from Elise' house. Elise screamed in surprise and excitement.

◆

Mae-Lei Komala sat next to Mark Jason on the couch in his Task Force office. They each held a snifter of brandy from his office wet bar. He took another savory sip while she stared at the small amount left in her glass.

"So, that's your plan," she said.

"There's poetic justice in it," he replied. "We have to eliminate everyone in his crew, doesn't matter where or how. They all made their choice, and choices have consequences." He glanced at the picture of the forged driver's license displayed on the wall touch screen. "I don't pretend to understand what made that young boy grow up into a serial killer, and frankly I don't care. Everything we have points to someone with a psychological problem."

He stood and walked to the world map that hung on the wall behind his desk. He looked at different locations as he spoke. "In all my travels across the world, all those different missions, there were two constants: an injured animal is the most dangerous creature in the wild, and a psychotic killer cannot be reformed."

He turned back to her. "That goes especially for psychotic killers who are dictators, cult leaders, or megalomaniacs."

"So, David DeVeaux is what? He's not a dictator. Is he a cult leader or megalomaniac then?"

"I don't think he fits in either category. But he could one day. All the people he's already killed over the past four years. For what? Psychopaths and most sociopaths don't need a reason anyone else can understand, they just have a reason that makes sense to them."

She shook her head, then picked up the outline of Jason's plan. "There are so many variables, how do you know he'll end up at your 'Destiny' target location?"

"Another thing about psychotic types. With the right guidance, they can go exactly where we want them, and they think it's their idea. As long as *they think* they're in control, we're the ones who actually remain in control."

"So why there, Mark? Why drive him there? Of all places?"

Proteus stepped in. She was in full uniform and knocked on the door for permission to enter. Jason gave her an entry wave without a word. She came in and stopped in front of Mae-Lei.

"Elise DeVeaux all safely tucked away?" he asked.

"Snug as a bug in a rug," Proteus replied. "She 'fell asleep' after our shopping trip, a little sleeping pill in her water, and should be out for about six more hours. I dropped her off with our Division psychologists and psychiatrists. They're ready to work with her when she wakes."

"Excellent. Now, I have a special job for you." He handed her a 5x7 manila envelope that was on his desktop. "I need you to make this for me."

She opened the envelope and withdrew a picture. Proteus' eyes widened in surprise, and Mae-Lei leaned forward to look, and smiled. Proteus nodded. "Yeah, I can do it. When?"

"You've got two hours."

"Sure, no problem," she mumbled as she headed for her laboratory. "At least it's not a Jem'Hadar."

**CHAPTER 60**
**OCTOBER 31, 2011, SUNSET**
**PLAN OF ATTACK**

Three matching, nondescript, black cars were parked on the sides of the roads at irregular distances from each other. Trick-or-Treaters were out in force, going from door to door collecting all the Halloween treats they could get.

Proteus arrived in her car and joined the team in its surveillance.

Spy was in the passenger seat in Hunter's car, parked two blocks from the house. He had spent nearly all his surveillance time watching the AVL GPS on his phone. David hadn't moved much from an apartment building on the west side, about two miles away. At 8:30 p.m., the Trick-or-Treaters were mostly dispersed because of the light rain. The flashing dot began to move, heading toward his icon on the map. He tapped Hunter on her shoulder. "You got a read on him?" She asked him from the driver's seat.

"GPS has him a mile away and closing," he said, looking at his phone's AVL. "Taking their time. But remember the Trick-or-Treat rule: you don't go to houses with the door light off. And the DeVeaux house light is very definitely off," he said as he pointed at the house. He pulled the hood over his head, very carefully, and sealed the collar seam.

"All set, boss," said Hunter. "We don't want to ruin the surprise later, do we?"

He nodded and removed a narrow pouch from beside his belt buckle. From the pouch he removed a pair of extra-flexible night vision lenses to slide into the hood's eyehole frames. When he heard them click into place the clip sensors in the hood activated the infrared-sensor system wired into the fabric, allowing him to see just as well as his teammates in the darkness.

Finally, he heard a voice over the comm system from Task Force Command. "Spy, Tactical, confirming. We've, uh, 'borrowed' a couple geographical-study satellites and have moved them into synchronous orbit over your position. These also have infrared cameras, so we'll be able to track movement provided the cover isn't too deep."

"No promise, we have residential tree ceilings here. Make sure you don't bump the satellites up there now; we don't want to send someone up to fix the paint job." Spy checked his phone and looked at Hunter. "You ready for this? They're almost here."

"I should be the one asking you that," Hunter answered. "You're pretty calm on your first mission in charge."

"I promise to panic after we're finished." Spy looked back at the DeVeaux house and saw two cars pull into the driveway: a red Hummer and a gray sedan. Spy said, "Tactical, confirm mobile target arrival, request status."

Everyone heard over their individual earpieces, "Spy, Tactical. We show a total of ten targets' heat signatures. Initially they all went to the front door and stopped for several seconds before separating. Satellite tracking marks two in the front behind bushes, three on the east street facing also behind bushes, three on the west by the cars that were driven, and the last two went inside."

"We could assume the two inside are the DeVeaux brothers," added Spy.

"That's our guess as well, Spy," Tactical continued. "Satellite imagery shows the back of the house faces a high fence, and there are two higher buildings at north and northwest, open to streets on east and front. We read no activity in the house to the west, nor to the houses across the street to the south. House across the street to the east has one signature on the far east side."

Hunter had been following Tactical's descriptions with a pair of mini binoculars from her belt. "They're all armed with big guns, look like rifles but can't make out model from this distance in the night."

Spy ordered, "Hunter, you've got the two in front. Take them out then keep anyone from going out the front door. Seeker you take the three on the east side, make sure there's no exit potential that way. Got the three on the west and will enter from there through the kitchen door at the rear. Proteus, if any of them get past us, stop them. But I definitely want the DeVeaux brothers alive. We don't want to deny David DeVeaux his invitation."

No one said a word.

Spy said, "OK, everyone, let's get to work." Hunter and Spy got out of her car. When Hunter looked across the roof of the car, her team leader was already gone. She never heard or saw him move away.

"Where's Spy?" she asked aloud. "Okay, I really gotta find out how he's doing that."

8:38 p.m. (Hunter)

It was easy enough for Hunter to get to the south side of the house undetected. She stuck to the shadows of houses across the street until she was in sight of her two targets. Using the night vision filter in her cocoons, she followed their movements as they patrolled the front yard behind the fence and tall bushes.

Hunter made her way across the street in the darkness. She crouched along the street side of the bushes. For silent assault she wore a black quiver with matching arrows on her back and carried a black compound bow in her left hand.

The front guards returned to their position across the bushes from her. They stopped, mumbled something to each other, then turned around and resumed their lookout duties. When their attention faced away from her, Hunter rose from hiding and fired two razor-tipped arrows in rapid succession, hit both men squarely in the back. They both fell dead without a sound.

With the front yard clear, Hunter softly stepped to and reached over the front walkway gate, released the clasp, and stepped forward. She heard shouting from the east side of the property.

"Update," she heard the Tactical voice in her headset comm say. "West side targets and inside are moving away from the house to the cars."

8:38 p.m. (Seeker)

Seeker snuck his way along the house's east side and proceeded to the two-story business building to the north of the house. He hid behind the privacy fence that separated the DeVeaux's back yard from the business' rear entrance. He climbed up on the crates stacked along the fence and peered over the top. With his night vision cocoons he made out the three guards in the east yard. He pulled the rifle that was slung over his back and took aim. Before his finger could touch the trigger, he saw the area around him suddenly glow with light, and a voice yelled, "Hey! What do you think you're doin'?" Alerted by the yelling, the guards from the DeVeaux yard began firing toward Seeker's position. Seeker lost his balance and fell to the side into the alleyway behind him. He ran forward and rounded the building corner, right into the next alley which was blocked by a commercial trash dumpster. "Shit!" he said. He turned to run back, but now the three guards were already firing over the fence in his direction. "Shit, again!"

The man who surprised Seeker ducked back inside his store when he heard the gunshots. Even though he had a pistol, he was not interested in being part of the firefight. He slammed the door, locked it, and turned around to a solid black figure standing in front of him. The store owner yelped in surprise.

"That really didn't help," said the figure as he reached out and gently took the pistol out of the man's hand. He opened the revolver and emptied the bullets into his gloved hand. "Now please stay inside for your own safety." He dropped the bullets and gun in the trash container behind him.

"Sa-safety?" The man was visibly rattled. He turned and pointed at the back door. "What's going on out there? What? He turned back and the black figure was gone.

Bullets continued to make miniature explosions of concrete and wood around Seeker's head. He pulled his rifle up and fired back until its load was spent. Rather than take time to reload, he dropped it to the ground and drew his handgun to continue firing back. Seeker saw a shadow movement out of the corner of his eye, then heard a familiar voice. "Got a problem?" he heard Spy ask.

"How'd you get here?" Seeker squatted low as he fired his last round. He quickly dumped his gun's magazine and reloaded from one of the many spares on his belt.

"I was in the neighborhood."

"Funny. So, who the hell got the drop on me?"

"An innocent bystander, of all things."

"He okay?"

"Yeah, just made sure he stayed innocent. I jammed his doors from the outside."

More bullets from the enemy sent sprays of wood and dust around them…

8:39 p.m. (Hunter)

Hunter heard the gunshots coming from the east side of the house. Over her comm she heard Proteus calling her for status. "Stay in position," she ordered Proteus, "continue original orders." Trees between the front yard and east side kept Hunter from seeing who was doing the firing. Sounds to her left caught her attention.

The three men on the west side ran down the driveway toward the cars. They were followed by David and Henri. Hunter said aloud, "Boss, main targets are leaving."

"Kinda busy back here," she heard Spy say in her ear. "Make sure they go where we want them."

With David at the wheel and Henri in the passenger seat, the Hummer backed out into the street after the sedan.

"Proteus, get over here!" she said into her comm. "Tactical, you got a read on the target cars?"

"Confirmed, Hunter," replied her tactical contact. "We have both cars on LoJack if needed and tracking with same."

Both DeVeaux vehicles drove away as Proteus pulled up in her car. Hunter jumped into the passenger seat. "Take me to my car, then we go make like cowboys."

"Don't you mean cowgirls?" said the smaller female agent.

"Oh, shut up and start chasing the bad guys."

## CHAPTER 61
## OCTOBER 31, 2011, 8:48 P.M.
## TRICK OR TREAT, SMELL MY FOOT, GIVE ME SOMETHING GOOD TO SHOOT

"Spy, report?" came the Tactician's voice over the headset woven into his hood.

"I'm a bit busy here, Tactical!" Spy shouted back. This was one time he was glad to wear the full-head mask. He didn't have to hold a phone to his ear, and the flying splinters from incoming bullets didn't hit his skin. "Unless you want me to ask these guys to stop shooting at us so I can take a call?"

Seeker couldn't help but smile at Spy's sarcasm in the middle of a firefight. *You're really growing on me, pal*, he thought to himself. "You think the rest of us could get head gear like that?" he asked. "Gonna be a bitch washing all this shit out of my hair."

"Put in a supply request," Spy bellowed over the gunfire. "And tell the police to stay back. I don't want to have to deal with them in the middle of this war here." He peered around the side of the building; his night-vision lenses cast a jade color to his view. He saw a face peek out from behind a trash can. Spy raised his gun and fired once. He watched the face fall back and heard a thud from behind the can. "I got mine," he said.

"Good shot, boss," Seeker replied.

Another hail of bullets assaulted their position. The two agents were well-protected in the alley, but discovered they had no way to escape, at least, conventionally. Looking up the side of the building, Mark assessed their position. *Only two stories, good*, he thought. "Keep us covered," he ordered Seeker as he changed places with his partner.

Spy holstered his gun and detached one of the pouches from his belt. He opened the Velcro-sealed front flap and removed a short coil of nylon cord connected to a collapsible rod. He extended the rod fully and locked the joints in place. Withdrawing his gun, he released the bullet magazine into his opposite hand, and slipped the end of the rod into the barrel. He reached into the cuff of his right boot top and extracted three short narrow steel rods from the shin area and attached them to the cord-end of the rod. His makeshift grappling hook assembled, loaded a compressed gas bullet into the chamber. He aimed and fired at the rooftop with the specially retrofitted weapon. He heard it land on the roof and pulled the cord slack until it held fast. "You go," Seeker told him. "I'll join you when you're up." Seeker resumed firing at their enemies.

Spy nodded and returned his equipment pouch and gun to his belt. He placed one boot sole against the wall to start his ascent. It took only a minute to reach the roof. "I'm up, get your ass up here, I'm not getting any younger." A minute later the two agents were rejoined at the roof edge and looked down.

Below they saw the man who Spy killed minutes before, lying on his back. The remaining two men were glancing around their cover, wondering why the shooting stopped. Spy and Seeker both drew their weapons. They nodded to the other, looked down, and fired. Three shots later their opponents were all dead on the ground below. "You had to shoot twice?" Spy said. "Sign yourself up for target practice when this is all over."

Seeker saluted with his gun barrel from his forehead. "Aye, aye, boss," he smiled.

Spy said, "Hunter, Proteus…status."

In his ear, Hunter spoke, "We're in pursuit. They took off in both cars and then split up a mile from you."

"Can you route them to 'Destiny'?"

"Already on it," everyone heard Tactical say in their comms. "Changing traffic lights and patterns ahead of both cars to force them to 'Destiny'."

"ETA?" Spy asked in a firm tone.

"Six minutes projected."

"Copy." Spy turned to Seeker. "What say we join the fun?"

"I'll call in a cleaner crew for here on the way," Seeker said as he holstered his pistol. He looked up and Spy was already gone. "How in the hell does he DO that?" When he was back on the ground and running for his car, he noticed on the way that Spy's car was already gone.

◆

The Trick-or-Treaters were done for the night. She drove in high-speed pursuit, and Hunter noticed adults at Halloween parties in their yards and through house windows. She sped through residential streets after the sedan. Her target car wouldn't willingly go the direction she needed. She said aloud, "OK, I'm done playing nice. Time for the bitch to get to work." Snickers were heard from unknown Task Force staff across the team's comm feed.

Hunter studied the map on her console. She saw where the next intersection was on the display, a press of her finger on the screen programmed the destination into the weapons system. She pressed a virtual button on her dashboard display, arming her car, and pressed the "fire" button.

The driver's side parking light pivoted down, and a short-range rocket burst from the opening. It soared ahead, trailing a line of fire and flame-lit smoke, landing, and exploding a few dozen yards in front of her target car. The non-destructive detonation forced the driver to turn right without slowing down, then accelerate down the next residential street.

"Tactical, Hunter," she said aloud. "Get the PR guys workin'. There's gonna be a lot of fireworks in this subdivision over the next few minutes."

Using the rest of her front-end rockets (two on the driver's side, three on the passenger's side) she succeeded in steering her target car onto the street toward its "Destiny".

◆

Proteus followed behind the Hummer at whatever the speed limit was on the road. The Hummer's driver seemed more interested in paying attention to traffic signals and not getting into traffic wrecks. "Lucky me, I get to chase a safe-driver bad guy. Let's see if we can get things moving a bit." She swerved back and forth behind the Hummer as the two vehicles raced down the roads, keeping it from being turned onto another street. "Easiest pursuit I've ever had…"

◆

Spy parked his car, exited, and stood in the middle of the street. "Everybody accounted for?" he asked.

"Confirm, Spy," said the tactical voice in his hood. "The five bogeys downed at the house have been recovered and taken in. Tracking shows Seeker, Hunter, and Proteus are guiding both vehicles to you."

He checked the AVL on his phone and watched the blinking lights. There were two red lights for the target cars and three blue for his team. "Nice of Seeker to join the party," Spy said. The two red lights eventually came together back-to-back on the road, heading toward him, and the three-blue bordered them in a triangle pattern. He looked up and saw all the headlights coming at him. He put the phone back on his belt and drew his .45 automatic. He brought up his gun and aimed…

◆

From the passenger's seat Henri looked ahead. In the headlight beams he saw something, "David, look! What's that?"

David looked ahead and made out a black human silhouette. "Oh, my, God! It's an Avatar!" He floored the accelerator. A sudden barrage of bullets pierced through the windshield and whizzed past their heads. He turned the steering wheel hard in reflex, veered the Hummer to the left and crashed into a streetlight. The sedan reached Spy, who had already ejected his spent clip from his gun and reloaded. Bullets tore through its windshield also, and the car swerved to the right, crashing into a store front window. Airbags deployed in both vehicles, momentarily preventing any of the DeVeaux gang from exiting.

David and Henri, with guns in hand, exited the Hummer through the driver's door. The door faced away from David's Avatar in the street. They realized they'd come awfully close to being killed and were desperate and panicked. "Through the yards, Henri, let's run through the yards! He won't shoot if we're near people's houses!" Hunched down, they ran through the dimly lit neighborhood and down an intersecting street.

The crew in the sedan managed to open the driver's and back doors and bombarded the Task Force team with a hail of gunfire. Hunter, Proteus and Seeker stayed within the safety of their armored cars while the DeVeaux gang unloaded all their bullets at them.

Over the comm Proteus spoke. "This isn't gonna mess up the paint job, is it?"

Hunter responded, "Na, I'm pretty sure your deductible is safe with that."

Seeker chimed in, "Well, I'm getting pretty bored, I wanna shoot back."

"Enjoy yourself then, I got your back," Hunter said.

Seeker grabbed his rifle and opened his driver door. In a relaxed movement he stood, aimed, and fired three shots, killing all three gunmen. He lowered the rifle scope from his eye. In a disappointed tone he spoke aloud, "Well, damn, that was anticlimactic…but, now I don't have to report for target practice."

**CHAPTER 62**
**OCTOBER 31, 2011, 9:37 P.M.**
**REDUX**

Henri and David ran to the end of the block, turned, and looked back. The dark figure David referred to as an Avatar walked unhurried down the street toward them. Henri raised his .38 and fired all six shots at their pursuer who continued to walk forward, then disappeared into the darkness between streetlights.

Three lights away Henri and David watched as the Avatar stepped out into a cone of light that glowed down onto the paved street.

Panicked, and with shaky hands, Henri reloaded his .38 and raised his gun to fire. He knew at this range there was no way he could miss. He aimed…

The figure raised his gun and fired once. Henri fell to the ground a second later. "Henri!" David yelled and dropped to his brother's side. He watched as blood streamed out of Henri's left eye. David was horrified and furious at the same time. He thought his heart would pound out of his chest. Without time to think, he drew his trophy pistol from his back waistband, looked up and fired into empty space.

The Avatar was gone.

David howled in fury as he still knelt beside his dead brother. He fired the rest of his bullets randomly at the street and hoped the figure had only moved into the shadows and was hit. He continued to squeeze the trigger long after his bullets were spent. The only sound he heard was the echo of the hammer clicks in the night.

David watched as the Avatar reappeared and swung his arms, first his left hand then his right hand, but he didn't see the Avatar throw anything. The silence was broken by two thunderous explosions behind him, followed by three more. David covered his head with his arms, holding tight to his trophy gun as he curled into a fetal position and particle debris rained down on him. His mind counted---TWO explosions, THREE explosions. "TWO, THREE," David said softly.

He held his breath as the staccato of pebbles hit him, the ground, and Henri's body. They eventually stopped and silence returned, but David's heart continued to race. He unfurled his body and pointed his gun forward. He still didn't remember the weapon was empty. The Avatar was gone again.

All was eerily quiet. A light rain began to fall again, and he started to shake from the wet and cold. David realized that Henri didn't react or flinch from the raindrops that splattered on his face.

He watched as blood pooled from Henri's wound and spread outward. The raindrops spattered the blood onto his shoes. He waited for it to start flowing up his body, just like in his nightmare.

David heard something snap, then a cracking noise to the right of the large building. His head spun sideways; the empty gun raised as he stepped away from his brother's body. All of David's senses were on fire. He could hear every movement, smell his brother's blood. The odor was iron and tin, mixed with asphalt and dirt from the street. "Damned rain! I can't think!" He ran slightly crouched toward the concrete sidewalk.

An uneasy feeling grabbed David in his stomach, and his eyes searched the darkness. There was a rustle in the shrubbery to his right, and he turned and pulled the trigger…nothing.

There was a powerful impact to his face by something large and black, and David fell backwards, watching rain move in slow motion as he fell. He felt his body hit the ground, though the impact was numb. He was only out a few seconds. The rain hitting on his face awoke him suddenly. He'd panicked that he'd been unconscious. He tried to get up and a curl of nausea washed over him while his world blurred in and out. He shook his head, tried to clear the fuzziness from his vision, and stumbled to his feet.

Another powerful blow assaulted him from behind. It hit him in the middle of his back, the impact lifting him off his feet, flinging his body forward. He watched as the sidewalk flew up and collided with his face and body. The force knocked the air out of his lungs, and he was momentarily blinded.

He desperately tried to catch his breath and sucked in drops of water that flowed down his face and waited for his vision to clear a second time. A punch of reality set in when he realized where he was…

He was behind the arts center building, where it all began a few months before…

It was the very place he'd completed this year's sacred THREE.

David's mind reeled. "This is where I killed Father's first damned Avatar! The one with the perfect diamond symbol, the one I got this gun from, my ONE trophy."

David sat up. A motion detector light activated at that very moment, above the back door of the arts center. The black figure stood there, gun in his right hand, pointed at the ground. David saw him clearly, the gun belt around his waist. He stared at the flat metal buckle, with the diamond symbol in its center.

"NO!" David screamed. "It's not possible! I killed you! I sent you to hell with Father!" Spittle flew from his mouth as he yelled.

The Avatar moved forward; his gun hand remained pointed at the ground. David blinked hard, wiping the rain from his eyes, and listened to the repetitive sound of the slow measured footsteps in the soggy grass. He finally remembered the extra bullets in his jacket pocket. His hand shook violently as he took out the handful of bullets and fumbled as he tried to load the ammunition.

David looked up the Avatar holstered its own weapon, then as two black-gloved hands reached forward and gently took the gun from David's right hand and bullets from his left. David sat and stared up at the figure. He began to scoot backwards toward the garden shed, the same shed he hid in months before.

The Avatar followed, partially illuminated by the lights. He loaded the gun, spun the cylinder, and closed it. He reached around behind his back, retrieved another gun from his belt and tossed it at David.

David recognized the automatic as his own, the one he left behind the night he killed the first Avatar.

The figure tossed a magazine clip on the ground. David picked it up, and realized the clip was fully loaded. The Avatar stepped full into the light, only feet away from David. The black figure reached up with his free hand and pulled upwards at his neck. The fabric covering its head was pulled free and tossed to the ground.

David screamed.

He looked into the face of the Avatar he'd killed months before. He looked at the grime on the face, blood streaks on its cheek and temple. The black glasses, with the left lens marred by a circular hole, were covered with dried blood. The Avatar stepped backward several feet.

"No! You're dead! I killed you!" His hands shook violently, but David loaded the clip into the handle of the automatic and forced himself up. He was hunched over from the pain in his chest and back, his left arm holding broken ribs. His hands trembled as he readied the weapon to fire. His breath came out in short misty clouds.

"Time to join us in hell," the Avatar said in a dry, raspy voice.

David shook his head back and forth violently, trying to clear the confusion and rain at the same time. He remembered himself as a five-year-old...

*---watching the man at the front of the bus yell "I'll see you in hell!"...so terrified he wet his pants in front of everyone...flash of light...thunder...fire...heat...flying and falling...Mommy and*

*Daddy not moving...I'm your new father...we'll get along just fine...do as I say or there'll be hell to pay...hell's been paid, dear brother...you are a threat to my THREE so you must die---*

Humiliated by Father, defeated by his Avatar, terrified...David wet his pants.

Again.

The avatar raised his weapon, thumbed back the hammer, and said, "Time to get on the bus—"

With a horrific scream David raised his gun, aimed...

## CHAPTER 63
## NOVEMBER 5, 2011, 9:00 A.M.
## FINAL FAREWELL

Mae-Lei stood at the headstone of Marshall Gray, mourning the loss of her fiancé. She was somber, reflective, and missed him terribly. She placed a red rose at the base of the marble stone.

Mark stood nearby with Jan and Angela. To their right, Calvin and Harri stood. Several feet away Tom Michelson held a black canvas bag. All were dressed in black suits or dresses, and winter coats. It was a chilly 40 degrees.

Mae-Lei dropped to her knees and placed both hands atop the headstone. She hadn't given herself permission to truly grieve for Marshall. Now that his killer was found and killed, she was able to release what had been buried deep inside for months. She wept quietly at first, but the hurt turned into heavy sobs full of anguish.

Jan looked at Mark and squeezed his arm. She nodded her head toward Mae-Lei. With a silent nod in reply, Mark stepped forward, and knelt on one knee beside her. Mae-Lei felt his powerful arm grasp around her back and his hand rested on her right shoulder. She gave in to the sorrow, allowing herself to fall into his arms and wrap her arms around him. She was wracked with uncontrollable shakes, and he held her tight. Jan then also knelt beside her, to offer comfort and shield her.

No one moved.

The Team grieved together.

Minutes passed, and Mae-Lei's sobs slowed and finally stopped. Mark looked into his wife's eyes, the request unasked. "We'll wait for you in the car," Jan whispered. Jan rose, Angela joined her, and together they left the gravesite.

Harri and Calvin came up to give Mae-Lei a hug. "You made one helluva mask there, girl," Mae-Lei said to Harri in a soft whisper. "It was really over the top, but it was like Marshall really did avenge his own murder."

"Yeah, it was cool, wasn't it?" Harri replied, grinning.

"I know who I want to do next year's Halloween office party," Calvin said as he smiled. "Can you make me look like a zombie?"

"Just look in the mirror, boyfriend," said Harri.

"I think Marshall can rest in peace now," Mark offered. He waved to Tom to join them. When he arrived, he handed Mark the bag. Mark took it and placed it in Mae-Lei hands. "This is his gun, and his glasses and the last of his released Task Force items." She nodded, hugged him again, hugged Tom, accepted the bag, and left the graveside. Mark and Tom watched her walk away with Calvin and Harri.

"Good job," said Tom.

"Nothing really good about it actually, Tom. A cold heartless father created two murderers, and now their last victim is their surviving sister. She's all alone now."

"Elise DeVeaux will get the best care and guidance possible. And two psychotic serial killers have been eliminated. Think of the justice for their victims and the future lives you saved…two years from now."

"Fine," said Mark. "Justice has been served. In two years, Richmond will be worried about the return of 'The Biblical Bomber' and nothing will happen. No one will ever know what happened to him or who he was or why he was."

Tom turned and faced Mark. "That's the job we do."

"Yup. Just like the old days in the SEALs." Mark crossed his arms, looking at Marshall's grass-covered final resting place. "So, Mae-Lei got some leave time coming?"

"Yeah. She's on administrative leave until she's ready to come back."

He stood at attention and saluted Marshall's headstone, then he began to walk toward his wife and daughter.

"Mark, one moment." Mark stopped and turned. Tom said, "Yeah, they were kids. But they were murderers, and psychiatric killers at that. I know you had to kill them both. We saw the video from your belt camera."

Mark looked at him with cold eyes.

Tom looked at him with searching eyes.

They stood silently for several seconds.

Tom had never seen that expression on Mark's face. For everything he had read about Mark's SEAL missions and all he had done training to command the Task Force field team, he had never once felt fear around Mark. He was now feeling it…a lot of fear.

"What are you?" Tom finally asked.

Mark simply nodded curtly, his terrifying expression never changing. "I am my father," he said, and he left Tom perplexed alone at Marshall's grave...

## ABOUT THE AUTHORS

**Jack Gannon**

Jack Gannon began his literary career with high school best friend Cyndi Williams-Barnier after they were both retired from their respective careers, writing the stories they talked about way back in high school.

YBR Publishing was born when Jack wrote and published his first solo book, "I WALKED IN SANTA'S BOOTS", a coffee-table-sized autobiography about his quarter-century as Santa Claus for Beaufort, SC. "SANTA" was entered into the Beaufort County Library Historic District Collection as an important book reflecting the history of Beaufort, SC, as well as the Columbia State Library as an important book in South Carolina history.

His decades in print media gave him the experience to put together that first book in a unique and attractive scrap-book style, and now serves as the Production Manager for YBR Publishing. Jack works one-on-one with each author to create a distinctive visual signature in the book from cover to cover, a trademark style individual to each author with YBR Publishing. In addition, Jack is YBR Publishing's webmaster and finance manager.

Jack also serves on the Liturgy Committee for St. Peter's Catholic Church in Beaufort as its chairman and the Proclaimer Ministry chair.

He is retired from The Beaufort Gazette & The Island Packet after 24 years in management plus another ten years prior as a motor route delivery carrier and intern reporter.

In January 2021, Jack was double honored by Marquis Who's Who with inclusion in the Marquis Who's Who Top Executives and the Albert Nelson Marquis Lifetime Achievement Award for his lifetime careers in print media and publishing.

Jack lives in Beaufort, SC, with his wife Mendy; Tasia, a 15-year-old Pomeranian; and Mister Grey, an 8-year-old Russian Blue who is "a lot of cat"!

## ABOUT THE AUTHORS

**Cyndi Williams-Barnier**

Cyndi Williams-Barnier, a Beaufort, South Carolina native, brings to YBR Publishing 25 years of county government service in Emergency Management, including writing and managing grants, writing training programs and detailed multi-agency operations manuals for disaster preparation and recovery. Her detailed programs are still used as guideposts for county, state and federal agencies including FEMA, Homeland Security and the National Guard at the Pentagon.

As co-founder of YBR Publishing and co-author of nine books, she brings a unique personal perspective and experience to maximize marketing opportunities for YBR and its authors. Her eye for detail and creative skill brings the emotional connection to every manuscript.

Cyndi was awarded a plaque and flag flown over Camp Phoenix, Afghanistan, from the Department of Defense; plus, she was awarded a retirement plaque from the Beaufort (SC) County Emergency Management Division for her 20 years of service.

Cyndi lives in Ridgeland, SC, is married to Bill and has one adorable cat, Scooter (who serves as her personal YBR critic)!